TOO LATE
FOR
REDEMPTION

TOO LATE
FOR
REDEMPTION

A Britannia Bay Mystery

SYDNEY PRESTON

RYE PUBLICATIONS

Rye Publications
800 Kelly Road
Victoria, BC V9B 6J9

Printed and bound in Canada by Printorium Bookworks

ISBN 978-1-7753157-1-1 (Paperback)
ISBN 978-1-7753157-0-4 (e-book)

"Evil must be driven out with evil. Where there is no justice, it must be created."

From *The Fifth Woman*
by Henning Mankell

Chapter One

He gazed at the fountain pen lying next to the bottle of blue ink. Blue, not black. The pen was a beautiful writing instrument, perfectly weighted to his hand and fitted to his slender fingers. Its shiny black surface was clean of any embellishments or bodily oils.

Taking up his notebook, he returned to his final poem. It had been a difficult piece. All the others had come easily. But not this one. Was the task ahead clouding his mind?

Everything had been done. All the preparations made. He turned to look at the clock. He would have to leave in a few hours to make his five o'clock appointment. As thoughts of the aftermath came to him, he felt a sense of exhilaration, and along with it, freedom and peace.

He picked up the pen and set to writing in his long, thin script. The final few lines began to flow as though waiting to be written.

Max Berdahl looked over the Kendall property proposal for the hundredth time. It was quiet in the office. He had given his cousin, Ingrid, the day off for a family event. It was grad weekend, and her daughter would be graduating from the local high school. From time to time he would glance out the window to watch the activities on the streets. Although he saw the comings and goings, they did not register with him. His mind was on figures, trying to fiddle with them one last time so as to be fair to Kendall while making a profit for Berdahl Brothers. Property Developers.

He yawned. His eyes watered. It had been a long night. Most of his energy had been spent playing squash. Even though he had been flagging at bedtime, he could not sleep. The possibility of failure kept him awake.

The sound of his cellphone interrupted his concentration. His brother's voice boomed into his eardrums as he talked over the squeals and laughter in the background.

"Hi Max. I'm just wondering what time you're coming by the house tonight."

"I'm not sure. I don't know what time I'll be finished showing that house to Mr. Fitzgerald. He's not arriving until five o'clock. And I'm dog tired. I couldn't sleep last night thinking about these two deals." He paused, mouth suddenly dry. "I think I'll just get an early night."

"Oh." Jaxon's voice dropped. "I don't think you should do that, Max."

Max's ears burned with the veiled admonition. With effort, he kept his voice even. "I'm already struggling to stay awake, bro."

"Everyone's going to be there. They'll expect you."

"Yes, I know, but I'm still working on the Kendall proposal."

"I understand how important it is for us. But everybody's going to be disappointed if you don't show." When Max didn't respond, he continued. "And don't forget tomorrow morning. You'll be there, won't you?" It was a family tradition to meet for prayer Saturday morning and Jaxon's tone was more of a command than a question.

Max waited a moment before answering, thinking about the time line. Those prayer meetings could drag on. "Yes. I'll be there."

Jaxon heard his hesitancy. "Faith and family come first, Max. Don't forget." The intensity of his words reminded Max of his precarious position within both. He understood their desire to watch over him. But it rankled.

"I know that," he said quietly, smarting under the soft rebuke.

"Good. See you later then."

Max hung up without saying goodbye. He needed his family. They were essential to his well-being and direction; had patiently and lovingly guided him back to the fold. But wheeling and dealing gave him a buzz. Got his juices flowing. Made him feel alive.

With that thought, he went back to what turned him on the most. Well, almost. And as a flashback popped into his head he felt the familiar tug at his crotch. His mind wandered dangerously to a time and place he had diligently tried to delete from his memory. But the lurid scenes kept reoccurring, reminders of powerful feelings he would never forget. He knew his rehabilitation would be hopeless until he could cleanse his thoughts. *Damn it! Damn her! Damn her to hell!*

Shortly after four o'clock the grad parade started snaking its way up from the high school and around the main streets. Max came out of his office and watched as the cars passed by then continued toward the Community Centre. As occupied as he was, he loved this parade. It was a shame that his religion prevented the children from taking part in it. It was just another prohibition that he didn't dare question. He had learned early that putting some of his thoughts into words was not a wise thing to do. The result was swift condemnation, or worse, from his family and church elders. Thank God they didn't know about *her*. A business transgression was one thing. But the other? He shuddered to think of the consequences if that had come to light.

It was time to go. With the main roads blocked off, he took side streets down to the bay. During the drive, he thought about his extended family and Jaxon's little kids, who loved their Uncle Max.

He always enjoyed them, but at the same time he was glad when he could leave them behind. Marriage and children were not for him. *No time for that. No time at all.*

Approaching the turn off to Townshipline Road, he noticed the For Sale sign leaning over the ditch. *Jeez. When did that happen?* Then he realized he hadn't been to the house for a month or more. Should he straighten it? He glanced at his tasseled loafers and decided it could wait. He began the slow drive up the hill, his SUV bumping over humps in the asphalt.

He turned at another sign advertising the property for sale and curved around a narrow gravel road covered in dry leaves and needles. A tunnel of trees cut off sunlight, casting dark patches in his path. It gave Max the creeps, but what could you do about some peoples' taste? Dappled light soon broke open to a bright treeless clearing. An A-frame cedar house poised on a rock shelf provided a viewing point for the spectacular sight of the bay curled into the mainland mountains.

He shrugged on his jacket and approached the stairs leading to a large deck. It must have been a beautiful place at one time. Now it was neglected and deserted—but not by everything. When his foot touched the bottom stair, he heard the sounds of scurrying feet. *Oh rats! Mice.* Giggling at his own joke, he ascended the stairs, pulled out the key and inserted it in the lock. The door creaked open. He was about to go in when he thought he heard a noise behind him. *Maybe Fitzgerald?* Turning around he saw no one. Straining to hear anything, he heard nothing. He shivered and the hairs on the back of his neck stood up. *Why am I so jumpy?*

As he angled his way into the house, he heard a rustling noise. He turned. A vision of something sliced through the air. His skull split open, scattering blood and bits of brain and bone, eyes shooting out of his head. His body slumped against the wall, leaving a ribbon of red as it slid to the floor.

The killer reached into Max's jacket pocket and removed the

cellphone. Stepping carefully around the body, he took the key and closed the door. Then he got about the business of leaving no trace behind.

Chapter Two

The Previous Day

Something shapeless but pungent penetrated Jimmy's dream, disturbing his sleep. Instantly awake, he recognized the smell of burning wood seeping through the open window. Wildfires raged through vast swaths of the country, but with the exception of occasional smoke blowing across the strait from the mainland, the small community of Britannia Bay had been spared. What it hadn't escaped was the devastating drought and hot weather baking the area.

Checking the clock radio, he saw that it was almost time to get up. He pressed the OFF button before the alarm sounded and glanced at Ariel, dead to the world and snoring softly. He slid quietly from under the sheet not wanting to wake her just yet.

Roger, who had wedged himself between Jimmy's feet, felt movement. The black long-haired cat stretched, hopped off the bed and padded toward the kitchen. And food. Roger was Jimmy's cat. Molly, the Siamese, answered to no one but Ariel, if she answered at all.

Closing the window against the acrid air, Jimmy slipped on his robe. Bad idea. It was too damned hot. He shuffled down the hall in slippers and pyjama bottoms.

Seeing that all superfluous creatures had left, Molly leapt onto the bed from her cat perch, nestled into Jimmy's pillow and buried her nose in Ariel's curls.

In the kitchen, Jimmy peered at the small wireless weather station. Inside and outside temperatures were the same—twenty-four degrees with no precipitation expected. The last real rain had fallen more than a month ago. Everything was parched and thirsty. Leaves curled and shriveled. Needles turned brown and dropped. Grass and ground crunched underfoot.

Filling the kettle, he plugged it in then dumped beans into the coffee grinder and turned it on. The racket didn't seem to bother Roger, who sat watching, lifting one paw and then another to a rhythm in his head and the thrum of his own purring.

Jimmy looked down at him while he shook the ground beans into the cafetière. "Now, what do you want, beastie boy?" Roger answered with a few slow blinks. "There's kibble in your bowl, you know."

Roger was having none of it and continued with his two-step dance, conversing telepathically with his owner until he got the message. Jimmy opened the dishwasher and pulled out a bowl decorated with the three little pigs. "I think this is the perfect bowl for you." Opening a small can of food, he put half in the bowl. "Here you go, you little oinker."

Roger dove in. "Thank you very much. You're welcome," Jimmy said as he poured hot water over the grounds. While the coffee brewed he stepped outside to scan the smoke-stained sky. Due to the onshore winds, blue skies prevailed all summer long in this beachside village. But this morning the air was still. Behind an ocher veil, a pale mustard dot outlined in red disguised the sun.

The seven o'clock news updated the fire situation, listing new fires, containment percentages and growth. The announcer

reminded listeners of the latest water restrictions. No watering at
all from sprinklers. From 7 PM until 9 PM, bucket watering only.

There was no mention of overnight murders, assaults, rapes,
B&Es, or vandalism. Why would there be? This was a small, law-
abiding town.

Jimmy gently pressed down the plunger, filled two mugs and
returned to the bedroom. He gingerly elbowed aside a biography of
Dietrich Fischer-dieskau on Ariel's bedside table and placed the cup
down. The fragrance awakened her. She sat up, stretched, and
reached for her coffee.

"Thank you, sweetheart." She blew across the top of the mug
then took a quick sip. "Mmm. Wonderful."

Molly shifted slightly, grunted and went back to sleep.

"I see you closed the window. There was only a hint of smoke
last night."

"There's more than usual out there now. And the sky is yellow."

"It'll blow away by this afternoon when the winds pick up," she
said with conviction. "It's like clockwork."

For a few moments, they drank their coffees in shared solitude.

"I guess all the news is about the fires."

"Pretty much. Some new ones overnight."

"Nothing bad happen around town?"

"Course not."

She put the mug on the table and opened her arms. "Come here
you delicious piece of ass. I need my morning glories."

Jimmy laughed, throwing off the sheet and startling Molly who
meowed her annoyance and jumped off the bed. Hormonal
harmonizing was not on her agenda.

After a cool shower, Jimmy stood in front of the bedroom mirror in
his socks and underwear. During the process of dressing, he felt
himself falling away as, piece-by-piece, he became Detective
Sergeant Jimmy Tan. Mentally preparing for the day ahead, he

knew he was only spinning his wheels. The day was bound to be the same as yesterday, and the day before that and the day before that. Nothing would require any "detecting." He sighed and headed back to the kitchen.

He heard Ariel singing Schubert in the shower. He had long ago stopped marvelling at the big voice belting from her petite body. She put her talents to good use, unlike himself. What did all of his training accomplish in this burg? Questions about his decision to leave Vancouver and move here seemed to be arising a lot lately.

Roger and Molly were waiting to go outside. Jimmy accommodated their wishes then placed a sliced bagel in the toaster oven.

Ariel strolled in wearing shorts and a T-shirt, and began preparing her usual breakfast. It was one less thing to think about before her brain and body began firing on all cylinders simultaneously. "That idiot across the street had his sprinklers on last night. They were still running at midnight."

"What were you doing awake at midnight?"

"What do you think? He woke me up walking around yelling on that freakin' cellphone." She poured soy milk into the bowl and began munching her muesli. "I could murder that man!" With her mouth full, the invective came out muffled. But it was clear to Jimmy, not being her first complaint against their neighbour. Since Max Berdahl's arrival on the quiet street, his strident voice had raised the ire of all the residents. Noisy table tennis games and weekend barbecues only added to his list of crimes. Ariel was not alone in her detestation of the man.

Jimmy poured a half cup of coffee and spread peanut butter on his bagel. As he took his first bite, he watched the cats meticulously grooming themselves. Caught in the sunlight, Roger's hair was shot through with gleaming bronze and gold, again reminding Jimmy of the hidden beauty of black cats. Now clean and bored, the two approached the glass door. He slid it open. "Dogs have masters. Cats have staff," he said, as they made their way in. Roger thanked him by brushing against Jimmy's pant leg leaving behind a silky stream of hair.

Molly vocalized her plaintive greeting to her mistress. Ariel absently reached down to fondle her ears, but her mind remained on their neighbour's misdeeds. "I hope the town fines him big time. But that probably won't happen. Sometimes I wonder if Council is turning a blind eye while he snubs his nose at the law. His freakin' family are such big shots around here. It seems the mayor is doling out indulgences their way."

"Pieter's not the Pope," he laughed. "And first of all, it's not a law. It's a bylaw."

She stopped eating and drilled him with her eyes. "Honestly Jimmy. You're splitting hairs. You know what I mean. Just because it's a new house doesn't mean everything has to be picture perfect right away. Why didn't he wait until the fall to lay sod?"

"Maybe because he's a real estate agent?"

"He's a *sod*, is what he is," she spat out.

"Don't let it get to you." He leaned down and kissed her damp hair, breathing in traces of lily-of-the-valley. "What's on your plate today?"

She heaved a sigh and looked at her husband resignedly. She knew when he had had enough of her tirades. "Not much. I have one student this afternoon. And then there's that meeting tonight."

"Oh, right. I forgot about that." He laced on his shoes.

Two government hydrologists had been invited to the Town Hall to speak about the drought situation and water conservation. Mayor Pieter Verhagen had been urging his community to take it more seriously. Senior citizens in particular, who made up the majority of the population, were not convinced that this rain forest part of the world could possibly be experiencing a lack of water.

"Clive is positively apoplectic about the possible loss of flowers and trees. He's already tearing out what's left of his hair over the brown grass." Clive Abernathy was President of Heritage Gardens Society, a position he wore like a royal robe. "He's practically ordered the board members to go to the meeting and voice our displeasure at the town's directives. But on this issue I think he's wrong."

"So you're going?"

"Of course. I feel I *have* to put in an appearance because *he* won't be there. He's off to Vancouver for *something more important*," she huffed.

Jimmy grinned at her umbrage then noted the time. "Speaking of going ... Oh, and just to make you feel better, sod is given a special permit."

She stared at him. "Is that what I think it means?"

"Yep. Berdahl got a green light, so to speak."

"Oh, thanks a lot for that bit of good news," she muttered.

He opened the door and snuck a peek at the sky. "You may want to take a look at this."

She joined him. "Oh my gosh. Isn't that weird?"

"Don't stare at the sun," he warned, and brushed a soft kiss across her cheek. "See you later."

"I'll see you, too ... and your adorable little ass."

Wiggling his behind, he headed off.

"Hey," she called out. "Have a safe one."

Without turning, Jimmy waved as he walked the few short blocks to the station. She had said the words lightly, but they were packed with meaning. When they lived in Vancouver with its violence—sometimes random, often targeted—she never knew if he would come home at all. And then there was his family.

Chapter Three

"Hey, Dave. How's it going?" Max plopped a pod of coffee into his Tassimo machine as he spoke on his Bluetooth. "GREAT. How soon will you be here?" Coffee poured, he filled a watering can, grabbed the cup and can and pushed the door open with his hip. A wall of heat stopped him dead. Fleet-footing back to the air-conditioned kitchen he removed his jacket. *Stupid to wear a suit in this weather. But hey, if you wanna do business you gotta look sharp.* Continuing the conversation, he made his way around the house, drinking his coffee and watering his hanging baskets. At the price he paid for them, there was no way he was going to let them die. He picked up a ping-pong ball and put it back on the table. *Last night's match had been AMAZING.*

At the front of his property he gazed at the last empty spot. His landscaper had convinced him to use a massive boulder as the fountain feature, and it was on its way. Everything about building this house had gone smoothly. Except for a nudge here and there. Trees, shrubs, and sod were in place. *The sod looked DY-NO-MITE! So what if it had required a special permit. It was a small price to pay.* He realized Dave was about to say goodbye. "That's AWESOME! JUST AWESOME! See you in a few. Ciao."

Next door, Delilah Moore was still asleep, but Max's shouting jolted her awake. Sitting up, she blinked rapidly for a few seconds waiting for her eyes to clear before focusing on the clock. Some of the numbers were dulled by the grey ghost in the centre of her pupils, but after adjusting the angle of her head, her vision captured the time. Coming up on eight o'clock.

She rolled to the edge of the bed and sat with her feet on the floor. At least she could still reach it. Her doctor had told her that she was just over five feet tall now, but that couldn't be right. She had always been five foot two, eyes of blue.

Sensing that she was finally getting up rather than making another trip to the loo, her tortoise-shell cat slipped daintily off the duvet.

Delilah waited until she felt steady then pushed herself up. "Mmph." She looked down at her beloved pet. "It's getting harder every day, Tabitha." She threaded her spotted and bony arms into the sleeves of her pink robe, inched her feet into her pink mules and carefully made her way along the rose-coloured carpet to the front window. Raising the blinds, she saw her neighbour watering his hanging baskets and yelling into something hanging around his neck.

That damned pipsqueak. Why is he always shouting on his phone? Morning and night. Does he think it's made of tin cans and string? I'd like to string him up. There must be some kind of noise ordinance in this town. I should complain to the mayor.

She returned to her pink palace—her en suite with its pink tub, sink and "throne." She used to make a joke about being in the pink when people commented on her colour scheme that carried throughout the house. Clutching the edge of the counter for support, she reached for her face cloth. Frailty and failing eyesight were beginning to encroach on her day-to-day activities. She would have preferred that it was her hearing that was going because she couldn't be bothered listening to what most people had to say anyway. "Am I being too grumpy, Melvin?" she asked aloud to her dead husband. "I know I should be grateful. No aches or pains. Well, except for a bit of arthritis."

Tabitha already had her nose in the kibble when Delilah stepped carefully into the kitchen, wary of the change from carpet to vinyl. Putting water on to boil, she spooned instant coffee into her Royal Albert cup then poured corn flakes into a bowl and sliced in half a banana. Her milk was nearly out. *Time to get more. Wonder what else I need? Maybe a dozen eggs. I'll pop down to Bayside Foods. Have a chat with Barb. She's always good for a laugh.*

She turned on her little battery-operated radio just as the news began. She only listened to one station—one that had been on the air since 1944. The station started up in her home town and in its infancy had live music. On the day of her twelfth birthday, she had sung *Whispering Hope* on air.

Vivid recollections of that day remained with her. She had taken the bus to the radio station and back home again by herself. Parents didn't mind if you did that in those days. There didn't seem to be any perverts around—and if there were, someone would give them a good sock. Not like today. Everybody too busy looking down at their cellphones tweaking, not paying attention to their surroundings. A youngster could get carried off in a second while their stupid mothers wandered around holding a phone instead of their child's hand.

Plagued by 3 AM anxieties while visualizing all the evil and sadness in the world, she would lie awake praying to Jesus to protect the vulnerable, and wondering why there were so many times when He wasn't listening. *Where was He when our Scott died in that frozen wasteland?* Her heart gave a little lurch. *Don't go there, Delilah.*

The radio announcer broke her reverie. "We begin the newscast with the unfolding wildfire situation across the west. First to the Elaho Valley fire which has grown to 650 hectares…"

A hectare. What the heck's a hectare? Why can't they say acre? People know what an acre is. Is a hectare smaller or bigger than an acre? She had looked it up, but now she couldn't remember. *It's like millimeters when they measure rainfall. Fifty millimeters! Good God! It must be a deluge. Then you find out it's only two inches.*

"Smoke has now covered Whistler where visitors are packing up and leaving. And there's no relief from the warm weather as the temperature is going to rise to twenty-five today."

At least Delilah knew that twenty-five Celsius would be about eighty degrees. *It's too hot and too dry. The world is turning into hell.*

Max read over the document for the hundredth time looking for any impediments to the possible purchase of ten acres of cleared land in the next community. He had put in an offer, and now he was waiting to hear from the owner. It would be an amazing opportunity for himself, his brother and his father whom he would contract to build the houses. After all, the Berdahls built some of the finest houses in the whole area. And solid, too.

While he worked, only the click, click of a wall clock broke the silence. After a half hour or so, he picked up his cellphone. "Hey Jari. If you're not doing anything, you wanna play squash later? ... Right on. I'll catch up with you mid-afternoon or so. Okay? ... Ciao."

As he ended the conversation, the call he had been praying for came in. "Hi, Dan. How are you this morning?" At that moment, the explosive hiss of air brakes announced the arrival of his latest acquisition. He high-tailed it out the front door. "So have you had anymore thoughts on our offer?" Listening with anticipation, he heard the words he desperately wanted to hear. "Sounds great. Can we meet Saturday morning, say around ten? Super. See you then." He ended the call and let out an ear-splitting whoop.

Tabitha, who had been sitting on the sofa back gazing out the window, fled into the bedroom, tail down, ears back. *Now what?*

Delilah got up to see what had frightened her. *Oh, no. Not again,* she groaned. All that spring large trucks and heavy equipment spilled onto the street. First came the caterpillar tearing out all the old trees—the last treed lot on the street stripped down to dirt. Neighbourhood cats had explored all the nooks and crannies, nosing aside branches and under leaves to see what lay behind or below. Sometimes they would come out with a mouse. Deer had bounded in and out eating whatever appealed to them. All gone. Birds and critters lost their playgrounds, foraging places and worse, their homes. *I could wring that man's neck!*

She crept part way up the driveway to get a good look at the shenanigans. The heat almost drove her back inside, but her curiosity prevailed.

A flatbed truck had parked in front of Max's house. Its cargo secured on all sides with thick nylon winch straps. Aboard, a huge chunk of angled rock sparkled shades of silver and blue in the early morning sunlight like a slice of the Canadian Shield. Another flatbed arrived carrying a Bobcat with a lift loader. As soon as it came to a juddering halt, a man jumped on board. He started the engine and drove the machine off the ramp. Everyone busied themselves with the work at hand. Delilah watched, fascinated, as a crane operator picked up the boulder. As it was lowered, workmen slid it into place as easy as a hot knife through butter.

By the time Delilah returned to the kitchen, her corn flakes had sunk into a soggy, milky mess and the newscast had switched to the sports report. The announcer repeated what she already knew—the Toronto Blue Jays had won another game, a game she had been watching the previous evening. They were having a terrific season. *It won't last. That's what Melvin used to say. And by George he was right.* Except when he was wrong. Twice.

She turned off the radio, threw out the cereal and put two slices of bread in the toaster. While she waited, she went back to watch the goings-on. Then something caught the corner of her eye. *There's that motorcycle again.* She had seen it a few times in the past couple of weeks and thought he would stop at the house on the other side of her where cars pulled up and left their engines running while someone dashed in and out. Thinking dope deals were going on, she had mentioned it to Ariel hoping she would pass it along to Jimmy. It was bad enough having that nincompoop destroy a wooded lot on one side of her, but then that slovenly cow moved in on the other and began throwing parties that lasted all hours of the day and night. And people throwing up in the driveway. *That place is nothing but a flop house. A blight on the neighbourhood.*

But the biker never did stop. *Maybe he's checking out houses to rob while people are at work. There's too much traffic using this street to get to the Community Centre. We should have local traffic only. Or speed bumps. The kids on their bicycles and skateboards could get hurt or worse. What's wrong with the zoning laws in this town? I should complain to the mayor.*

Chapter Four

A black BMW SUV pulled up on the side street. "Max and Jaxon. Your Go-To Property Guys," painted on the doors. On the back was a stylized logo of a house with "Berdahl Brothers. Property Developers" in large script. Out stepped a man who could have been Max's twin, dressed in a similar suit.

"Hey bro," Max greeted his younger brother. "You're just in time."

"Gosh. It's already in place. I thought it would take at least a couple of hours."

"Heck, it only took about a half hour. It was BRILLIANT."

"I'm sorry I missed it."

"Well, you're here for the countdown. That's the main thing." He punched him on the arm.

Jaxon flinched. "Where's Dad?"

"I don't know. I thought he'd be here by now, but I can't wait." He led him over to where the trades people had gathered. "EVERYONE READY?"

They formed a semi-circle. Max put his hand on the water faucet. "THREE! TWO! ONE!" He turned on the water and after a few seconds a stream shot up through the centre of the rock and began gurgling down the sides. Everyone cheered.

"AWESOME. JUST AWESOME," Max shouted.

At that moment, a white pickup threw out gravel as it slid to a stop. A tanned and fit man jumped out and rushed over. "Sorry I'm late, Max. Had a slight problem to take care of."

Max gave him a quick hug. "No problem, Dad."

The senior Berdahl strolled over to the fountain. "This is pretty darn nice, isn't it?" He surveyed the property, now complete. Father and sons stood together for a quiet moment.

"You built me a beautiful house, Dad."

Stefan Berdahl's eyes glistened. Max had been nitpicking every detail during the construction, and there were times he wanted to walk away. But the result was worth the petty annoyances. He cleared his throat. "It does look wonderful. Everyone did a great job."

"But they were your plans," Jaxon said, noting his father's reluctance to take credit for anything.

Jaxon's comment caused a rush of resentment to take hold of Max. "Be right back. I gotta go distribute some cheques," he said abruptly and walked away, his mind filling with dark thoughts. *The house plans might have been Dad's, but* I *am the one who brought them to fruition. It was* my *vision that turned it from a pretty house into a beautiful house. All the finishes and the landscaping had been* my *idea. Except for the fountain.*

He motioned to a few people to follow him and disappeared into the house. The others waited around, shielding their eyes from the relentless sun.

Jaxon took his father aside. "Dad, Max doesn't want me to be at the meeting with Dan Kendall. He says it will give the impression we're pressuring him."

"He could be right, Jaxon."

"But he could blow the deal. I've been told that Mr. Kendall doesn't like high-powered people and Max comes off that way."

Stefan smiled at the difference in his sons' temperaments.

"Jaxon, if he blows the deal, he blows the deal. It'll be on him." He looked straight into Jaxon's eyes. "And he has to redeem himself. You know that."

Jaxon, surprised by the quiet force of his words, looked off into the distance for a few moments. "I know."

"Then, just step back and let him have a free hand. We will live with the results."

"But it could be worth a couple of million," he protested.

"It's only money, son. It's not God's Heaven and Earth. And there will be other opportunities."

Carrying his jacket and a briefcase, Max came back out with the few contractors, who distributed cheques to their employees. As quickly as they had their payment in hand, they were gone. Rather than rejoining Jaxon and his father, Max inspected his newest addition.

Berdahl gently squeezed Jaxon's arm. "I need to get back to the job. I'll go say goodbye to your brother. You take care."

"I will, Dad." He watched as his father said a few words to Max and pulled him in for a bear hug. Jaxon felt a momentary stab of jealousy, but quickly chastised himself. He loved his big brother. He knew Max had strayed and needed watching, but he needed support and encouragement as well. Negative emotions must not worm their way into his thoughts. He would pray about that.

As his father drove away, Jaxon walked over to Max. "I'm off."

"Me too. Got lots of figures to look at."

"Well, don't burn the candle at both ends. Life is more than work, you know."

"Not with this family," Max laughed.

They knocked fists and headed to their vehicles. Driving off, Max looked in his rear-view mirror and frowned at a Harley heading up the street.

Chapter Five

"Good morning, everybody." Detective Sergeant Ray Rossini manoeuvered his way through the swinging double doors, a Styrofoam tray of coffees in one hand, a box of pastries in the other. Outgoing, cheerful and frank, he filled the room with his presence. He placed the items on the raised counter above the dispatcher's work station.

"Oh. Fresh coffee *and* goodies from Catalani's," Mary Beth McKay beamed. "You darling."

"You are wrong about that, Miss McKay. *You* are the darling."

She raised her eyes heavenward and grinned.

He opened the box with a flourish revealing an assortment of pastries.

"Mmm. They look scrumptious."

"Napkins are in my pocket." He stuck out his hip. "And don't get fresh."

Mary Beth blushed, took a napkin and chose the crostata with its rich pastry and tart cherry filling.

Glancing around the room, he noticed the empty desks. "McDaniel and Novak on patrol?"

"Yes," she mumbled, mouth full of sticky goodness

Picking up the box, he wove his way to the kitchen. Passing

Jimmy on the way he gestured with the box, and got the expected head shake.

Constable Simon Rhys-Jones was hard on his heels. "Thanks, Ray. I didn't have breakfast."

"Erin still laid up with morning sickness?"

"Yeah." He grabbed a coffee and piece of pastry. "I'll die of starvation before this baby is born."

"You need to learn how to cook," he lectured the young Welshman. *Like that's going to happen.* He returned to the squad room and plunked down in his chair opposite Jimmy. "How's it going, partner?"

"It's going," Jimmy answered tightly, thinking, "*Nowhere.*"

Ray picked up his mood, but let it slide. He noticed the open door to Chief Wyatt's office. "Chief not around?"

"He's in a meeting with the mayor."

"Oh, oh. That's not good."

The meeting would be about money. The police chief, not known for his serenity, would return with a blacker cloud than usual over his head. The tight-fisted mayor treated city funds as though they came from the famous little change purse tucked into his vest pocket. But he was re-elected time and again because he kept taxes low while maintaining infrastructure

In the last ten years, Mayor Pieter Verhagen had managed to swing a new fire hall, town hall and police station, the latter of which almost everyone agreed was far too big for this small town. But Verhagen argued that they needed a large, fully staffed station because it was not only the town they patrolled, but the entire township. This was the main source of taxes. Not the homes or small businesses in the village. The township contained the industrial and commercial operations generated by the fishing and agricultural base of the area as well as the airport and hospital. Surrounding it all were several square miles of family farms and forest.

To mollify the council's misgivings, the mayor constantly put off purchasing state-of-the art equipment for the police department. Even so, what they had was far superior to what was available in similar small-town stations. Thus, Wyatt did not have a lot of rocks in his slingshot when he faced off with the mayor.

Although early in the day, a call came in. Mary Beth quickly swallowed a piece of half-chewed pastry. "Police headquarters. How may I help you?" She listened for a second or two, and then turned to face the squad room with a grin. "Oh, good morning, Mrs. Hoffmeyer." Everyone groaned. The constant caller was considered a meddlesome mischief-maker around town.

Ray spoke in a high-pitched voice, "I just saw Eugenia No-Last-Name, walking a big hairy dog and she didn't pick up the poop."

After listening for a few minutes, Mary Beth said, "Thank you Mrs. Hoffmeyer. We'll deal with it right away ... Yes I'll call you back to let you know."

"What is it this time?" Ray asked.

"She smelled smoke coming from Chester Hansen's place."

"That stupid old bat." Ray shook his head in disgust. "He's probably smoking salmon. But we'll have to send someone." Being senior officer in the chief's absence, he pointed to Rhys-Jones who sighed, gulped down the last of his coffee and, as he headed out the door, lobbed back a Welsh curse resulting in nothing but laughter. He was small, knobby and dark. It was as though dust from the slag heaps of South Wales had drifted onto his body at birth leaving him with black hair, glittering coal black eyes and olive skin.

Ray retrieved the coffee that was meant for the chief. "Would you like this coffee, Mary Beth? It's only going to get cold."

"Thanks, Ray." She took the coffee in one hand and held out the other.

"What?"

"So, what do I dunk in it?"

He laughed, returned to the kitchen and brought back the pastry box. "Here you go. If you're not careful, you'll turn into a real cop," he warned her.

Mary Beth was one of the many civilians who worked for the police department in Information Management positions. This could mean anything from manning the phones to transcribing statements. She had been with the department for several years, and was respected for her calm ability to redirect non-emergency calls, gather information, relay messages to police officers, and to sit for hours at a time. Her ample behind was proof of that.

Ray sat and pulled a file from his bottom drawer. "So, tell me what's on your mind, Tan."

"Thrilled by all the excitement and criminal activity."

"Yeah. Really hard to take, isn't it?" He waved the file. "I got a real doozy here. Seems like someone may be stalking Bryony Shepherd," and he guffawed.

"Isn't she the cook at Abernathy's B and B?"

"Yeah. Picture this. She's waddling down the street after eating one too many waffles—"

"—I'd rather not."

"— and there's some perv trailing behind her. And then she says she sees the same guy standing in front of her house."

"Probably someone walking their dog and waiting for it to do its business."

"Whatever. I think she just wants a man to come and talk to her." He paused. "I think I'll send Tamsyn instead. That'll shut her up." He looked around. "Where is Foxcroft, by the way?"

"Probably beating up her ex."

"Nah. I heard he's scared shitless of her—runs when he sees her coming. She could freeze the balls off a brass monkey with one look."

Jimmy laughed then returned to his report on the harassment of an elderly woman. Two young boys, about thirteen, had been running up and pounding on her door or ringing the bell over and over and then running off. She was fearful, but he had told her that it was a childhood prank and she should ignore them. Sooner or later they would either become bored or outgrow it. He didn't mention that if that was the worst thing that happened to her she was lucky. After making a few notations he filed the document away then glanced at the clock. "The chief should be coming back soon."

Ray nodded. "A long meeting is better than a short one."

No sooner was the remark out of his mouth than Chief William Wyatt stormed in. Without a word, he strode to his office, slammed the door and yanked his blinds shut. Ray, Jimmy and Mary Beth looked at each other as they heard something slam against something. "Ooh. Must have been pretty bad," she whispered.

Ray nodded. "Yeah. Think I'll just keep my head down." They knew that the chief would simmer down and eventually come out and report on his head-to-head with the mayor.

Wyatt recognized the importance of keeping morale high. One way he accomplished that was to keep his officers and civilian personnel in the loop. The only thing he could not do was keep his temper in check. That aside, he was respected and liked by his crew.

Simon returned with Constables Gene McDaniel and Tim Novak in tow. They sensed the atmosphere and spotted the chief's closed door and closed blinds. Needing no other explanation, they were heading for their desks when Mary Beth quietly intercepted them holding out the box of pastries. McDaniel, a tall black man with charm and good looks to spare, chose one, gave her a big smile and thanked her, causing her heart to flutter and her skin to flush.

Novak watched with a wry grin. He felt sorry for Mary Beth's involuntary blushing around McDaniel. He knew such a thing would never happen with him, but he did not mind. Small in stature with an almost imperceptible lisp, his appeal arose from his natural charm and sense of humour, which bordered on the mischievous. He seemed like a grown-up Cupid. During breaks, he entertained everyone with jokes and stories and singing songs in his beautiful tenor voice. Genuinely sweet, he was loved by everyone on the squad. Why he chose to become a cop baffled them all—unless it was his heart-felt desire to serve and to make the world a better place.

Mary Beth saw Simon taking out his report form. "Simon, did you talk to Mrs. Hoffmeyer?"

"No, I didn't. There is no way I'm going to deal with that old biddy face-to-face. I might punch her out."

"You'd need a ladder," Ray added to the laughter in the room.

"So what do I tell her when she calls back?" Mary Beth asked him. "You know she's going to call again."

"Just tell her that Chester was smoking salmon. She won't be happy until we throw someone in jail until they rot," Simon groused.

Rhys-Jones's reluctance to talk to the complainant arose from spitting matches between her and his wife. Mrs. Hoffmeyer had been incensed that Erin had replaced their lawn with drought-resistant plants that didn't "fit in" with the neighbourhood. He began to write up his report running what remained of his fingernails through his wavy black hair. Should he mention that Chester had given him a chunk of smoked salmon? No. Chester hadn't done anything illegal so it wasn't a bribe. He omitted the gift from the report and smiled. At least this time Mrs. Hoffmeyer's complaint had backfired.

As noon approached, Jimmy stood up, stretched and picked up a pad and pen. "I'm taking lunch orders," he announced.

"It's not your turn, is it?" Ray asked.

"No. I just need to shake out my legs."

Ray looked at Jimmy sharply. There was something off with his partner—had been for some time. He hoped everything was okay at home.

After taking their orders and cash, Jimmy looked at Wyatt's door.

Ray smiled. "You gonna chance it?"

"Yeah, I think so. He's had time to cool down." He walked over and tapped on the door.

"Come in," Wyatt called out.

Jimmy stepped in, leaving the door ajar. "I'm doing a lunch run to Justine's, Chief. Can I get you anything?"

Wyatt, whose salt-and-pepper head was bent over a ledger sheet, took a few seconds to answer. "Yeah, a club on white toast but leave out the middle slice of bread. And ask her to make a fresh pot of decaf, will you?" He stood and reached for the wallet in his back pocket. "And top up the tip. She can get real cranky with cheapskates," he added, handing Jimmy a ten-dollar bill.

Jimmy stuffed the money in his pocket and was about to close the door.

"You can leave that open," Wyatt told him.

Overheard, those few words eased the tension in the squad room. Jimmy signalled a subtle thumbs-up as he passed through. When he returned loaded down with bags, the familiar squeak of the chief's chair as he got up was almost comforting.

Wyatt had grown up in Britannia Bay and been its Chief of Police for eight years. It was not his first posting, but he was planning for it to be his last. He intended to retire early. After that, he and Sherilee would take their fifth wheeler and travel all over North America. They had spent their evenings at the kitchen table poring over maps, plotting their route, and adding some out-of-the-way places they had heard about from friends. When he was at work, he viewed the lone jail cell and felt as if *he* were a prisoner. Was it any wonder that he was a grump?

He came into the room and cleared his throat, garnering their attention. "Let's gather in the kitchen. I want to bring you up to speed on my meeting with the mayor."

They got busy unwrapping their sandwiches and getting drinks from the fridge. While the station had been built five years before, it had yet to acquire a comfortable, well-worn ambiance. It was not a home yet. Not that that anyone would want it to be. But the kitchen with its toaster and microwave ovens, apartment-size fridge and automatic coffee maker was as close as it came, which is why officers could often be found there when they weren't at their desks.

Novak threw out the coffee that had been stewing since first light and made a fresh pot. McDaniel spread napkins and paper plates around the table. Wyatt inspected his club sandwich. "How much tip did you splash out on this, Tan?"

"Twenty percent."

Wyatt winced but nodded. He bit in and started chewing. They all did the same, enjoying their sandwich of choice. Justine's Joint was only open from eight until three, and even though she had no competition to speak of, she never took advantage of the fact, giving her customers Grade A food and service. Justine's bespoke cafe was a little goldmine.

Finishing first, Wyatt walked over to three different-coloured bins where he deposited his leftovers into the appropriate receptacles. The town had strict recycling and garbage rules, which people now viewed as SOP. He waited until everyone was settled then blew out a long breath. "You know, I've been on to the council umpteen times about replacing our crime scene equipment. Well, it appears that that is not going to happen yet again. The Capital Budget is unchanged." His sagging shoulders displayed his disappointment. "There was nothing I could say that convinced Verhagen. He said there's no crime here that demands it." He paused for a moment. "I suppose he's right."

Ray chimed in. "At this point we should count ourselves lucky that we even have a photo lab, and someone who knows how to use it."

McDaniel wanted to say something witty about how often his skills had been called upon, but decided he would just keep his mouth shut. No one was in the mood for mirth.

"The only good news is that our Operating Budget for next year will be bumped up. And depending on the town's overall fiscal condition, we may even get a pay raise over and above the usual cost of living increase."

"Well, that's something coming from that tight wad," Ray said.

"Well, to play the Devil's Advocate, I don't have to remind you who his constituents are, Ray. Some of these people were around during the Great Depression. They're frugal, and appreciate a mayor who's the same. That's why he keeps getting elected."

"All the same," Ray muttered.

"Okay. Enough of that." Wyatt wanted to change the narrative before it descended into a time-wasting, mayor-bashing, belly-aching session. "On to something more upbeat—this weekend's activities."

Chapter Six

"Aww, Mom," Marcus complained as his mother struggled with his bow tie.

"Don't 'aww Mom' me." Georgina warned. She had watched a bow tie demonstration on the Internet, but it was trickier than it looked.

"But I'm going to look so … so … gay."

"Don't use that word, Marcus Rossini," she admonished him.

"You know what I mean. The guys will laugh at me."

"You? I seriously doubt it," she said, taking in his broad shoulders. "They *are* going to be jealous, though. The girls will be all over you like white on rice." *Maybe Umberto will have to do this. He's tied enough of them.*

"But it's so old fashioned. Nobody dresses like this anymore."

"Ah hah! Got it." She stepped back and examined her handiwork. "Hmm. Maybe not." *Umberto it is.* Seeing her handsome seventeen-year-old son in the tux with its cutaway jacket, white vest, shirt and bowtie almost made her cry. But she contained herself. "Perfect. All you need now is the panache to carry it off."

"What's panache?"

"Watch a Fred Astaire film and you'll know what I'm talking about. He had style and elegance. He was the epitome of cool."

"Who's Fred Astaire?"

Georgina sighed. "Okay. Then *The Godfather*. See how beautifully they dressed and you'll understand what I mean."

"*The Godfather*? That old movie? Those guys were all gangsters. I don't want to look like a gangster."

"That movie is a classic, Mr. Know-Nothing, and this tux is the same. It's very sophisticated. You want to look like some sixties R and B group with their powder blue tuxes and frilly shirts? That's what a lot of your friends are going to look like. You'll stand out."

"Yeah. Like a big pimple on the end of my nose."

"Wrong. I'll make a bet with you, young man. I'll bet your picture will be on the front page of *The Bayside Bugle*."

"That's not saying much. It's a rag."

"It may be a rag but it's our rag."

"So what's the bet?"

"If you don't get on the front page as the hippest grad of the year, I'll personally take out an ad and say that I forced you to wear it. How's that?"

Marcus pondered this for a moment. "So you think the girls will like it?"

"They'll be elbowing each other to get to you."

"Yeah. Right," he snorted.

"Now stand over there. I'm going to take your picture to show your dad when he gets home."

Marcus stood awkwardly, not knowing what to do with his hands or feet. He faced the camera full fronted.

"Oh, for goodness sake. It's a photograph. Not a mug shot," Georgina said. "Do this," and she struck a "ta-dah" pose, which he copied. She had to be quick because he started laughing.

"I feel like a jerk," he told her as she took the shot. "Now I'm gonna put on some *real* clothes," he announced.

His sister approached him in the hall. "Oh, dude. You look so lame."

"Gabriella!" Georgina yelled at her.

"See Mom? I told you!" He shouted back at her.

Gabriella punched him on the arm. "I'm just kidding, Marc. Actually, you look kinda cool."

"Huh. Some vote of confidence coming from you." He opened his door.

Georgina stepped into the hall. "Marcus, don't be rude." He slammed the door.

She turned to her fifteen-year-old daughter whose eyes were now level with her own. She had shot up in the past year. Up, not out, thankfully. Too many of her friends were overweight. But that didn't stop them from swanning around in yoga pants with their big butts hanging out and thongs in full view. "Honestly, Gabby."

"Sorry, Mom."

"Oh, never mind. It's what I expect from you guys." They went into the kitchen where Gabriella eyed a plate of pastries.

"Is that all there is?"

"I sent most of them with your dad this morning. There wasn't much left from last night."

"No wonder. Lana's pastries are amazing. She's *so* much better than Bruno. And *he* was Italian."

Georgina recalled the summer evening four years before when two stylish women walked into Catalani's, the restaurant owned by Ray's parents, Umberto and Silvana. Busy greeting and seating other customers, Georgina had not taken special notice of them during the evening. When they asked her about desserts, she apologized and explained that the pastry chef had left, so their selections were limited. Fall came and went, and with Christmas approaching, Georgina and Silvana prepared *zuppa inglese*, tiramisu and cranberry almond crostata. They were exhausted from all the extra work.

Then in early spring, Georgina received a call from a Lana Westbrook. She mentioned her visit to Catalani's the previous summer and asked if they were still without a pastry chef. That was when Georgina remembered the conversation she had had with the woman with enormous brown eyes. She thought she was going to pass along the name of someone. But when Lana said she was a *maître pâtissier* trained in Paris, Georgina wondered if she dared hope.

Lana said that she had been over to Britannia Bay a few times since that first visit. She was planning to leave Vancouver, and the town seemed a lovely place to live. At the moment she was teaching at *École Gastronomique* but the semester would be over soon. If they were interested, she would like to come over for an interview. She would bring her credentials with her. Georgina suggested that if she were serious, she should come prepared to bake. Lana took up the challenge.

Her arrival was greeted with the enthusiasm they might have given Pope John XXIII, the last pope the Rossinis had any use for. Umberto approved of her instantly, claiming later that it was obvious she came from *buon allevamento*. Good breeding or not, Silvana first wanted to see her *maître pâtissier* certificate. After they had watched her working and tasted her Italian pastries, they realized she was the real deal. But it was her lemon pie that sealed it. They had rarely tasted such a refreshingly authentic pie, and there had to be chocolate cake and a pie for the diners used to those desserts. Later, on the menu, it was called Lana's Legendary Lemon Pie.

After filling in all of the necessary employment forms, she asked if it would be all right if she did the baking in her own home. All right? It would be wonderful as long as it passed health inspection. Their kitchen was already bursting through the walls. She then requested that her information remain confidential. They said they would keep her employment as confidential as they could in a town that thrived on gossip. They wondered if she were hiding from a man.

Chapter Seven

Mid-morning and already hot. Lana began opening the windows to get a cross breeze. But smelling smoke, she closed them and turned on the air conditioning. As she grated lemon zest, she glanced out at Pascal lugging around buckets to water the flowers and shrubs. Her appreciation of him had grown as he gradually took on more of the decision-making, thereby leaving her time to bake.

Throughout her first summer in Britannia Bay, Lana had managed to get one area of the garden cleared and planted. The struggle to rip up ground cover had taken a toll on her hands and they hurt when she kneaded dough. In spite of all she had done, there was still a mountain of work awaiting her. In early September she threw in the towel and started advertising for a gardener. She was specific about what she wanted. But when applicants began arriving, she wondered if they had even read the ad past "Gardener Wanted." No one was willing to do anything except cut grass, prune and mulch. Lana had despaired of finding someone when, one afternoon, her doorbell rang. A petite woman with wild curls and a wide smile stood on the stoop, a bouquet in her hand.

"Hello. Gosh, what beautiful dahlias."

The woman held out the flowers. "A belated welcome to the neighbourhood."

"Thank you very much." Lana was touched by the gesture.

"I've already shaken out the earwigs." she said, laughing. "My name is Ariel Tan. My husband, Jimmy, and I live in front of you on the other side of the lane." She nodded in the direction of her house.

"It's nice to meet you. I've seen your garden. It's gorgeous. I hope to have something similar in a few years. Oh, I'm forgetting my manners. I'm Lana Westbrook." They shook hands.

"I already know your name. Don't forget. This is a small town. You're the Lana of Legendary Lemon Pies."

She laughed. "That's me." She was wondering what to say next. *Here was a neighbour coming over unannounced. Was she simply being neighbourly? Or nosy?* There was just enough space in the conversation to create an awkward pause.

Ariel flushed. "Um ... I'm probably interrupting you." She turned to leave. "If you need anything ... like information about the town, pop over. I'm usually home. I'll be off now."

Lana made up her mind. "I have some biscotti cooling. Do you have time for coffee?"

"Well, if I didn't before, I do now." She giggled.

As they walked through the airy living room to the kitchen, Ariel noted all the changes. She remembered the original house, and what she saw bore no resemblance to it. A wall had been knocked out, and when she entered the enlarged, gleaming stainless steel kitchen she knew why. "Wow! Is this ever fabulous! It's like something out of a TV cooking show." No slouch in the kitchen herself, she regarded everything with admiration tinged with envy. Then she checked out the biscotti on a cooling rack. "Mmm. These smell wonderful. What's in them?"

"These are pistachio, and these are cranberry chocolate," Lana pointed out. "Actually, I'm just learning to get them right. I'm not sure what they'll be like when they're dunked."

As they dunked the biscotti into mugs of dark-roast coffee, they agreed that they were damn fine. The subject of gardening naturally arose. In passing, Ariel mentioned that she was a member of a garden organization.

Lana seized on the words. "A garden organization?"

"Well actually, it's the Heritage Garden Society, but that sounds so formal and stuffy." She paused a second. "Well, in fact, it is." Then she let out a raucous laugh that ended in a snort.

Lana chuckled, enjoying this woman. "Tell me about it."

As Ariel launched into a description, a lightbulb lit up inside Lana's head. "Can I ask you something?"

Caught by the tone in her voice, she looked at her with interest. "Sure."

"I'm in desperate need of a gardener. I've advertised, but no one wants to do the grunt work. And I need someone who also knows something about garden design. Would you happen to know of anyone?"

"I know what you're up against," she said, recalling the overgrown areas visible from the street. "Let me put on my thinking cap. There may be one or two prospects who work at Heritage Gardens part time."

"That would be wonderful."

"I'm not promising anything."

"I understand." She did, but she was still hopeful.

"Well, I'd better shift myself."

"Just a second." Lana wrapped and packed two each of the biscotti and handed them to Ariel. "A trade for the flowers."

"Ooh, lovely. Thanks."

About a week later, Lana received a call from a man with a Québécois accent. He told her he worked part time at Heritage Gardens. They set up an appointment for the next day. When he arrived, she tried not to prejudge him. His lean body was clothed in dirt-encrusted jeans and a soiled, sweat-stained T-shirt. That was to be expected. After all, he was a gardener. What gave her pause were the tattoos of flowers growing up both his arms.

As she showed him around the property pointing out what she had already done and what she wanted done, she took in his close-cropped black beard and dark eyes under an old Montreal Expos baseball cap. Other than listening intently and nodding now and then, his comments were sparse. When they completed the circuit, he revealed, in somewhat broken English, his knowledge of plants and soil and gave her some suggestions. Impressed, she hired him on the spot. Ariel's inquires had borne fruit.

That was how the two women had become friends and Pascal Nadeau her gardener. Lana loved how he treated the garden as though it were his own. It was thriving and filled with all manner of unusual plants. Something else unusual was that they rarely discussed anything except plants and the weather. During the early days of his employment, she would say things that she hoped might lead him to be more revealing. But he was tight lipped. She wondered if he would be more comfortable speaking in French. But when she tried conversing in her Parisian French, he laughed and said, "*Votre français est trop rapide.*" And wading through his Québécois patois was a cultural minefield for Lana. She was loath to insult him by saying, "*Je ne comprends pas.*" When nothing was forthcoming in either language, she ceased the exercise. She recognized a person who wished to remain private.

Turning from thoughts of Pascal to her chocolate cake, she tossed a couple of bottle caps of brandy into the ganache and waited for it to cool. The cake and a lemon pie were going to Justine's, who was staying open because of tonight's meeting. Justine often asked her to provide a few items for special occasions. Lana's contract was with Catalani's, but Georgina never had any objections.

Tomorrow morning she would have to bake enough pastries to cover the evenings she would be away. Every two months, she spent three nights in Vancouver with her friend, Charlotte, her husband and young children. Lana relished the ferry trip, the relaxing visit and the chance to get her hair cut. The trip also kept her attached to the city and mentally, if not physically, detached from Britannia Bay. Maintaining her distance from the residents of the village was a struggle. Their nosiness, even if not meant to be intrusive, irritated her—Ariel excepted.

When she purchased the house and had the interior gutted, people began to talk. They speculated that all the renovating "didn't come cheap." Guesswork had become the latest diversion for seniors drinking their morning coffee at Justine's. When free top-ups kept their lips lubricated, some carpenters and dry-wallers passed along what they knew.

It was soon determined that she was divorced from a wealthy entrepreneur, high-powered lawyer, plastic surgeon, celebrity chef or sports super star. News that Catalani's had hired her as their new pastry chef resulted in patrons pumping Georgina for information, who told one and all the same thing: "If you want to know, knock on her door and ask her." They were horrified at the suggestion. It was not until the following spring that someone took Georgina's advice.

Lana had just put the finishing touches on two tiramisus and was looking forward to sitting down with another Donna Leon mystery when she heard the doorbell. On the doorstep stood a florid-faced man with a well-trimmed moustache above a snaggle-toothed grin. Tiny red veins traversed his nose like rivers on a miniscule map. Even in the heat he was dressed in a linen suit and sported a bow tie. He doffed his straw hat, revealing thin grey hair combed over his freckled scalp.

"Good afternoon, Miss Westbrook," he greeted in a plummy British accent while holding out a business card. "My name is Clive Abernathy, and I'm President of the Heritage Garden Society." Lana now knew what Ariel meant by formal and stuffy.

She took his card but did not look at it. "Yes?"

A breath as chilly as an Arctic winter blew onto his face. Undaunted, he carried on. "It has come to my attention that you are doing extraordinary things with your garden, and I wondered whether you might give me a tour."

What cheek. "I'm sorry Mister—" and she now made a point of looking at his card, "—Abernathy. But I *am* busy. You are free to look around on your own, however." She suspected that touring her garden, when it was nowhere near "extraordinary," was only part of the reason for his visit. She pointed to the right. "You can start there," was all she said.

It would have been enough to put off a more sensitive soul but Abernathy had a brass neck. He bobbed his head, thanked her, donned his hat and trundled off in the direction indicated. Seconds later, Pascal dashed around to the kitchen.

"That man is—," he started.

"Yes, I know," Lana said, showing him the business card. "Does he know you?"

"No. I do not see him in the garden. *Jamais.*"

"Really? That's interesting. Well, just let him look around. *Mais pour l'amour de Dieu*, keep him away from here," she indicated the patio and kitchen. As he was about to move off, she called him back. "Pascal, if he asks anything, just pretend you don't speak English."

He grinned conspiratorially, did a swift salute and headed back to where Abernathy was poking about. Of course the President of the Heritage Garden Society could not pass up an opportunity to illustrate how much he knew, so he asked Pascal a question that he was sure he wouldn't be able to answer. And sure enough he couldn't. "No spik Inglese," he said, and Abernathy hit one more brick in the wall.

He left, armed with only fragments of information. Nevertheless, he instantly passed them along to his wife who shared them with her book club. Within a matter of days, dozens knew that her garden had been transformed into the style of England, Japan, France, Italy, and Arizona. And that her "swarthy" gardener was Mexican, Italian, Portuguese or Spanish. And so it went.

Two years had passed since then, and by the time the locals sat down with a piece of chocolate cake or lemon pie, the only thing they truly knew about Lana was that she was one hell of a baker.

Chapter Eight

Ingrid had already left for the day when the phone rang. Max checked the call display. *Private caller.* Curious, he picked up. "Berdahl Property Development, Max Berdahl speaking," he answered tentatively.

The caller apologized acknowledging the special weekend in Britannia Bay, but he and his wife were on their way up island to visit their daughter and son-in-law who were interested in the Schwindt property on Townshipline Road. They wanted him to have a look at it. Would Max have time to show it to him tomorrow?

Max punched the air. For almost a year he had been trying to rid himself of this property on the edge of town. It was his final residential listing. Schwindt had already moved into his new home and twice had lowered the asking price. "Have you seen the place yourself, Mr...?"

"Fitzgerald," he offered. "No, I haven't."

"But your daughter has?"

"Yes. She and her husband have been by a couple of times, and I think I know what you are getting at," he said with smile in his voice. "She said it needed a bit of cheering up."

Max laughed. "That's a good way to put it. The owners have been doing their best to maintain it. The front steps need replacing, but overall the fundamentals are sound. The interior is in good shape. And the view is spectacular."

"So I've been told."

"I could meet you there after lunch, say one o'clock?"

"Oh, we won't be leaving Victoria before two o'clock. I don't expect we would arrive in Britannia Bay until around five."

Max was thinking. All he had on his plate was the gathering at Jaxon's and he could still make that. "That would work for me. Do you know how to find the place?"

"Yes, my daughter gave me a detailed map."

"Excellent. I'll meet you there tomorrow at five o'clock."

"Thanks very much. If we can't make it by that time, I'll give you a call."

"Great. I'll be here all day. But let me give you my cell number just in case," which he read off.

"I appreciate you doing this on such short notice, Mr. Berdahl."

"No problem at all. And please call me Max."

"Right you are. Goodbye for now."

Max was jubilant. The acreage deal with Kendall looked imminent, and now maybe this millstone would be off his neck. He'd been looking for an opportunity to set things right with the Schwindts. Perhaps his efforts were finally being rewarded. Or perhaps it was divine intervention. Whatever. Things were looking up.

When Ray pushed open the kitchen door, Georgina greeted him in her usual way. She hugged him, said "*baciami*," and puckered her lips waiting for him to plant a big kiss on her mouth.

"Usual day?" she asked.

"Usual day," he replied.

A smile lit up her face. "I want to show you something."

Wiggling his eyebrows, he gave her the glad eye. "Do I need to undress?"

"Tsk! You lothario." She picked up her cellphone and opened the gallery. "Look at this."

Ray took a few seconds. "This is Marcus?"

"Yes," pride ringing in her voice.

"He looks sensational. Like a movie star."

"That's what I told him."

"Where did you get the tux?"

"I rented it from the costume department at the little theatre."

Ray continued to stare. "Jeez, Georgie, he's so handsome and he looks so grown up."

"Yeah. I know," her voice echoing the nostalgia she heard in her husband's words.

"He's gonna be beating off the girls."

"That's what I told him but he didn't believe me."

"I'll tell him." He took the cellphone and looked again at his son. "We made beautiful children, didn't we?"

She snuggled in his arms. "We did that."

"Is it too late to make more?"

She poked him in the ribs. "You know it is, you goon."

"Maybe we could challenge nature." He looked at her expectantly. "Where are the kids?"

"Never mind that. I have to get ready to go to work."

He pretended to pout. "You're no fun anymore."

She ignored him. "Are you coming by the restaurant for dinner?"

The thought of a delicious meal perked him up. It used to be sex and food. Now it was food and maybe sex.

The evening shift filed in while Jimmy walked out.

"Hi, Jimmy. How's it going?" Constable Craig Carpenter greeted him.

"Going okay, Craig." Jimmy never failed to feel like one of the Seven Dwarfs next to the former professional middle linebacker.

Constable Dalbir Dhillon followed behind. "Detective Tan. How you doin', man?" he boomed and bumped fists with Jimmy.

"Same as always, Dal," he replied. Jimmy didn't want to hang about and shoot the breeze. He just wanted to get away from the claustrophobic atmosphere. All day long he had been enveloped in ennui and a desire to be anywhere but the station. Outside, the sky had changed from yellow to blue. Trees swayed and dipped. Westerlies blew across the bluffs pushing out the offending smoke and trailing the tang of salt air in their wake. Just as Ariel had promised.

At the thought of her, he crossed the street to Bayside Foods and looked at the selection of bouquets and cut flowers. Ariel hated to see her own blossoms die an early death, so she never picked them unless they were for friends. He chose two bunches each of carnations and gerberas and a bunch of baby's breath. That was his first mistake.

As he approached the check-out counter, he saw Barb's bead on him.

She frowned. "Are these for Ariel?"

"Who else?"

She nodded at the chosen flowers. "Well, she doesn't like those."

One of the original employees, Barb was blunt to a fault. She spoke that way to everybody, and if they were offended, then they could damn well go to another cashier. But she had a following because of her ear to the ground and ability to make people laugh.

Jimmy realized she probably knew more about Ariel's floral preferences than he did. Coming out from behind the counter, she snatched the flowers from his hands and marched back to the display. She gathered up several different colours of alstromeria and hybrid lilies. "These are what she would buy," she told him. He could see that his selections paled beside her colourful and exotic-looking bouquet. "They last a long time, which is one reason she likes them." She slipped them into a cellophane sleeve and dropped two packs of preservative inside.

When she began to wrap them in decorative paper, Jimmy made his second mistake, "That's not necessary, Barb. Ariel will just toss it in the recycle bin."

She withered him with narrowed eyes. "Are you thick as a brick? You're bringing your wife flowers, and you're not going the whole nine yards?" She clicked her tongue. With pursed lips, she wrapped the flowers, took his money, and gave him his change and receipt in one fast and fluid motion. "Now, if she doesn't kiss you when she sees these, my name ain't Barb."

Jimmy bowed deeply to her.

"Oh, go on with you," she laughed, which led to fits of coughing. Barb was last of the long-time smokers.

Sauntering home, Jimmy reflected on his detachment. It was not as if his mind had been on anything else. It just hadn't been there. He recalled this morning when Ariel had been complaining about Berdahl that his thoughts had wandered to the cats. Maybe the flowers were a subconscious apology for something she probably hadn't even noticed.

Barb's words were prophetic. Ariel threw her arms around him and kissed him on his cheek. "Oh, what a nice surprise!"

Jimmy looked sheepish. "Yeah, I guess I don't buy you flowers that often, do I?"

"Let me see." She held up a hand and began counting on her fingers.

"Okay. Okay. Don't rub it in."

"Never mind. You thought about it today." She reached into a cupboard for a vase. "These are my favourite cut flowers. How did you know?"

"I had a little help." He sat down and removed his shoes.

Ariel laughed. "Barb?"

"One and the same."

While Ariel dealt with the flowers, Jimmy went into the bedroom where he began the transformation back to being himself.

As he removed his clothes, he wondered what that was. He inspected each item. *Almost unused. Sort of like me.* He sank down on the edge of the bed. *Is that it? Am I becoming useless?* He pulled on some shorts and went into the bathroom to clean up. That was his image in the mirror, but it looked lifeless. After he splashed cold water on his face, he patted his cheeks. The sound triggered an image and maybe a remedy for his bland state of mind. He hurried back to the bedroom, coming out soon after carrying a duffel bag. "Ariel," he called out.

"I'm in the living room."

He found her placing the vase of flowers on a console table. "I'm going down to the do-jo."

"What brought this on? It's not Saturday afternoon."

He tapped his head. "I've been feeling weird all day, like there are cobwebs up here. I need to clear them out."

"Okay. I'll be at that meeting. You can heat up the butter chicken when you get home."

"Right." He rushed out leaving Ariel in the tail of a passing tornado.

Chapter Nine

The evening was warm. The hall was stuffy. Even so, Mayor Pieter Verhagen had anticipated a large crowd, but this was unprecedented. A backside adorned every chair in council chambers. Those unfortunate enough to arrive after the eager beavers had to find a seat in the hallway and listen through the open doors. But at least they had seats. He watched as people gave up their chairs to older residents and joined the many already jostling for a place to stand.

Britannia Bay was a noted garden town. It boasted the Heritage Garden Society and the Britannia Bay Horticultural Society, two entities known for their petty jealousies and slanging matches. There were flower competitions leading to acrimony, subterfuge and all manner of hurt feelings. Flower gardens required lovely lawns to set off their beauty. Britannia Bay didn't get its name by accident. It had been settled by immigrants in the early 1900s that came from a country known for its lush green lawns. And all newcomers, irrespective of nationality, embraced the custom. Thus, water resources were a hot issue.

Mayor Verhagen looked at his watch. Seven o'clock sharp. He stepped up to the podium and tapped the microphone. Hearing the echo, he cleared his throat. "Good evening, ladies and gentlemen," he said, his voice reverberating around the room. The chatter abated somewhat, but not entirely. He pressed ahead, nevertheless. Waiting for this crowd to settle down on protocol alone was too much to expect. "We are fortunate to have with us tonight two eminent hydrologists from the provincial government who are going to speak about the drought situation and to offer some suggestions on water conservation." At the word "drought," people stopped in mid-word.

"They will also take questions at the end of the meeting. I'd now like to introduce Professors Bob Browne and Alan Cunningham." A smattering of applause greeted the two experts.

Browne took the podium. A tall, slim man, about forty-five years of age, he had a neatly trimmed beard and thinning sandy hair that was slightly longer than most of the inhabitants of Britannia Bay. His rugged appearance was more like that of someone who spent his time outdoors rather than in the rarefied air of a university campus.

"Good evening. Professor Cunningham and I are pleased to be here in this lovely town tonight, although we wish the current circumstances hadn't been the cause for the visit. As you know, we are facing a unique weather pattern in British Columbia this year—in fact, not just here, but along the entire west coast of North America and even eastward across the continent.

"I'm sure many of you have heard of El Niño. I'm going to get a bit technical right now. It may be interesting for those of you who find meteorology fascinating. The rest of you can tune back in when it suits you." There were a few chuckles and nods of appreciation.

Then he launched into the details of El Niño and its impact on global weather patterns. As predicted, he lost a few listeners along the way. When he touched on a local issue, however, faces turned up at him.

"I'm sure you are aware of the reduced snowfalls this past winter." People's heads started bobbing up and down. "So that brings us to the situation here. As you know, Mt. Washington, which is not that far away, usually averages about four hundred seventy centimeters of snow every year."

Someone shouted, "How much is that in inches, or feet?"

At that point, Alan Cunningham spoke up. "It's approximately one hundred eight inches or fifteen-and-a-half feet." His British accent endeared him to more than half the people in the audience. "I don't know if you are aware of this, but Mt. Washington has some of the deepest snowfalls in North America." People looked at one another with surprise. It was news to them. "Last season it had to close due to lack of snow." Everyone knew that. It had been a shock and a financial disaster for the ski hill operators.

Browne spoke up again. "Right now there is no snow pack anywhere on Vancouver Island. And there has been a dramatic drop in rainfall since May first. We are coming up to July and so far only fifteen millimeters have fallen. It's usually in the hundreds of millimeters."

People were shaking their heads, worry sketched on their faces.

"I am trying not to be an alarmist here..." And then he proceeded to alarm everyone about the ramifications of low water levels, particularly as they affected the fishing and agricultural industries, both central to the region.

"So, that leads us to what you, as an individual, can do to help in conserving water. I'll now turn over the meeting to Doctor Cunningham."

Delilah turned to Ariel. "He's a doctor? I thought he was a professor."

"Professors are called doctors, too, Lilah."

The old woman frowned, not understanding.

Cunningham took the podium. "It is unfortunate that it takes a disaster to change people's attitudes towards water, which has been so abundant here. But you are fortunate that in this township you have deep well sources and a superior distribution system. However, the drought management plans and water conservation programs that are already in place may have to be adjusted if this dry weather pattern remains in place."

Someone stood up, clearly annoyed. "Well, what more can we do? We've already got restrictions on watering our lawns and washing our cars. In fact, it's after seven o'clock right now and that's when we get to water our gardens."

"At this point, you shouldn't be watering your lawns at all," Cunningham said.

Everyone gasped.

Cunningham pressed on. "There's nothing bad about letting grass go brown. It will turn green again once it begins to rain." He might as well have said they should murder their first-borns.

"If you feel that strongly about your grass and your cars, you can use water you normally would see run down the drain. When you shower or bathe, plug the drain so that you can scoop out the water and use it on your garden. Just be sure to use an all-natural, detergent-free soap or shampoo. That way the water you use won't be contaminated."

"Where would we get something like that?" an elderly woman asked.

When no answer was immediately forthcoming, Jade Errington stood up. Locals called her the resident hippie, but not in a pejorative way. Somewhere along the line she had amassed enough money to buy acreage in the township where she raised chickens and kept a few bee hives, then selling the eggs and an occasional jar of honey. Residents also benefitted from her vast vegetable garden as anything she did not use fresh, can or freeze was put out in a little makeshift hut with a sign: "Take only what you need."

She spoke. "I don't see Helmut or Ursula here, but their store sells all kinds of natural products for cleaning everything—even your fruits and vegetables." And then she promptly sat down. Jade was reluctant to speak at any time as she had a prominent overbite.

Delilah turned to Ariel and whispered: "She might try using some of that soap on herself."

"She just *looks* unkempt, Lilah," Ariel corrected her. "She's very clean and smells wonderful. She makes her own lavender soap."

"Good thing too, with all that chicken shit on her property."

Ariel covered her mouth as she choked down a laugh. In the meantime, Cunningham had been offering some other hints, which she missed. "And don't forget that leftover tea can be used to water plants," he was saying.

"Not the way the wife makes it," an older man interjected loudly. "It'll kill anything."

"Obviously I haven't succeeded," his wife said, straight-faced.

Cunningham continued over the laughter. "Last but not least, a thin layer of wet coffee grounds can be placed around larger plants and shrubs. They're a good slug deterrent."

Delilah turned to Ariel. "I've never heard of slug detergent."

"Slug deterrent," Ariel explained, smothering yet another laugh.

"Oh," Delilah giggled.

Vivian Hoffmeyer, President of the Britannia Bay Horticultural Society stood up. The society's long name belied what it was in essence; a small group of prune-faced women ready to pounce on any alteration to the town's hanging baskets or sidewalk containers. The women abhorred the move to graceful grasses mixed with drought resistant heliotrope and coleus.

"Used coffee grounds are also a very good fertilizer for roses," she said with her usual aura of authority. She looked around for acknowledgement of her expertise. Getting none, she sniffed and sat down. She shouldn't have expected otherwise. There would be more than one local in attendance who had been annoyed at her interference in what they chose to plant in their own gardens. She doled out unsolicited advice like dandelion seeds blowing in the wind—and with the same results.

At this point, Verhagen stood up and subtly edged Cunningham aside. "Are there any more questions?" As there weren't, he thanked the two men for their appearance, leading the applause. "Before you

all leave, I want to remind you that the grad parade starts at four
o'clock tomorrow. So don't park in the town centre after two. Don't
forget the dinner dance later at the Civic Centre. We were going to
have fireworks, but it's too dangerous."

At the sounds of dismay, he held up his hand. "I know, I know.
We are all disappointed. But there will be fireworks on the beach on
Canada Day. And don't forget the market and street fair and live
music all weekend. Lots of vendors and art work and ..."

People started to get up and file out at this point and he took his
cue from that. "Thanks very much for coming," his voice trailing
away. He shut off the microphone and was about to leave the dais
when a short, stocky, red-faced woman came charging up. She
shouted to the departing backs. "Hey, everybody! Justine's is open
for coffee, tea and dessert." Then she turned and glared at the
mayor who had stopped in his tracks. "You were supposed to
announce that, Pieter."

"Oh, gosh. I'm sorry, Justine."

"Just for that, no more free pie for you." She flounced off and
hurried to her café.

"Damn!" he uttered. Now he would have to pay like everybody
else, and grimaced at the thought. He absent-mindedly fingered his
vest pocket.

As Ariel kept abreast of Delilah shuffling along with her walker,
she realized she wanted some human company. "Delilah, do you
want to go to Justine's for a cup of tea and a piece of pie or cake ...
on me?"

Delilah, surprised at hearing Ariel call her by her full name,
stopped and gave her a long look. "That would be a real treat. I'd
like that."

And the warm evening became warmer. But in a better way.

Chapter Ten

Friday, June 26th

On a cloudless, smokeless afternoon the town buzzed. People milled about in a holiday mood taking in the farmer's market, looking over art work in the town square and buying hot dogs and ice cream cones from street vendors. Next to the antique car show, the grad parade was *the* big event as family members descended from wherever to congratulate whomever. All police officers were on duty, even those who normally worked nights and weekends. Overtime pay would be one perk. The pleasurable day would be the other.

"Okay, boys and girls," Wyatt announced. "Let's hit the streets." They filed out, chatting and laughing. The atmosphere was contagious.

Ray had shown everyone the picture of Marcus in his tuxedo that Georgina had sent to his cellphone. They all agreed he looked *swayve* and *deboner*.

Gabriella was on watch at the living room window. "Here they come!" She ran to the front door and opened it before her grandparents could ring the bell. "*Ciao Nonna, Ciao Nonno. Come stai?*"

Umberto and Silvana Rossini, a handsome and energetic couple who remained true to their Italian culture, stood on the landing.

"*Bene, grazie, bella ragazza*," her grandfather said, a bit out of breath. "*Dov'è tua madre?*"

"She's in the bedroom with Marcus." Umberto hurried off as he knew his services were required.

Gabriella took her grandmother's arm, pulling her into the dining room. "*Vieni, Nonna.* I want to show you something,"

Silvana looked around the room. With an expert eye, she surveyed Gabriella's handiwork. "What? I see nothing."

"Oh, *Nonna*," she chided her grandmother. "You do, too."

Silvana smiled. Gabriella had set a table worthy of Cantini's. "If you're not careful, we'll put you to work."

"Honestly? I would love that!"

"Maybe for one night you would," she said, quickly squelching her granddaughter's enthusiasm. "It's not like having all day to make a table look beautiful like this. You'd be rushed off your feet and maybe getting in the way. So I don't think it's something for you."

"Aww," Gabriella pouted.

"Well, we'll see," she relented, and put her arm around her. "Now let's go see what your grandfather is up to."

What he was up to was tying Marcus's bowtie. He had just finished, and was looking at the results. He stepped back and took in the whole picture. "*Madonn'!*"

"*Mamma mia!*" Silvana gasped. "What a handsome boy!" She pinched his cheek.

"Ow!" he laughed in mock pain, dodging out of her reach in case she planned to pinch the other one.

"You will make all the other boys *geloso*," Umberto told him.

"See?" Georgina says. "What did I tell you? He kept saying it was old fashioned."

"Sometimes old fashioned is better," Umberto said.

"Old fashioned is *best*," Silvana corrected him.

Marcus looked at his watch. "Holy cr... uh, cow! Mom! We've gotta get going. I have to be at the parade car in fifteen minutes."

"I'm coming with you," Gabriella announced, and they both ran out.

"I'll be back in about twenty-five minutes," Georgina told her in-laws as she snatched up her keys and chased after them.

Umberto poured himself a Campari, sighed as he sank into the sofa and watched his wife preparing a plate of antipasto. She moved with such grace. At sixty-seven Silvana was as beautiful as she was at twenty-seven. When she glanced over at him, he blew her a kiss. She giggled like a little girl. Not for the first time, he thanked God for his blessings.

Delilah was excited. She enjoyed every activity put on by the town. But the grad parade was her favorite. Seeing those beautiful children dressed to the nines trying to look like anything but teenagers brought tears to her eyes. They'd be perched on fancy convertibles, smiling as they searched amongst the bystanders for friends and family. It was all so lovely.

Her walker waited by the door. She would sit at her usual place one block from her house where the parade would turn into the Community Centre parking lot. Wearing her big sun hat, she would chat to anyone within ear shot, or to herself. Sometimes it was the same thing. She liked to be in the thick of things, to laugh and make silly jokes.

"It's going to be fun, isn't it Tabitha?" Resting back in her overstuffed recliner with her feet on the footrest and her purring kitty on her lap, she began to nod off. She might have slept through the entire parade, but as promised the previous evening, Ariel arrived to accompany her. She knocked on the screen door, setting Tabitha running for refuge.

"Are you ready, Lilah?"

"Of course I am," she said with forced energy. She didn't want Ariel to think she had fallen asleep. She pulled on her hat, collected her walker, and shuffled out. She turned and locked the door. "We never used to have to do this, you know." Ariel nodded. How many times had she heard her say that? "Is Jimmy coming to watch with us?"

"No. He's working. He'll see it in town."

They trudged slowly up the street, Delilah's liver-spotted hands gripping the handles like a raptor's talons clutching its prey. One time she had tripped and almost fallen on the uneven road. When she told the council to tell the mayor about it they said they would. But nothing was ever done. *I should talk to the mayor myself.*

Everybody had already staked out their territory. Chairs, walkers, boxes, anything that worked as a fanny rest, lined both sides of the street. The neighbourhood regulars saved a space for Delilah knowing where she sat. She and Ariel got settled just in time.

Around the corner came the old convertible fire engine resurrected for public events, with volunteers winding the siren and clanging the brass bell. People got their cameras ready. Mayor Verhagen sat on the back of the engine waving and smiling in anticipation, but there were not many pointed in his direction. All the attention was focused on the graduates dressed in their finery. Being a small town, it was a small class, but the organizers devised a way to stretch out the enjoyment. Only one grad per car.

"Oh, there's Mark Rossini!" Ariel exclaimed, pointing to a young man sitting atop the back seat of a vintage black automobile smiling and waving. "Doesn't he look fantastic?"

"That's Ray's boy?" Delilah asked, dumbstruck. "My gosh. He looks like someone out of *The Godfather.*"

Ariel was busy taking photographs. A black 1937 Packard coupe with white sidewall tires and silver hubcaps was the perfect car for Mark with his black tux and white shirt. She turned to Delilah.

"What were you saying about *The Godfather*?"

"Never mind." She was afraid Ariel would say something to Jimmy and it might get back to Ray. She didn't want to offend the Rossinis. They could be connected to the Cosa Nostra.

As if on cue, Georgina could be seen coming along the street. She was beaming as she strode up to Ariel and Delilah. "Did you see Mark? Didn't he look fabulous?"

"He sure did. Like a movie star from the nineteen-forties," Ariel agreed. "Very dashing and handsome."

Georgina turned to Delilah. "What did you think, Delilah?"

"He reminded me of Fred Astaire."

The 5:30 ferry left without Lana. It was her own fault. When she arrived at the crammed terminal, she realized that people were taking advantage of a special weekend price, a rarity with the ferry company that monopolized all the routes between the island and the Lower Mainland. And she had forgotten to make a reservation. She called Charlotte to apologize, picked up a *Bruno, Chief of Police* mystery and got comfortable. Finally on board, she decided to stretch her legs before trying to find something remotely edible to fill the hole in her stomach. She joined the throng walking around the outside deck marveling at the stunning scenery and watching for breaching Orcas. Passengers were keeping their cameras busy as the occasional killer whale put on a show. Lana was trying to do the same but people kept popping into the frame or jiggling her elbows. She managed a half dozen shots at best.

After a while she queued up at the cafeteria. Selecting the least greasy calorie-laden meal, she began searching for an empty table—a seemingly hopeless task in the packed dining area. When she noticed a couple getting up, she made a bee-line for their table and waited as they cleared away their dishes. "I feel like a vulture," she said to them.

"Like waiting for a parking spot at a mall," the man laughed.

She hunkered down with her book and her meal, and soon was oblivious to the chatting and laughing that bounced off the echo-friendly room.

"Excuse me, miss," a man said.

Lana looked up, not sure if the voice was directed at her. It was. A very tall, good-looking man in motorcycle gear was standing in front of her table holding a tray, his helmet strap looped through his arm.

"I'm sorry to interrupt you," he said apologetically, "but would you mind if I shared your table? You seem to have the only available chair in the room."

Lana glanced around. He was right. "No, I don't mind. But just a warning—I don't chat when I'm reading." She had already eaten most of her food.

He laughed. "No problem. I hear you. Books are to be savoured."

Lana blinked. *That was a surprise.* As were his eyes—startling turquoise blue with long black lashes under thick, black eyebrows. While he busied himself placing his plate and utensils on the table, Lana gave him a quick once-over. He didn't look like a biker. No long hair, outrageous moustache or beard. No earrings in his ears, nose or eyebrows. No missing teeth or tattoos of HATE and LOVE on his knuckles. No colours or badges on his leathers announcing his allegiance to the Hell's Angels or Red Scorpions.

He looked around for a place to put his tray. A cafeteria employee approached him with her hand held out. "I'll take that," she said. "We're short of trays."

"Well, that was fortuitous," he said, causing Lana to smile.

When he shook out his napkin, she caught the cleanliness of his hands. And as he looked down, strands of shiny brown hair shot through with gold fell across his forehead. She dragged herself back to her book and tried to read. But the unnatural silence between them made her uncomfortable and she began gathering up her dishes.

"I'm sorry. I didn't mean to drive you off," he said.

"You didn't. I should give up my seat. I don't want to be a table hog when other people are looking for a place to sit. I'm only drinking this sorry excuse for tea, anyway." She smiled

Later, as she sat in the lounge, Lana scrolled through the pictures she had taken earlier and was surprised to see him in two shots. She didn't remember taking them. It must have happened when her finger was on the camera icon and someone jostled her. She was about to delete them, but changed her mind. *It might be fun to show Charlotte and Martin my dinner companion.*

Chapter Eleven

Saturday, June 27th

Jimmy sat at the patio sipping his morning coffee, a national newspaper opened to the cryptic crossword. Birdsong crisscrossed the air threatening to drown out Mark Murphy be-bopping in the background. Ariel and the cats were in the garden. Later she would sit down with the puzzle while he was at the do-jo. He scanned the clues and jotted down answers on a piece of paper, which he tucked into his shorts pocket. He was hoping she would be stumped by one or two. His uncanny ability to see outside the box annoyed her and amused him. But she was game for the challenge.

His cellphone buzzed. He barely had time to answer before Chief Wyatt's voice burst through the line. "Tan! Get your ass in gear! There's been a homicide. Ray's on his way to pick you up." He rang off without waiting for a response.

A homicide! Christ! He ran to the bedroom, flung off his shorts, and threw on pants and shirt. He grabbed his duty belt and dashed out the door looking for Ariel while keeping an eye out for Ray.

"Ariel, where are you?" he shouted.

"Over here." Standing near the street with a trowel in her hand,

Ariel frowned. *Now what's biting his butt?*

"Honey, Ray's coming. I gotta go. There's been a homicide."

"What?!" She stared at him incredulous. "Here?" Her face blanched.

The police van swerved into the driveway, lights and siren off. Jimmy held her briefly, feeling the tremors in her body. "I love you." And he hurried to join his partner.

Ariel, still as a statue, remained fixed to her spot.

"Jesus. A homicide," Jimmy said, as he jumped in. Glancing in the side mirror, he saw Ariel staring after them, her face filled with fear as they roared off.

"It's bloody unbelievable," Ray agreed. "I was just enjoying a quiet moment with Georgie, you know? We were talking about last night and looking at some pictures of all the kids." He flicked a quick look at Jimmy. "She's terrified."

"So is Ariel. It's been a long time ..." his voice trailed off.

As they drove down side streets to avoid the busy town centre, the radio came to life. "Base to unit one."

"Unit one. Over," Jimmy responded to Robyn Lewitski, the dispatcher.

"Chief Wyatt and SOCOs on scene." She paused. "RCMP Ident Officers on the way."

"Thanks, Robyn. Ten Four. Out." He looked at Ray. "Well, I guess that was to be expected."

"Gonna be some ruffled feathers," Ray turned to him.

"Do we know who the victim is?"

Ray chanced a quick glance at his partner. "Yeah. It's one of the Berdahl boys."

"Holy crap!"

"You're not kidding. The chief was lobbing information at me, thick and fast. From what I could make out, Stefan Berdahl phoned him. I don't know all the details, but he and one of the brothers discovered the body when they went looking for him. The place we're going to is the last place they looked. It's a house they were flogging. Apparently the brother who was murdered told the other brother that he was showing the place yesterday around five o'clock."

It didn't take long for Jimmy to put two and two together. "Grad night. Jaxon has a family. Max hasn't. Who would be more likely to be showing a house?"

"Right," Ray acknowledged. Reaching Bayside Drive, he put on the lights and siren as he wove his way around the road, bay on one side, steep hillside on the other. Treacherous in the winter when the wind sent waves flying over the seawall, it posed a different danger in the summer as joyriders decided to treat its twists and turns like a horizontal rollercoaster.

"Do you know where this place is?"

"I do. Good thing cuz the GPS may not be accurate. The place is sorta remote."

As they reached Townshipline Road, Ray braked hard. A real estate sign leaned over the ditch. "This is it," he said. The shocks on the van were sorely tested as he wrestled his way up the steep and narrow road over heaved pavement.

"Have you been up here before?" Jimmy asked.

"No. But I know there used to be a picnic site from the early twentieth century at the top of the hill."

"How the hell did they get up?"

"They didn't. They came down. There was a road from town, but it pretty well got washed away when Little Man Creek changed course after a rock slide."

Another For Sale sign appeared. "This must be it." He inched along a driveway littered with leaves. "Jeez, look how dry everything is. One match and poof!" He parked behind the official vehicles, both of the Berdahl brothers' SUVs, and a silver Volvo sedan.

Stefan Berdahl sat in the Volvo, face ashen and tear-streaked. Jaxon occupied the passenger seat, but the tinted glass shielded his face from view. Chief Wyatt, dressed in white crime scene overalls, was leaning into the open window, mask dangling from his neck. He turned and signaled the detectives to wait.

They approached Constable Adam Berry standing near the steps with a sign-in log, looking sour faced. He wanted to be inside where the action was. This was as close to being "a real cop" as he had ever been, and standing around manning crime scene tape in the middle of nowhere blackened his mood. Who did they think would be up here wandering by and poking their noses in? No one. Zip. Zero. Zilch.

"What's the skinny, Adam?" Ray asked.

Instead of answering, he pointed to pools of vomit strewn near the stairs. Ray and Jimmy exchanged a look.

The Volvo started up. Stefan Berdahl edged around the other vehicles and made his way off the property. The sound of sobbing could be heard as the passenger side window slid closed.

Wyatt joined them, dark-faced. "This is a brutal murder, boys. I've seen some awful stuff in my day, but this ..." He shook his head. "His skull has been smashed to a pulp. Rats have already been at him. The place is full of flies and God knows what else. "

"Jesus," Ray gulped.

"Is there a murder weapon?" Jimmy asked.

"No. I've got Hastings and Carpenter searching the area." He turned his head in both directions. "Going to be damned hard to find in all this underbrush."

"I'll go get our kits," Jimmy said and headed back to the van.

"Don't forget gum," Berry advised.

Wyatt motioned with his head for Ray to follow him for a more private conversation. "I had to bring in the RCMP," he said dejectedly.

"So why is Atkins here?"

"I wanted him here first so that he could begin the walk through and then set up the ALS. McDaniel is photographing everything.

That way the RCMP can't steal all our thunder," which perfectly described his glowering face.

"Jimmy and I think the victim is Max Berdahl."

"Yeah. You're right," he said and nodded to where Jimmy was lifting two crime scene kits from the van. "He lived across the street from Berdahl, didn't he?"

"Yeah." Ray followed Wyatt's gaze. "Pretty close to home for him." He wondered about the ramifications of that.

As Jimmy returned with gear and gum, their heads turned at the sound of a car. Wyatt's face broke into a rare smile as a flashy red SUV pulled in.

The woman who stepped out was a bit of flash herself. A shapely woman with skin the colour of cinnamon, Dr. Dayani Nayagam was the medical examiner for the mid-island district. Exotically beautiful, but more important, brilliant, she was welcomed wherever she placed her Prada pumps.

Wyatt walked up to her. "Well. Aren't you a sight for sore eyes?"

"Hello, Chief. Long time no see," she greeted in a velvety voice tinged with remnants of a BBC accent.

"Yes. I don't know if that's a good thing or a bad thing," he said teasingly. Wyatt's history with the doctor went back several years when he was chief in another community. He had attended her lectures and been smitten by her combination of beauty and intelligence. Only on two occasions had they worked a case together. Unfortunately, they involved the RCMP as well, and it seemed there was a spark between her and a corporal from the detachment.

"What have you got for me today?"

Wyatt eyed her fashionable clothing. She must have been planning to attend a fancy lunch somewhere. Why else would she be dressed in such finery at this hour? He didn't even want to consider the alternative. "Something that requires an outfit a little less fetching than what you're wearing, Dr. D." Because her name twisted his tongue, he rechristened her immediately after their introduction. It spread throughout the policing community and quickly became her moniker. She didn't appear to mind. Or if she did, she was too well bred to say anything.

For all her attributes, Dayani Nayagam seemed to have no personal life. Her extended family was scattered from Vancouver to St. Stefan's and from Britain to Sri Lanka. As for men, most were intimidated by her or believed she must have some superman in the wings. So what was the point of making a move on her?

Replacing her high heels with comfortable loafers, she reached into her kit and pulled out a folded Tyvek suit, booties, mask and gloves. "Do we know who the victim is?"

"Yes. It's Max Berdahl. And I want to warn you, it's a gruesome sight. There's nothing left of his skull."

"Oh my God!" Quickly zipping on the overalls, she grabbed her medical bag and hurried up to the deck where she added the rest of her protective items then disappeared inside.

Moments later an RCMP mobile crime scene van pulled in.

"Here comes the cavalry," Wyatt announced under his breath, a scowl on his face.

Two Ident Officers, a female officer and civilian, also female, got out of the vehicle. Jimmy recognized Constable Eric Lindquist. But a rangy man that he was sure Ariel would describe as a "dish," was a stranger to him.

The officer walked leisurely up to Wyatt. "Chief Wyatt," he said in a soft, deep drawl, his mouth barely moving. No hand was offered.

"Corporal Griffin," Wyatt nodded once. Freeze-dried air filled the space between them.

After shooting a quick look at Ray, Jimmy took in Griffin's square jaw and dark eyes. As far as he could tell, the only flaws in his handsome face were the residual marks of teenage acne.

Griffin indicated his team. "I believe you know Constable Lindquist." Next he gestured to two women. "This is Constable Cassidy MacLean, our photographer, and Dr. Poppy Langstone, of

True North University. Dr. Langstone is an entomologist."

Wyatt ignored the entomologist and zeroed in on Constable MacLean. "We have our own excellent photographer on scene," he protested, setting his course full speed into the storm.

Griffin, sensing Wyatt's irritation, sought to take some wind out of his sails. "No problem. I'm fine with two photographers," he countered diplomatically. "Cassidy can work with me. The information I received seems to indicate that there will be enough work for both." He casually turned his intense eyes on the young Constable. She froze like a deer caught in headlights.

The cause and effect were not lost on Jimmy.

Pacified for now, Wyatt reflected on the carnage inside. "Unfortunately, you're right about that. I'll have my men working on the grid and crime scene log. D.S. Atkins will do the blood pattern analysis."

Griffin hesitated. He had planned to do the BPA himself, but he didn't want to get into a tug-of-war over turf, so he nodded. "That's fine. I would request one thing, though, and that is all data and evidence be turned over to me ASAP."

Wyatt chewed this over for a moment. "You'll get the bagged and tagged material today, but I'll want to read the log and look at the photographs first."

"When could we expect them?"

Wyatt thought through the time line. "Tomorrow morning. That should be time enough for your report by Monday." He knew he was pressing Griffin.

Aware of Wyatt's tactics, Griffin remained unfazed. "Sounds feasible." He nodded to the red Honda. "I see that the lovely Dr. Nayagam has already arrived. I'd better get on my horse." The sly retort put Wyatt on notice that his references to Griffin had reached their mark. Without another word he returned to the van for his materials, his crew behind him.

So, Griffin knows about my cavalry remarks, eh? So what! But was that a needle about Dr. D.? Wyatt's feelings for her were more proprietorial than sexual. Nevertheless, he was unable to squelch the little green monster that tapped on his shoulder. *Why did he let that cowboy get to him?* He stormed over to his car, his annoyance spilling over into the radio. "Where's that damn ambulance, Robyn?" he snapped.

"It should be there momentarily, Chief," he said, trying to soothe his irritation.

He harrumphed a response and returned to the house.

"That was some pissing contest," Jimmy said as he handed Ray his kit.

"That was mild. Their few run-ins have become urban legends. Pistols at twenty paces. A duel at dawn." He chuckled.

"What's the source of their animosity?"

Ray waited until Griffin and his crew passed by. "The usual. The RCMP's feeling of superiority. Trampling on our investigations like we're local yokels. And then there's the fact that we have to go begging to them for special equipment. During the arson investigation a few years back, Griffin handed the chief a HAZMAT suit because we didn't have them. Wyatt was so humiliated he nearly threw it back at him. That's why he gets so pissed at Verhagen's stinginess. It makes him have to suck up to the RCMP and accept whatever crumbs they throw us."

"And what's with his accent? He sounds like an American from the south."

"You caught that, eh? Yeah. When Wyatt says, 'Here comes the cavalry,' he doesn't mean the Mounties. He means the Texas Rangers. Griffin is Canadian but he spent his childhood in Texas. Came back to Canada when he was draft age. That's all I know about him. But I do know he draws women like flies to honey."

Wyatt hopped down the stairs, his bulk causing a board to crack. "Jesus," he shuddered, yanking down his mask, his ruddy face gone grey. His waxy appearance unsettled Ray.

"How's it going in there?" he asked anxiously as he zipped up the overalls.

"As good as can be expected, I guess. Atkins seems okay with the arrangement. And McDaniel's nose is not out of joint."

"Well, we've put it off long enough," Ray said to Jimmy. "It's time to go in there. You coming?"

"In a minute."

Ray smiled. "Postponing the inevitable, eh?"

"No. I just want to check something with the chief first."

"Yeah. Yeah. A likely story," he said as he walked off.

Wyatt turned to Jimmy. "What?"

"Any damage to the front door?"

"No."

"Has anyone done a search of the exterior yet?"

"No. Everyone's been inside. You want to do that?"

"Yeah. The killer had to get in somewhere."

Chapter Twelve

Ray stepped warily into the house. His stomach churned at the sight and the smell. It had been a long time since his last murder and he was no longer inured to the putrefaction of a rotting body. He tried to fight the nausea by breathing through his mouth. But after a few moments the stench and the heat of bitter bile burning up his throat won out. He ripped off his mask, barreled back out the door and spewed his breakfast into the accumulating pool of vomit. Berry, nimble and quick as Jack, jumped out of the way just in time.

Jimmy, carrying his kit, began a circuit of the house speaking all the while into his cellphone. A carport sloped down to an entry under the large deck. He tried the door. Locked. He walked toward the back of the house, eyes scanning everything along the way. Bypassing the stairway leading up to the back deck, he continued until he reached a corner of the house. Stacked dry rounds of felled trees, bucked and cut into quarters, reached the roof of a lean-to. A space tucked between the wood and the house contained a scarred chopping block. He snapped off a picture.

From here the pathway split. To the right, it narrowed and veered off along a ridge where the land fell away steeply to the dry boulder-strewn creek bed below. To the left, it led behind the house but ended abruptly in a tangle of blackberry brambles. Doubling back, he walked up to the landing where the back door hung on its hinge. It had been smashed in with a heavy instrument—more than likely the murder weapon. Wood splinters were scattered about.

Unpacking his kit, he zipped into the overalls. He slapped a pair of self-adhesive pockets onto the suit, slipped on the shoe covers and pulled on a mask, leaving it hanging for the moment. Tugging on nitrile gloves, he stepped through the door into a mud room, a common sight in rural areas. There were no shoe prints on the dusty floor. But there were visible tracks going through an open doorway and into a hall.

Before checking them out, he descended a flight of stairs to a clean and well-insulated basement containing a wood stove, a workbench, large freezer, washer and dryer and ladder. He peered inside the unplugged and empty freezer, and then opened and closed the ladder. Although old and made of wood, it was sturdy. Spiders had already constructed homes inside the washer and dryer. After a good look around and recording everything notable, he went back up the stairs.

Jimmy picked his way along the edge of the hallway avoiding the trail of smudges in the dust—the killer's pathway. In the bathroom, the shower showed signs of use—but not the sink. It was dull under a coating of dust.

After a cursory inspection he double backed and climbed a stairway to an empty and undisturbed loft above the living room. The view out the window was spectacular—a calendar picture no matter the season. Framed by the tall cedars and spruces, the mountains of the mainland rose up from the blue waters of the bay and stretched into infinity. Turning around, he looked down through a grilled opening to the grisly scene below, guaranteed never to grace the pages of a calendar.

Jimmy joined Ray, still green around the gills and furiously chewing gum. He offered a piece to his partner but Jimmy shook his head then stood watching, still and emotionless. Ray wondered how he could be like that—so unmoved, stoic. Was it a wall built up after viewing one too many murder scenes? Was it his Oriental upbringing? Or did it have something to do with his martial arts training? Whatever it was, it left Ray puzzled and not a little disturbed.

They observed Novak and Dhillon meticulously collecting evidence square by square with tweezers and swabs, which they then bagged and tagged. McDaniel worked alongside, documenting each item and each square on his old reliable Nikon. So far, their cache seemed to contain jagged bits of bone and pieces of soft tissue, slivers of hardwood, rodent feces, a lot of short black hairs—probably from a dog—and a few cloth fibres. Earlier, McDaniel had photographed the entire house. Except for dust balls, it was as bare as his bald head.

During college, McDaniel had been a lifeguard and played football. To earn tuition money, he had tried being a bouncer, but got fed up with the ignorance of what he called PWT—poor white trash. Realizing he was a team player, had intelligence, and could bash in heads with the best of them, he decided to become a cop. Along the way, he studied photography and added it to his resume. That had turned out to be a big bonus because he got to work with people like D.S. Josh Atkins, who was setting up his equipment and preparing to do his magic.

Impervious to the foul smell, Nayagam and Griffin crouched by Max's body, now stiff with rigor. There was nothing left of his cranium. It had been crushed with such force that only the jaw remained intact. His hands showed no defensive signs. Nayagam spoke softly into her recorder while making notes in a small notebook. She looked up at Poppy Langstone. "Have you got all the photographs from this side?"

"Yes."

She turned to Griffin. "Could you turn him over, please?"

Griffin nodded to Lindquist, and the two men gently turned over Max's remains. Although now a corpse, he had been a human being and was accorded as much dignity as possible—until the pathologist began the autopsy. Cause of death? Would a head smashed to smithereens do?

"Any guess as to how long he's been dead?" Ray asked.

"Judging from the rigor and lividity, I would say sixteen or so hours. But in this heat, it's hard to say. It could be shorter. The pathologist will be able to be more precise. In the meantime, I think the best estimation would come from your entomologist," and she nodded toward Dr. Cassidy McLean.

At this point, Ray and Jimmy agreed that there was nothing more for them to do. They thanked her and as they began to leave the house, Jimmy turned back to look at the door. The key that Berdahl must have used to open it was not in the lock.

"Corporal Griffin," Jimmy said.

"Yes?"

"Did you find a house key in Max's pockets?"

"No. Just a wallet and a handkerchief."

"And no cellphone?"

"No." He understood where Tan was going.

"Thanks."

Blowflies had already laid their eggs in what remained of Max's brain—a grey pulpy mush of veins and blood vessels. Dr. McLean had been busy preparing all the paraphernalia she needed to collect, preserve and package the adult flies, or their eggs, maggots, pupae and empty pupal cases. She desperately wanted to step outside for fresh air. *Will I ever get this smell out of my nose?*

"Okay, Cassidy," Griffin said to her. "You can stop holding up the wall now."

She walked over and quickly snatched two beetles that were scurrying under the body. She placed them in separate vials to prevent the tiny cannibals from eating each other.

Dr. Nayagam packed up her bag. "I'm finished. He's all yours ... what's left of him," she grimaced then walked toward the door, Griffin beside her.

He spoke to her in a quiet voice. "This weekend's shot. How about next weekend?"

"I think I can manage that," she purred, and walked to her car thanking her lucky stars that Ike Griffin had the jam to take her on. After removing her protective clothing and stowing her bag, she approached Wyatt. "We'll do our best to get that autopsy report to you as quickly as possible, Bill."

"I know you will, Dr. D. And thanks for that. We'll be sending D.S. Atkins to observe."

She nodded. Neither being in the frame of mind for idle chit chat, she returned to her car and drove off.

The ambulance finally arrived. Two paramedics rolled out a stretcher on which was placed a folded body bag. Jimmy knew one of the men from the do-jo. "Hi, Owen."

"Hey, Jimmy." He assessed the officers dressed in white coveralls. "Not a good scene, I'm guessing."

"You guess right."

"I'll see if they're ready for you," Wyatt said. Attaching his mask, he headed back to the house.

"There are not so many homicides around here," the other paramedic said nervously in a Québécois accent. "It must be very bad if you are dressed in your gear."

"Yes it is. I suggest you put on a mask," Ray warned him.

"But *you* are not wearing one," he argued. "You are holding it."

Ray locked his eyes on him. "That's because this is a clean one, *monsieur*. The first one is in a bucket filled with puke."

Owen heard this, went back to the ambulance and came out with two masks. "Here, hot shot. Put this on."

The Frenchman stiffened and an angry flush suffused his face. He resented being spoken to with disrespect in front of others. His umbrage gave way the second they walked into the house, however. Galvanized by the sight, he was glad he had done as advised.

Griffin watched the removal of the body. Next, he followed up on something Atkins had told him but which he hadn't been able to get to. He motioned for Poppy to accompany him to the bathroom stepping carefully around the grid pattern set up by Novak and Dhillon, who were now packing up their equipment.

Already feeling nauseous from the smell and with no time for breakfast, Poppy groaned audibly. Griffin fired a stern look at her. Chastened, she followed in his footsteps.

Atkins had mentioned a bright pink spot in the hem of the shower curtain. Griffin pointed it out to Poppy. After she took shots of it, he carefully removed the curtain, folded it inward and deposited it into his evidence bag.

"Okay Poppy, you're free to leave."

"Thank you, sir," she said, being careful not to register her relief.

Griffin took one last look around. Satisfied, he walked outside and up to Wyatt and his officers. "We've completed our work."

Jimmy stopped him before he moved off. "We may require a tracker dog at some point."

Griffin nodded, and without looking at Wyatt he added: "We have a wonderful hound called Barnaby."

Wyatt mumbled, "Of course you do."

Griffin ignored him. About to walk away, he turned back. "Atkins found something on the shower curtain. It'll be in the report."

Wyatt nodded, trying to say something that didn't choke him.

Ray, noticing his conflict, spoke up. "Thanks."

Griffin gave them a curt nod. "I hope you find this fucker."

They watched silently as the RCMP Corporal returned to the van, stripped off his crime scene gear and took out a bottle of water, drinking greedily. A moment later he hopped in the van and drove away.

Jimmy turned to Ray and Wyatt. "The murder weapon was probably a long-handled ax or a wood-splitting maul. There's a chopping block behind a pile of wood at the back of the property." He showed them his cellphone picture. "I'll have McDaniel take some better shots."

Wyatt said. "A maul would make sense. But they're heavy suckers. The perp had to be strong."

"What I'm wondering is, why would the killer take the house key?"

"Some keep mementoes of their crimes," Wyatt said.

"Yeah, he needed something small," Ray said. "He couldn't very well haul around a maul."

Chapter Thirteen

The sun was now well into the west and Wyatt's stomach was
rumbling. Food had been the last thing on his mind, but now he was
ravenous. He ordered his team home to clean up and eat before
returning to the station. Wyatt wanted their minds on their work,
not their personal discomfort, and that included himself. He walked
over to the van where his two detectives were waiting. Max's SUV
had been towed to the RCMP garage for forensic testing. Jaxon's
was waiting to be ferried to his father's house. "Time to get Jaxon's
SUV back to where it belongs. Jimmy, you drive it and follow me.
Ray will follow you, and the three of us will meet at Berdahl's house.
I'll introduce you as the investigating officers and tell Stefan that
you need to question him tomorrow."

"But—" Ray started to protest.

"I know, I know. It's a little unorthodox. But this is a small
town, and we don't want to push any buttons unnecessarily.
Particularly Verhagen's. The Berdahls are an important source of
tax income. The family needs some time together, too, and Jaxon
needs some rest." He paused. "He probably needs psychiatric
counselling, but he won't get that."

"Why not?" Jimmy asked.

"Their religion," Ray said with disgust.

"What are they, Scientologists or something?"

"Jehovah's Witnesses," he sneered. Having been raised a Roman Catholic, he disparaged any offshoots of traditional Judeo Christian beliefs. This, however, didn't hinder him from criticizing the tenets of his own religion.

"Never mind that right now," Wyatt interrupted. "Let's just get the show on the road. The sooner I can get something in my belly the sooner I'll feel like getting back to work."

"No argument there, boss," Ray agreed, hurrying to the van.

Before leaving in Jaxon's car, Jimmy called Ariel. "Hi sweetheart."

"Hi darling. Are you on your way home?"

He heard the hope in her voice. "Not quite. Have to make a detour. Might be an hour yet. I'll shower and have something to eat. Then I have to return to the station."

She knew that. It was a given. "I'll have some warm comfort food for you."

"Some warm comfort would be nice, too" he added.

"It will be on the menu," she said.

Placing the phone back in its cradle, Ariel felt her heart in her throat. All day she had moved about on automatic pilot, trying to come to grips with a murder in this small community. She hoped it would be random, some person here for the weekend festivities. The thought that it might be someone from Britannia Bay filled her with dread.

Ray curved his way around the pea-gravel driveway flanked by giant rhododendrons, many varieties of which were still in full bloom. He whistled when the Berdahl family home came into view. A modern adaptation of a two-storey Colonial style mansion sprawled across a vast expanse of perfectly manicured lawn. "Welcome to the one percent," he muttered to himself. Parking next to Wyatt's car, he took in the half-dozen or so tradesmen's trucks and late-model cars off to the side of the house near a coach house big enough to hold four vehicles. *It probably has its own postal code*, he thought.

As the three officers walked toward the wide colonnaded landing, the crunch of their shoes on the gravel seemed unnaturally loud. Wyatt pressed an illuminated button. They heard the far-off echo of chimes. After a short wait, the door opened.

Stefan Berdahl greeted them, grey-faced, red-eyed.

After offering his condolences, Wyatt indicated Ray and Jimmy. "Stefan, these are Detectives Sergeants Rossini and Tan. They will be the senior investigating officers."

The two men nodded and Jimmy handed him Jaxon's key. Berdahl thanked him, and then scrutinized the two detectives. Although both men's eyes were brown, those of the Oriental reflected compassion, while the Italian's were glazed with a patina of suspicion. *Good cop, bad cop?* he wondered.

"We'll need you to come to the station for an interview while your recollections are still—" he struggled to come up with a word.

"Clear?" Berdahl responded bitterly. "They'll be vivid until the day I die."

Wyatt looked down. *God I hate this.*

Berdahl gave him some relief. "Will tomorrow afternoon be all right?"

"Tomorrow afternoon will be fine."

"I'll be there."

Ray jumped in. "Not just you, Mr. Berdahl, but Jaxon, too. We'll need a statement from him."

Berdahl stiffened. *Definitely bad cop.*

Wyatt shot Ray a blistering look before turning back to the bereaved father. "How is Jaxon?" he asked gently.

Berdahl turned to Wyatt. "As you would expect. Completely shattered. We're doing our best to comfort him."

"Would he be able to be there tomorrow?" Wyatt asked,

tramping on Ray's demand.

"I'm honestly not sure."

Ray interjected. "Any delay hinders the investigation."

Jimmy had been observing the interplay. It was his first time partnering with Ray on a major crime and what he was seeing left him with a sense of unease.

"If you could come after lunchtime, it would be appreciated. And if Jaxon is up to it, so much the better." Recognizing his detective's point, he decided to be a bit more hard-nosed himself. "But we do need to talk to him no later than Monday while the details are still fresh in his mind."

"His mind is what we are trying to heal at the moment, Chief Wyatt."

Wyatt held up a palm. "Even so ..."

Berdahl sighed, "Yes, I understand."

"In that case, we'll expect you tomorrow afternoon and Jaxon too, if he's up to it. If not, then Monday," Ray confirmed.

"All right. Now, if you'll excuse me ..." He reached for the door handle.

"One other thing," Ray stopped him. "I'm assuming he had staff in his office. We'll need to talk to them too. If you could provide us with their names and numbers we'd appreciate it."

"There was only his cousin, Ingrid."

"Fine. We'll need to talk to her. And we're going to need the files and computers from the office and Max's home."

Berdahl's eyes hardened. "Why would you need either of those things?" Anger began rising through his pain.

"Because there may be information in them that might lead us to a suspect," he explained.

Berdahl hesitated before answering. "I'm not sure about this. I'll have to call my lawyer."

"Of course. You do that. In the meantime, we'll make sure no one goes inside and tampers with anything."

"Why would you even suggest that? We wouldn't do that."

"*You* may not, but we don't know how many people have access to the office or to Max's home—cleaners, janitors, that sort of thing. Or what they may remove. Perhaps some memento they think has nothing to do with the investigation. Something may seem innocent to one person, but it may have significance to another. Everything matters in an investigation."

Berdahl's ire evaporated as he strained to deal with his competing emotions. "I'm sorry. I just can't think about any of this right now. You do whatever you have to do. I have to get back to my family." He turned and closed the door.

Wyatt glared at Ray. "Your impatience and lack of compassion will be noted in your file," he launched at him and marched to his car and drove off.

"Oh, shit." Ray knew he had crossed a line, but he wasn't expecting to be written up.

"Okay, Detective Jackass," Jimmy said. "Now get me home to Ariel."

For a good part of the drive they said nothing. Ray broke the silence angrily. "I hate the idea of giving them extra time, especially if they wait until Monday for Jaxon to come in. It gives them a chance to circle the wagons and get their story together," Ray said.

Jimmy's jaw dropped. "What story?"

"I think the family is involved," he stated flatly.

"How do you figure that?"

"Because it looks like revenge to me. And who more likely than a family member? I mean, JWs kick people out. Prevent fathers or mothers from seeing their children. Shun them for life. It can cause a ton of grief."

"On the other hand, it could be about losing money in a business deal."

"Whatever. It's revenge for something. That we do know."

Chapter Fourteen

At the station, officers were setting up the Incident Room. Dormant after years with no serious crimes, it was now a hive of activity. Computers were booted up and the evidence board stretched open. Adam Berry bustled about like an old woman even though his shift had ended hours before. He had appreciated Wyatt's thanks at the scene and was hoping that he would take more notice of him.

Dhillon and Novak were entering data from the grid pattern. Atkins had turned in his crime scene notes to Jimmy and was analyzing the blood spatter pattern while McDaniel was placing enlarged photos on the board. When he tacked up the grisly picture of Max's torso, silence enveloped the room. Berry, who had not seen the victim on site, felt faint and grabbed onto the back of a chair. Embarrassed, he concluded that being outside the house had been the better option.

Ray and Jimmy sat at a long table piecing together the killer's movements and poring over photographs. Jimmy added information into the case book. It had been decided that he would be the writer of record. Ray was good at a lot of things. Writing down details was not one of them.

"There's no shoe prints in these pictures," Ray asked.

"He took off his shoes, either on the deck or at the foot of the stairs. I would guess the latter. And there's no evidence of bare feet in the dust. So he must've been wearing socks."

"Right. So he takes off his clothes outside so that nothing from them lands inside the house."

"He was taking a chance with hairs falling off his body."

"Then maybe he was wearing overalls. You can buy polypropylene ones easily enough. And latex gloves."

"And a face mask and some kind of goggles," Jimmy suggested.

"Right. So he comes in carrying some kind of holdall and the weapon. Does the deed, washes off the weapon in the shower. Stows the overall and other stuff in the holdall, walks back out—"

"— Wait a second, Ray. This guy was meticulous. He would have showered and washed his hair, too. Then he would have put on *clean* socks before walking back out naked."

Ray nodded. "Makes sense. But where's that damn weapon? A weapon that size must be somewhere around the site."

"I'm going to ask Drew and J.D. to take another look tomorrow. If they can't find it, we'll have to call in the dog. We're going to have to talk to the Schwindts pretty soon, too."

Ray cleared his throat. "Have you told Ariel who the victim is?"

They were at the table, Jimmy enjoying a second bowl of split pea soup; Ariel enjoying his appetite. His shower had been long, hot and restorative. Sitting in the warmth of the evening sunshine, he felt human again. The cats were curled in their corner beds.

"You could have put a blowtorch between Wyatt and Griffin and the ice wouldn't have melted."

"It has to be something more personal than a turf war," Ariel said.

"That's what I think."

"So you say he is handsome."

"Very. He had that poor photographer just about coming in her pants."

"Jimmy! That's gross. First you're swearing. And now you're being disgusting. You're hanging around Rossini too much."

"Can't do much about that."

Noticing how he had talked about everything but the victim's identity, she hesitated to ask. But she had to know. "Are you allowed to say who the victim is?"

Stalling, he picked up the napkin and rubbed it across his mouth. "We're trying to keep a lid on it," he began.

Her eyes widened. "It's someone local then. That's what you're saying, isn't it?" Her voice tightened.

"Yes. And for you and me, it's even more so." He paused. "It's Max Berdahl."

"Oh my God!" She let the initial shock set in. Then she started to giggle. "Well, I guess I wasn't the only one wishing him dead," she said, morbidly delighted.

Ray laughed. "Man. That was cold as a Butterball turkey."

"Keep it under your hat, you goofus."

"Yeah. Yeah. But can I tell Georgina?"

"Why not? You tell her everything, don't you?"

"Pretty much." He thought about his life with his teenage sweetheart. "You know, it's a funny thing. You would think that after being married for twenty years you would run out of things to say to each other. But we yammer about everything all the time." He paused. "And then, of course, there's body language," he said with a leer.

Jimmy shook his head. "You juvenile."

"Speaking of body language, there's not much more we can do tonight, so I'm going home to a warm bed and even warmer woman." He yawned.

Jimmy yawned in response. "Ariel said you were a bad influence on me. First, I'm swearing more, and now you're making me yawn. If I didn't know better I'd say you were my doppelgänger."

Ray chuckled. "Your what?"

"Look it up in your Funk and Wagnalls," Jimmy told him.

"She's right. You *are* swearing a lot."

McDaniel had spent the night labelling his photographs and forwarding the batch to Corporal Griffin. His adrenaline had kept him going, but now he flagged and felt the need of a nap. He locked the door to the deserted Incident Room and dropped the key in his pocket. In the changing room, he rolled up the towel from his locker, stuck it under his head, and stretched out on one of the wooden benches. Seconds later he fell into a deep sleep.

Wilma Young, the oldest person employed at the station, had arrived a few minutes before her weekend graveyard shift. She had been given details of the day's events but didn't know what to expect. Jacquie Tomlin, the evening dispatcher, relieved her apprehension. Everything was quiet. The identity of the victim was unknown and the Incident Room remained locked. She told her McDaniel was asleep in the changing room. The murder had rattled her. All she wanted was to get home and climb under the covers. Wilma gave her a hug.

Mike Heppner and Frank Paulson arrived for their midnight to eight patrol. When Paulson tried the door of the Incident Room and found it locked, he exhibited his usual crankiness. "Why is the Incident Room off limits?" he carped.

"To keep the name of the victim from getting out," DC Nathan Quinn said.

"Why? What's so special about this one?"

Quinn's shrug further aggravated the short-fused constable. In a mood to throw someone in jail, Paulson left for patrol searching for troublesome stragglers. Finding none, he settled into his funk. Heppner, on the other hand, was relieved. It would have meant a stack of paperwork as well as a grilling from the chief, who believed that arrests for minor infractions were a last resort. A firm but diplomatic talking-to would suffice in most cases. They finished up what reports were outstanding and filled their remaining time with busy work.

The night dragged on. The switchboard stayed silent. Wilma worked on a quilted blanket for her newest great-grandchild. At four o'clock, she got up. "I'm going to make some fresh coffee," she told them. It was time for her regular mid-shift snack. After she prepared her plate of food and got the coffee maker going, she went to check on McDaniel. She found him snoring softly, an arm flopped over the side of the bench. How he could sleep on something so hard was beyond her. Near retirement, she felt protective of her "boys." *Why is he here? He should be in his own home with a good woman.*

Chapter Fifteen

Sunday, June 28th

Jimmy got up, his mind in turmoil. Being plunged from six years of tedious routine into a full-fledged murder investigation required serious mental adjustment. His brain was still working on it at 4 AM. Roger remained on the bed, nose burrowed in his behind. After quietly gathering his clothes and dressing in the bathroom, Jimmy texted Ray. Not expecting a response, he was surprised with an immediate answer. At the kitchen table, he began a note to Ariel, but before putting pen to paper he heard the swish of her nightie.

She leaned against a wall. "Planning on running out on me, big boy?" she drawled.

"Sorry, honey. I couldn't sleep. I'm off to meet Ray."

"At this hour?"

Jimmy shrugged.

"No breakfast? No coffee?"

"I'll get something at Justine's later on."

"Then … I'll see you when I see you?"

He got up and gave her a long hug. "That's all I can promise for now."

She opened her right hand, revealing a crumpled piece of paper.

He grinned. "Going through my shorts again, eh?"

"Yes, and this time without you in them."

"So, are they right?"

"What do you think, mister know-it-all?" she said, turning down her mouth.

He laughed. She punched him in the arm.

"By the way, did you know Max was a Jehovah's Witness?"

"Of course. Everyone knows the Berdahls are JWs."

"Everyone but me, apparently."

"Guess you're not a know-it-all after all," she said, laughing.

Ray and Georgina were sharing continental breakfast and information. Savouring the prosciutto and cornetto, he listened as she gave him a run-down on the previous evening.

"Gabby did the greet and seat, filled the water glasses, and so on," she said through a yawn.

"That's what she wanted. So how did she make out?" he asked, slurping his cappuccino.

"Well, she did get in the way of the wait staff now and then. But it didn't take her long to learn to keep an eye out. I think she was a bit overwhelmed, frankly."

"A lot of jobs look like a slam dunk until you start doing them." He helped himself to a wedge of crostata.

"It was busier than usual with all of the out-of-towners. I'm glad Silvana agreed to give her a taste of what it's like. Maybe now university will look more appealing."

"Hmm, I don't know about that. She doesn't seem academically inclined."

"No she doesn't, does she? She would rather be doing than thinking."

"Did you tell her anything about why I wasn't here when she got home?" he mumbled through a mouthful of food.

"I don't think she even noticed. She was dragging her butt and just wanted to hit the pillow."

Ray grunted his understanding as he got busy making himself another cappuccino. "You know, Georgie, I'm really ticked that Wyatt wouldn't let us ask Stefan Berdahl a few questions yesterday. He had talked to him at the scene, but I don't know what he learned. The whole family has probably gotten together by now and come up with a story to protect Max."

"Didn't you always tell me it was wrong to go into an investigation with preconceived ideas?" She ignored his sharp look. "Don't you think that's what you're doing now?"

Over the years Ray had learned to listen to her level-headed advice. He sat down. "Yeah, I have said that. But I'm sure this murder is personal. And personal means family."

"Does Jimmy agree with you?"

"He thinks it might be a business deal gone sour."

"Losing money is personal, too. Maybe it's a combination of both."

He took a last bite of pastry, drained his cup and rose. "Yeah. Maybe it is." He leaned down and kissed her upturned cheek. "If you're right, you'll be the first to know."

As Ray and Jimmy pushed their way through the station doors, Paulson accosted them. Stewing all night, his anticipation and anger overrode any semblance of social niceties. "So, who's the victim?" he demanded.

Ray raised both arms to the sides of his head and wiggled his fingers. "Only the shadow knows," he said spookily. Then he went to his desk and removed a set of keys.

Not to be put off, Paulson appealed to Jimmy. "C'mon Tan. Don't keep us in the dark," he whined.

"What do you know so far?"

"Just that a victim was discovered Saturday morning in a

vacant house on Townshipline Road."

"That about covers it," Jimmy said.

"Well, shit!" Paulson exploded. "The biggest story to hit this town and we don't know nothin'."

Jimmy followed Ray as he walked down the hall jingling his keys and whistling, *I got plenty o' nuttin'.*

"Don't be so impatient, Frank," Heppner tried to reason with his partner. "We'll find out soon enough. Right now, they've got to be tight-lipped. It won't be long before the whole town will be banging down the doors and calling us about suspicious people in the neighbourhood, wanting us out there fighting a crime wave."

Paulson, disgusted, uttered an oath. Not for the first time he felt left out of the loop.

McDaniel awoke, groaned and peeled himself off the bench. He spent a few minutes limbering up his muscles, having a quick pee, and rinsing out his morning mouth before returning to the Incident Room. When he unlocked the door, he was surprised to see Ray and Jimmy, heads together, conferring.

"What are you guys doing here?"

Ray looked up. "Jesus, McDaniel. Never mind us. What are *you* doing here? You look like hell. Go home and get some sleep."

"I just had that, sort of. What I need is a shower and some food." He threw the extra key in a drawer. "I'll be in later."

"You don't need to come back. You've already done yeoman's work," Jimmy said.

"'Yeoman's'?" McDaniel laughed. "Where do you come up with these words?"

"From my wife. One of the perks of being married to a clever woman."

"Whatever," he tossed back, shrugging off the jab as he left. Being the only unmarried male member of the squad made him a target of barbs—some envious, others piteous.

After he left, Ray locked the door and the two detectives began discussing the upcoming interview with Jaxon Berdahl and his father.

"We're going to get pushback from them, you know," Ray said.

"Does it have something to do with their religion?"

"Religion, my ass. It's nothing but a cult." He sat back and cracked his knuckles. "Nope. We definitely won't get a lot of help from them."

"Not even when the victim is of one of their own?"

Ray thought for a moment. "They probably think that any member who does anything to bring in people from the so-called *outside* causes them shame. At least that's what Georgie told me. She reads up on all of this stuff cuz one of her relatives got caught up in Scientology."

"But then why protect him? Why not co-operate fully to find out who did this and why?"

"Because I think it's the 'why' part that worries them. There may be something in Max's background that is anth ... anthema to them."

Jimmy smiled. "You mean anathema?"

"Shit, Jimmy," he laughed. "Give us a break."

"It's your word for the day. Use it with the crew."

"Are you nuts? I'd be target practice for doughnuts."

There was a knock on the door. Ray got up and opened it an inch to see Heppner standing there. "Yo, Mike. What's up?"

"Robyn has just arrived. Should I send her back here or do you want to come out and tell her about ...?" And he left the rest to their imagination.

"I'll come out there."

Heppner turned to go.

"Mike?"

"Yes?"

"Good thinking," Ray told him.

Heppner nodded and returned to the front. He had heard Ray's laughter and envied the camaraderie between the two detectives. How many times had he wished he had not been paired with someone as cynical and ignorant as Paulson?

"I'm going to bring Robyn up to speed," Ray said.

"Okay. I'm going to Justine's for breakfast." When he stepped outside, Constables Drew Hastings, Dalbir Dhillon and Marina Davidova were making their way to the front door. Davidova, Special Municipal Constable, dealt with the press. Dark-haired, dark- eyed and beautiful, she was the ideal foil for male reporters who were too busy looking at her rather than asking hard questions.

"Good morning guys and gal," Jimmy said.

"Oh, never mind that PC crap," Davidova said. "I like to be included with the guys."

"Why not? You have more balls than most of them," Hastings said.

She gave him a look. "Present company excepted, of course."

"But of course," he replied, grinning.

Jimmy halted them from going inside. "About this homicide. You know who the victim is, right?"

"No," the two men said as Davidova said, "Yes."

Hastings rolled his eyes. "Why am I not surprised?"

"Hey, mister put-upon. It's based on need to know," she pointed out. Chief Wyatt kept her apprised of everything so that the press wouldn't catch her flat-footed.

Jimmy backed her up. "Once you learn the victim's name you'll realize why we're trying to keep our cards close to our chest. We don't want anyone blabbing. And Paulson is already dogging us."

They groaned.

"Can you tell *us* who it is?" Dhillon indicated himself and Hastings.

Davidova got a nod from Jimmy. When she told them, Dhillon whistled. "All it's going to take is one person and this town is going to boil over."

"Drew, I have a special job for you today."

"You mean, on top of my regular job?"

"Yeah, your regular job of sitting around on your ass all day," Dhillon chuckled.

"What do you want me to do?"

"I've called J.D. I want you two to go to the crime scene. We need fresh eyes looking for something like an ax or a maul. We believe it was the murder weapon."

"Holy shit!"

"We may have to bring in an RCMP sniffer dog if you're not successful. And you know how much Wyatt would love that."

"So, in other words, no pressure," Hastings said.

"Sorry. But someone's got to do it and most of the crew was at the scene yesterday."

"Okay, then."

As predicted, Paulson was waiting to pounce on the arriving officers. "Davidova, you always know everything. Why is the victim's ID a secret?"

Before she could deflect his question, Ray strolled over, placed his body close to Paulson and poked him on the chest a couple of times. Paulson backed up. "To keep guys like you from being a wise ass. That's why. You brag like some big shot in the know. You spew out details Davidova tries to keep from the press. You're as leaky as a rusty faucet."

Paulson moved his mouth as though to say something, then thought better of it. Grabbing his belongings, he stomped out to smatterings of applause. "Good going Rossini," someone said.

"Happy to be of service," he said with a bow, hoping the incident wouldn't get back to Wyatt, who was already on his case.

Delilah had been so energized by two nights of restful sleep that she sang the hymns with gusto, and shouted out "Hallelujah" during the sermon. It was not uncommon in her church, but people were surprised at her rambunctiousness. The congregants looked for her in the basement kitchen after the service. She never missed helping herself to the squares and tarts, but this particular morning she was nowhere to be found.

She was on the road rushing home as fast as her walker would take her. After changing clothes and eating a quick lunch she got out into the garden with her gloves and empty ice cream bucket. She didn't know where Max was, but she didn't care. "It's heaven, isn't it, Tabitha? Well, maybe hell in this heat. But we've got to take advantage of the peace and quiet before he comes back, don't we?" Tabitha responded by gagging up a hairball.

Chapter Sixteen

Ray and Jimmy ran down the list of points they wanted to raise. "What're we missing?" Ray asked.

Jimmy shook his head. "I don't know. But I'm willing to bet something will turn up during the interview."

Ray checked his watch. "They should be here soon."

"I haven't heard if Chief Wyatt is going to be around for this."

"No, he's not. He wants to be arms-length. I'm glad, because he might try to play nice. And I'm not about to do that."

Unlike Ray, Jimmy did not relish tearing away people's defences leaving them exposed, but sometimes it was the only way to get to the truth. If Ray was right, it was going to be doubly difficult with a doctrinaire religious group.

"We need to go back to Townshipline Road, too." Jimmy said.

"Why's that?"

"I saw what looked like a driveway onto another property. Maybe there's someone living there who saw something."

"Okay. Let's check that out after we finish with the Berdahls."

Shortly after one o'clock, the Berdahls arrived. Ray was already walking toward the reception desk. "Mr. Berdahl, if you'll just come this way," he said, softer than he intended, and motioned toward the squad room, deserted except for Robyn and Marina.

Stefan Berdahl started to proceed then realized that Jaxon remained rooted to the floor, his head swinging left and right, whites of his eyes like those of a colt about to bolt from the barn.

Jimmy shuddered at his shriveled resemblance to Max: the same height, the same build, the same hair and eyes, and almost as lifeless as his brother.

"Come on, son," Berdahl murmured, gently taking his arm.

Jimmy stepped forward. "Actually, Mr. Berdahl, you will be interviewed in separate rooms."

Stefan Berdahl glared at Jimmy. "But Jaxon's hardly in a state to be answering questions. Never mind alone."

"We want his answers in his own words, Mr. Berdahl. No one is supposed to get special treatment, yet Chief Wyatt gave you time with your family last night and several hours this morning. It's unusual and does not help the investigation. Nevertheless you were given that courtesy."

Berdahl was about to argue the point when Jaxon surprised them, speaking in a halting voice. "Dad, please. Let's just get this done."

"All right, son. If you're sure." He searched his face.

Jaxon nodded.

"I'll be interviewing Jaxon," Jimmy said.

Berdahl was visibly relieved. At least it would be himself locking horns with Rossini. That decided, he left his only remaining son in the hands of a non-believer.

With no second room for formal interviews, Jimmy showed Jaxon to the comfortable visitor's lounge. It would serve a second purpose by being a less threatening environment.

"Sit anywhere, Jaxon."

Jaxon sat on one of the chairs and began rubbing his thighs and looking around.

Jimmy moved another chair so that he was facing him. "Thank you for coming in. First, let me say how sorry I am for your loss."

Jaxon nodded.

"I know this is a very sad time, but we need to get as much information from you as possible so that we can find the person who did this. Do you understand?"

"Yes," he answered quietly.

"Just so you know, I'll be taking notes."

Again, Jaxon nodded.

"Could you tell me when you realized that your brother was missing?"

Jimmy watched Jaxon's eyes as he called up his memory. "I phoned Saturday morning." His voice was hoarse. He cleared his throat. "Around seven thirty. He didn't answer. It went to message." He swallowed and looked down.

"Was it normal for you to be calling him so early on Saturday morning?"

"We have a family prayer meeting every Saturday morning. I always call him to make sure he's up. I waited for him to call me back."

"Do you remember how long you waited?"

"Maybe ten minutes. I thought he might be in the shower. I called again and when I didn't get him I phoned the office. I thought he might be there. But the answering machine was on."

"What did you do then?"

"I drove to his house."

"Do you remember what time it was?"

"About eight o'clock."

Jimmy recalled what he himself was doing at that time. Reading the paper, eating breakfast, having a coffee. Normal everyday things. And there was Jaxon, right across the street from him, looking for his missing brother.

"And when he wasn't there, what did you do next?"

Jaxon grew more ghostlike as the story unfolded. "I called my dad. I told him Max wasn't at home and that he was not answering his cellphone or the office phone. So I was going there."

"Is it normally open on Saturday morning?"

"Yes, but not until nine o'clock. Sometimes he works when it's closed."

Jimmy noticed the use of the present tense.

"And when he wasn't there ...?"

"I was sure he had been in a car accident."

"Was there a particular reason why you thought that?"

"He told me on Friday that he was tired, that he hadn't slept. I thought he might have fallen asleep at the wheel. So I called my dad again. I told him I was going to go to the house that Max had been showing. Maybe I would see his car along the way."

"Do you know who he was showing it to?"

"A Mr. Fitzgerald."

"Do you know him?"

"No. Max got a call from him on Thursday. He said the man wanted to check out the house for his daughter."

"Did Max get his address?"

"I don't know, but he wasn't from here."

"How do you know that?"

"Max said he was driving up the island."

"Do you know when they arranged to meet?"

"Yes. Five o'clock on Friday."

Jimmy now had an approximate time of death.

"When you told your father you were going to the house, what did he say?"

"He said he would meet me there."

"Did you get there before or after your father?"

"Just before."

"Did you see anything?"

Jaxon gulped a few times. "I saw Max's SUV." His breathing became shallow and fast.

Jimmy did not want him jumping ahead to the murder scene, so he quickly asked another question. "Did you check out the SUV?"

"Yes. The key was still in the ignition. Then Dad arrived. As soon as he looked inside, he phoned the police chief. He told him we had found Max's car and he was going in the house because he might be lying inside injured." Jaxon struggled to stay together. "So we went in." He swallowed several times. Unable to hold himself together any longer, he broke down, anguish tinging every word. "How could someone do … that?" He put his head in his hands and sobbed.

After a minute or so, Jimmy spoke in a quiet voice. "Every once in a while we face horrific events and try to comprehend why they happened. Sometimes we find the answer. Sometimes we don't." He had to ask the next questions, but he needed to be able to see Jaxon's face. He handed him a box of tissues. Jaxon pulled out a handful, wiping his eyes and blowing his nose.

"Jaxon," Jimmy said softly. "Can you think of any reason why anyone would do this?"

He sat straight up. "No!" he choked out. "What reason could anyone have for doing something so … evil?" Expending his last bit of energy on the outburst, he fell back into the chair.

"Whoever did this was very angry. If you look back, was there some incident in his personal life that might have led to this?"

A flicker of anxiety crossed his face. Weight settled on his shoulders.

"Jaxon?" Jimmy prompted. He waited through a long, uncomfortable silence. Jimmy was happy to wait. Silence had its own way of speaking.

Jaxon stared at his hands as they twisted the soggy tissues around and around. Abruptly, he stopped and glanced up like a small child caught in a punishable act.

Something is definitely going on there, Jimmy thought, but chose not to press the issue. Not then.

Jaxon finally shook his head. His voice waivered as he

answered. "No. There was nothing."

"What about a business deal that might have gone wrong and someone blamed him for it?"

This time the answer was immediate. "No."

Jimmy had managed to get a few pertinent details from Jaxon and looking at the state of him, he decided it would be cruel to carry on. "Thank you for your co-operation, Jaxon."

Jaxon just nodded. He was wrung out.

"Just a moment. I'll be right back." He went looking for Davidova, who was in the kitchen nursing a cup of coffee and reading some documents.

"Marina," he said quietly.

Surprised, she looked up expectantly. "Yes?"

"Jaxon looks like hell. Could you please direct him to the visitor's bathroom? He's been crying. Maybe ask him if he wants to wash his face, or something. Give him a few minutes."

When she saw Jaxon, Davidova was moved with tenderness. "Come with me, Jaxon." He got up and shuffled along beside her, unquestioning.

Jimmy knocked on the door of the interview room. After a moment, Ray came outside, closing the door behind him. "What's up?"

"Ask him about his calls to Chief Wyatt."

Ray nodded and went back in. "So Mr. Berdahl, we have just about covered everything."

Berdahl, thinking the interview was over, made motions to leave.

"There are just a couple of other details I want to go over."

"Oh?" He resettled himself.

"What prompted you to call Chief Wyatt so soon in your search?"

"As I said before, Jaxon had been to Max's house and when he wasn't there he called to tell me he was going to check at the office. He phoned again to say he wasn't there either and that he was going to go to the property. That's when I called Bill … uh, Chief Wyatt."

The use of Wyatt's first name didn't surprise Ray as they were both long-time residents of Britannia Bay and about the same age. "Why would you call Chief Wyatt instead of the police department to report a missing person?"

"Because I didn't think the police would give much credence to a young man missing overnight," he replied testily.

Ray let that statement pass for the moment. "But Max could have been in an accident."

"Yes. That was my concern. Jaxon told me Max said he hadn't slept well on Thursday night and was very tired. When he didn't show up for a family gathering on Friday night, we assumed he just went home and went to bed. But then on Saturday morning when he didn't come to the prayer meeting and when Jaxon didn't find him at home or at the office, I was afraid that he might have had a car accident. I told Chief Wyatt where I was going and that I would take a look along the route."

"Didn't he offer police help at that point?" Ray was baffled by this information.

"He did, but I told him to wait. It might not be necessary."

"But then, why call him at all?"

"I just wanted to alert him."

Ray rubbed his chin as he tried to comprehend Berdahl's statement. It was a strange way to handle a MISPER case.

"And the second call was after discovering Max's body?"

"No. It was just before. I told him about Max's empty vehicle. I thought Max might have had an accident inside the house—maybe a rotting floor board or a tumble down the stairs from the loft or in the basement. Something."

"So, the door was open?"

"No. It was closed, but it wasn't locked."

"And you went inside."

Berdahl paused before answering in a barely audible voice.

"Yes."

Ray could only imagine his reaction on seeing his son brutally murdered. "Did Jaxon go in as well?"

Berdahl's head went down as he nodded.

Ray waited.

"And that's when you called the chief to report the murder?"

Berdahl cleared his throat. "Yes. He said he would be right there, that he was sending his crime scene team, not to touch anything and to leave the house immediately."

"Thank you very much for your co-operation, Mr. Berdahl." A beat. "And may I say that I am very sorry for your loss."

Berdahl finally saw compassion in the bad cop's eyes. "Thank you." He reached into his pocket and handed Ray a piece of paper. "Ingrid Berdahl's phone number," he explained, then left the room.

As father and son filed out the front, Wyatt slipped in the back. "My office," he motioned to Ray and Jimmy. They joined him and he closed the door. "Did you learn anything useful?"

"Not much. It was like pulling hen's teeth."

"I did get a bit of something," Jimmy offered. "Jaxon was hesitant when I asked him if he knew anything of a personal nature that might have led to the murder."

"That's interesting, because I got the same kind of reaction when I asked Berdahl about Max's *business* dealings." Ray shot a glance at Jimmy, then turned back at Wyatt. "But there was one thing that caught our attention."

"Which was?"

After a second or two, Ray responded, "The phone calls to you."

"Okay. So why is this so important?" Wyatt asked, voice neutral, face blank.

"Only that Mr. Berdahl called you before Max had been missing for twenty-four hours. He said you would understand. He didn't think the police would have taken the call seriously."

"I'm ashamed to say he was probably dead right about that.

They wouldn't have. Most of the fellows on the squad don't have a clue about how young men seriously involved in a strict religion behave. They would automatically assume the guy would be shacked up overnight. I mean, what man in his thirties checks in with his parents? And remember, it was a celebratory weekend. So they wouldn't have given the call the time of day." He paused. "These JW young people are aggressively managed. They're expected to lead a chaste life. They don't call it The Watchtower for nothing."

"Well, when you put it that way," Ray said.

Wyatt grunted as he worked his way out of his chair. "Well, boys, it's in your hands. Mine are going to be busy with the press and the townspeople. Don't know which will be worse."

Chapter Seventeen

Back on Townshipline Road, Ray drove the police cruiser while Jimmy looked for the opening he thought he had spotted the day before. "There it is."

Ray stopped and looked. "It's almost invisible, isn't it?" He turned into a narrow entrance cut into heavy brush and trees and followed a curving dirt road that ended abruptly at the foot of two gigantic cedars that all but swallowed the single storey house. As they got out of the vehicle, they heard barking dogs being shushed. The front door opened and a burly man with long hair, bushy beard and sideburns came out, closing the door firmly behind him.

"Good afternoon, officers," he greeted them affably. "What brings you to my humble abode?" Although his beard was heavy on the salt and light on the pepper, his voice and energy were that of a younger man.

"Good afternoon, sir," Ray replied. "We're making inquiries about any strange cars on this road lately."

"Strange looking or unfamiliar?"

Jimmy smiled at the man's discernment. "Unfamiliar."

"Hmmm. What kind of information are you looking for, exactly?"

"A vehicle that's been up and down the road on more than one occasion recently," Jimmy explained.

The man thought for a moment. "Well, other than all of the police vehicles that were here yesterday, the only car I ever see is the Jeep belonging to the people who live near the top of the road in Rose Cottage. It's not that easy to spot cars from here." He pointed to the curving driveway.

They turned and realized what he meant. "What about in the winter?" Jimmy asked, thinking how much clearer it would be without all the leaves blocking the view.

"We don't spend our winters here. We're long gone by the time October rolls around. Don't come back until the beginning of April."

"Where do you go?"

"Mexico. We have a fifth wheeler. So we close up the house and head on down."

There was a pause in the conversation. "Well, thank you very much Mr. ... uh?"

"Phillips. Warren Phillips," he came up and shook their hands.

"Just a thought, Mr. Phillips," Jimmy said. "What about a motorcycle? Have you heard a bike more than once or twice?"

"*A* bike? How about a half dozen of them? They race up and down all the time. It's like a bloody motocross."

"Does it happen often?" Ray asked.

"All the time. But mostly on the weekends. It drives us nuts. The animals run inside." He laughed. "And so do we."

"Thanks again, Mr. Phillips." He gave him a card. "If you think of anything ..."

"Okay. Don't mention it." As they began to walk off he called after them. "Are you asking because of the goings on at the Schwindt place yesterday?"

"Yes, as a matter of fact, we are." Jimmy said.

"That place has been vacant for a long time." He paused. "What happened? I saw an ambulance, too."

"We can't really say at the moment," Ray said.

"But you're asking questions about a strange vehicle," he said apprehensively. "Do we need to be locking our doors?"

"My advice to anyone is always your doors," Ray said. "But as for any danger to you, you don't need to worry."

"Okay, if you say so. It seems there's no security anywhere anymore. We're safer in Mexico," he muttered.

"Thanks again," Jimmy said.

The man nodded and went back inside.

As they pulled out of the driveway, Ray turned to Jimmy. "I doubt that."

"Doubt what?"

"That they're safer in Mexico."

"Yeah, there seem to be more and more murders at so-called *exclusive* resorts," Jimmy said.

"We've been there once. It was okay. The food was phenomenal, and the people were friendly. But I like Hawaii better," Ray said. "By the way, what made you think of a bike?"

"I don't know. It just came to me. If you were wanting to scope out the house, it would be easier to get up and down on a bike than in a car. And less obvious."

"Yeah, and what a perfect cover ... all the other bikes."

"And that would mean the weapon would have had to be left behind."

Ray gave him a knowing nod.

They turned up the hill, slowing down as they passed the entrance to the crime scene. Ray said that the only saving grace about the murder site was that it was too far off the beaten track for ghoulish gawkers and the rapacious press. "I mean, why would anyone want to live here? It's so far from town. Say you needed an ambulance. By the time they found you, you could be dead," Ray observed.

"That's one of the reasons why Ariel and I like living in town. Everything's close."

"Yeah. Georgie and I thought of that, but decided we didn't want to be that available to neighbours. Don't they ever bother you with police stuff?"

"Not yet ... well, we do have one neighbour who's a sort of one-person block watch. She's been over to talk to Ariel about what she thinks is a dope house next to her. But that's been the only time."

Near the hilltop they easily spotted the wide entry to Rose Cottage. Alongside a paved driveway, abundant flowerbeds were set amongst grass that was managing to remain green. At the end, a two-storey house of faded brick topped by two dormers in a hipped roof, stood solidly facing them. Masses of yellow roses hugged the façade, curling around both corners. Hence, the name. Except for the newish Jeep parked at the side, the whole effect was something out of *Miss Marple*.

"Wow. Who would have expected this?" Ray said. "It's pretty over the top, even for Britannia Bay. And brick. It must have cost an arm and a leg."

Ray rapped the rose-shaped brass knocker on the gleaming black door. After a few minutes with no reply, he stepped off the stoop. "Maybe they're outside." He called out a hello as they headed toward the side of the house.

A grey-haired couple came running. She was holding secateurs and wearing gardening gloves. He had on a long leather apron. They quickly took in their visitors and their vehicle.

Her hands flew over her heart. "Oh, my goodness! Police!"

The man's eyes bugged out.

"Good evening," Ray said. "We're sorry to trouble you, but we're making inquiries about traffic on this road."

After a moment of shocked silence the man said: "Traffic?"

"Yes. We're wondering about suspicious automobiles or motorcycles that have been in the area lately."

"Suspicious?"

His wife latched onto his arm, a look of alarm on her pretty face.

"Yes. There's been an incident at the Schwindt property."

"Incident?"

Jimmy thought he would start over in an effort to quell their anxiety. "Yes. The Schwindt property has been accessed by someone other than the owners or the real estate company that's handling the sale," Jimmy said. "We're trying to find that person."

The woman, who resembled a delicate bird, finally spoke. Unlike her husband, she managed to use words of more than one syllable. "Oh, I'm sorry, constables, but we don't pay much attention to the goings on around here," she replied in a strong British accent. "We keep ourselves to ourselves,"

"I see." Since Ray had the feeling they were going to get a quick brush off, he tried a page out of Jimmy's book. "You've put a tremendous amount of work into this place. It's lovely."

Jimmy pressed his lips together to keep from smiling.

She beamed, and her husband relaxed. "Yes, we have," she agreed, "but it's what we enjoy."

"Is it an old house that you renovated?" Ray asked.

"Oh, no. We had it built. We knew what we wanted and where we wanted it." She turned to her husband with a smile. "We're happy here, aren't we Tommy?"

"Yes. Very," he responded, as though obeying a command.

"What about the noise from the motorcycles?" Ray asked.

There was a beat before she answered. "Oh, that," she laughed uneasily. "We are used to that. You see, we used to live on the Isle of Man and they have one of the most famous motorcycle races in the world—the T.T. it's called. The Tourist Trophy. Mind you, that was only for a couple of weeks at the end of May and into June. But I suppose it inured us to loud sounds."

"How do you manage such a beautiful green lawn with this drought?" Ray asked.

"Well, actually, we collect rainwater. When there's rain, that is. We've been doing it for years and it has kept our garden flourishing." Again, it was the woman taking the initiative.

"I can see that. Very clever of you. Too bad other people don't do that."

"Perhaps this drought will have them considering it," she said.

Ray nodded. "Well, thank you very much. We're sorry to have troubled you."

"No trouble at all, I assure you," she smiled. They watched until the officers cleared off. "That was a bit scary, wasn't it, darling?"

"When I saw the police car, my heart nearly stopped," he said, apparently capable of uttering more than one word at a time. "I thought it was …" his voice trailed off as she nodded. "And then I was afraid they would want to see how we harvested the water. That cistern is so close to the greenhouse."

"What worried me was their asking about the motorcycles," she said, nibbling nervously at her lips.

"Hmm. Yes. But I don't think they know anything, petal," he said, as they moved to the back of the house. "Remember, they mentioned something that happened at the Schwindt property. And there *were* police cars there yesterday. No. I think we are fine."

And they returned to the greenhouse where they were presently harvesting their latest crop of B.C. bud.

At the crest of the hill, the detectives got out and looked around. "Hey, Jimmy! Get a load of this!" Ray yelled from behind a stand of fir trees. Jimmy, who had been walking among signs of human use, joined him. "Someone's been busy," Ray said. An old outhouse had been haphazardly repaired, with new hinges on the door, and the wooden shelf for the open seat replaced. A bag of lime with a scoop inside sat on the floor. "Looks like the old picnic ground has become a kind of campground."

"Not a bad site," Jimmy said, his eyes sweeping over the location. "And fresh water when the creek is full." The creek bed bore fewer boulders than at the Schwindt property and was easily accessible. He pointed to a weed-flattened rutted roadway alongside.

"I guess this was where the old road used to be. Looks like only the dirt bikers use it now."

"We'll need to talk to some of those riders." Ray said. "They might have seen something or someone."

"Bike shops might be able to help. We should start there."

"Yeah," Ray sighed. "Just add it to the list."

Chapter Eighteen

Monday, June 29th

Early Monday morning. Blessedly, tourists and participants at the weekend party had cleared out and the town returned to its normal routine. So far, the news of Max's death had been contained. Although police officers patrolling the area around the office had not attracted undue attention, the arrival of police vehicles was bound to generate intense scrutiny. News that something was up with the Berdahl boys would spread like an oil slick.

The coroner's report was pending but faxed copies of the forensic reports had already arrived. Griffin had been both quick and thorough. In this case, the results were unusually prompt due to the dearth of evidence. And yesterday's search for the murder weapon had been fruitless.

Wyatt, Ray and Jimmy were reading through the reports. "The pink residue in the shower curtain was Chlorhexidine Gluconate. It's used as a pre-surgery scrub," Jimmy said.

"Is this something you can only get in hospitals?" Ray asked, hopeful.

Jimmy punched the query into his computer's search engine.

"Nope. It's available on pharmacy shelves."

"Oh, great. And even if and when we get DNA results, the hairs and fingerprints won't help until we find this guy," Ray said. "Looking for clues at this point is like pissing in the ocean."

Wyatt threw down a report in disgust. "Damn it! Now we're going to have to borrow that sniffer dog. No evidence and no weapon are crippling this case."

"Well, we haven't found anything on *site*," Jimmy said. "But there may be something in Max's files. Or one of the bikers may have seen something suspicious."

"Hope springs eternal." Wyatt gave his thighs a little slap and stood up.

"Thanks for getting the warrants, Chief," Ray said.

"Yeah, I have a feeling it's going to cost me," he said with chagrin and walked out.

Jimmy looked at Ray with raised eyebrows.

"Judge Silverman was probably on the golf course when Wyatt called," Ray explained.

"So, what do you want to do? Get the files or go to the bike shops?"

"You have to ask?" Ray grinned, got up and made his way to the garage.

Jimmy addressed the officers in the squad room. "I've got a task for you," he said, handing a search warrant to Tamsyn Foxcroft.

She looked at the warrant then up at Jimmy. "Really?" There was a gleam in her eye, and the thought of a smile on her otherwise implacable face.

Jimmy picked up on it. "Now, Tamsyn. Behave yourself. Don't get 'All White Men Bad' on me."

She laughed. "No worries, Sergeant."

"And take one of the unmarked cars. Don't want to get the neighbours gossiping." Delilah came to mind.

As she grabbed her gear and left, Rhys-Jones asked, "What was that about?"

"She's removing files and any computers from Max's house."

"What have you got for us?" Novak asked.

"His office. I'm meeting Stefan Berdahl there at nine thirty." He looked at his watch. "You have time to load up about four dozen transfer boxes."

Berdahl arrived as scheduled, opened the office door, quickly motioned everyone inside, and promptly closed the door behind him. Jimmy handed him the warrant, which he carefully read. "Good grief. This is asking for records covering the past ten years. Why do you need to go back that far? Max had barely started working then."

"We can't rule out anything," Jimmy told him, holding out his hand for the keys to the filing cabinets.

Berdahl gave him a sour look before handing them to Novak. Jimmy ignored the snub and nodded at Novak, who began opening the drawers and extracting the contents. He handed each file to Rhys-Jones, who wrote the name on a list, which Berdahl then signed. As expected, it wasn't long before the activity around the office became a source of curiosity. People who had stopped across the street to watch were now pulling out cellphones, making calls and taking photographs.

Rhys-Jones noted the crowd as they drove away. "We'd better tell the chief right away."

"Yep. The doo-doo is about to hit the fan."

Inside the office, Jimmy turned to Berdahl. "Thank you very much for your co-operation."

"I didn't have much choice, did I?"

"But you understand that we are on your side, Mr. Berdahl. We are trying to find your son's killer."

Berdahl rubbed his close-cropped hair. "It's so savage. I can't get my mind around it. It's beyond understanding."

"That's why we need to search every document. There may be a minor detail in one of them that can give us a clue. And that's why we need information from your family and anyone who had more than a passing acquaintance with Max. Someone must know something," Jimmy suggested.

Berdahl shook his head back and forth. "Well, perhaps someone else does, because I've told you all I know."

Jimmy doubted that.

Ariel stood at a front window drinking coffee, waiting for the expected activity at Max's house. From what Jimmy had told her, she knew that police cars would soon be arriving. A car pulled up—a white Lexus. Out stepped an attractive middle-aged woman wearing a pale green dress that fell below her knees. Ariel thought it must be Max's mother. Rather than going in, she stood by the fountain, its water still gurgling. A black unmarked police car parked around the corner. Ariel recognized Tamsyn Foxcroft making her way to the front door.

Mrs. Berdahl was as different from Foxcroft as chalk was to cheese. One—blond, pretty and plump. The other—dark, striking and sculpted. Coming from one of the oldest of Vancouver Island's First Nations, Foxcroft had the imposing stature of one who was proud of her heritage and what she had achieved. Some of her own people, whose opinion of law enforcement bordered on the hostile, vilified her for joining an organization that was seen by them as racist, a belief she once held herself. But over time, she decided that wasn't the case and was convinced she could turn those biases around. It had been a hard road, but she was making headway as a role model for younger First Nations women.

Ariel watched Foxcroft hand over the warrant, which Mrs. Berdahl read, talking and gesticulating all the while. Foxcroft remained still, and only after the woman went silent did she speak. The woman's shoulders drooped. She nodded and opened the door.

Delilah had put out her recycle box first thing, but as she finished her breakfast, the radio announcer said it was Monday, not Tuesday. Except for Sunday, one day was the same as the next to her. But not wanting people living on the street thinking she was senile, she retrieved it. Curious at the activity next door, she sat at her living room window watching the goings on. She saw a female police officer carrying a box and walking around to where a black car was parked. The exercise was repeated twice. Then she brought out a computer, placed it on the passenger seat, and drove off in the direction of town. A woman came out of the house, got into the white car and sped away.

So, the cops are sniffing around, eh? Maybe Max is in jail. Maybe that's why it's been so quiet around here. I should ask Ariel. She went into the bedroom where she rummaged in her closet, tugging down a blue and purple muumuu from a hanger. "What do you think, Tabitha? This will be cool. Nice and loose and I won't have to wear a bra in this heat."

She pulled on the shapeless dress and took out a pair of flip-flops with pink plastic flowers on top. The shiny petals wiggled as she slipped on one sandal. Tabitha, catching sight of movement, pounced from the bed and landed on Delilah's bare foot, her back claws digging in and drawing blood as her front paws batted at the flower.

"Get off, you crazy cat!" Delilah shouted and shook her leg. Nearly losing her balance, arms flailing around, she grabbed the closet handle as the doorbell rang. "Jumping Jehosaphat!" she yelled, then caught her breath, righted herself, and hobbled to the door, throwing it open with all the energy she could muster. "Ariel! What are you doing here?"

Ariel, who had seen Delilah at the window watching the activity, thought it might be best to bring her up to speed before she got on the phone to anyone and set tongues wagging. Instead, she stared at the chaos that was her neighbour. Delilah stood there, hair sticking up in all directions, one flip-flop on, and a bare foot with blood trickling out.

"My God, Delilah. Are you all right?"

"Yes. Tabitha decided to use my foot as a launching pad."

"Here," Ariel said, slipping her arm under Delilah's elbow. "Where are your bandages?" She guided her toward the hall bathroom.

"I have a little first-aid kit. It's in an old camera bag."

"Where is it?"

"Hmm." Her eyes grazed the ceiling and she pressed her lips together. "It's been so long since I used it I've forgotten where it is, but I think it's in one of the cupboards. Or maybe a drawer. Anyway, it doesn't matter. My blood congeals fast and this scratch is nothing. I'll just slap some Kleenex on it. Maybe use a bit of scotch tape."

"That's not very sanitary, Delilah."

"People worry too much about germs. A little dirt is good for you. Never mind that right now. I was on my way to your place, as a matter of fact."

Ariel, not surprised, ignored her comments and instead searched for and finally found the first-aid kit. "Sit down while I put these on."

"Oh, all right," she said grumpily. "And if you're so worried about germs, there's some rubbing alcohol under the sink and some cotton balls in that top drawer."

Ariel cleaned the scratch and affixed the bandage. Delilah was right. Her blood coagulated quickly.

"So, don't you want to know why I was coming over to see you?" Delilah asked, impishly.

"I have a pretty good idea."

"Who better to ask than a policeman's wife?" she asked expectantly.

"Well ... I do know a bit, but—"

"I know. You can't spill the beans before it's official, right?"

"Right. What I *can* tell you … and Delilah, you must keep this under your hat until the press has—"

"Who am I going to tell?" Delilah interrupted, dying for the details.

"What about Val?" As soon as she had spoken, Ariel cringed remembering the fraught relationship between Delilah and her daughter. When Val and her husband moved to Vancouver, the number of visits between mother and daughter, which were already sparse, dropped precipitously. Delilah called it elder abuse.

"That daughter of mine would be the *last* person I would tell," she snorted. "She's got a mouth the size of the Grand Canyon."

Ariel thought about how big her *own* mouth was about to be. "Well, here's what I know so far." She paused. She wasn't going to pretend she was sad. "Max Berdahl is dead," she said, straight and to the point.

Delilah drew in a sharp breath. "Holy doodle! Dead!" After taking in the information, she squinted at Ariel and grinned. "I can see you're all broken up about it."

"Indeed. So *dreadfully* upset," she mocked. "I'll be reading his obituary with a great deal of satisfaction."

They were having a good laugh when Delilah abruptly stopped. She screwed up her eyes and thought for a moment. "Dollars to doughnuts he was murdered."

Delilah's deduction startled Ariel. "Why do you think that?"

"Because he was just itching to be bumped off." She paused, thinking. "I'll bet one of his real estate deals went sideways. Lost peoples' money. He was a two-bit crook under all that flash. It's probably pay back."

Ariel grinned. Delilah's colourful language reminded her of the woman's penchant for watching police dramas. "But he couldn't have stayed in business in this small town if he had been crooked, Delilah."

"Maybe not here, but he didn't always live here, you know."

"He didn't? How do you know that?"

Delilah tapped her index finger on the side of her nose. "I know lots of things about people in this town."

Ariel didn't hesitate. *Nothing ventured. Nothing gained.* "So why don't we have some tea and talk about it?"

Delilah giggled and rubbed her hands together. "I'll get my slippers. You put the kettle on."

As Ariel made tea, she thought about what sort of information Jimmy might ask Delilah if he were here. She wasn't sure, but she would follow one of Jimmy's tenets: *Don't interrupt when people are speaking. You'd be surprised what you learn when you listen.*

Chapter Nineteen

Ray was clearly out of his element. There had been a time when he felt comfortable in a bike shop, but that was years ago when he and Georgina toured around on his big Honda Gold Wing. When he walked in the door of Dirt Riders, it was if he had stepped into a scene from Star Wars or become an avatar in a virtual reality game. Although stationary, every bike seemed to be moving.

A bell sounded as he entered, and he smiled because there were CCTV cameras everywhere if you knew where to look. The short, wiry man now approaching him would, no doubt, have had a good look at him already. "Good afternoon, sir." He had on a salesman's smile. "How may I help you?"

God, another Brit, Ray thought. *Was there an Anglo left in the U.K.?* "I'm Detective Rossini of the Britannia Bay Police Force." He showed the man his ID. "We're investigating a situation that occurred on Townshipline Road recently, and hoping you can help us." He noted that the man was in his sixties and wondered what his background might be that he was selling the latest in sport and motocross bikes.

"Oh, yes," the man said, showing not the least trace of curiosity. Whatever the "situation" was, it had nothing to do with him.

"It's our understanding that a group of bike riders race up and down that road at least once a month, and we'd like to talk to them."

Realizing it might indeed have something to do with his business, he became cautious. He wasn't about to trash any of his loyal customers. "And?" he asked, defensively.

Ray, sensing the sudden shift, quickly spelled out the details in order to smooth the prickly atmosphere. "We are not looking *for* a particular person from this group. What we are looking for is information about anything unusual or anyone unknown to them, either on the road or up at the picnic site. So we are contacting all the bike shops."

"There aren't that many of those around here. At least, not the kind that carry this sort of bike," and he gestured at the rows of gleaming machines. Feeling no threat, he lowered his mental drawbridge. "I know there are some fellows who frequent Townshipline." He paused. *Oh, what the hell. In for a penny, in for a pound.* "So how can I help you? By the way, my name is Nigel Wright." He held out his hand, which Ray shook.

"Maybe you could speak to one or two of them. Tell them what it is we are looking for, and ask them to pass it amongst the group. And have them contact the Britannia Bay detachment." He gave him a half dozen cards.

"So anything out of the ordinary, or some person or bike they hadn't seen before. Something like that?" he asked.

"Yeah, something like that."

"And from when to when?"

"That's a good question. We're not sure, but at least in the last two months or so."

"Hmm. What sort of incident was it, if you don't mind me asking?"

"Unfortunately, I can't tell you that. But it is serious, so we're looking for anything that can help with the investigation."

"I see. Well, good luck. I hope one of the riders will have something to add to it."

"So do I. Thank you for your co-operation."

As he was walking toward the door, he spotted a classic bike mounted on the wall. "Wow. That is a beauty," he exclaimed.

The man, obviously pleased, came up to Ray. "This is a 1946 BSA Gold Star. I bought it in 1972 when I was just a shaver. Rode it all over England and brought it over with me when I immigrated. At the end of World War 2, BSA was the largest producer of motorcycles in the world and one of the largest companies in the British Empire. I still believe that BSA made the finest bikes. But now the damn Japs own the market."

Ray looked at him quizzically, astonished to hear someone say that in today's politically correct world.

Wright took the look as a silent rebuke. "Pardon me, I usually only use that language at home. Good thing they don't have a Speakers' Corner here like they do in London or I'd be covered in rotten tomatoes."

Ray gave him a grin. "Maybe so. But it sure would be entertaining."

On his drive back to the station, he thought about what the man had let slip. His father often displayed similar sentiments, his target shifting with the times. And truth be told, he carried over some of the same prejudices while adding a few more of his own. He hadn't always been that way. In fact, there had been times he railed against his father for being bigoted. But after years in the force and seeing some of the things he had seen, his views changed. Now he saw political correctness as stifling freedom of expression—a kind of oral hand-cuffing.

Chapter Twenty

By the time everyone returned to the squad room, the first phone call had come in. When Mary Beth heard who it was, she wanted to tell him that Chief Wyatt was unavailable. But she knew better. When she announced his name, Wyatt's expletive could be heard through the walls.

"Put him through," he growled.

"Good morning, Chief Wyatt. Malcolm McDonald here." No response. "*Bayside Bugle?*"

Malcolm McDonald had landed in Britannia Bay after leaving behind a series of jobs on small town newspapers from one end of Canada to the other. He fancied himself a hard news reporter, but when there wasn't any such thing to be had, he would create something out of nothing in order to sell the paper, thus hoping to keep his job. Readers and editors alike soon recognized his flights of fantasy and it wasn't long before he was out on his ear. Never seeming to find his "*niche*," he kept moving on. So far, his two-year tenure at *The Bayside Bugle* seemed to have gone well enough since he was learning to temper his flair for the dramatic.

He had been in the process of finding a photo for the front page of Tuesday's issue. Looking at all the graduates and imagining himself at that age around all of those young hotties, he decided to go with something completely different. Readers would be expecting yet another picture of a pretty teenager. Instead, he chose the image of a handsome young man—Marcus Rossini—who looked studly indeed; something as far from Malcolm as Brad Pitt was from Mr. Magoo.

As he was writing up a caption, the phone rang. Alone in the office, he answered, and a man informed him that police had been removing computers and boxes from the Berdahl brothers' office. About to head out, McDonald sank back in his chair on being told that everyone had just packed up and gone. But the caller had pictures on his cellphone.

After reintroducing himself to the police chief, which he seemed to have to do each time, McDonald waited for an indication that his name was recognized. When he was greeted with silence, he carried on. "I'd like to ask you about the activity at the Berdahl Brothers' offices early this morning."

Wyatt imagined the smarmy little man slavering at the other end of the line, nearly orgasmic at the thought of scooping a headline. "Oh yes. That." he said laconically. "At this point, it's not much. We're in the early stages of an investigation, and that's all I can say right now."

"What kind of an investigation?"

"I can't tell you that right now."

"So it's a *mysterious* investigation?"

"If you want to put it that way."

"But I can't write a story based on conjecture," McDonald protested.

"When has that ever stopped you?"

Momentarily taken aback, he chose to ignore Wyatt's rebuff. "When will information be forthcoming?"

"I don't know. I can't see into the future."

"I have photographs of police officers carrying out boxes. If I print them, readers are going to want to know what it's all about."

"Then perhaps you might not want to print them," Wyatt cautioned him. "Is that all?"

"For now," came the crisp reply.

Wyatt cut the line. He felt he had manoeuvered that mine field for now, but there would be other calls. *Crap. Better have a press conference.* He thought about how to inform the media while keeping residents from raining down on the police station. After coming up with a roughed-out plan, he gathered his crew together.

"So, let's sit down and decide what we're going to reveal to the public." He knocked his head with his knuckles. "Jeez, I've got to get Davidova in here."

"I'll call her," McDaniel said, pulling out his smartphone. Wyatt, sharp-eyed, wondered why McDaniel had Marina on his personal device. *This guy's a dark horse—in more ways than one.*

"Chief," Ray caught his attention. "Should we send someone out to get lunch?"

Wyatt laughed. "Seems every time we have a discussion it's lunchtime. Yeah, okay. But I don't think we should send anyone over to Justine's. There may be curious townsfolk wanting to ask questions."

"We could order Mexican from El Coyote," Rhys-Jones suggested. "Miguel delivers."

"Good idea," Wyatt said then looked at McDaniel. "Gene, call Marina back and ask her if she wants to join us for lunch." He had a smirk on his face.

McDaniel's face did not reveal a blush, but the sudden awkwardness of his body language telegraphed his embarrassment. He cursed his reckless stupidity.

As Rhys-Jones took the lunch orders, Wyatt went over to speak to Mary Beth, who scribbled down notes. They were engaged in a serious discussion when another call came in. It was the mayor. Wyatt took the call in his office, closing the door behind him.

Jimmy was not having any luck reaching Gunther Schwindt. With word beginning to spread, he was anxious to notify him of the situation. But he was not answering his telephone and had no answering machine. There was a Curt Schwindt listed. When he called, it did go to message. He asked that someone there please contact him.

After finishing their lunches they filed into the Incident Room. "Okay, let's begin with the essentials," Wyatt said. "How much are we going to reveal to those vultures?"

"Name, rank and serial number," Novak called out.

"That might be the only thing they get right," Ray remarked.

Wyatt held up a hand. "Okay, we all know what we think of the press. So, to make sure they get the information right, let's make it as plain to them as possible. And we need to make it snappy because the mayor wants details. Apparently the report I gave him yesterday wasn't enough. His friends have already been on the blower demanding to know what the Berdahls have been up to. He's trying to preserve the family's reputation. When people find out it's a homicide rather than fraud, they'll relax because then they won't have to avoid the Berdahls."

"Yeah. Better a body than feeling uncomfortable for chrissake," Ray griped under his breath.

"So I'm going to do this tomorrow. With short notice, I'm hoping there won't be that many reporters. Marina, you're sending out a brief statement late this afternoon to the media, right?"

Davidova had arrived and taken a seat as far from McDaniel as possible. "Right, Chief. It may make the early evening news." Her job, as she saw it, was to decide what to release and what to keep within station walls. Right now, that was nothing and everything, in that order.

"What about the incoming calls?" she asked.

"Unfortunately it's going to fall on our dispatchers to field calls.

I've already given details to Mary Beth, and she'll give them to the others."

"Do they get hazardous duty pay?" Novak threw in.

"Just working with you guys is hazardous enough."

Back at the newspaper's offices, Editor Keith Kittridge had arrived and was arguing with his hapless reporter. "Look, Malcolm. All you have is some photographs. Granted, there's a story here, but Chief Wyatt has already said the equivalent of 'no comment'. And where else are you going to get credible information? You certainly can't call the Berdahls."

Frustrated, McDonald paced around the small room. "It's bloody maddening. We won't have another edition out until Thursday, and by then the story will be all over town and we'll have missed a scoop."

Kittridge looked at his reporter and wondered why he had hired him. Then he remembered. No one else had applied. So for now, all he could do was put the brakes on McDonald's wild imagination. There had already been threats of lawsuits for incorrect reporting causing embarrassment and worse.

"It's more important to get things right than trying to get a scoop." Then he changed the subject. "By the way, your decision to run with the picture of Marcus Rossini for the front page is brilliant."

Momentarily assuaged, McDonald thanked him.

"Now put this edition to bed," Kittridge ordered.

Just as he was leaving for home, Jimmy was halted by Liz Haversham's raised hand. She was taking a call. "I'll put you through, Mrs. Schwindt." She turned to Jimmy. "It's the son's wife," she advised him.

Stephanie Schwindt was calling from her mother's house in Vancouver. She had checked her messages and heard that the police

had called. Jimmy gently explained that he was trying to reach her
in-laws. She said they were on a cross-Canada train trip. Upon
hearing the reason for the call she gasped. Would the media
publicize that it was her in-laws' house? She didn't want to tell them
while they were enjoying their dream trip. But they would be calling
her because she had just had a baby. She would call Curt. He was
up north logging. Jimmy apologized for having to land such tragic
news on her lap, particularly as she was dealing with a new baby.
He walked home with a heavy heart.

As McDonald sat on his worn sofa watching the news and eating a
Chinese takeaway directly from the container, he heard the reader
announce "breaking news." He sat up.

"We have just learned that a prominent land developer in
Britannia Bay has been found dead under suspicious circumstances.
Police Chief William Wyatt will hold a press conference tomorrow
morning at eleven o'clock with further details."

McDonald, enraged, threw the remaining food at the screen. He
knew it! Maybe his last chance to make a name for himself and
Kittridge had blown it for him. All he could do now was cover the
press conference and write up a story for Thursday's edition. The
phone rang. As he ran to the kitchen where it was charging, he
tripped on the corner of the coffee table upending his soft drink. It
was Kittridge. "Malcolm, I'm assuming you've been watching the
news."

"Yes. I just heard the announcement," he said with anticipation.

"Well, I'm going to cover this story. So I'll be taking the press
conference tomorrow morning."

Speechless, McDonald stared at the phone.

"Malcolm, did you hear me?"

He croaked out an assent before hanging up. Returning to the
carnage in the living room, he curled up on the sofa, gripped with
despair.

At the same time, Ray was reeling after researching the practices of Jehovah's Witnesses. His mind boggled at the number of things they were not allowed to do. He wondered how they could even be a part of modern society with all of the prohibitions in place.

Georgina returned home, clothes smelling of food. For her, it was the worst thing about working in the restaurant. "Hi honey," she called out. "I'm just going to get out of these glad rags." A few minutes later, dressed in her robe, she came in and gave her husband a kiss on the cheek.

"Look at this bullshit, Georgie." He pointed to the screen.

"What is it?"

"These are some of the things you aren't allowed to do if you're a JW," he told her. "There are a hundred forty-one of them."

"Didn't I tell you that?"

"Yeah, but do you know what they are? Look at this." He returned the cursor to the top of the page, and as he scrolled back down they read in silence together.

"My God. Can you imagine being a teenager and not being allowed to go to a party or the prom? That would be heartbreaking for girls," Georgina said.

"Not to mention some of the guys. When Marcus saw his picture on the front page of *The Bugle*, I thought he was going to hyperventilate he was so excited."

"He bought a dozen copies."

"Yeah. A couple of days later and it would have all been about the murder," Ray said. "Grad night would have been forgotten." He yawned and rubbed his eyes. "I can't read any more of this crap right now. It's enough to give me nightmares." Nightmares were the least of his worries. First he had to get to sleep. It had been a long time since a case had kept him awake. He wondered how many sleepless nights were in store for him.

Chapter Twenty-one

Tuesday, June 30th

Arriving exhausted but exhilarated after her weekend away, Lana
weaved her way through the house dropping her purchases in their
appropriate places—brioche and pain beignets on the kitchen
counter, hand-crafted lavender soap in the shower, and a picture
book of San Francisco next to her bed. She looked forward to reliving
her memories of the Bay Area.

She opened windows and threw together a light meal.
Afterwards, she walked around the garden drinking a cup of tea and
watched the day burning itself out. The tranquility refreshed her
spirits. She had found the hectic pace of Vancouver enervating. It
was good to be … home? Could it be that this little town would be
her last stop? Would she be satisfied? She and Charlotte had spent a
long evening discussing the pros and cons.

At the thought of her friend, she remembered the photographs
she had promised to send her. It had been ages since she had
cleaned out the gallery and now was a good time to upload them
onto her laptop. Leaving the transfer program to run, she immersed
herself in a lavender-scented bath.

Later she scrolled through the photographs, fascinated. Had she really taken them? Some brought back memories of people and places she had almost forgotten or forgotten entirely. How could it be that a brief gap of years seemed like a chasm? Maybe this *was* her final home after all.

She composed a message to Charlotte. The weekend photos were in sequence, and as she selected which ones to attach, she spotted the two of the biker whom she had found so intriguing. When she had shown his picture to Charlotte and told her about the encounter, Charlotte had agreed that he seemed interesting. He was certainly handsome. In a way, it was too bad she would never see him again. Hesitating, she removed her finger from the delete option.

When she awoke on Tuesday morning no snippets of leftover dreams awoke with her. Feeling rejuvenated, she was eager to get back to work. When she was up to her elbows in flour singing along to *Heard it Through the Grapevine*, the doorbell rang. At first she was not sure if that was what she heard because the music was blasting through the speakers. She continued her duet with Marvin Gaye. Then she heard it again.

"Oh, damn!" She decided to ignore it. It was not worth interrupting her work, washing up and going to the door just to find someone peddling something. She reached for the sugar. When there was a rap on her patio door her hand jerked, spilling a few granules. Surprised to see Ariel, she motioned for her to come in. The duet instantly transformed into a trio with two back up dancers. The song ended and they burst out laughing.

"I'm surprised you knew that song," Lana said as she washed up and turned off the CD. "I thought you just liked lieder. You know, serious stuff."

"Oh, no. Not at all. I like all kinds of music. And I just happen to love that song. But I prefer CCR's version."

"You're just full of surprises, aren't you?" Lana laughed. "What brings you here so early?"

Ariel sat at the table while Lana returned to her recipe. "It seems I'm the bearer of bad news in this neighbourhood. Pretty soon someone's going to shoot the messenger."

Lana, concerned, stopped what she was doing. "What bad news?"

"Max Berdahl was murdered last Friday."

"Oh, my God! The guy across from you that you were always complaining about?"

"One and the same. Totally incapable of speaking below a hundred decibels." She took a breath. "It broke on the news last night."

"It did? Gosh, and there I was taking a long, hot bath. Do you have any details you can share?"

Ariel filled her in with what she knew, leaving out the vital bits that Jimmy warned her to keep to herself.

"At least you won't have a noisy neighbour anymore. So maybe it's more good news than bad news."

"That's the way I see it, although that sounds pretty cold. By the way, how was your trip?"

"It was really good. But I was glad to get back."

"Yeah. It's always nice to come home."

There was that word again. The one Lana had been wrestling with. No matter how many times she tried to knock it down, it kept popping back up like a roly-poly doll. She poured the batter into pans then placed them on oven racks. "Do you have time for a café au lait and a beignet?"

"What's a beignet?"

"The French version of a doughnut only without a hole, and just as bad for you."

"Sounds wonderful."

"Keep talking while I clean up. Then we can dish the dirt."

Chapter Twenty-two

The press descended on the town like a murder of crows. Or so it seemed to Chief Wyatt. He had been expecting a few reporters but was taken aback by the arrival of three mobile television units that would feed the news to their national stations. Their presence was already creating curious onlookers and traffic chaos.

"McDaniel. Novak. Get out there and keep those old farts from running into cars and God knows what else with their golf carts."

The small room set aside for such an occasion was jammed. Lights, cameras and microphones encroached on available space. Reporters searching for a place to sit or stand shamelessly elbowed aside their competitors. The last press conference had been several years before during a string of arsons and the number of reporters hadn't even filled the seats.

As Davidova stepped up to the microphone the hubbub died down. "All right, everybody. Let's get started, shall we?" Her beauty combined with her no-nonsense manner hushed the chattering. "I am Constable Marina Davidova, Media Liaison. The correct spelling of my name is in the press handout. Chief William Wyatt will now make a brief announcement, after which he will take questions." She took a seat behind him but with a view of the room.

Wyatt was already agitated, and when a furry boom microphone came close too close to his head, he almost swatted it away. He began by reading a prepared standard statement telling them who the victim was, when he was killed and when the body was discovered. "We are actively looking for the suspect. We do not believe that this is a random event. Therefore the residents of Britannia Bay need not worry for their safety. The relationship between the suspect and the victim is still being explored. As the investigation is in its early stages there is nothing further to report at this time." Then the questions began.

Where was the body found? "We are not releasing that information for time being."

Who made the discovery? "We are not releasing that information."

How was he killed? "He died of blunt force trauma."

Did you find the weapon? "No."

Do you have any idea what kind of weapon it was? "Forensics has not determined that as yet."

Do you have any leads? "We are pursuing every line of inquiry."

Any idea who did it? "No."

He comes from a well-known family. Have any other members of the family been threatened? "No."

Any idea why he was murdered? "That is part of our inquiry. At the moment we have no answer to that." Wyatt was trying to live up to his reputation as a master of earnestly not answering questions.

So the killer remains at large? Wyatt looked at the reporter, stone-faced. "Obviously."

As light snickers broke out, a woman stood up. "Dee-ann Marie Goudron, Radio Canada," she pronounced *à la française*. "According to my source, it was a particularly savage murder. Can you tell us anything about that?"

When he heard the word "source" his hackles went up. Wyatt contemplated the woman. She was like an exotic bird amongst seagulls with her spiky hair, tight sweater tucked into designer jeans on a boyish frame and a silk scarf tossed on with a certain insouciance that only French women seem to have mastered. Sadly, the hardness of a once-handsome face marred her otherwise casual elegance.

His length of time in answering caused some reporters to think he was finally about to give up some information. There would always be one or two who had a morbid appetite for details.

"No."

"You mean no, it was not a savage murder? Or no, you can't give us any information," she persisted.

"As they say, 'No means no'." *I'm going to be raked over the coals on that one. She looks like a bloody feminist.* "And your source is questionable."

"My source has it on good authority that—"

"—I rather doubt that." While seething inside, Wyatt interrupted her without a flicker of expression. "My chief investigators and myself are the only ones with all the information. Anyone else would be questionable." *Dammit. Who's her source? Gotta get a jump on that.*

Davidova, realizing that the Chief might be close to snapping at whoever asked the next question, stepped beside him, which was her signal that she was taking over. He relinquished his place with relief.

"That will be all the questions for now. As information becomes known to us, we will make it available to the public. Thank you." As they left the room, some reporters rushed to give their hastily scribbled commentaries to the live feed, while others spoke on their mobile phones. All were grumbling. What was the point of this press conference?

Dianne Marie Goudron found a quiet area outside the station, took out her cellphone and spoke in French. "Were you listening? I was made to look a fool. Are you sure about your facts?"

Gratified with the reply, she left to file her report.

Watching on live television in the Incident Room, Ray and Jimmy exchanged a look when the Radio Canada reporter said she had a source. "Who the hell would be leaking details to the press?" Ray asked.

"No one in our squad. I'm sure of it."

"Not even Paulson?"

"Especially Paulson. He might be a jackass, but he'd be the first one we'd suspect. He knows it. Besides, can you see him approaching that French-Canadian reporter?"

Ray smiled envisioning it. Then he picked up a file. "I haven't found diddly squat in any of these that would point to a reason to off Berdahl. Have you?"

"No. But I'm missing files from 2007 to 2012. Do you have them?"

Ray looked at his list. "Nope."

"Okay. That bears out what Delilah told Ariel. Max did not always live here. We have files from 2004 into 2007. After that there is no record of him doing any business here again until 2013."

Wyatt barged in, red faced, slamming the door against the wall. "So, who the hell is this 'source'? That's what I want to know. That damn reporter must know something. They don't go spouting stuff like that without back up."

"We were talking about that, Chief," Ray said, "and we don't think it's anyone from the unit."

"No, probably not. It would be too obvious," he conceded. "So who else?"

"There's any number of people," Jimmy said. "Any husbands, wives, lovers ... you know, pillow talk. A slip of the tongue."

"But who would benefit from that kind of leak? And why do it?"

"Maybe it's not a benefit. Maybe it's just someone who doesn't like the Berdahls."

"Or maybe just a general shit disturber," Wyatt said. "I can see the headlines now. 'Gruesome death rocks Britannia Bay.' And we'll have even more goddamn reporters on our doorstep." He shuddered.

"And more phone calls," Ray added.

"Thanks for that, Rossini," and he charged out like a bull with a red flag in its face.

"You just keep stepping in it, don't you?" Jimmy needled.

Mike Heppner had been correct when he told Paulson what would happen. No sooner had the press broadcast wound down than the callboard lit up. Mary Beth took a page from her early training as a customer service clerk. She handled each call calmly and methodically and ignored anyone waiting until she was finished with the call at hand. She remained unfazed. Each caller was given assurance that she or he had nothing to fear. Few believed her. These were people afraid of everything, anticipating the worst, and keeping their doctors busy writing prescriptions for Ativan.

"All right, Mrs. Carstairs. I'll have someone come by to check that out." She was scribbling on a post-it note. "Yes, as soon as possible." Before answering the next call she turned, holding out the note and looked imploringly at Novak.

"Another sighting of a suspicious stranger?" he asked.

"Yes. Everyone is freaking out, Tim."

"That's understandable, Mary Beth," he said, taking the piece of paper.

"After nothing but innocuous calls every day it's hard to believe a murder has taken place here." She sighed. "It's been the safest place to live."

"There's no safe place anymore," he said. "All you have to do is watch the news. You see it every day. People saying: 'We can't believe it would happen here. It's such a safe community'."

Rather than phone, the brave individuals who tried the direct approach found the front doors of the station impassable. Once again Adam Berry was called upon to man the barricades. This time he had help from Craig Carpenter, and no one would be getting by Carpenter. No one would even contemplate it.

The flurry continued for a few frantic days. The panic dissipated at last. The disquiet, however, remained. Everyone agreed that it was turning into a terrible summer.

Chapter Twenty-three

Wednesday, July 1st

It might have been the Canada Day holiday, but for Ray it was just another working Wednesday. Apparently it was the same for Jehovah's Witnesses since they did not celebrate holidays. In fact—as Ray recalled from a list of 141 prohibitions—they didn't seem to celebrate anything.

The funeral for Max Berdahl had taken place. Ray decided it was now time for Ingrid Berdahl's "Hail Mary" pass to be intercepted. There would be fireworks tonight at the beach, but he was hoping for a few fireworks during the interview.

When Ingrid arrived at the police station in the company of an adult male, the only fire was the slow burn in Ray's belly. He had specifically suggested that she come alone and perceived her refusal to do so as pushback. Rather than let it get under his skin, he decided to push back in his own way and called on the gracious side of his Italian heritage. Even Michael Corleone had been polite before killing someone.

"Good afternoon, Mrs. Berdahl. I'm Detective Sergeant Rossini," he said with a smile from some sycophantic memory that he dug up and dusted off.

"Good afternoon. This is my husband, Robert," she said in a small voice.

There were perfunctory greetings from both men. Ray had already researched the Berdahl family and knew that Robert was not only an elder in the church but also a corporate lawyer. Ray bet that he was involved in the family business.

Broad-shouldered and slightly bald with a bull neck, the man, dressed in a dark suit and crisp white shirt, carried himself with authority. Ingrid, on the other hand, was barely there. Wearing a muted print skirt and pale sweater set, she was washed out like a faded watercolour print. Her oval face was pretty but pinched with worry.

"Let's go in here, shall we?" Ray opened the door to the visitor's lounge with a flourish. "Please take a seat anywhere. Can I offer you coffee or tea?" *Am I laying it on too thick?*

Robert spoke up. "No, thank you," he said, making the decision for both of them.

After they sat on the sofa, Ray noticed the significant space between them. If it had been himself and Georgie, their derrières would have been cheek to cheek. He sat back in an overstuffed chair and rested an ankle on the opposite knee hoping his comfortable position would convey a casual tone to the conversation. His file folder and a pen lay on the table beside him, but he made no move to make use of either as he began.

"The reason I have asked you to come in, Mrs. Berdahl, is to get a sense of the routine in the office." He made a point of singling her out as being the important person here.

"What do you mean?" she asked nervously, colour rising to her face.

"Well," he flicked one hand, "give me an example of a regular day, and what Max might be doing." This was of no interest at all to Ray. While she gave the information in short, halting phrases, he snatched glances at her husband, who hadn't taken his eyes off his wife from the moment she opened her mouth. Ray realized why she had brought him with her. It wasn't pushback on her part. It was a case of being terrified of saying something that might cause censure, either from the family or her husband. Ray recognized in Ingrid Berdahl the signs of a psychologically abused woman.

"Do you know if he took work home with him?"

"Yes, he did."

"Would that include files?"

"Yes."

"Now, as you know, we have removed the files and computers from the office—"

"—Yes," Robert Berdahl interrupted. "And we want them back. You've had them for a week. There are ongoing projects involved and we need those documents."

"Of course," Ray said smoothly. "I wasn't aware that you worked for the company."

"I don't."

"So you are not an employee."

"Certainly not," Berdahl bristled. "I have my own law practice. It handles their corporate interests."

"I see." At this point, he took his file folder and pretended to write something on the pad inside. *This ought to ruffle his feathers.* "I apologize for the delay in returning everything. We had to make sure there was nothing in them that might point to a reason for Max's death. We are finished with those files," he paused.

"Oh. Well ... uh ... good," Berdahl stammered.

Ray continued. "The thing is, we also removed his computer and all the files from his home and we cannot find any documents from most of 2007 to the end of 2012. Files for him start up again at the beginning of 2013, which seems odd. I wonder, since he sometimes took work home, is there another place where they could be stored, Mrs. Berdahl?"

"No."

"Why is that?"

She hesitated. "There aren't any for Max for those years," she said, her voice faltering.

"Wasn't he working for the company during those years?"

She shook her head sharply seemingly unable to speak altogether. Ray waited. She looked at her husband almost beseeching him to answer. But he had deliberately avoided her gaze the moment Ray had mentioned the missing years.

"Mrs. Berdahl?"

She dragged her eyes away from her husband and looked at Ray. He felt sorry for her, but like a lion pursuing the straggler in a herd of wildebeests, he went after her. "Mrs. Berdahl, was Max not working in the office between those years?"

Ray waited in painful silence for her cringe-producing responses. She worked her lips as though trying to form words.

Berdahl finally flung out the answer. "No, he wasn't." He had assumed his natural role as his wife's voice.

Ray nodded. "Well, I guess that explains it," Ray flashed his most engaging smile and scratched his head. *All I need is a rumpled rain coat and an old Peugeot.* "But there are almost five years missing. Where was he?"

There was a slight adjustment in the man's posture. Ray recognized an offensive move when he saw one.

"He was on the mainland, but what has that got to do with Max's routine here? That's why you asked my wife to come in, isn't it?" he asked icily.

"Yes, you're right, of course," Ray said, feigning an apology. "But it seemed a logical question when we saw such a gap of years. We wondered where he was and what he was doing. Perhaps something that happened in those intervening years is the reason he was murdered."

Upon hearing the word, Ingrid Berdahl's hand flew up to her

mouth. Her husband patted her on her shoulder as if to say, "there, there."

Ray itched to grab him and give him a good belt. He looked at the woman, who had by now blended in with the beige walls. He had to calm down before he carried on.

"You said on the mainland. Where, exactly?"

"In the Fraser Valley."

"What was he doing there?"

"Developing a property," Berdahl said tersely.

"The Fraser Valley covers a lot of territory, Mr. Berdahl. Can you be more specific?"

"It was somewhere around Langley."

"Okay, so he goes somewhere around Langley to develop a property, and after that he comes back here. By the way, was this development his or was he working for someone?"

"It was his project."

Ray thought about that for a minute. "I'm assuming it was completed. Is that correct?"

"Yes."

"Did it take all of the five or so years?"

"Yes."

"Well, there must be files on it somewhere."

They remained silent. Berdahl's phlegmatic face gave away nothing.

"Right. Well, if we find during this inquiry that we must see them, I'm sure they will turn up." He fixed the man with a hard gaze. Rather than pursue the subject, Ray returned to Max's activities in Britannia Bay. "So he completes this property development, returns home and picks up where he left off." He waited a couple of beats. "And his father builds him a house." He leaned back in his chair and smiled. "It reminds me of that story in the Bible. You know, *The Return of the Prodigal Son.*"

At the inference, both of the Berdahls blanched. Deciding he had gleaned enough from the charade, Ray got up. "Well, I can't think of anything else we need from you, Mrs. Berdahl. Thank you very much for coming in."

Stunned at the abrupt end of the interview, Robert Berdahl lost no time in getting up and leading his shell-shocked wife out the door.

Instead of looking triumphant, Ray wore a scowl as he returned to his desk. He threw down the folder and pen. "*Che stronzo!*"

"Didn't go well?" Jimmy.

"No, it went fine. But she's totally cowed by that bastard of a husband. I felt so bad for her. She was petrified, Jimmy. Could barely string three words together." He plopped into his chair. "But at least we have another piece of the puzzle. Max was on the mainland developing a property, 'somewhere around Langley'," he said framing the words with his fingers. "And magically, the files have disappeared. I don't know how relevant that is, but we'll probably have to go over and do some digging."

Thoughts of the mainland opened a wound in Jimmy's mind. He had unfinished business there. The question was, had enough time passed?

Ray interrupted his thoughts. "You know what really freaked them out? When I mentioned the story of the Prodigal Son who lived the life of Riley and then comes crawling home. Seems to really fit."

"Ray, don't we first have to find out *why* he went over there? You don't suddenly interrupt your career and go away for five years. Maybe he did something *here* that caused him to leave—something involving his personal life that the family's keeping secret."

"Yeah. Maybe. For sure we have to find out more about his personal life here *and* on the mainland. Same goes for his business activities. I think his working life is going to be easier to sort out than his personal life." He grinned. "So I'll get busy on that."

"Leaving the hard work to me, eh?"

"But you're so much more diplomatic than I am, Jimmy boy."

"Yeah. Forget about trying to sugar coat it."

Ray lifted his hands, palms up. "It's true. You'll get answers where I would get a door slammed in my face."

"First I have to find the right door to get my foot into."

Chapter Twenty-four

"Maybe I can help you there," Ariel said after listening to the afternoon's events.

"You can? How?" Jimmy asked, as he dug into his *melanzane alla parmigiana.*

"Max has a relative living up the street," she told him.

"He has? Where?"

"That house with the hockey net in the driveway."

"Tikkanen? The guy who does flooring? So, he's related to Max, eh?"

"That's what Delilah told me a couple of days ago."

Jimmy smiled. "Delilah again, eh?"

"Uh-huh," she chuckled.

"At the rate she's going, she may wind up cracking this case." He looked at the wall clock. "I'll go over as soon as I finish this and see if I can get some information out of him."

Almost everyone on the street had a Canadian flag flying somewhere on their house or property, but not the Tikkanens. Ray had pointed out that Jehovah's Witnesses did not celebrate national holidays, so Jimmy had no compunctions about talking to them. The sound of bagpipes came to him as he walked up the street. Britannia Bay's celebrated pipe band had already led the Canada Day parade and was now marching its way to the evening performance at the local Legion. Jimmy often questioned his inner thrill when he heard the hum of the drones and the rap and the flourish of the drums.

He knocked on the Tikkanen's door. A woman in a sleeveless top and shorts answered. Jimmy quickly took in her muscles and pale Nordic features then introduced himself as the neighbour from down the street. "I hope I'm not interrupting your dinner."

"Not at all, Mr. Tan." She called him 'Mister,' but knew he was a policeman. And with Max's murder, she no doubt had a good idea why he was there. "I'll get Jari." She left and a minute later her husband appeared.

"Hi," Jari Tikkanen said cordially. Except for his height and broad shoulders, he could have been his wife's twin, all blond and blue eyed and shiny cheeked. "I remember you. You needed some work done on your floor just as we were leaving for Finland."

Jimmy smiled. It was like that with most tradesmen. They didn't remember you, but the job you wanted done or what model car you drove. "That's right."

"Did you ever find someone decent to repair the laminate?"

"Eventually."

"So what can I do for you?"

"Well, this time it hasn't got to do with a repair job, Mr. Tikkanen. I'm afraid it's to do with the death of Max Berdahl."

Jari's face fell. He shook his head slowly. "Terrible tragedy. Just terrible."

"Yes, it is." Jimmy said, knowing there was at least one person who would not agree with that assessment. "We're trying to get some idea of his habits, his movements. Who he might have come across that would want to harm him. Someone with a grudge. That kind of thing."

Jimmy could have been talking to a wall for all the impact his words had. Either Tikkanen hadn't heard him or he was avoiding the request. "It's hard to believe he's not around. He was such a force, you know? He had so much energy. We used to work out together. I don't really need to, but it was something I enjoyed doing with Max."

Jimmy nodded but said nothing, deciding to let him talk rather than shape the conversation.

"My work keeps me fit. Max just sat around on a computer all day, but when we played squash, he beat the pants off me."

"Where did you play squash?"

"Down at Weight of the World."

Jimmy chanced a faint smile. "I always thought that was an interesting name. Get the weight of the world off your shoulders by lifting weights."

"Yeah. That's right, come to think of it," he smiled.

Jimmy slipped in a question. "Did Max have any weight on *his* shoulders?"

Jari hesitated, realizing it was a leading question. But the shutters did not suddenly drop down over his eyes. "No. Not at all. He was in good spirits, always." He paused. "I would say, though, there was a bit of pressure on him to get married. His family wanted him to settle down and raise a family."

"Is that why his dad built him the house?"

"I don't know. Maybe. But Max uses ... uh ... used it as a centre for social events. There was always something going on there. But I don't have to tell you that," he laughed. "You live across the street and probably had to put up with all the noise."

Jimmy thought again about all of the gatherings at Max's place. Were they set up in order for him to meet a future spouse?

Jari continued. "I think he just liked his life the way it was and didn't see any reason to change it. He loved his work. He never talked about anything else." Jari chuckled. "It got boring, frankly."

"Do you know anyone who might want to harm him?" Jimmy asked again.

"No. No one. He was a good guy. Lots of fun. Generous. It's

really puzzling."

Jimmy waited for more information, but realized that that was probably all he was going to get. "I appreciate your candor, Mr. Tikkanen." *What little there was of it.* "Any relation to the hockey player, by the way?"

"I'm sure down the line there's some connection. Finland is a small country and we're probably all related."

"How are you related to the Berdahls?"

"It's through Kirstin—my wife—on Max's mother's side. Don't ask me how. I get confused listening to her try to explain it."

"Well, thanks for your help."

"If I've helped you to find out who did this, then you're more than welcome."

"If you think of anything, will you let me know?"

"Absolutely. But don't hold your breath, if you know what I mean."

Jimmy understood, but if Tikkanen and Max were that close, the big Finn might have a nugget of useful information that Jimmy would need to dig up later on. His next stop was Weight of the World. He wondered if they would be open on a holiday. Returning home, he called and learned they were open until nine o'clock. Ariel was at the piano playing and singing. He stood in the doorway listening. Realizing he was back, she stopped.

"What were you singing?"

"*Morgen* by Richard Strauss."

"It's beautiful."

"Yes. It's gorgeous music." She reluctantly removed her hands from the piano. "Did you get some answers from Jari?"

"Not really. He was cooperative in his own way, but I think he's obfuscating. I'm going down to Weight of the World to check on something."

"Okay. See you later." Ariel knew jazz was Jimmy's favourite music, but she was pleased that he heard the beauty in Strauss's composition. *Music has charms to soothe a savage breast,* she thought. Maybe that's what the killer had needed. Maybe he had no music in his soul. She gave thanks that music was embedded in her being. It was as close to praying as she would get.

At Weight of the World, a fitness centre full of machines and thumping sounds pretending to be music, Jimmy spoke with the manager and one personal trainer. Neither had anything to add. Max and Jari arrived together. They didn't engage in conversations. Rather than memberships, they paid the drop-in fee. They used the machines and weights, played squash and left.

Jimmy phoned Ray and gave him an update, and then made his way home. As he drove along Bayside Drive, he spotted a small, neat building; one of the many cottages that had been converted into businesses. It sported a sign, Greenwood Realty. *There's an idea. Why didn't I think of this before?*

Chapter Twenty-five

Thursday, July 2ⁿᵈ

"Would you like another cup of coffee, Bill?" Sherilee Wyatt was clearing away the breakfast dishes.

Wyatt, busy opening up *The Bayside Bugle* to the front page, did not glance up. "No thanks, honey. I'll grab a cup later at the station."

She was about to load the dishwasher when he slammed his fist on the table. "For chrissake! What does this fool think he's playing at?" No explanation was forthcoming nor would it be necessary. She knew he would be referring to Malcolm McDonald.

"This headline will have the whole town apoplectic."

"Not to mention you."

Eyes ablaze, Wyatt tossed the paper onto the table, shoved his chair back and heaved himself up. "Honest to God, Sherilee, I would strangle that bugger with my own hands if I thought I could get away with it." He picked up the paper and handed it to his wife. "Look at this. I've got to get ready." He thundered down the hall.

Max Berdahl Brutally Murdered, she read, inwardly groaning. She could care less about the town's reaction. Her husband's blood pressure, however, was another matter. Then the byline caught her attention. "Honey," she called out and walked into the bedroom where Wyatt was struggling to fasten the buttons of his jacket. She waved the paper at him. "It wasn't McDonald. It was Kittridge."

"Really?" He took the paper. "Huh. I thought he had more sense. Seems he's just as irresponsible as that other git. Come to think of it, I did see him at the press conference. But he didn't ask any questions. The mainland bloodhounds probably beat him to the punch." He handed the paper back to her and abruptly changed the topic. "Look at this, Sherilee," he said, pointing to his widening girth. "You'd better put me on a diet."

"Are you crazy? You'd be even crankier than you are right now."

The headline had everyone in the squad room airing their unprintable opinions of the press, and agreeing that it was an *effing* shame that public pillorying had passed into history.

Wyatt blew through the door. Before addressing his crew, he spoke to Mary Beth. "Have we heard from the mayor yet?" fearing the response. He knew Verhagen would be worried how the news would affect the town's tourism trade.

"Not yet."

He sighed. "That's a relief. But I'm guessing a deluge, right?"

"Yes, but not a flood, Chief," she said soothingly, thinking his knickers would be tightly wrapped in a knot. Visualizing what that might do to his nether regions, she blushed. "I thought the board would be lit up like a pinball machine, but it's been pretty quiet."

"Well, that's a bit of good news, anyway," he said, wondering why her face had turned red. He joined the officers grouped around Ray's desk. "Apparently the headline hasn't set off any alarm bells yet," he told them. "So, where are we on this case?"

"At the moment we're dropping goose eggs," Ray said.

"That's a polite way of putting it."

"But Jimmy's come up with an interesting idea."

Wyatt looked around. "Where is he?"

At that moment, Jimmy was stepping through a screen door into Greenwood Realty, a tiny bell dinging his arrival. By the looks of it, the office had been a living room at one time. Cozy and comfortable, it was unlike most real estate offices familiar to Jimmy. The man who entered the room was also far removed from the salon-tanned and Botoxed agents dressed in leather and laden in gold. His clothing was tasteful and casual—linen trousers and a short-sleeved checked shirt—and the only gold was the bezel on his watch. When he smiled, Jimmy was not blinded by bleached implants. His neatly parted white hair crowned a naturally tanned face and deep-set grey eyes. Jimmy guessed his age to be around seventy-five.

"Good morning," he said in a normal voice, not the forced charm of a salesman working on commission. He came forward, hand outstretched "I'm Gordon Greenwood. How can I help you?" His handshake was warm and solid.

"I'm Detective Sergeant Jimmy Tan from the Britannia Bay Police Department." He handed him his card.

After a quick glance, Greenwood tucked it into his shirt pocket. "Would I be wrong in thinking you are here about Max Berdahl's ... demise?"

Recovering quickly from his initial surprise, Jimmy almost smiled at Greenwood's description of a murder. "No, you wouldn't be. That's exactly why I'm here. As a real estate agent, you might know something about Mr. Berdahl that could shed some light on why he might be a victim of homicide."

He turned a steady gaze on Jimmy and waited a moment before answering. "How much time to do you have?" he replied calmly.

A spark of excitement charged through Jimmy. At last!

Chapter Twenty-six

Greenwood ushered Jimmy through the office into a sunlit room that opened onto a patio containing flower pots of all sizes, shapes and colours. Overflowing blossoms spilled their scent into the room. Paintings of stylized tropical beach scenes dotted the walls. Upholstered rattan furniture completed the picture of a lanai on some south sea island.

"What a cheerful room," Jimmy said.

"It's my little piece of paradise."

Jimmy nodded at the paintings. "Are these your work?"

"Yes. A hobby of mine. I try to do a bit every day."

"They remind me of the Impressionists."

"You have an appreciation for art?"

"Some of it. My wife took some art history courses. She's taught me quite a bit."

"Does she paint?"

"In a way," Jimmy smiled. "She's a wonderful gardener." *And she paints pictures when she sings,* he thought.

"I used to garden. Now all I do is prune the shrubs. Bending over weeding has taken its toll over the years." He indicated a love seat behind a glass-topped coffee table. "Why don't you sit down? Would you like a cold lemonade?"

"Sounds perfect, thanks."

While Greenwood was out of the room, Jimmy took in more of the surroundings. There were no personal photographs, and no obvious signs of a woman's presence in the room. He was curious about the man's marital status.

Greenwood returned with the lemonade and handed a glass to Jimmy. "Cheers."

"Cheers." Jimmy took a sip. "Mmm. This is really good."

"I make it from scratch. And don't ask me for the recipe. It's a trade secret." He chuckled.

"Too bad. Kids could make a small fortune selling this." They sat in companionable silence for a few minutes enjoying their refreshing drinks.

"Well," Greenwood began, placing his glass on the table, "you probably want to get to the matter at hand."

"If you wouldn't mind. And I do appreciate you taking the time to do this."

"Time is no problem. It's not as if anyone's trying to reach me."

It was then Jimmy became aware that there hadn't been one phone call since his arrival.

Greenwood paused, his demeanour darkening. "First of all, I will preface what I say with this. And I won't apologize for it either. I am not sorry that Max Berdahl has met his maker." When he saw that the detective did not even blink, he carried on, warming to his subject. "There is a rather old-fashioned word to describe him. Bounder. He was a bounder. A cheat. And he did something that in our business is considered the lowest of the low. It's called block-busting. Do you know what that is?"

"Not in detail." Jimmy did know, but he gave people the opportunity to reveal what they knew, and at the same time reveal something of themselves.

"It's a way to scare people into selling their homes. In a majority of cases, people are told that undesirables are taking over the

neighbourhood and driving down property values. And these
miscreants will set up scenarios to prove it. Or they'll hire lackeys to
make life so miserable for home owners that they finally throw in
the towel and sell."

"So you're saying that Max did this?"

"Yes, but not here. The incident I'm talking about occurred in
the Fraser Valley."

Jimmy interrupted. "Was this somewhere between 2007 and
2013?"

Greenwood cocked his head. "Yes, it was. Do you know about
that development?"

"We've only just heard about it and we don't have any details.
What can you tell us about it?"

"A lot, as it happens. There were three five-acre parcels. An
elderly widow owned the centre piece. Max had purchased the two
on either side and he wanted hers. But she didn't want to sell
because it was the family homestead. Her sister was living with her
at the time. But the little ... so-and-so found a way to squeeze her
out."

Jimmy could feel the heat of Greenwood's growing anger.

"Max started clearing the first parcel. That meant heavy
equipment on the road day after day, six days a week. The noise
level was so bad that the women complained to the police and the
municipal government. When they got no help there, they went to
the press. The story created a lot of interest. But of course
everything Max was doing was within the law."

"'The law is a ass'," Jimmy said.

Greenwood smiled. "Ah, yes. Dear Mr. Bumble. How often has
he been misquoted, I wonder?"

"Legion."

Greenwood laughed. After the moment of levity lapsed, he
continued. "When he started clearing the second parcel, the widow
had a stroke, which meant she had to go into care. So her children

ended up selling to him."

The two men stayed silent, their black thoughts unspoken.

"Do you know happen to know her name?"

"I can't recall it at the moment. But it was something Ukrainian, I believe. The newspaper article might still be available in archives somewhere."

"What about her sister? Where did she go?"

"That I don't know."

"And did Berdahl finish developing that property?"

"He did. And I hate to give the little dirt bag credit, but the whole development is attractive."

"How do you come to know so much about it?"

"A friend bought a house there."

"What's the name of the development?"

"Sunnyvale Estates."

"Berdahl just did the one project?"

"Yes. It took about five years."

"And then he came back here."

"And he came back here," Greenwood echoed.

"And his karma followed him," Jimmy said.

Greenwood smiled. "It will bite you in the butt sooner or later."

"So I've heard." He took the last sip of lemonade. "I wonder why he went to the mainland. There's land here he could have developed."

"Ah. I wonder why indeed," he said through a sly grin.

"Are you saying you know something about that, too?"

"I do. And it's quite a story." He paused and drained his glass. "But the day is only so long. And there is a limit to how much detritus I can take. I apologize but I do need to get to my painting while the light is right. I know it's unorthodox, but would you be able to come back another time?"

The unusual request caught Jimmy off guard, but it only took him a second to answer. "How about tomorrow?"

"Same time as today would suit me fine," Greenwood said genially.

"Tomorrow it is, then."

They got up and went to the front door. Jimmy shook his hand. "Thank you very much for this information, Mr. Greenwood. It's been very useful."

"Really?" He seemed surprised.

"Yes. We were coming up against some roadblocks."

Greenwood's eyes narrowed. "Ah, yes. I understand."

"Enjoy your painting."

"More so than usual, I dare say."

Wyatt and Ray sat in rapt silence as Jimmy related the events, "He was a real shit disturber. No doubt about it," Wyatt said. "But if we're thinking this murder is based on revenge, we have to find out more about that family. For instance, what happened to the widow? Is she still alive? Was the fact that she was turfed out of her home a motive for revenge? If so, who carried it out? Not her, that's for sure."

"Maybe it hasn't anything to do with that," Jimmy said. "Greenwood promised to give me more information about why Max went over there in the first place."

"Maybe he just wanted to play with the big boys," Ray said. "After all, if you're thinking big, why would you want to stay here?"

Wyatt looked past them, thinking. Then he glanced first at Jimmy and then at Ray. "I think a trip to the mainland might be in the works for you two." He slapped his hands on the chair arms.

A glow spread across Ray's face. "Great!"

Jimmy's mouth set into a grim line.

Chapter Twenty-seven

Friday, July 3rd

Jimmy knew something was amiss when he arrived at Greenwood's home-office the following day. The door was closed and a slight, white-haired woman wearing an apron was walking about, stopping now and again and stooping to peer under bushes. He got out of the unmarked police car and approached her.

"Excuse me," he said.

She jumped. "Oh, heavens!" she gasped, gaping at Jimmy. "You gave me a start,"

"I'm sorry," he hastily apologized. "I didn't mean to. I guess you didn't hear the car." *Who is this woman and what's she doing?*

"No. I'm too busy looking for Gordon's cat," she explained.

"Is Mr. Greenwood out?"

Rather than answer, she viewed him and his car with suspicion. "And who would you be?"

Jimmy quickly introduced himself, retrieved his card from his wallet and handed it to her.

"Police? Then you're not here to bring me bad news," she said with relief.

"I'm not following you. Maybe we should start over, Miss ... uh ..."

"I'm Mrs. Haswell. I live behind Gordon." She instinctively pointed to her house on the other side of a white wooden fence.

A growing feeling of alarm pressed on Jimmy's chest. "Could you please tell me what's happened, Mrs. Haswell?"

"Gordon was taken to Raincoast General Hospital this morning. He had a heart attack."

"When was this?"

"Sometime after he had gone to bed." Her manner appeared straightforward, but there was a ripple of agitation beneath the surface. "I got a phone call from MedAlert. Gordon hadn't check in with them this morning, as he usually does ... as he's *supposed* to do. So they phoned me. I'm one of the people they notify if he doesn't answer when they phone to find out if he's all right and just forgotten to check in."

After rushing out the words, she stopped as her breathing became laboured. "I came over with my key and let myself in and he was on the floor in the bedroom. The telephone was making that awful sound when it's been left off the hook. He may have been trying to call for help." She paused and fished in a pocket for something. Jimmy thought it might be a handkerchief or tissue as her eyes were tearing up. But she extracted an inhaler. She promptly pressed it taking in a long breath, after which she held it for a few seconds, exhaled and put the device away.

"I get anxious and it kicks in my asthma. That's why I have this thing," she explained. "It's always at the ready. Now, where was I? Oh, yes. Gordon was lying on the floor, white as a sheet. I threw some blankets on him right away and called nine-one-one. They told me to put up his knees and prop up his back so that he formed a kind of W. So I did that. You know, he doesn't weigh more than a pea pod."

Jimmy appraised her shape and decided that neither did she.

"You're certain it was a heart attack?"

"I *know* it was. He told me he had had one once before and that's why he had the medical alert set up."

Thinking it might be more than a coincidence that he had just visited him the day before, he wanted to check inside. Jimmy asked her if she would let him in the house.

"Yes. But I won't go in with you because I'm going to carry on looking for Felicity. She ran off when I came in this morning. She was probably upset when Gordon fell. I've got to take care of her while he's in hospital."

She opened the doors for him, jingling the little bell over the screen door. "The bedroom is just off the office to the left," she told him, and returned to her searching.

To Jimmy's eyes, the only things out of order in the bedroom were the blanket and pillows in a heap on the bed. He returned to the room where he and Greenwood had discussed the case just twenty-four hours before. Something had been added—an easel in the corner. A painting in progress revealed the portrait of a woman of incredible delicacy and beauty. Her black hair piled on top with tendrils trailing down alongside a peaches and cream complexion, evoked images of Pre-Raphaelite femininity.

"That was his wife, Elizabeth," he heard Mrs. Haswell say. Her quiet entry surprised him as he hadn't heard the bell. "Beautiful wasn't she?"

"Was?"

"She died in a sailing accident off Barbados." She shook her head. "Such a tragedy."

"How long ago?"

"Let me see now." She looked up, thinking. "It must be thirty years."

"Did you know them then?"

"No. I've only been here ten years."

"And he never married again?"

"Now tell me, would he still be painting pictures of her if he had?" Her eyes twinkled as she poked fun at him.

"Good point," Jimmy chuckled. "So I'm assuming there are more pictures of her"

"I can see you'll not be giving Inspector Morse any competition. I'll just get a key." When she returned, she opened a door on the north side of the house. "You can see for yourself," and gestured into the room.

Jimmy entered a miniature museum whose walls were covered in pastels, water colours and oil paintings—all of his wife. In one, wearing a diaphanous sundress, she leaned against a white veranda railing framed by vibrantly coloured tropical flowers. In the background was a turquoise sea and white sand beach.

Returning to the room that Greenwood had called his paradise, Jimmy viewed it with a new appreciation. Its tropical theme and exposure to the southern sun was clearly another way of remembering the past. Was he another of those souls who could not bear the thought of moving on?

Mrs. Haswell had locked the door and was on her way out when Jimmy asked: "Did you find Felicity?"

"No. I gave up. But she'll show up on my doorstep eventually. I always keep some of her food on hand."

"You're a good neighbour."

"Not good enough for the hospital staff," she said with asperity. "They won't give me any information and won't let me visit him. Have to be family. Well *I'm* the closest thing to family he's got," she complained.

Jimmy had an idea. "I'll be visiting him. They'll let a policeman in. I'll let you know his condition."

"Oh, would you? I hate not knowing."

She gave him her phone number and saw him out.

"By the way, how did you get in the house right now without the bell ringing?"

"You caught that did you? You must be a decent detective after all," she teased. "I'll show you." Closing both doors, she picked up a long stick lying under a shrub. It had a tiny piece of rubber attached to one end. She cracked open the screen door and reached up with the stick. The rubber pressed the clapper against the lip of the bell, and she held it there while she opened the door completely. "Piece of cake."

"Once you know how."

"You just have to be thin and agile."

"But why would you need to enter without sounding the bell?"

"Because on sunny days I bring Gordon his tea. That's when he paints. And he doesn't like to be disturbed. So I just come in quietly and put it in the kitchen."

He assessed Mrs. Haswell. She had a charming down-to-earth manner, a flair for fun and was warm and kind. It was no surprise that Greenwood had come to rely on her and entrust his cat to her care. Jimmy wondered if Mrs. Haswell wished that Greenwood would leave the past behind and focus on the present.

Chapter Twenty-eight

Ray caught himself hunching over the computer screen and promptly straightened up, rolling his shoulders and moving his neck. He could hear Georgie's words warning him to take breaks every twenty minutes. It had already been more than an hour.

The screen was opened on an archived article from *The Fraser Valley Times*. It corroborated Greenwood's statement. The two sisters had brought their complaint to the paper after the city council could do nothing to mitigate the noise. Berdahl was breaking no laws or bylaws. Only one woman's name was given in the article: Edna Pitchko. But it was a start.

He began running the name Pitchko on PRIME, the Police Records Information Management Environment system. Personal information of anyone who had ever had any interaction with the police was recorded on its database. While the automatic search began, Ray got up and walked over to Novak.

"Is there anything in Berdahl's computer that point to anything like a normal bachelor's life?"

"No. It's like the guy was a monk. No Facebook. No Twitter. No diary. Just a calendar with reminders of birthdays, anniversaries and so on."

Ray thought about that. "Except for the last thing, that could be me," he told Novak. "I don't do social media, and Georgina looks after important dates."

"Me too, come to think of it."

"Have you had any luck on the press leak?"

"Oui," he said with a twinkly grin. "I have a hunch our culprit is the new paramedic at the scene."

"No kidding. What are you basing it on?"

"The reporter was a French-Canadian by the name of Goudron, right?"

"Right."

"And for first prize, can you tell me the name of the paramedic?"

"No shit!" Ray said.

"Well, in this case that would be *pas de merde*," Novak smiled.

"It was that easy?" Ray shook his head. "Unbelievable they would be that transparent."

"And stupid. He'll lose his job, for sure."

"And she'll probably get a raise," Ray said with disgust. He grabbed a cold drink from the fridge and went back to his desk where he started reading the details on the few Pitchkos that popped up. And there she was. Edna Pitchko, nee Sutherland. Born, 1931. Died, 2010. *So, she died. Probably thanks to Berdahl,* he thought.

Scanning the obituaries he found it, and a surviving sister was listed—Lettie Ashton. As he began a search for her, his phone rang. Glancing at his watch, he was surprised that it was mid-afternoon.

"Sergeant Rossini, this is Nigel Wright, the owner of Dirt Rider. You asked me to call you if I heard anything about a biker on Townshipline Road."

Ray's ears pricked up. "That's right. What have you heard?"

"Apparently an unknown rider has been spotted a couple of times, as recently as ten days ago," he said.

"Would the person who gave you that information be willing to talk to me?" Ray was trying to keep the excitement out of his voice.

"I don't see why not, but he's just left for a motocross event in Ontario. He'll be gone about a week."

Damn! "That's unfortunate."

"It's my fault," Wright admitted ruefully. "He told me a couple of days ago, but I got caught up in a problem with Canada Revenue, and as you know, when they say 'jump' you ask how high."

"Ouch. I hope it's not serious," Ray said. "They can be miserable buggers."

Wright laughed at the officer's forthright observation. "No. It's not serious, but regrettably it will cost me the price of a new bike," he said ruefully.

"Oh. That's not good. But at least you're not in jail," he quipped.

"Not at the moment. Anyway, for what it's worth, I hope that my not getting back to you sooner hasn't put a spanner in the works."

Ray thanked him and rang off. Nothing to do now but be patient, a virtue buried somewhere deep in his ethos.

Chapter Twenty-nine

As he stepped into the sounds and smells of Raincoast General Hospital, Jimmy was transported back to the many times he had spent in emergency rooms with a suspect or victim in various stages of trauma. Was it any wonder he hated hospitals? After showing his ID on the intensive care ward, he was accompanied by a nurse to Greenwood's room. Along the way, she said he was still heavily sedated.

"I just wanted to know how he was doing. Would the doctor who first saw him be available?"

"I'll see if Dr. St. Germaine is still in the hospital." She turned and walked back to her station, shoes squeaking on the shiny vinyl floor.

The only light in the room filtered through a sheer curtain pulled across the window. Greenwood was lying on his back, a drip inserted into his right arm. He seemed to be breathing normally and his colour was good. Jimmy had expected far worse and was encouraged by the signs. But as there was no opportunity to speak to him, he returned to find the nurse on the phone. Spotting him, she held up an index finger indicating him to wait. He was glancing about for a place to sit when she came up to him. "It's your lucky day. Dr. St. Germaine is on her way up from ER."

A moment later he heard his name. He looked toward the sound and saw a petite, stunning woman approaching him. Except for her startling green eyes, she could have been Gordon Greenwood's daughter. She had the same peaches and cream complexion, and white hair that was obviously premature. "I'm Dr. St. Germaine," she said with an engaging smile. "Pardon me for not shaking your hand, but it's a new edict from above." Jimmy recognized her South African accent. He wasn't surprised as there were many in the medical profession who had arrived in Canada from that troubled country.

Jimmy recovered from being struck by her beauty in time to answer. "How do you do? No need to apologize. It makes sense."

"I understand that you are interested in Gordon Greenwood's condition."

"Yes. Thanks for taking time to see me. Is there some place we can talk privately?"

She pointed to nearby chairs. "Actually, right here should be fine. People are so busy coming and going and concerned with their own problems that two people talking quietly won't attract any attention."

"I'll be quick."

"I appreciate that," she said, grinning. "Other than cardiomyopathy, Mr. Greenwood is in good health overall."

"So, not a heart attack."

"No. We are more concerned with his concussion."

"Concussion?"

"Yes. It appears he hit his head when he fell and it knocked him unconscious. He wasn't unconscious because of his heart condition. Well, let me take that back. He could have experienced dizziness when he got up during the night, and fell. There is a rather large bump on his head. And blood had been coming out of his ear. It had dried by the time we saw him. So we'll be running some tests."

"How serious it is and will it impair his memory?"

"It depends on what we find after the CT scan."

"When will you be doing that?"

"As soon as he's stable."

"How soon do you think that'll be?" Jimmy was beginning to feel stonewalled, but he understood patient confidentiality

She laughed. "You're persistent. Right now all his vital signs look good, so it may be sooner than later. It's up in the air at the moment."

Jimmy backed down. "Okay."

"I see that you're eager to talk to him."

"Yes, I am. How can I be kept informed of his progress?"

"I'll have my office call you straightaway of any change."

"That would be great. Thanks." He took out a card and handed it to her, which she scanned.

"Oh. I thought you were from the RCMP."

"No. Does it make a difference?"

"Not at all. It's just that we don't meet many municipal police officers. They're quite rare."

"Yes, and soon we'll be extinct," he said.

Her laughter caught the attention of a few visitors. She put a hand to her mouth. "Oops." She ducked her head, eyes sheepishly peering around. "So much for not attracting attention."

Jimmy found himself charmed and felt a need to suppress his growing attraction. "Thanks very much for your time, doctor," he said more formally than he intended. He quickly stood.

She did the same. "You're welcome."

"Goodbye."

"Goodbye then." She watched him leave, puzzled at his abruptness.

In the car, he thumped his head with his knuckles. "You dickhead." Then he punched in Mrs. Haswell's number and passed along the information on Greenwood and his present condition.

"Oh," she said, her voice dropping. "I was hoping that he would be awake. But at least it wasn't a heart attack."

"No, it wasn't."

"Well, I guess I'll just have to wait until he comes home," she sighed tremulously.

"No, you won't," Jimmy assured her. "I'll keep you posted. In the meantime, I need to get into his house and check something in the bedroom."

"Are you coming now?"

"Yes."

"I'll be waiting at the front door."

Still wearing an apron, Mrs. Haswell was good to her word. Together they went into the bedroom. "Can you tell me exactly how he was lying when you found him?" he asked her.

"His legs were there and his head was here," she said pointing to a spot beside the bed.

Jimmy began looking for signs of blood and it wasn't long before he noticed a brown smudge and a few tiny hairs on the corner of the bedside table. Chagrined, he turned to Mrs. Haswell. "I should have noticed this before."

She patted his arm playfully. "Don't worry. I won't turn you in."

Chapter Thirty

Monday, July 6th

Something strange was happening with the weather. Humidity, unheard of in the area, had settled upon Britannia Bay. Compounded with the high temperature, it was creating churlishness and petulance among the citizenry. Feelings flared at the tiniest affront. "Stolen" parking spots led to insults or cursing. People couldn't cope with the discomfort. The beach was packed. Along the quay a small breeze did what it could to cool down hot bodies and even hotter tempers. Officers on duty had been expecting altercations requiring their attention, but the weekend was quiet. That was a relief as was the comfort of the air-conditioned squad room.

On Monday morning, Ray contacted a supervisor of the telephone company and inquired about a listing for Lettie Ashton. He was on hold when Jimmy arrived and told him he was going to try another real estate office. He couldn't sit around waiting for the recovery of Greenwood and the return of the biker form Ontario. He had to do something.

Ray understood. "Okay. I'm looking for a phone number for the younger sister." As Jimmy headed out the door, he heard the voice on the other end of the phone.

"Sorry to have kept you waiting, Sergeant Rossini, but there is no listing for a Lettie Ashton."

"Oh. That's too bad." His shoulders slumped and he was about to end the call when she continued.

"However, I do have a listing for a Barry Ashton."

He sat up. "Whereabouts?"

When she told him, he was sure he had struck gold. She gave him the number.

"Could I also have the address?" And when he had that, he thanked her profusely. He ran Barry Ashton on PRIME and came up with one entry. A speeding ticket in 2006 when he was nineteen, and nothing since then. He might be Lettie Ashton's grandson. If so, that meant there had to be a son somewhere. Maybe a very pissed-off son. There had to have been more than a little bitterness about the way Berdahl had run roughshod over the family. But enough to commit murder? Lots of people lost everything, but it didn't turn them into killers. *On the other hand, if someone in the family had a screw loose ...*

Noting Ashton's date of birth, he called the government service responsible for registering births. Hunkering down and diving into drudge work, Ray soon found that Barry's parents were Dean and Gloria Ashton. After that it was a walk in the park. He found records for the family up to 2010 when Dean and Gloria divorced. At the time there were three children: Barry, Tyler and Angelina. Searching the web for Dean Ashton, he found a listing for him at a brokerage in Edmonton, seven hundred miles away from Langley.

"I expect salt crystals to start forming on my body pretty soon," Ariel said as she swiped a palm across her forehead wiping away beads of sweat. Ariel and Lana were enjoying cold beers in the small gazebo Pascal had built amongst the cedars and rhododendrons.

"The Japanese call heat and humidity *mushi atsui*," Lana said. "I drank a lot of beer when I was in Japan. That and cow piss."

"What!?"

Lana started laughing. "There's a non-alcoholic drink called Calpis, but it sounds exactly like cow piss."

"What's it made of?"

"It's a lactic acid fermentation concoction," Lana said.

"It sounds disgusting."

"Not at all. It's very refreshing. Sort of reminds me of runny vanilla yogurt with a twist of lemon."

"I'm not convinced. I'll stick to beer."

"How's the investigation going, by the way?" Lana asked, steering the conversation away from Japan and unpleasant memories.

"They seem to be getting little pieces of this and that. Sort of like assembling a quilt." She took a long drink. "They've had some setbacks, though. First, a pretty spotless crime scene. And second, a biker who might have had some information for them has gone to a kind of motorcycle racing thing in Ontario. He may have seen an unfamiliar rider on Townshipline Road around the time of the murder."

"A biker?" Lana said, her interest picking up.

"They think the killer rode a bike because a car would have been too conspicuous."

Lana nodded. Then a sudden shiver swept through her body.

"Did someone just pass over your grave?" Ariel joked.

Jimmy was on his way to find another realtor who might have some personal knowledge about Max Berdahl when a call came in from the station.

"Jimmy. We just got a call from the hospital. Mr. Greenwood is able to take visitors now."

"Thanks, Mary Beth." He punched a hole in the speed limit all the way to the hospital.

Greenwood was sitting up reading when Jimmy strode in. "Ah. Officer Tan. How nice to see you," face creasing into a smile.

"Good morning, sir. I'm glad to see you looking so well. I hope I'm not disturbing you."

"Do I look disturbed?" He put his book aside and extended his hand. Jimmy, expecting the usual hand shake, was surprised when Greenwood clasped his hand and held it.

The gesture touched Jimmy. He looked at the two intertwined hands, swallowed and blinked, recalling his own father's distance, emotionally and physically. Greenwood gently released his grip. "I expect you're here for that follow-up conversation."

"Actually, my visit is personal as well as professional. I wanted you to know that Mrs. Haswell is very concerned and I promised to keep her up to date because the hospital won't tell her."

"Oh, that's kind of you. Their policy about next of kin is ridiculous. She's almost like family. Who knows what might have happened without her swift action?"

"Indeed."

Greenwood grinned broadly. "I've noticed that you don't talk the way I would expect a policeman to talk."

"So I've been told," he smiled.

"Speaking of talking, shall we pick up where we left off?"

"Yes. Do you mind if I take notes?"

"Not at all." After Jimmy took out a notebook and pen, Greenwood began. "There was a real estate conference in Vancouver in the spring of 2007. It was a relatively new event held on a weekend, and everyone came from all over B.C. Of course, a lot of us were already acquainted. Max, though, wasn't well known. He hadn't been in the business that long, but he was turning into a mover and shaker pretty quickly. He was more into land development than selling houses. That's where the big bucks are."

"He was only twenty-five at the time, so he must have been a fast learner," Jimmy said.

"It's easy when you grow up in a family that sleeps, eats and drinks real estate." Greenwood paused. "There was a motivational speaker on Friday night. Max was sitting at a table with a group from the mainland. Harry McFadden and I—he's a local realtor I've known for years—were sitting at another table, and we had a beeline view of Max."

Jimmy's forehead furrowed. "The name McFadden is familiar to me for some reason."

"I hope it's not in relation to a crime," Greenwood teased.

"I'm sure it's not. It'll come to me. Please go on."

"Well, there was a woman at Max's table who had quite a reputation, so to speak. She hadn't been paying much attention to him until he started chatting with the other people. He quickly had their ears. When the man sitting next to Max got up, she took his chair." He laughed briefly. "Harry and I looked at each other. He said something like, 'This should be interesting.' We had a name for her: Carlene the Cougar. She liked young men and ... well ..." He cleared his throat.

"I get your drift," Jimmy said.

"Exactly." He paused, recalling the scene. "But then the speaker began his spiel and Max focused on him. After the speech, she spoke to Max and began displaying her, uh, charms, shall we say?"

Jimmy chuckled at Greenwood's choice of words, a facility he admired.

"After a while, he was paying attention to everything she said," he chortled. "She left at one point and came back. They had a brief conversation, and then they went out together. Harry and I got a great laugh out of it." He paused and took a sip of water.

"Saturday was spent in separate seminars so I didn't see Max until lunchtime. He was lined up at the smorgasbord when Carlene came up to him. She had a man with her, a rather swarthy-looking character. But dressed impeccably. Possibly an Italian. Max had already met him because no introductions were made. When they sat down, their conversation was animated. Max was nodding every which way to September. Shortly after, the three of them left. That was the last I saw of the man. I did see Max and Carlene on Sunday at the closing dinner."

"Any idea who this other man was?"

"No. Neither of us knew him. But we think he had something to do with that parcel of land in the valley because not long thereafter, Max purchased it."

"So that's what got him to the mainland," Jimmy mused.

"Well, more than likely it was Carlene," he smiled.

"What makes you say that?"

"Because on Sunday he was a changed man. He was like a puppy dog following after his master, tail wagging." He paused. "Harry and I were convinced that Max had been well and truly bedded the previous night. It seemed so obvious. For a guy who probably had never had sex, being worked over by her would have been as intoxicating as downing a dozen glasses of champagne."

"Never had sex?" Jimmy asked with some astonishment.

Greenwood tilted his head to the side and grinned. "You don't know much about Jehovah's Witnesses, do you?"

"No, but I'm learning," he said with distaste.

"They are exhorted to remain virgins until they marry. Any transgression of that and they are given the boot."

Jimmy didn't say anything for a few minutes, letting this new information weave its way into the narrative. "So how did he avoid the scandal and the ramifications with his church?"

"Well, first off, we know there were no other JWs there because they stick together. So who would tell? I don't think anyone noticed other than Harry and myself. A few of the guys she had slept with before might have been watching the events play out, but after the weekend it was forgotten."

"Obviously Max didn't forget."

"Exactly. The possibility of developing that parcel of land might have been the impetus for going over there, but I believe the driving force was sex, pure and simple."

Jimmy found it improbable. But men's appetite for sex had been behind the fall of nations. "Do you know her last name?"

"Corrente. She was a realtor in Vancouver. May still be."

Jimmy smiled to himself. *An Italian from Vancouver. What are the chances?*

"Carlene Corrente! *Madonn*!" Ray's voice blasted throughout the room.

Everyone's heads shot up.

"*Che puttana*! I can't believe it." Ray stopped and thought for a moment. "Well, I can. She went to the same school as Georgie and me and she was a slut even then. I played hockey with her brother, Bobby." He kept shaking his head. "So *she's* the reason Max left. That bitch got him all fired up. Well at least his *pants* were on fire," he guffawed.

Novak and McDaniel wanted to hear stories, but Jimmy wanted to work. He left them to their tittering and went back to the Incident Room. He was entering the latest information when Ray walked in. "You said you had another lead?" Jimmy asked.

"Yes. I've tracked down the Ashton family. Lettie has a son, Dean. He lives in Edmonton. And there's a grandson, Barry. He lives in Langley."

"That sounds promising."

"I think the Chief's right. We need to go over and talk to Ashton. And now that Carlene's involved, we should talk to her as well."

Jimmy realized that a trip to the mainland couldn't be avoided. That this murder was leading there seemed to be a cosmic intervention. And sooner or later he would have to deal with his family. The two events were coming together as inexorably as day follows night.

Chapter Thirty-one

"I just hope Jimmy won't want to rush right back," Ray said as he and Georgina savoured a glass of *mistrà* after a rare evening meal together. Monday was the only night of the week the restaurant was closed. "After we interview Carlene I want to check out Joe's. See who's playing pool. And I want to go to Mom and Pop's old place for dinner."

"You're trying to cram too much into two days, honey. Jimmy might not want to go to Joe's. He doesn't know your old gang. Besides, he may have plans of his own. Dinner at Rossini's would be enough."

"Yeah. You're probably right. He probably wouldn't enjoy Joe's anyway. To tell the truth, I think he has a hard time just hanging out with people. It doesn't seem to be his thing."

"What is his thing?"

"Work. You know. The job." He took another sip of the *digestif.*

"Then he must be loving this investigation."

Ray nodded. "It's interesting you should say that. I've noticed a change in him lately. For a while there he would leave the station right on time. Now it's hard to get him to go home. It's a good thing he loves his wife or he'd probably be camping out there."

"Doesn't he have other interests? You can't live your job. Well, not if you want a balanced life."

"I know he does martial arts, but I don't know how regular that is. I think everything else he does is cerebral."

"How long has he been here?"

"Six years."

"And that's all you know about him? For a detective, you aren't much of a detector, are you?" She laughingly flicked her napkin at him.

Jimmy was reading information he had printed out from the Internet when Ariel walked in with a cold drink. She plunked it on the table, splashing a few drops on the desk.

"You know, Jimmy, you're beginning to be a bit of a bore."

He put down the document and looked up at her. She was glaring at him, arms akimbo. He laughed at the unfamiliar sight. "Who are you?" he asked.

"'Woman with Spunk', that's who," using the Scrabble nickname Jimmy had given her during their university days.

"You look ticked off."

"I *am*!"

"What did I do now ... or not do?"

"Don't you remember? I asked you to go for a walk after dinner," she said, reproachfully.

Jimmy turned back to the screen and looked at the time. "Oh, cripes."

"Yeah. 'Oh cripes'."

"We still have time. It doesn't get dark for a while. And besides, it'll be cooler now," he grinned.

She fixed him with a stare. "Well, you managed to wriggle your way out of that one."

He grabbed the glass and took a few gulps. "So what are we waiting for? Let's go."

Outside, he took her hand, which was warm and soft and fitted

so comfortably into his. They began a brisk walk that gradually
settled into a gentle stroll.

"You seem happy today," she said.

"I'm happy we've got another lead, one that I hope will point us
in the right direction," he told her.

"And you think Greenwood's information is valid?"

"Yes. I've already checked out some of the things he told me.
That's what I was doing when you so rudely interrupted me to take
some lame walk."

She punched him. He laughed.

"If I didn't get you out, your behind would fuse to that chair!"

"I know. I know. Now give me your hand, you badass woman."
They resumed their congenial perambulation. "It feels good being
able to do something meaningful again."

She nodded, knowing how he relished sinking his teeth into a
case.

"Greenwood is a nice man, Ariel. The kind of guy you like to
spend time with. And he has a cat."

"Then he *must* be a nice man!" she pronounced.

As they circled around the neighbourhood, Ariel pointed out the
flowers that had already bloomed or faded far earlier than usual.
"And look at those cedar hedges. You can already see the green
turning to brown. They will all die unless we get some real rain."
She seemed as stressed as the shrubs.

"Don't worry. Nature is resilient," he said. "By the way, we've
had Carpenter surveilling the house next to Delilah. He thinks
there *are* dope deals going on there."

They continued in silence, and then Ariel decided to ask the
question that weighed on her mind. "Jimmy?"

"Mmm?"

"Will you see Tess when you're in Vancouver?"

They walked a few steps before he answered. "I'm not sure."

It wasn't what she was hoping to hear. She pressed. "But after that phone call, don't you think it will be all right now?"

"I'm not sure about that, either."

She was sorry she had brought it up. Her spirits sank along with the sun.

Chapter Thirty-two

Wednesday, July 8th

From the elevated Sea to Sky Highway, taupe haze in the distant sky was evidence that wildfire smoke had invaded the Fraser Valley. But Vancouver lay untouched, glittering like an emerald jewel on the blue satin waters of Burrard Inlet.

"It's a beautiful city," Jimmy said, his eyes rarely leaving the scene.

"Yeah. A great camouflage for crime and corruption."

Jimmy turned to Ray. "How did you feel when you were posted to the Island?"

"At first I was pissed and Georgie was heartbroken because we were born and raised here and had friends up the ying-yang." He glanced over at Jimmy. "And before you correct me, I know it's yin-yang."

Jimmy grinned. "I wasn't going to say anything."

"Yeah. Well, anyway ... as I was saying ... I played shinny hockey with guys I grew up with. The Italian community was a big part of our lives. Georgina was really close to my mother and she loved working in my parents' restaurant."

"Ariel and I ate there a couple of times."

"Anyone who appreciated *real* Italian food ate at Rossini's." His mind drifted momentarily. "At least we got posted before the kids started school. Marcus was five and Gabriella was two. And Mom and Pop decided to move over not long after. They missed us, and the business taxes and red tape were getting ridiculous."

"Why did they call the new place Catalani's and not Rossini's?"

"Catalani is my Mom's maiden name. The guy who bought Rossini's wanted to keep the name. So Pop sold that for a small fortune with a caveat that the place had to have the same standards. Anyway, we brought some Italian culture with us." He turned to Jimmy with a smile. "I like to think we improved the town."

Because Jimmy expected Ray to ask him why he left Vancouver, he swiftly switched the topic. "So the RCMP is okay with us talking to someone on their turf. And no grief?"

"Nope, and if their information is correct, Ashton should be home from work around four thirty ... if we're lucky, and he comes straight home. The Staff Sergeant was curious about the investigation when I talked to him yesterday. So I thought a courtesy call wouldn't hurt."

"Ray Rossini?" a male voice called out. "Hey, *commilitone!*" An RCMP officer rushed out from behind his desk.

"Oh, for chrissake. Aidan! You old son of a gun!" Ray gave him a man hug. "Jeez, what a surprise."

"How the hell are you and what are you doing here? I heard you were on the Island."

"I am. This is my partner, Jimmy Tan. Jimmy this Aidan Kelly. We worked together about ten years ago."

"Pleased to meet you," Jimmy said.

"Likewise." He pumped Jimmy's hand. "How do you put up with this guy?"

"I drink a lot."

Ray laughed, rolling his eyes. "Tan here used to be with the VPD. So, how's it hanging?"

"Good. Good. Come on into the back. You want a coffee or cold drink?"

"A cold drink sounds good."

Kelly introduced the two officers to his colleagues, after which they sat in the cramped lunch room, discussed the wildfire situation, and caught up on family and former co-workers. Kelly's curiosity finally took over. "So, what brings you here?"

Ray gave him a brief overview of the case and the reason they were in the Fraser Valley.

Kelly nodded thoughtfully. "When I heard about that murder, I wondered if you might be involved."

"I thought we should meet Staff Sergeant Stewart and thank him."

"For what?"

"For allowing us to work in his territory."

"He's out right now. So you've got a pass to work on our patch?"

"In a manner of speaking. We'll only be conducting a couple of interviews. Stewart said he was okay with it. Even provided us with some information. He sounds like an all right guy."

"He is. Very straight arrow."

"We thought there might be a problem because we're not RCMP."

"Yeah, I heard you left. Why, if you don't mind me asking?"

"No, I don't mind. I just didn't want to get transferred anymore. Of course, that policy's changed now. But after we were transferred and bought a place in Britannia Bay, Georgie and I knew we never wanted to live anywhere else. It's a little hideaway, Aidan. A real bit of Heaven on Earth."

Jimmy stared at Ray, open-mouthed.

"What? What's with the face?"

"I've just never heard you waxing on so poetically before."

"Waxing on?" Kelly repeated with a grin.

Ray nodded. "Yeah. Tan's our resident linguist."

"It doesn't hurt to bring a little class to the squad room."

"See?" Jimmy needled Ray.

"Okay, Chomsky."

"So, what's your schedule?" Kelly asked.

Ray looked at his watch. "We're gonna grab an early bite and then talk to our guy. So I think we should hit the streets. Please give our regards to Stewart and tell him we're sorry we missed him."

"It was great seeing you, Ray. Give my best to Georgina."

"I will. She'll be tickled pink I ran into you. Do the same with Rosie, would you?"

"Absolutely. Nice to meet you, Jimmy."

"Same here."

As they exited, Ray turned to Jimmy. "That was a stroke of luck. There's no way we'll get any interference now. Aidan will have our backs."

"Doesn't sound like we'll need it."

"Not if the head honcho is as cooperative as Aidan says. But you know how territorial cops are."

Jimmy's mind rewound to the spat between Wyatt and Griffin. "Yes, indeed."

"Yes, indeed," Ray mimicked and jabbed Jimmy's arm.

Something was nagging Lana as she kneaded dough, and every once in a while a vision popped into her head. It was the biker she met on the ferry. Since Ariel had mentioned the almost sterile crime scene and the possibility that a motorcyclist might have committed the murder, she went over things about him that had seemed antithetical to a biker. But then, he might simply have been a fastidiously clean person who liked to ride bikes. She washed her hands, picked up the phone and called Ariel. When it went to message, she asked Ariel to return her call.

Ariel, Molly and Roger were mucking about in the garden, taking advantage of the sudden drop in temperature and lack of humidity. Jimmy would be gone for two nights at least. Being on her own to do whatever she wanted, however, didn't sit well with Ariel. Too many years joined at the hip with a man she loved, and too wedded to her routine.

Except for being outdoors amongst her flowers, summer was not her favourite season. For Ariel, the year began in September when choir practice started up again, her contingent of singing students returned, and regularly scheduled meetings of the Heritage Gardens Society dotted the pages of her diary. She would get up every morning at the same time and go to bed at the same time every night. Ariel, for all her free-spirited ways, loved regularity and being rooted like the roses in her garden. Doffing her gardening gloves and straw hat she went into the house. Upon seeing the blinking message light and hearing Lana's request, she returned the call. "Hi Lana. What's up?"

They sat again in the shade of the gazebo. "I want to show you something," Lana said, holding her cellphone. She found the photos of the man on the ferry. "This man shared my table on the ferry a week ago Friday."

"Oh? Have you met someone?" Ariel asked conspiratorially.

"No. It's nothing like that." Then she gave the cellphone to Ariel. "Look at that picture. It was taken the same evening Max Berdahl was killed. Check out what he's wearing."

After Ariel examined the photograph, she looked at Lana. "So he's a biker. So what? All kinds of people ride motorcycles. Especially in the summer."

"Yes, but didn't you say the person who murdered Max might be a biker?"

"Um, yes. So?"

"And didn't you say the crime scene was spotless?"

Ariel was having second thoughts about sharing this information—even with her tight-lipped friend. "Uh huh," she replied cautiously.

"Well, when he sat down, I noticed how clean he was. His hair. His hands. Even his fingernails. Wouldn't you expect a biker to look a bit greasy and have dirt or oil under his fingernails or ...?" She stopped short when she saw Ariel's quizzical gaze. "I'm being stupid, right?"

Ariel sat back and ran through her head what Jimmy had told her. Then she looked at her anxious friend. "Well, the fact that this guy was extremely clean and riding a bike is interesting. But until they find the suspect, they don't know what he looks like." Then a lightbulb went on. "I have an idea. Forward these pictures to Jimmy with an explanation."

Concentrating on his burger, Jimmy barely heard the buzzing of his cellphone. Pulling it from his pocket and seeing that Lana was the sender, he wondered if Ariel was all right. He read the message, looked at the pictures and handed the phone to Ray. "Look at this."

Ray took a minute or two. "This is interesting. If we zero in on a suspect, and he looks anything like this, we'll have something solid to work with. Too bad BC Ferries only keep their videocam records for a week. We might have gotten the guy's licence plate number." He took a sip of coffee, looked at the picture a second time and handed back the phone. "A coincidence like this would be more than weird."

Chapter Thirty-three

Barry Ashton's bungalow was situated in a modest family development built in the late 1960s. Tricycles, bicycles and skateboards littered sidewalks and lawns. Some homes were well kept while others were sliding into disrepair. Ashton's was in the former camp. A significant difference was the chain link fence surrounding his property. The reason for it became evident the second Ray rang the doorbell. A substantial dog was behind that door, barking fiercely.

Moments later there was silence. The door opened on a man bending to one side holding the collar of an agitated dog primed to pounce.

"Are you Barry Ashton?" Ray asked over the animal's growls.

The man regarded the two men and spotted what looked to be an unmarked police car at the curb. "Yes I am," he answered, his pale blue eyes examining them warily.

That affirmed, they sized up Ashton. Standing about six feet, he was whippet thin. Other than that, there was nothing remarkable about him. He had regular features in a round face with fair skin showing signs of sun damage. He was wearing running gear.

They introduced themselves showing him their ID. Still holding the collar, he took a cursory look at the cards. "Britannia Bay?

Where's that?"

"It's on Vancouver Island," Ray said, almost cringing. He knew it was small, but not *that* small.

"You're a ways from home, aren't you?" he asked, more curious than provocative. "What brings you here?"

"We're investigating the murder of Max Berdahl," Ray said.

Ashton's face registered the news. A smile transformed his face. "You mean that s.o b. finally got whacked?" He looked down at his panting dog and released his grip. "Bonnie, go lie down." The dog looked up at him then turned and trotted off.

"Bonnie?" Ray laughed.

Ashton joined in. "Yeah. People think she's a male called Thor or something like that. She's unusually big for a female."

"Is she a cross with a German Shepherd?" Jimmy asked.

"No. She's a purebred Belgian Shepherd."

"I've never seen one before."

"I got her because she's a perfect breed for marathon runs. She trains with me."

Ray noticed the dog's chest. "She looks strong."

Ashton smiled. "These dogs pulled around machine guns in the Second World War."

"No way!"

"Yes way," he laughed. He stepped back and held open the door. "Come on in. I think the neighbours have already figured out you're not Mormons or Jehovah's Witnesses."

Ray and Jimmy exchanged a glance.

Ashton pointed to a sofa behind a coffee table laden with scientific journals. "Take a seat, if you don't mind dog hairs. She sits where I sit."

"No problem," Ray said. The cleanliness quotient wouldn't pass Georgina's inspection, but he had seen a lot worse.

Ashton sat across from them, his body relaxed, face open. "So he was murdered, eh?" He almost laughed.

"You didn't read about it or see it on the news?" Jimmy asked.

"No. I don't do news anymore. It's too depressing."

Ray agreed and noticed there was no television set in the room, but it could be elsewhere.

Ashton took a better look at the two men dressed in casual and cool summer clothing. "How come you're from Vancouver Island?"

"That's where Berdahl lived," Jimmy told him.

"He did? When did he go there?"

"He was *from* there, and returned some time in 2012," Jimmy explained.

"Oh." He nodded. "So he was murdered there?"

"Yes."

"Then why are you over here?"

"We're wondering if there's a link to Sunnyvale Estates," Jimmy told him. "It seems Berdahl bullied your family during construction of that project."

A shadow passed across Ashton's face. "You can say that again," he said, sourly. "When was he killed?"

"Recently," Ray said.

The reason for their visit dawned on him. His face suddenly slammed shut. "Well, I'm not your man if you're thinking I did it. That development didn't directly affect me. I was away the entire time Sunnyvale was built."

"Where were you?" Ray asked, bluntly.

"McGill." Something hard had crept into his voice.

Jimmy sought to soften the tone of Ray's questions. "What did you study, if you don't mind me asking?" he inquired with genuine interest.

"Materials Engineering."

"Do you work in that field?"

Ashton visibly relaxed. This was his comfort zone. "Yes. I work in a lab that's in the process of developing new products from bamboo."

Jimmy nodded. "Apparently it's the next great thing in biodegradables."

Ashton eyed Jimmy with interest. "That's right. There's a whole new range of products that could make landfills obsolete ... or almost."

Ray watched as Jimmy wandered off topic. It was time to get back on track. "But you must have had some idea what was going on with your family during the construction of Sunnyvale."

Ashton reluctantly dragged his eyes away from Jimmy. "I got letters from Grandma. She told me a bit but didn't go into too much detail. She probably didn't want to bother me. But I read between the lines. She did tell me that when the homestead was sold, it broke her sister's heart. And hers too." His shoulders sagged. "I felt bad because there was nothing I could do."

Bonnie had been watching her master during the interview. When she saw his demeanour, she got up and came to him, laying her head on his thighs. He began stroking her head. "She reads me like a book," he said, then straightened up. "If you want details on Sunnyvale, you should talk to my Grandma."

"Where does she live?" Ray asked.

"She's in a care home not far from here called Fraser Terrace."

"How is her mental acumen?" Jimmy asked.

Ashton smiled. "She's eighty-one but sharp as a tack. The only reason she's in care is because she has advanced rheumatoid arthritis."

"Could you tell us where you were on Friday, June twenty-sixth?" Ray was at him again, focusing on facts.

"Where I am every day. At work." He glared at Ray.

"We'll need addresses and phone numbers."

"I'll get them and give you the name of the person to talk to at the lab. Eyeball scanners are the only way you get in and out. So there won't be any equivocation about where I was that day," he added with a jab.

He left the room briefly—Bonnie tagging along behind—and returned just as briefly—Bonnie with a ball in her mouth. Ray stood up too quickly and reached out for the paper in Ashton's hand. Bonnie dropped the ball, stood between Ashton and Ray and let out a soft, low growl. Ray quickly withdrew his arm. Jimmy laughed. Ashton followed. "She's very protective," he said.

"And that's a good thing," Jimmy mocked Martha Stewart. Ray wore a lopsided smile. Ashton seemed baffled.

"Thanks for this," Ray said. "And thanks for your time."

Ashton managed a sharp nod, still bristling from Ray's cop talk. Opening the door, he turned to his running companion "Just sit here for a second, Bonnie. We'll go soon." The dog sat, expectant. Then Ashton said: "Max Berdahl caused our family a lot of grief. So I'm not sorry he's no longer taking up space on the planet."

Jimmy gave him a straight look. "You're not the first person to express those sentiments."

Chapter Thirty-four

Fraser Terrace wouldn't have been out of place among the boulevards of Bel Air. Situated on a partially forested hilltop overlooking the Fraser River, it sat at the end of a long driveway accessible through tall wrought-iron gates. It reminded Ray of the stately mansions he and Georgie had seen during a tour of famous actors' homes. "Are we at the right place? This doesn't look like any care homes I've seen."

"That's what the plaque says." Jimmy indicated a shiny brass rectangle set into one of the stone pillars flanking the gates.

"It must cost a fortune to live here. I wonder how she can afford it."

After announcing themselves on the intercom, the gates slowly swung open. Residents who normally would be outside "taking the air" remained indoors due to particulate matter from wood smoke that could endanger their health. It was unfortunate because the heat of the day had cooled to a pleasant evening and would have enhanced their enjoyment of the spectacular view of the river flowing through the flatlands below.

At the locked entry doors, they had to identify themselves a second time. Ray had already counted a half dozen cameras. He looked down and uttered under his breath to Jimmy. "This is a bloody fortress."

When the buzzer sounded, they walked to the front desk. After showing their identification, stating the purpose of their visit and undergoing a mild third degree by the receptionist, they were shown to a small office where they sat, cooling their heels.

Several minutes passed. Ray looked at his watch. "These old folks go to bed early. If this snail's pace doesn't pick up, we could lose the chance to talk to Mrs. Ashton today."

Before Jimmy could comment, a buxom, middle-aged woman entered. A permanent frown and set jaw did nothing to soften her otherwise attractive face. While her clothes were stylish and looked expensive, the material struggled to fit properly over her big hips and equally big behind. Moreover, the muted colours only emphasized her sallow complexion.

They stood, ready to shake hands, but she did not offer hers. Perhaps it had something to do with the fear of spreading germs, Ray thought, as hand sanitizing dispensers were visible everywhere.

"I'm April Martin, the night nurse supervisor," she announced briskly after moving behind her desk. Not a smile. Not an invitation to sit down. "You're here to visit Lettie Ashton?"

Ray decided her officious manner must have something to do with her perceived self-importance.

"Yes, that's right," Jimmy said.

"So, being the police, I'm assuming this isn't a personal visit."

"No, it isn't," Jimmy replied with as much civility as possible. *What business is it of hers why they were here? This isn't a prison.*

"Could you be more specific?"

Her curt question caused Ray to give Jimmy a sidelong look. He knew his partner had no patience for rudeness and wondered what his response would be. Silence. Witnessing what looked like a Mexican stand-off, Ray enjoyed the moment,

April Martin caved first and carried on as though she hadn't been snubbed. "Lettie is on the second floor in room two-twelve." She glared at them. "Don't upset her." She picked up the phone.

The detectives were expecting a room, but what they stepped into was a beautifully decorated suite. The living room seemed larger with the addition of a small, flower-filled balcony. This was accessed by a door wide enough to accommodate a wheelchair. A small dining area next to a galley-style kitchen completed the main area and a short hallway led to a bedroom and bathroom. The mantel over the gas insert fireplace held several photographs in simple silver frames. The two detectives were hoping that among them would be the face of Dean Ashton.

Lettie Ashton was on the balcony facing outward and being fussed over by a care attendant. "Let me put this wrap around your shoulders, Lettie."

"I don't want it there, Teresita. It's too warm. Put it on my lap, please," came the reply.

On the way out, the attendant nodded to her supervisor and tossed a curious glance toward the visitors.

April Martin stepped onto the balcony. "Hi Lettie," she greeted the elderly woman.

"Are my visitors here?"

"Yes, they are, sweetie." And here, finally, was the warmth Ray expected from a woman whose job description would have contained compassion as a necessary qualification.

"Then, turn my chair around, please, and let's go in."

The voice was that of a young woman. But the body had been ravaged by the terrible autoimmune disease leaving it knotted and gnarled like an ancient olive tree.

Jimmy had heard of rheumatoid arthritis. Now he saw what it could do. He hurt in empathy as every joint appeared malformed, including her spine. It must have required a massive amount of medication to keep her from tortuous pain.

Ray, on the other hand, focused on her face still lovely at age eighty-one and framed by downy white hair carefully combed into a flattering style. Her blue eyes and rosy cheeks reminded him of colouring book pictures of Mrs. Santa Claus.

April Martin introduced them individually. When she said "Britannia Bay," Lettie cocked her head. "I won't offer you my hand because I don't want to frighten you," she said cheerfully. Her hands were hidden under the wrap.

Both men warmed to her immediately, admiring her ability to treat her infirmity like a mild inconvenience.

"Sit yourselves down. Would you like something cold to drink?"

"No, thank you," Jimmy said.

Ray was about to say, "Yes." The *q* and *a* with Barry Ashton had left him with a dry mouth.

Lettie spoke first. "Well, I would. April, would you bring that pitcher of lemonade from the fridge? And three glasses in case they change their minds."

The woman did so, placing everything on a coffee table and pouring a glass for Lettie, who was watching Ray. She could see that he was eyeing the lemonade like a parched rhino at a watering hole.

"Fill the other two. I can see they were just being polite. Anyone who would turn down lemonade on a day like today needs his head examined," she said, a lilt in her voice.

"Would you like anything else while I'm here?" April put a straw into Lettie's glass and then swung open a tray table on the wheelchair.

"No. That's all. Thanks, April."

"Anytime, Lettie," and she left.

With her hands remaining on her lap, Lettie leaned forward and drank through the straw. Then she smacked her lips together. "They make the best lemonade here."

After tasting it and comparing it to Greenwood's, Jimmy found it lacking. He doubted the institution used labour-intensive fresh lemons.

Ray drank it down like it was a cold beer then imitated Lettie, smacking his lips with gusto.

Her laughter rippled around the room. "Told you it was good. Help yourself to more."

Ray took her up on her offer.

She sat back and levelled her shrewd gaze at the two officers. "I believe I know why two handsome policemen have dropped in on me."

"You do?" Ray asked.

"Certainly. I have a big TV in my bedroom and put it to good use. I knew Max Berdahl was murdered on Vancouver Island, and when April said you were from Britannia Bay, I figured that's why you were here. I've been wanting to tell someone that he finally got what was coming to him. He was a nasty piece of ... uh ... something you scrape off the bottom of your shoes."

Ray nearly choked on his lemonade. He was trying to decide what cartoon character she had become because she sure as hell wasn't Mrs. Claus anymore. Since she was no simpering hothouse flower, he came straight to the point. "We believe it's a case of revenge."

"I'm not surprised," she said drily.

"Your family was seriously affected by his actions, wasn't it?" Jimmy asked.

"Absolutely. He as good as killed my sister, Edna."

"We have some background of what happened to her because of him."

"So. You've been doing your homework, eh? Good. But you won't know everything. It started long before Berdahl arrived on the scene," she stated.

"It did?" Ray asked, surprised.

She took another drink. "Do you have time to hear a story?"

An imperceptible glance passed between the two men. "Since you've been wanting to tell it, we'll make time," Ray said.

"Do you mind if I take notes?" Jimmy asked.

"Absolutely not. I'd be grateful if you did. There needs to be a record of it all."

He took out his notebook and pen and settled back on the sofa. Greenwood's outline was about to be filled in.

Chapter Thirty-five

"It started in 2001. I had been retired for a couple of years and was in good shape financially. My plan was to travel and to stay in my house for as long as possible. But Edna, that was my sister, needed help. She was living all by herself trying to deal with the house and all those chickens and the garden and so on after her husband was murdered."

She stated this so matter-of-factly that the two detectives almost missed it.

"Murdered?" Ray exclaimed.

"Yes. Murdered. The police said it was an accident, but we knew different. He was driving home at night in the rain. His car was found in a ditch. The police blamed it on the dark, his age and the road conditions. But we were convinced he was purposely run off the road."

"Why did you think that?" Ray asked.

"Because Johnny and Edna were being harassed by the owner of the land on either side of them. He wanted them to sell so that he could develop all of it, but they didn't want to."

"Who was the owner?"

"They didn't know because he lived in Italy. Another man came around who said he was 'representing' him. Crooked as a dog's hind leg, if you ask me."

"What was this man's name?"

"They couldn't remember. They said it was hard to pronounce."

"How were they being harassed?"

"A motorcycle gang rode around the property every day—all day and most of the night."

"How long did it go on?"

"For about half a year. It stopped right after Johnny was killed—which is interesting, don't you think?" Her eyes focused on them like lasers.

"Yes. Very," Ray acknowledged.

"Anyway, Edna was afraid of being alone, and she didn't have a lot of money. So I sold up and moved in with her. It was quiet for about a couple of years. Then, lo and behold, a real live person showed up. That was Berdahl. He wanted the same thing—Edna's parcel. When that little piece of pond scum offered her a pittance of what it was worth, she told him to take a hike."

Ray looked over at Jimmy, and they smiled imagining the scene.

She tightened her lips. "Of course, he didn't. He just kept coming around with offers. He said he would even throw in a new house as part of the deal. He was smarmy. Butter wouldn't melt. You know the type," she added scornfully.

"We do," Ray said.

"And when none of it worked, he cranked up the noise in hopes of driving her out."

She then verified what Greenwood had told Jimmy. He sat back and listened during her recounting, then picked up his pen as she provided new information.

"The city realized that the value of her property had increased because of the development. As a consequence, her taxes went up. That's when she had a massive stroke. Along the way she had had other TIAs. The long and the short of it is, her kids convinced her to sell the property to that loathsome wretch and go into care."

She paused for a few minutes, lost in thought. "She didn't live out the year." Her sigh filled the room. "Of course, that meant I had to look for my own place. But Dean suggested I move in with him and his wife Gloria and the two kids who were still at home. He had put in a basement suite that they were planning to rent out. So I offered to cover that and moved in. Then my arthritis got into my knees and ankles and it was impossible to climb the stairs. So Dean installed one of those automated chairs ... which I paid for, I might add."

When she continued, her voice dripped with acid. "Next thing you know, Gloria ups and leaves. Met a man from Alberta and took off with him, taking Tyler and Angelina with her. Angel was ten at the time and the apple of Dean's eye. He was beside himself."

"What year was this?" Jimmy asked, busily scribbling.

"It was 2011, the year I came here because Dean couldn't take care of me anymore. Everything just piled on top of him." Her voice dropped. "Then one day he told me he had decided to move to Alberta. The brokerage arranged for a transfer to their office in Edmonton. That's where the children were living and he wanted to be near them ... well, Angel, actually. It damn near killed me, but I knew how much he loved that little girl. He had never loved his sons that way."

"Why do you suppose that is?" Jimmy asked gently.

"I don't know. He did when they were young, but they were a handful as they got older and he didn't have time or patience for any nonsense. He was a bit hard-nosed. Barry gradually smartened up and did well at university."

"We met Barry earlier. He seems to be a fine young man," Ray said.

"He is."

"What about Tyler?"

She looked away briefly before answering. When she turned back her eyes were glistening. "Tyler is a different kettle of fish," she began, blinking back the tears. "He was caught in the middle. Big brother Barry, whom he idolized, and then Angel, who got all the attention later on. Tyler would do stupid things to get his father's attention, and of course, they always backfired. But I guess he figured any attention was better than none at all." She sighed. "He went from being on the honour roll to almost flunking out in the last year of high school."

"Being a teenager, it must have been hard trying to fit into a new school at that stage," Jimmy said.

"Yes, it was hard in every way. New kid on the block. Not being interested in sports. And you know, for boys, sports are *the* thing. If you don't play football or hockey, you're nothing in the eyes of your peers," she said bitterly.

Ray cringed.

"Fortunately, one teacher spotted a talent in him that he didn't even know he had. And she cultivated that."

"What was that?" Jimmy asked.

"He's a wonderful artist. He can draw anyone or anything. All it takes is a few lines and you can see what it is. I have a few of his sketches hanging in the hallway. Go take a look at them."

What they saw bore out what Lettie Ashton said. Simple sketches deftly put to paper—some black and white, others in pastels. Jimmy thought of Greenwood. He took out his cellphone and photographed Tyler's work.

Ray was more interested in the photographs on the mantel. "Are these pictures of Tyler?"

She turned her head and viewed them as though she had to reacquaint herself with the images. "Yes. And Dean. They were taken not long before they moved to Alberta."

Ray inspected them trying to imagine what the faces would look like after the addition of five years. Dean probably looked much the same. But Tyler would have grown from a teenager into a young man. He couldn't envisage the change.

"Tyler's a talented artist." Jimmy said and was about to put his cellphone away when Ray subtly cleared his throat. Jimmy looked at him. Ray quickly shifted his eyes to the photographs.

"Yes he is. He was accepted at Emily Carr University, you know," she said proudly. "It should have been the start of better days for him," she said with sadness.

"What happened?" Ray distracted her while Jimmy took a few shots of the photographs, tucked away his phone and returned to his chair.

"Dean made sure he had everything—a place to live and spending money. Everything he needed for his courses. We were so happy for him."

With sinking hearts, Ray and Jimmy listened, knowing that what was coming was not going to be good.

"He seemed to be settling in. When he visited me, he was always excited about his latest project, showing me pictures on his cellphone. That lasted about a half hour. Then he would become morose and say his art was rubbish, worthless—that he would never amount to anything. I was anxious about his mental health."

"Is there anything in the family history that would cause you to be concerned?" Jimmy asked.

"No. Then one day Dean showed up here out of the blue. He said Tyler hadn't been answering his calls or email messages. He went to his apartment. The landlord hadn't seen him for a while. When they went inside, they found food going bad, like he hadn't been there for a couple of weeks. Dean visited the school and spoke to an academic advisor, and what he heard shocked him. Apparently Tyler had been missing class and when he did show up his teachers believed he was exhibiting signs of mental illness. They finally expelled him." She stopped as though strained from relating the story. "You know, you should talk to Dean yourself. He can give you a better idea of what happened."

"I'm assuming he never found Tyler?" Jimmy asked.

She looked down and shook her head. "No."

"When did all of this happen?"

"Almost two years ago. But I heard from him last Christmas. He said he was fine and not to worry about him. He was painting and living in some kind of commune. Every once in a while he sold a painting. He told me not to tell his dad. But I had to tell Dean he was alive."

"Do you think Tyler blamed Max Berdahl for what happened to him and his family?"

"No. I doubt it would have occurred to him."

"What about Dean? Did he blame Berdahl?" Ray asked.

"I believe he did. I know *I* did! I would have gladly killed the little creep!" she said, vehemently. In her excitement, the shawl covering her hands slipped to the floor. Lettie was horrified. Ray and Jimmy were mortified. They knew how important it was for her to keep her infirmity covered up. Now it was laid bare.

Ray almost regretted that he had asked that last question. The pained expression on her face left him feeling sick. He picked up the shawl and placed it back on top of her malformed hands. "I'm sorry about that, Mrs. Ashton," he said softly.

"Don't apologize. No use hiding these hideous claws. I'm sure you've seen worse in your line of work."

Scenes of what they had witnessed not two weeks since streaked across their minds.

Jimmy asked if she remembered the dates of Dean's last visit.

"Sometime last month. There's a calendar on the kitchen wall. It'll be there."

Jimmy flipped back one page, he saw "Dean here" written in the square for June 17. *Three weeks ago. The murder was June 26th. That's just too close for comfort,* he thought.

"One of the care aides wrote that down for me," Lettie said. "I used to be a bookkeeper and now I can't even hold a pencil. Life can be cruel. You never know what you're going to be dealt, do you?"

"No ma'am," Ray said. He stood, ready for their departure.

"But I can't complain, really. This is a beautiful place. The food is delicious, too. I'm a heck of a lot better off than half the world." She smiled.

"Most of us are," Jimmy said. "It was a real pleasure meeting you."

"It sure was. You're an inspiration," Ray said.

"Thank you. I hope the person who wiped that piece of cow dung off the face of the Earth gets away with it."

Ray chuckled. "Sometimes I think the same thing, but it's our job to uphold the law."

"Then I hope the judge is lenient," she flashed another smile. "Goodbye. And have a safe journey home."

Chapter Thirty-six

"I think our work here is done, don't you?" Ray asked as they pulled away from Fraser Terrace. "We might as well head for Vancouver."

"We have to get in touch with Dean Ashton to establish his alibi. He was out this way close to when Berdahl was murdered."

"Yeah. He might be one of those goody two-shoes who turn ballistic and kill people."

They rode in silence as the car sped along a highway once lined by forests, now littered with malls. While Ray was eagerly anticipating the visit to his old neighbourhood, Jimmy was comparing the photo of Dean Ashton with the biker Lana saw. There was no resemblance. The thick eyebrows of the biker alone would have excluded Ashton. He scrolled to Tyler's sketches and as he admired them, he hoped the young man was safe in some artists' colony drawing and painting. And healing.

A message appeared on the computer catching Ray's eye. "Would you believe it?"

Jimmy followed his sightline. Dean Ashton had called the station.

"Barry must have contacted him."

"Well, he's left his number. Now's as good a time as any." He punched in the number and patched it into the Bluetooth.

Ashton picked up on the first ring. "Dean Ashton here," he responded.

"Good evening, Mr. Ashton. This is Detective Sergeant Jimmy Tan from the Britannia Bay Police Department."

"Hello. Thanks for returning my call. I understand you went to see Barry this afternoon in connection with the murder of Max Berdahl." No mention of them seeing his mother. "Why would you be contacting Barry about that?"

"One avenue we're looking at is a connection to the Sunnyvale development. Your family was heavily impacted by the actions of Max Berdahl."

"Yes, it was. But if you think Barry is involved in any way, you are sorely mistaken," he said, his voice calm but underlain with anger.

"I appreciate your concern, Mr. Ashton. But rest assured, Barry is not a suspect."

There was a long pause. "I'm glad to hear that."

"While you are on the phone, could you tell me where *you* were on Friday, June twenty-sixth?"

"I certainly can. I was here in our conference room videotaping a webinar for new users of iTrade."

Jimmy had already determined that Ashton was no longer a suspect, but needed his alibi nevertheless. "Mr. Ashton, I understand that Tyler has been missing. Have you heard from him recently?"

"Tyler?" he fairly roared. "For crying out loud. What next?"

"As I understand it he had to leave his home and begin a new life at a particularly difficult age. He might have had a grudge against Max Berdahl."

"That's stretching it," he stated flatly. "I doubt that Tyler even knew his name."

"Nevertheless, we need to eliminate him as a suspect." Ray and Jimmy waited for an answer. When he said nothing, Jimmy pressed him further. "Do you happen to know how we can get in touch with him?"

A deep sigh blew through the line. "No. I have no idea where he is. He's only contacted me once in the past two years."

"When was that?"

"Just before he left school. I have the date in my journal if you need that," he offered. Ray cast a quick look at Jimmy. According to Lettie, Tyler had been expelled. He hadn't "left."

"Yes, please."

"Just a moment." They heard the clack of a keyboard. Jimmy realized that the man did not have a silent chiclet keyboard, a type he himself cursed when his fingers slid off the keys, which was often.

"Here it is. May fifteenth, 2015."

Ray had exited the highway and was navigating the local streets toward East Vancouver. Something began fluttering in Jimmy's chest, but he needed to stay focused. "What did he say at the time?"

"He said he found out he was bi-polar but he didn't want to take his meds because they interfered with his creativity."

"How did you hear that he had left school?"

"When his phone calls and emails stopped, I got in touch with them. I was very disturbed about what I learned." Dean Ashton then reiterated what Lettie had told them. "That's when I began looking for him."

"Did you notify the police?"

"Of course. That was the first thing I did. They put up his college picture and details on their public database."

"Obviously he had sought medical help because he knew what his diagnosis was. Did you contact any hospitals or mental health facilities?"

"Yes. We were afraid he might try to commit suicide because my mother said he thought his life was worthless."

Jimmy remembered that Lettie had said Tyler thought his *art* was worthless, not his life. But then, perhaps for him, his art *was* his life.

"No unclaimed suicides had any similarities to Tyler. Then after I went on a wild goose chase putting up flyers and going on social media, I finally hired a private detective. Between us, we found nothing."

"You said 'social media.' Did Tyler have a Facebook page?"

"No. But Angelina has one and she uploaded the information about him. There were a few replies at first, but then nothing."

"So there were no postings from his friends?"

"It didn't seem like he had any."

"Did anyone ever get in touch with you with any leads or information?"

"No. No one. He just vanished." There was a catch in his voice. "Truthfully, the only thing I do know is that he was alive last Christmas because he called Mom."

Jimmy decided to tell him about their other visit. "You should know that we've just come from talking to your mother."

"Oh. That's probably where you would have heard the details about what happened to our family. Barry wouldn't have known them, unless she shared them with him. Which I doubt."

"She certainly bent our ears."

He chuckled. "She's an amazing woman, isn't she? All of that pain but she lives every day to its fullest … and with good humour. I hope if I'm ever in that position, I can be like her."

"We were very pleased to meet her, I can tell you."

"Before we end this conversation, there's something I'd like to say." Ashton sounded hesitant. "Max Berdahl was a son-of-a-bitch and I don't regret his death." When Jimmy said nothing, Ashton thought his silence was a rebuke. "You probably think I'm a terrible person for saying that."

"Not at all," Jimmy said. "We've heard similar statements more than once."

"I'm glad I'm not the only one who feels that way. Well, if you have no further questions ..."

"No, I don't. Thank you for your co-operation, and I hope you eventually get good news about Tyler."

"So do I. I have some serious amends to make," he said, the pain in his voice travelling through the line as it went dead.

"Sounds like he wants to make things right," Ray said.

"I just hope he gets that opportunity."

Chapter Thirty-seven

It was the dinner hour when Ray and Jimmy arrived at their destination. Commercial Drive, a diverse street of shops and restaurants, began as a place for post-WWII Italian immigrants to live, eat, shop and gather. A section of the street was still referred to as "Little Italy," but ethnic groups from Latin America and all parts of Asia were changing the tenor of the neighbourhood. In addition, creeping gentrification and a large counter-culture demographic that openly promoted the use of marijuana altered the community that had been rechristened, "The Drive."

Ray's initial enthusiasm on returning to his old neighbourhood began to fade as he passed each once-familiar spot. New owners, with no sense of history, had moved in making changes. On the one hand, everything was trendy and colourful and popular with tourists. On the other, pride of possession, so prominent among the first wave of immigrant families, had given way to a sense of impermanence.

"It's sad how this area is changing," Ray moaned as he cruised up the street looking left and right. When he spotted a café on a corner, his spirits picked up. "But *there's* something that hasn't. Joe's! Thank Christ for that. I told Georgie I might drop in, but I don't think there'll be time."

"We could make time. It would be nice to go back for a cup of cappuccino."

He glanced at Jimmy. "Go back? You know Joe's?"

"Of course. Ariel and I went there a lot when we were at SFU. It's an institution."

"You're just full of surprises, you know that?" As he drove around looking for a parking spot, his short-lived relief left. "Jeez, would you look at this junk yard?" He pointed to a park where elderly Italian men had once relaxed and played bocce. Grass that had been green and covered with bocce balls was now covered with garbage and dotted with dandelions and dog feces. The benches and public bathroom walls were defaced with graffiti.

"God, this is sickening. I'm afraid of what I'm going to find at Rossini's." His anxiety swiftly abated as they entered his family's former business. It remained a tastefully appointed, classic Italian *ristorante*. Every table but one was filled. People were sitting at the bar waiting to be seated and there were two groups in front of them at the *maître d's* desk, both with reservations, which Ray and Jimmy did not have.

"Oh, crap," Ray muttered, realizing his mistake. Then he had an idea. "I'll be right back," he said and went outside.

Jimmy, keeping their place in line, heard the desk phone ringing. The *maître d'* picked up, said a few words, went to the rear of the restaurant then came back. Ray returned and slid alongside Jimmy. "Jack Robinson," he whispered. Jimmy was about to ask him what he meant, when a short, corpulent man rushed toward the line-up.

"Rossini, *dove sei?*" he asked in a loud voice.

"*Qui a destra,*" Ray responded.

Everyone nearby turned to look at this man calling himself Rossini. Ray broke into a smile. "My family started this establishment," he announced. A few applauded. He bowed.

Vincenzo Gaglardi, the new owner, had the affable congeniality necessary to attract and retain loyal patrons. His kitchen did the rest. After giving Ray as much of a hug as his girth would allow, he continued in rapid Italian, hands flying off in all directions. When Ray introduced Jimmy, Gaglardi worked his hand like an ancient water pump. He ushered them around the waiting patrons then signalled to a waiter, who, with swift sleight of hand, caused a "Reserved" sign to disappear. Seconds later, they were seated and large leather-bound menus placed in their hands.

"Well, at least that hasn't changed," Ray snickered, recognizing the age-old custom when favoured clientele arrived without a reservation.

"Anything you want, it's on the house," Gaglardi announced with exuberance. He signalled again and this time a bottle of Adalia Valpolicella Ripasso Superiore 2011 appeared.

Ray reared back. "Whoa. This is too much."

"*Voi due non state lavorando ora, vero?*" Vincenzo smiled slyly at Ray.

"No, we're not on duty now," he answered. "But first of all, we can't drink a full bottle. Save it for the people with money. I'll just have a glass of the house red. And second, my partner here doesn't drink wine."

"So, perhaps some San Pellegrino for you?"

"That would be perfect," Jimmy agreed.

"*Bene. Bene.*" The proprietor's busy eyes looked about the room, observing everything.

"Vincenzo, we appreciate everything. Now get back to work."

"Very funny. Very funny," he smiled, tapped Ray on the shoulder and took off like a bullet to check on something that had caught his attention.

"God, that man is a whirlwind," Jimmy said.

"He's working his ass off, I can tell you."

"And apparently failing," he observed. "By the way, what did you mean by 'Jack Robinson'?"

Ray explained the saying and Jimmy shook his head. "English I can understand. But English idioms are beyond me."

"Christ, I hope to hell you never learn those or you'll be giving the guys even more grief."

Ariel was slipping into deep sleep when the phone rang. Like a programmed robot, she reached over to the bedside table in the dark and picked up. "Hello?"

"Hi honey, it's me, checking in."

"Who is this?"

Jimmy laughed.

"What time is it?" she asked

"Does it matter? Your lover is calling and all you care about is what time it is?"

"If it *was* my lover, I'd be worried that my husband would suddenly show up and find us in *flagrante delicto.*"

"On the phone?"

"Haven't you ever heard of phone sex?"

"Sounds pretty enticing right about now."

"Are you saying you miss me after only one day?"

"One day? Jeez, is that all it's been? Seems like a week." He related the events of the day and ended with the dinner at Rossini's."

"The food was fantastic. Just like it was when we were there. And it kept coming. I'm stuffed. I hope I can sleep. Ray had wine, so he's probably sawing away right now. The new owner is a real showman ... and generous. We had to turn down a bottle of wine that Ray said would've cost about sixty dollars at a liquor store. *If* you could find it. He was happy the place was the same because he'd been moaning about all the other changes in the area. He called them seedy."

"That's too bad. But The Drive was always a bit frayed at the seams."

"We were going to go to Joe's, but it was getting late."

"Joe's," she said dreamily. There was a momentary pause in the conversation as each of them remembered their times at the popular Portuguese café. "Will you be back tomorrow night?"

"Yes. We only have to interview Carlene Corrente. And Ray wants to visit a friend afterwards."

Once again, she posed the question. "And what about you? Are you going to see Tess?"

Jimmy hesitated. "Yes. I decided that with Uncle Beng dead, it's time to pay her a visit and offer my condolences."

"Do you think it's going to be as unpleasant as the last time?" she asked, her throat constricting.

"I hope not."

"What if it is?"

"I'd be surprised at this stage, Ariel," he said trying to soothe her. "It's been eight years. And in that time I haven't contacted anyone in Penang or breathed a word about my suspicions."

"Do you think *she* knows what happened?"

"I'm sure she does."

"And will she finally forgive you for becoming a cop?"

"I doubt it."

Ariel heard the hurt in his answer and advocated for his side. "What about the love she withheld? What about the respect you deserve? Will she own up to her mistakes?" Her voice broke.

"Ariel. Sweetheart. Please don't beat yourself up. Things might be different with Uncle Beng gone. But if they aren't, then that will be it. I have to move on. *We* have to move on."

"I hope not or else *both* our families will be lost to us," she said bleakly.

"If that's the case, it'll be you and me, babe—like always."

She sighed. "I love you, Jimmy."

"And I love you. Straight from the heart."

As Ariel placed the phone in its cradle, her thoughts darted back to the day she brought Jimmy home to meet her parents. She groaned and rolled on her side hugging the pillow, the words "some goddamn Chink!" echoing in her ears.

Chapter Thirty-eight

Thursday, July 9th

Ray ran a razor over his face. He had overslept. Not unusual when he had eaten and drunk too much the previous night. Georgina wasn't there to poke him and he had forgotten to put in a wake-up call. Hustling to finish his shave, he nicked his chin. "Damn!" He stuck some toilet tissue on the cut, jammed his shirttails into his pants and ducked out of the room. A post-it note on Jimmy's door announced to all and sundry that he was in the dining room. *Nothing like an open invitation,* he thought. Too impatient to wait for the elevator, he clattered down three flights of uncarpeted stairs and hurried into the dining room.

Jimmy had finished breakfast and was reading the morning paper. Feeling a disturbance in the atmosphere, he looked up, grinning. "Had a good sleep?"

Ray ignored the dig, plopped into a heavy vinyl-covered chair and poured himself a coffee. Looking around he spotted the breakfast buffet. Jimmy had pushed his plate to one side, remnants of a piece of bacon evident. Just the sight of it had Ray's taste buds turning to action. After eating an enormous dinner, he was surprised that he was ravenous. "I'm going to forage."

"You might want to remove the paper on your chin."

Returning with his plate heaped with scrambled eggs, bacon, sausages, hashed browns and a grilled tomato, he sat and tucked into his breakfast. "Looks like we're right back to square one," he mumbled through a mouthful of food.

Jimmy put the paper aside. "Yeah. After we talk to Carlene Corrente and you visit your friend, we might as well go home."

"Maybe we'll get something useful out of her." He sounded doubtful. "I was hoping to return with this case solved."

"The guy who did this was clever."

"Yeah. Damned clever." He expelled a puff of air along with bits of egg. "You think maybe it was a professional job after all, and made to look like a personal revenge thing? Like that horse's head in *The Godfather*."

"That was just a threat," Jimmy pointed out. "This was the real thing."

"Maybe Berdahl reneged on a deal." His energy picked up steam. "If that's the case, we follow the money. Carlene might know something about that. She was involved before Max got going on his grand plan."

They returned to Commercial Drive where Carlene Corrente had her small real estate office. A gritty itchiness clung onto Ray's skin within minutes of walking in. Even with the air-conditioner labouring to cool and clean the air, the scent of perfume permeated the room. There was too much of it. And there was too much of her.

Soft flesh spilled out of her low-cut sleeveless top. Mottled and dimpled arms were approaching the flapping point. Thighs packed into a skimpy skirt threatened to split the seams. Make-up *à la* Tammy Faye Baker had been applied with a palette knife. Ray couldn't imagine this shopworn Barbie Doll holding Max Berdahl in thrall.

Wearing impossibly high heels, she was perched on the edge of her desk scanning a sheet of paper. Upon seeing Ray, she dropped it and squealed. "Ray Rossini!" She ran to him in mincing steps, her arms open.

He cringed. *Lord. Take me now.* Standing rigid, he endured the hug and the huge breasts pressing into his chest. But the perfume was too much. He coughed, successfully dislodging her arms. "Hi, Carlene."

"Christ! I can't believe it." She stepped back and looked him up and down. "You haven't changed a bit. Just a bit more grey around your temples." She reached up to touch his hair but he dodged out of the way. "You're looking good."

When the compliment she expected was not returned, she shrugged. "What brings you here? And who is this handsome dude?" she asked, fluttering her false eyelashes.

Jimmy had long ago determined that anyone who used the word "dude" was a moron. His impression of her, which had been zero on a scale of one to ten, now slid into the minuses.

"This *handsome dude* is my partner, *Detective Sergeant* Tan." He emphasized the rank hoping it would give her a clue as to why they were there.

"How do you do?" Jimmy said politely.

Carlene, from a family hostile to police, didn't bother holding out her hand, sending waves of relief over Jimmy. "Detective Sergeant?" She frowned at Ray. "You're on the job?"

"That's right," he said curtly.

"What's it about?"

"Max Berdahl."

Her eyes widened briefly then quickly narrowed with caution. "Oh, yeah. I heard about what happened to him," she said dully. "What are you doing *here* then? He was murdered over your way."

"Can we sit down?" he suggested, pointing to the chairs inside the door.

"Oh, uh, sure." To her credit, when she sat, she tugged her skirt down and kept her legs together.

"We want to know about your relationship with Berdahl," Ray told her. "And this isn't an official interview. Just a chat."

"Hmmm, where have I heard that one before?" her tone sardonic. "First of all, I didn't have a *relationship* with him," she declared. "And even if I *did*, what would that have to do with his murder?"

"Maybe nothing. But we need you to fill in some holes in our investigation," Ray said calmly. "To begin with, can you tell me the circumstances of the weekend in April 2010 when you met him?"

She took some time to let this revelation sink in. That they had knowledge of this did not surprise her. They wouldn't have come without ammunition. But they couldn't know everything or else they wouldn't be asking her questions. She decided to cooperate, up to a point. "What do you want to know exactly?" she asked.

"Well, to begin with, how did you come to have such an interest in him?"

She recalled her first encounter with Berdahl. This was safe ground. "He was funny. Entertaining, you know? Full of enthusiasm. He had charisma."

"And he was young," Ray shot her a zinger.

She slowly licked her glossy lips. "Yeah. I like young guys. What's wrong with that? They're more fun than old farts," she threw back at him.

"And maybe more gullible?"

She cocked her head, and then snickered. "Berdahl wasn't gullible. He was sharp."

"Is that why you introduced him to the man who had property on the market in the Fraser Valley?"

Shit, how did they know about that? "He said he was itching to develop a large parcel. He had ideas. Plans."

"And you just happened to know someone who had just such a

parcel."

"Something like that," she acknowledged reluctantly.

"And you introduced him to Max. What was his name by the way?"

"Amadeo Curcio." She pronounced the Italian name slowly and correctly, and flipping the *r*.

Coor-chee-oh. No wonder the Ashton's couldn't remember the name, Jimmy thought.

"Did he own it?"

"No. He was working on behalf of somebody."

"Somebody offshore?"

"Yes"

"Offshore where?"

"Italy."

Ray nodded as he began to get a clearer picture of what was going on. "What was your relationship with Curcio?"

"Again with that word," she said angrily. "I didn't have a *relationship* with him, either. He was just an acquaintance I met at a wedding. We got talking and it sounded like he was trying to meet people in the business. So when he heard that I was a realtor, he suggested we could work together."

"Did he try to chat you up for other favours?"

She laughed. "You mean, was he trying to get into my pants?"

"You said it. I didn't."

"Of course. Men are always trying it on with me. But he was too old."

"Oh, yes. Pardon me. That seems to be your only criterion."

"And fat. They can't be fat, either."

"Well, *that* whittles it down."

She didn't miss the sarcasm. "I do have my standards," she said archly.

Ray had to bite the inside of his lip to keep from laughing. "Do you have his phone number?"

"No, I don't."

"You don't?"

"That's what I said."

"Do you have an address for his office?"

"As far as I know, he never had an office. He seemed to work from home."

"Do you know where he lives?"

"I don't know that, either." She smirked, enjoying her stonewalling.

"And I'm guessing you don't have a phone number for his residence either."

"You guess right."

"Well, how do you get in touch with him?"

"I *don't* get in touch with him."

Ray realized he had to rephrase that question. "Well how *did* you get in touch with him?"

"I had a cellphone number."

"Had?"

"You're batting a thousand."

Ray sneered. "So what was the deal? Were you supposed to suss out a prospect and then introduce him to Curcio?"

"Something like that," she admitted. "I told Max I knew someone who had just what he was looking for and asked if he would like to meet him."

"And I'm assuming he was interested," Ray surmised.

"He was. I called Curcio and he told me to bring Max to my hotel suite. So I did."

"Had you done this before?"

"Done what?"

"Worked with Curcio to find buyers for properties."

"No."

"So how was it that you paired up with him this time?"

"He heard that I was going to the conference and asked me to look for a possible buyer."

Ray was tiring of the sparring match. "So how much did you pocket from this arrangement?"

"What makes you think he paid me?"

"Oh, come on, Carlene!" Ray said, scathingly. "You don't expect us to believe that you did this from the goodness of your heart."

He faced a wall of stone.

"Did the deal include softening up Berdahl with sex?"

Under hooded eyes a slight sneer curled the corners of her mouth. Ray recognized the look and a chill crept into his bones. Her family was Calabrian, where the 'Ndrangheta held sway. They were vicious. You either became one of them, or learned to live with them. It suddenly struck him that Curcio might also be Calabrian and possibly Carlene was tied up in something bigger than even she realized. He didn't like where this was going.

"What are you implying?" she asked, coldly.

"What do you think? Are you going to tell me that a roll in the hay wasn't part of the deal?"

"That's right. I introduced them. That's all." Her chin rose defiantly.

"No. That's not all." He looked at her levelly.

"What do you mean?"

"We *know* you and Max had sex."

Christ. Where are they getting their information? She was beginning to feel trapped but decided to bluff it out. "You couldn't know any such thing."

"We know that by Sunday evening, he was following you around with his tongue hanging out. Anyone at the conference who knew you would know what happened. So, do you want to tell us what went down?"

She began fidgeting with the hem of her skirt, her long nails threatening to unravel the threads.

Ray waited her out.

She folded. "It started out as a lark. Honest. He was cute. When I brought him back to my room on Saturday night one thing led to another. And then he told me he was a virgin. I couldn't believe it. I thought it would be fun to give him the thrill of a lifetime. But he wouldn't go the whole nine yards."

"So you gave him one of your trademark BJs, and whatever else you pulled out of your bag of tricks."

Her face flushed.

"So, surprise, surprise, he winds up buying the property. Where did he get the money, I wonder? Could Curcio have pressured Max to borrow it from him?"

"That didn't have anything to do with me. That was between him and Curcio," she protested. "My part in it was finished."

"Was it? Do you think an innocent man who has had a taste of that kind of sex would just walk away from it? He knows he'll never get it back home where he's watched, morning, noon and night. When he came back here, was he begging for more?"

"Yeah, and he got it," she said, gloating.

Ray's evident disgust didn't faze her.

"What happened after that, Carlene?"

"He became a real pain in the ass is what happened. I finally had to tell him to shove off."

"Oh, a real class act, Carlene." For the first time, he felt some sympathy for Berdahl.

She brushed aside his comment and inspected her manicure.

"Well, somehow Max came up with the money," Ray continued. "And somehow he wound up dead a few years later."

Her dark eyes shot daggers at him. "That hasn't got anything to do with me. I told you, all I did was introduce him to Curcio," she said, ice in her voice.

"Sounds like nothing has got anything to do with you," he snapped off.

She stood up abruptly. "This so-called chat is over."

"Before we go, I want to give you some advice. And this is from an old friend. If Curcio should ever get in touch with you again, don't have anything to do with him. What do numbered companies and offshore money sound like to you? This guy is mixed up in money laundering, which, as you know, is a criminal offence. Worse, he could be behind the murder of the man who owned the last piece of land that Max finally got his greedy hands on." He paused then looked at her pointedly. "And I wouldn't be surprised if Curcio doesn't have your sexual liaison with Max in that hotel room on video somewhere."

She flinched. Ray had finally touched a nerve.

He pressed on. "He could blackmail you into working with him in the future."

"I don't need your advice," she said rigidly, but there was a tremor in her voice. She nodded toward the exit. "Now get out. And don't let the door hit you in the ass."

"Nice seeing you again, Carlene."

"Yeah. Fuck you, too." She flipped him a finger as she slammed the door.

Stepping from the air conditioned office into the outdoors was like stepping into a blast furnace. Shimmering spirals of heat rose from the pavement. Ray jerked his hand toward a small grocery store across the street. "Let's wait inside there for a few minutes and see what happens." They dashed through vehicles waiting for a light to change and entered the surprisingly cool store protected from the sun by a large cloth awning. In an instant, Ray and Jimmy were struck with the smells of fruits, vegetables and age still fresh in their memories from their days visiting Chinatown. To their ears, the sound of the creaky wooden floor was a refrain from an old familiar tune.

Startled by the appearance of two men in crisp short-sleeve shirts and dress pants, the ancient-looking Chinese man behind the counter stared at them, sharp eyed. While Ray took up a spot by the window, Jimmy quickly but surreptitiously displayed his badge and told him in halting Cantonese that they'd be leaving soon. The man was pleased to be addressed in Cantonese, however mangled. The policeman could have spoken to him in English. He shrewdly pegged his ancestry as Straits Chinese, which had its own dialect. He nodded, saying nothing, but curious about whom they were spying on. Gathering around the till, he and his few shoppers whispered animatedly.

It wasn't long before Carlene locked up, got into a light metallic blue Mercedes convertible and drove off. Ray headed for the street. Jimmy turned to the owner, bowed briefly and said "m goi." The excitement and the polite gestures made the day for the old man. And his customers.

"I can't figure out why she didn't threaten to call her lawyer the minute you asked about Curcio. I wonder what stopped her."

"Probably thinking about him. I'll bet she's peeing her pants right now. Just the mention of a video camera rattled her more than anything else."

"What do you think she'll do?" Jimmy asked.

"She'll go to her family for help," Ray said. "She stepped in it, and now they're going to have to clean up after her." Reaching the car, he stood thoughtfully by the passenger door. "I'll see if there's something I can do for the family's sake. Drop me off at my friend's place, would you? I'll probably be an hour or so."

Ray directed him to an old, well-kept house a few blocks away. Jimmy noted the address and took off for his own unscheduled meeting.

Chapter Thirty-nine

Ray almost fell back into believing it was a dozen years ago as he chatted with his old friend. Handsome in a Paul Newman sort of way, with the same blue eyes and warm smile, David Sanders radiated good health. Except now he sat in a wheelchair, immobilized from the waist down. What had begun as a routine traffic stop rapidly escalated into a drug take-down involving gunfire. During the melee, Sanders took a ricocheted shot in the spine from a .44 Magnum.

Rather than being pitied, he had become a role model for anyone suffering a major spinal cord injury. From the moment he began his rehabilitation, Sanders had focused on sledge hockey as a way to keep him motivated. After playing on adult teams and realizing how essential the game had become to his own mental and physical health, he became immersed in children's programs. Not content to simply coach, he wanted to do more. As a participant on championship teams and former public relations face for the police department, he became a speaker on the national stage, promoting the game and helping to raise thousands of dollars for equipment and team trips. It took him across the country to wherever an ice rink could be found.

Ray looked around at the many cups and awards, and marveled

at the resiliency, courage and generosity of his friend. "I gotta tell you, David, these honours of yours make me feel like a lay-about."

"Don't be a jerk, Ray. Where would we be without cops?"

Ray accepted the explanation, but was not placated. Even his own coaching contributions to peewee baseball now seemed to fall somewhere between dubious and incidental. "During the time you've been doing this, has there been one thing that stands out?" He thought Sanders would have to take a moment to think about it, but he answered without hesitation.

"Yes. A few years back, I went to Metula, Israel, which has an Olympic regulation ice rink. Interestingly, it's in The Canadian Centre. Of course, with a name like that you can guess which country built it. There are jerseys of Jewish players in the NHL hanging from the rafters. I put on a demonstration hoping to get some adults interested. There are a lot of Russian immigrants in the country and some are ex-soldiers who are in the same boat as I am. And most have played hockey at one time or another."

After closing his dropped jaw, Ray asked: "How did it go?"

He took a few moments before answering. "It's a work in progress. That's about all I can say. But lots of parents of kids with lower body injuries were enthusiastic. And that's showing more promise. Hockey in Israel gets a lot of support from Jews in Canada. There's a regular team of boys and girls from all faiths who are crazy about the game. They were in Canada a couple of months ago, and I tell you, Ray, there was absolutely no animosity between the kids or their parents, Jew and Arab alike. All they cared about was the game. The kids were billeted in homes and more often than not, there would be one kid from each faith in one room."

"You hear stories like this all the time. Makes the world seem like a better place."

"In my opinion, sports and the arts are going to be the saviours of this world in the long run."

"Isn't that the truth? Too bad we can't get more Arab kids

involved, then maybe they would stop blowing themselves up."

David's wife, who had been in the backyard watering the vegetables, walked into the room, pushing stray strands of wavy grey hair away from her olive-skinned forehead. "Hiya sweetie," she said to Ray, who got up and gave her a big hug.

"Hello gorgeous."

"Are you guys ready for some coffee and cake?"

"Depends," Ray teased. "I'm sorta spoiled in that department."

"Don't look a gift-horse in the mouth, Raimundo," she ordered, voice at full volume. Devorah Sanders was the rock that shored up David after he awoke from surgery convinced he was now only half a man. Her strength in her faith and belief in her husband kept the family from falling apart. The children had become proud of how their father had turned a tragedy into a triumph. As far as Ray was concerned, her name should have been etched on every cup and written on every award alongside the name of her husband.

"So, what you got, Rebecca of Sunnybrook Farm?" he asked cheekily, as she came in and stood looking down at him.

"Apple cake. My bubbeh's recipe," she said, hands resting on her hips.

Ray thought she had probably eaten a few of those cakes herself, but the extra pounds did not diminish her beautiful face and flashbulb smile. "I remember that cake. I wouldn't say no to a piece … or two."

"I didn't think you would." Her nose crinkled in laughter as she left for the kitchen.

The two men smiled at each other in shared thought.

Sanders shifted in his chair. "You said something about a case you were working on."

"Yeah. It's damned frustrating. We thought we had a strong lead, but everything fizzled out after we finished with our interviews. However, something did come up, and I want to run it by you. "

"Okay." Sanders looked intrigued.

"It's to do with Carlene Corrente."

"Carlene!? How is *she* involved?"

"About eight years ago she got herself mixed up with a guy called Amadeo Curcio. It looks like he's mixed up in money laundering through real estate schemes. She said that she didn't have anything to do with him anymore. I don't know how true that is. But I warned her not to do any more business with him—if you want to call it that—because the guy could be damned dangerous. He may even be behind a murder made to look like an accident. Does his name ring a bell with you?"

"No, but then again, I'm not connected anymore."

Ray knew how quickly retired cops were eased out of the loop, shunted aside like a piece of useless furniture. For some, it was too hard to take. Without a family or interests outside of work, they often took to drink or committed suicide. Sanders was fortunate to have both a supportive, loving family, and a passionate cause that gave him a reason to get up every morning. He didn't seem the slightest bit bitter that he was no longer included in cop gossip.

"Give me some background."

Ray drew a sketch of the case and Carlene's activities. He mentioned her reaction after he pointed out some home truths. "I don't know if she's going to take my advice, but I did put a little scare into her. At least I hope so. If it was anyone else, I wouldn't care so much, but…" he let his words trail off.

"You want me to talk to Bobby?"

"I would appreciate it, David."

Bobby Corrente had been their friend since childhood, playing hockey together into their adult years. Even so, they had a hunch that it was going to be an awkward conversation.

"I don't have to tell you that the Correntes are a tight clan and they've had some dodgy dealings with the authorities over the years."

"But Bobby's clean?"

"As far as I know. I haven't heard anything different."

"He's a good guy. Doesn't seem to be from the same family."

"Remember their reaction when they found out we were going to join the RCMP?"

"I do, and I had to hand it to Bobby who never bought into their belief that we were suddenly the enemy."

"Even so, he had to deal with the pressure on him to take sides."

"I thought he stick-handled that pretty well."

Sanders chuckled. "Now that I don't play regular hockey anymore, I don't see him much. But every once in a while he'll call just to shoot the breeze."

"Do you have any idea what his relationship with Carlene is like?"

"He hasn't mentioned her. But she's family, so he would be concerned. I'll call him and find out if he's heard from her. If he has, I'll see if she's said anything to him. If not, I'll ask him to drop by to make sure he gets the full story."

Devorah brought in a tray and wordlessly set out the coffee and cake, utensils and napkins. There was a noticeable change in her. As she turned to leave, Ray stopped her. "Aren't you going to join us?"

"What? And interrupt all your *fun*?" she snapped, dark eyes throwing out sparks. She emphasized the word with a flourish of her hand and walked out.

Ray looked at Sanders. "She's not happy that I came, is she?"

"It's not you, buddy. It's just the mention of anything to do with police work."

"I shouldn't have asked for your help," he said ruefully. He poured coffee for the two of them.

"Don't worry about it, Ray. It's not the first time an old colleague has been in touch for one reason or another. Usually something to do with a cold case. Devi knows that I'm not in any danger anymore, but it's still hard for her. She's a pretty rational person, but when she begins every day by looking after me, she's reminded of that night."

As though she had been listening at the door, Devorah edged back into the room. "I'm sorry, Ray." Her eyes glistened. "I really do love you and am happy to see you. I was just hoping that *the job* wasn't the reason for your visit."

Ray gestured apologetically. "It wasn't. Believe me. Something came up during an interview before I got here. Time is tight, so I thought I'd ask David for help. I guess it was a mistake."

"Devi, all I have to do is have a meeting with Bobby. It's not like I'm going to be out in the streets in the thick of it."

"Oh, I know, honey. I know. It's just me being meshuga. Just do what you have to do. If you need to see Bobby, have him come here. God knows we haven't seen him in ages."

"Anyone ever tell you that you're a mensch?" Ray said.

She grinned. "I'll bet you don't get to say *that* in your little British town."

They broke up in laughter.

No longer stressed, she joined them for coffee and apple cake. Moments later they were talking about their children, families and friends—as they had done so many years before.

Chapter Forty

When Jimmy pulled up to his childhood home, he was struck by the changes on the street. The two-storey house, which had once been considered large and grand, appeared dwarfed by the "monster homes" surrounding it. The new structures ignored the scale of the neighbourhood and size of the lot, taking up every available inch of space leaving room only for a few shrubs. In the face of such desecration, the Tan house remained intact, defiantly reminding everyone of what had been the norm—family homes with flower and vegetable gardens and neat lawns bordering the sidewalk. It was now an anomaly.

With his heart hammering, Jimmy walked with trepidation to the ornately carved front door, the only embellishment in an otherwise unadorned façade. He wasn't sure what to expect. The acrimony during his last visit was still fresh in his mind. But at least one person would be in his corner. He turned the tiny lever on the brass bell ringer and waited.

Moments later the movement of a lace curtain on one of the narrow windows at either side of the door was followed by the click of locks. The face that finally revealed itself spread open with joy. "Baba Tan Chi Mi," a scratchy voice greeted as he bowed.

Jimmy was embarrassed by the deference from the old man. He

was the house man who had served his aunt and uncle in various capacities for nearly fifty years. Jimmy returned the courtesy out of respect for the man's age and position, but sensed his discomfort.

Mr. Lim was Jimmy's childhood bane, meting out punishment as the traditional household tried to control and contain the rambunctious boy. To counteract the strict discipline, he also doled out as much love as necessary. That he was entrusted to raise the child and safeguard the secret of Jimmy's true parentage indicated the high regard in which he was held. As far as the authorities knew, Jimmy was the son of Tan Beng Siang and Tan Teck—Benny and Tess to English speakers.

Slipping effortlessly into Penang Hokkien, Jimmy greeted his former guru. "Lim Sin Seh." It was Lim who also taught him the martial arts of China. "Is Aunty at home?" Of course it was a rhetorical question because his aunt rarely stepped out of the house except to visit the barber who cut her hair. Even mah-jong games with her old friends took place in the dining room. Lim did everything "outside," the word she used to describe anything that did not take place within the house.

Lim's response to Jimmy's query was to lead the way to the back porch. Filing through the main room filled with finely carved rosewood furniture, painted screens, and artifacts of exquisite beauty. Jimmy was once again reminded of the glaring difference between the interior and exterior of the house. A large jade carving of a dragon, which had been removed during Jimmy's exuberant youth, had been returned to its honoured position. Had it been there eight years ago? He couldn't remember. He hadn't noticed much of anything then.

Lim motioned Jimmy to wait while he continued to the back verandah. The familiar odours of *nyonya* cooking filled the house, overwhelming Jimmy and returning him to the years spent within its walls. Sadness seeped into his soul.

"Chi Mi!?" His aunt's shocked voice broke his reverie.

Lim signalled to Jimmy.

Teck was sitting upright in a high-back rattan chair, queen of her domain, as it were. A small table held a red iron tea pot and two porcelain cups. It was obvious that the old man had been keeping her company. And why not? Her husband was now dead. Why should she sit alone?

As Jimmy came into her sightline, she stood. A rare honour.

So the respect is here. What about the love?

Her bearing was that of the aristocratic Straits Chinese of Malaysia. But any resemblance to the forbidding figure of Jimmy's early years faded away as she clasped his hands. "Chi Mi. It is good to see you."

Such a small gesture. Such commonplace words. But they bridged a canyon. Jimmy relaxed.

Still holding his hands she stretched back and let her eyes take him in. "And you are looking well."

"And you too, Aunty," he replied. "You never change."

Healthy and spry at seventy-three, Teck had a face almost free from lines, a secret she attributed to drinking a cup of hot water with lemon juice first thing every morning and great amounts of green tea thereafter. She released his hands and wordlessly waved away his compliment "Lim, get a cup for Chi Mi." To Jimmy, she indicated a chair nearby. "Pull up that chair."

Jimmy did as ordered.

"This is a surprise. Of course, I expected you before this," she admonished him, before settling back into her chair. "It's long past the mourning period and your uncle's ashes have already been returned to Penang." She paused. "How did you hear, by the way?"

"I phoned him," Lim said, returning from the kitchen with a tea cup. "He had to know. And *you* wouldn't call. You think the telephone will infect your ear drums," he teased her. He looked at Jimmy as he twirled a finger around the side of his head. "Ear worms," he laughed. The sound came out like crinkling tissue paper.

Jimmy wondered if Lim's years of smoking had led to throat or lung cancer.

"Oh, you silly old man. I just don't like them. You can't see the person so you don't know what they are really thinking. People lie on the telephone," she explained as she poured tea for Jimmy.

"There's a lot of truth in that," he agreed, enjoying the bantering in the relaxed atmosphere. Was this the same house?

"You would know, being a policeman. That's why you have to have face-to-face talks, isn't it? To get to the truth."

"And sometimes that doesn't even work. Some people are very good at lying."

Their eyes met in recognition of the lie they had lived for forty years. She looked down before replying. "That is very true, unfortunately."

Jimmy used the uncomfortable silence that followed to sip the tea. It was hot, but his aunt believed that drinking hot liquids in hot weather cooled a person down rather than a cold drink, which turned up the thermostat inside the body.

"Are you here long?" Lim asked.

"No. We will probably return to Vancouver Island later today."

"Who is 'we'?" she asked.

"My partner and I. We were here investigating a crime that took place over there. But we thought it might have originated here."

"So your reason was not to visit us," she stated, studiously avoiding any display of disappointment.

"No, Aunty, but I did need to talk to you to find out what the situation is within the family now."

She nodded. "They may still be concerned, Chi Mi. They wonder if you will return to Penang and take your rightful place. Beng Siang told wife number two that it would not happen, but her son still thinks that you will try to oust him and take over the family business."

"So Uncle Beng couldn't persuade them?"

"He did try."

"But it's been eight years since Father died," Jimmy argued. "Doesn't the fact that I haven't made a move to go back mean anything?"

"But there's so much money involved, Chi Mi," Lim said.

"Money doesn't interest me. Neither does running the business. I tried to tell Father that. I thought he finally understood."

"He understood, but he never accepted it. He kept hoping you would give up the foolish business of being a policeman and return home."

"Trying to make things right is not foolishness," Jimmy pointed out.

"And that is the other thing. They are afraid you will use your police background to ask the Royal Police to investigate his death."

Jimmy snorted. "I wouldn't ask that corrupt organization to investigate a dog napping, never mind a murder."

"You believe it was murder?"

"Of course it was!"

"Don't you want to find out who did it?"

"No. I already know who is responsible, and I don't want to get muck on my hands dealing with them. They've probably been bought off, anyway."

Her eyes fluttered briefly toward Lim. "So you will let sleeping dogs lie?"

"Yes. Father was not a father to me, so it's not important," Jimmy said bitterly. "All he was was a bank. Uncle Beng was my father. And you as well, Lim. Maybe even more so. And a fraudulent birth certificate might *say* you are my mother, but to me you are." He paused as thoughts clouded his mind. "What kind of father ships off his young son to a foreign country?" he asked, his voice vehement and filled with sorrow.

Teck kept her emotions in check, a skill honed after a childhood of knuckle rapping and nose pinching. This time she struggled, but her training prevailed. "It was because your mother died, Chi Mi," she said gently. "If she had lived, you would not have come to Canada." Then she reached over and touched his arm. "Don't you know your father sent you here because he loved you?"

Jimmy looked her, astonished. "What do you mean?"

"Your position as the firstborn son was a great threat. He sent you here to try to keep you safe. Didn't you know that?"

Jimmy's mind worked furiously, processing what he had just heard. "No, I didn't know that. I thought he just wanted me out of the way. That I reminded him of my mother."

Teck was crestfallen. "Oh, Chi Mi. My poor boy. I was sure Beng Siang told you." And now she could not control her feelings. Her eyes filled with tears. "You have lived with that thought all of your life." She reached into a pocket for a handkerchief and wiped her eyes. "It is my fault. I should have made sure you knew that."

Lim spoke up, the weakness in his voice gone, "It is *not* your fault! Beng Siang was responsible for this household. *He* is the one at fault. He should have told him!"

Jimmy saw that his visit was creating a rift between them. "Please. It is not the fault of Beng Siang or you, Aunty. It lies with my father for getting tangled up with that woman. She used her wiles to get a strong hold on him."

Lim and Teck exchanged a look acknowledging Jimmy's correct assessment. The three of them then sat quietly thinking of the tangled history of the family and how the rapaciousness of a woman led to separation, misunderstanding and murder.

"Anyway, after that family gathering here, I never did feel safe. I never knew if a relative or one of their minions would come here to kill me."

After some minutes, Lim caught the eye of Teck. Whatever passed between them was slight and subtle. He cleared his throat. "Chi Mi. With your permission, we will contact them again and tell them they have nothing to fear from you."

"Yes. Please do that. I've spent too much time looking over my shoulder. I just want to live a quiet life, doing my job."

"You like what you do?" she asked.

"Yes. Very much."

"Then, that is good. It is good to be happy in your work. But I think you don't make much money."

"It's not a lot, but it's enough for the two of us."

Another look passed between Teck and Lim. "Chi Mi. There is money here for you."

A buzzing cellphone broke into the conversation. Teck moved her head from side to side and looked up, agitated. "What is that?" Her hands flew all around her batting at some invisible bug. Lim and Jimmy threw back their heads, laughing. Any remaining tension vanished like fog in warm air. Jimmy pulled the still-buzzing phone out of his pocket as he stood. He quickly showed it to her then went to the end of the verandah where he took the call. Ray was ready to be picked up.

"You know, Chi Mi," she said to him when he rejoined them, "those things will give you cancer."

"*Now* who is silly?" Lim said. "You listen too much to babbling old ladies."

Jimmy made motions to leave. She stood up.

"The phone call means you must go now?" she asked.

"Yes, I'm afraid so," he replied.

She held out her arms, and they embraced for a long time. *And here is the love.* He felt the sting of tears and blinked them back.

She playfully pinched his waist. "No fat. That's good. You're a strong man."

"I have Lim to thank for that."

"Maybe your wife is a good cook, too?" she asked.

"She's an excellent cook."

"But no *nyonya* cooking," she jested.

He laughed. "We probably couldn't even get most of the

ingredients where we live."

They made their way to the front door. "Will you come again?"

Jimmy, touched by the simple request, promised that he would.

"Bring missus next time. I'll show her *nyonya* cooking."

"Her name is Ariel," he told her.

"Strange name."

"It's the name of a kind of angel," he explained.

She nodded. "And still no little Tans?"

Jimmy lowered his head. "My job. My situation. It was too dangerous. Now it's too late."

"But now you are safe. It's not too late. You must have children."

It was almost an order and Jimmy laughed. "I will talk it over with my wife."

"Good. Good." She squeezed his hand.

"We look forward to seeing you again," Lim said

As Jimmy drove off, he watched them in the rear view mirror waving until he was out of sight. His heart and spirits were light. The undercurrent of fear that he had lived with for so many years was swept away.

Lim turned to Teck. "What are you going to do about the money?" he asked her outright.

"I told him there was money here for him."

"I think he did not hear you."

"He's a policeman. He hears everything."

Chapter Forty-one

After Ray made a quick stop at an Italian bakery, they headed back toward the ferry. They were quiet. Their minds, rather than being focused on the case, were centered elsewhere. Neither seemed keen to talk. Loud rumblings from Ray's stomach finally broke the silence. Two pieces of apple cake weren't lunch.

"Do you want to eat something now or wait until we get on board? The thought of ferry food puts me right off."

"Yeah, let's eat first. I haven't had anything since breakfast."

Ray wondered what Jimmy had been doing while he was visiting David and Devorah. But he didn't ask. And Jimmy didn't offer.

"Right. I know a nice little French bistro just up a ways."

"Why am I not surprised?"

Ray laughed, patting his stomach. "Food is my life. Or haven't you noticed?"

"I wasn't going to say anything."

"Eh! Watcha yo' mouth." He peeled off the highway onto a busy street. Manoeuvring across two lanes of traffic, he ignored blaring horns and deftly drove into a shopping plaza. "That's it." He indicated a tiny café with a small French flag by the entrance. "Not a huge menu, 'but what's there is cherce'."

Jimmy grinned at Ray's imitation of Spencer Tracy. "I'll take your word for it, you being a gourmand and all."

The patio was deserted. Even sun lovers were taking cover from the heat. A young waitress poured ice water with sliced lemon into their glasses and read off the three items on the *table d'hôte*. They ordered, then immediately slaked their parched throats. As she walked away, Ray wondered if this was a summertime job for her—perhaps saving money for university. He thought about Gabby. She was becoming more and more interested in the restaurant. Maybe university wasn't in her future. It was a discussion he and Georgie would have to have with her pretty soon.

Jimmy interrupted his thoughts. "It was nice to meet David Sanders after hearing about what happened to him. I don't know what I would have done in those circumstances. Probably curl up into a ball and hope to die."

Ray put down his glass and shook his head. "No you wouldn't, Jimmy. You're not that kinda guy."

"I'm not so sure, Ray. That's a life-altering injury. It takes a special sort of courage to deal with it every single day."

"What's the alternative? Suicide? Drinking yourself to death? Overdosing?" He saw Jimmy do a quick surveillance of the room and realized his voice was rising. He continued, *sotto voce*. "You know, being a cop takes courage."

"Yeah, but it's not the same kind of courage," Jimmy countered. He thought of how vividly this played out in his own life. He had been only too eager to dump his job in this city and rush off to a little town because he feared both for his life and for Ariel, worried that she would wind up a widow. How courageous was that? It was just the opposite. It was cowardly. He was relieved when their food arrived and the discussion ended.

During the remainder of the journey they hashed over the case and their next moves. By the time Ray dropped off Jimmy, they had agreed on two things: the Berdahls would have to be questioned about the Sunnyvale project. If that proved to be on the up-and-up, then Max's life needed further examination because the motive for his murder had to be in there somewhere.

When he walked into the kitchen, Jimmy took hold of Ariel without a word and hugged her hard, nestling his nose into her neck. "Mmm. You smell so good."

"Wish I could say the same about you," she laughed. "You're a bit on the ripe side."

He hushed her with a long kiss. "Then let's get really ripe."

"Race you to the bedroom!" She pushed him off and dashed down the hall.

It wasn't until after they had showered together and shared a light snack that they talked about his visit to his aunt.

"So you think your family in Penang will finally believe you're here for good and not interested in going back?"

"I hope so. I'm sure that after Lim talks to them once more, they'll get it."

"What a relief."

Roger jumped up on his lap and began purring. Jimmy rubbed his cheeks and the cat settled down for more. "I couldn't believe how different the atmosphere was in that house, Ariel. You know, I wouldn't be surprised if Tess and Lim are lovers."

"With Benny barely cold in the grave?"

"Well he wasn't the hottest coal in the fire. Aunty Tess is relaxed now. Not stiff the way she used to be. The kidding between her and Lim reminds me of an old married couple who love each other a lot."

"Like us," she smiled.

He took her hand and kissed the palm. "Yeah. Just like us."

"I brought you a present," Ray said, almost shyly, handing Georgina a white box tied with string.

She gave him a shrewd smile. "I bet I know what's inside." She went to the counter for her scissors, cut the string and opened the box. "*Brutti ma buoni!* You sweetheart." She hugged him then popped one of the misshapen sweets into her mouth. "Yum. These really take me back."

Ray was glad he had made that little detour. He sighed and dropped into a chair. "Other than these and the visit to the Sanders, the trip was a total bust. This investigation is as cold as a well digger's ass. We've got sweet F.A. We've picked all the low-hanging fruit. Now we need a goddamn ladder!"

"That's too bad, Ray. But it did fall into place too neatly, don't you think?"

"Yeah. Seems like it now. We went steaming full speed ahead up a blind alley. But I'm gonna find whoever did it, no matter what. I still believe the Berdahls are hiding something. We're gonna bring them in again. And this time I'm not gonna pussy-foot around. Maybe I can rattle their cages a bit." He got up from the table. "I'd better call the Chief right now. Then I'm gonna take a hot shower. Wash off this grime."

"Do you want me to heat up a piece of lasagna for you?"

"No thanks, honey. We ate. But better open a bottle of wine. A few glasses are calling out to me."

Georgina watched him stomp off leaving a trail of gloom in his wake.

Wyatt sat at his wooden desk, one he had owned for many years. It was his first real desk. Solid oak and weighing a ton, it had been sitting on a street in front of someone's house with a "Free" sign stuck to it. The couple who owned it told him they were moving and it was too big for their new home. After no one had answered their ad, they decided to put it out front with the hope that someone would take it and look after it.

He did both. While he appreciated its sturdy appearance, what he most loved was the warmth in the wood grain striated with golds and browns. He placed it away from windows to avoid bleaching from the sun, and every three months he rubbed it with linseed oil. Sherilee teased him in the beginning but, sensing that it meant something more to him than simply a piece of furniture, she stopped.

Wyatt placed his elbows on the gleaming desk and folded his hands together to form a comfortable resting place for his chin. And brooded. Rossini's phone call meant that Max Berdahl's life would now be stripped bare. And Wyatt would no longer be able to protect the Berdahl family from scandal.

But first he had to rein in Rossini.

Chapter Forty-two

Friday, July 10ᵗʰ

Sober faces greeted Jimmy when he walked in at mid-morning. Tim Novak caught his eye, nodded toward the kitchen and got up from his chair. *Now what?* Jimmy wondered.

"There's been a dust-up between Wyatt and Ray," Novak whispered. "He went barreling out of here with his ears smoking."

"Okay. Thanks." He had barely put *derrière* to chair before Wyatt came out.

"Tan," he said, jerking his thumb toward his office. Jimmy obliged him. "Close the door." Wyatt pointed to a chair. Jimmy sat. "I've arranged for the Berdahls to come back in for a formal statement."

The fact that Wyatt had called Berdahl bothered Jimmy. This was supposed to be their investigation, and Wyatt's sensitivity to the Berdahl family could muddy the waters.

"You'll be handling the interview."

Jimmy let that bit of bombshell sink in. No wonder Ray had bolted. "Okay. When is this happening?"

Wyatt relaxed when he realized Jimmy was not going to protest.

"Monday, at one o'clock." He gestured with an open palm. "You understand, I had to keep Ray out of it. His biases are just too obvious. His ham-handed ways won't get us anywhere. We need kid gloves here. That doesn't mean we let them off easy, Jimmy. We need to put the screws in, but as gently as possible. I trust you to do that. You're more cool-headed than Rossini."

"That would include almost everyone in the squad," Jimmy ventured a bit of humour.

"Myself excepted, of course," he said, grinning. "I think that's why I'm able to put up with him. I've been known to boil over on occasion."

"I hadn't noticed," Jimmy said blandly, causing Wyatt to laugh.

"By the way, Ray gave me some background on the family involved in the Sunnyvale Estates situation. But he didn't get to the details. What's the story there?"

Jimmy recounted the tangled tale of the Ashton family, holding Wyatt's attention. "I visited Gordon Greenwood earlier this morning since he gave us what we believed was our first lead. As it happens, he thinks he saw some of Tyler's drawings at a local café called *Cupcakes and Coffee*."

"Wouldn't it be something if the boy turned up here?"

"It would. And better yet if father and son could mend their broken fences. It would be a nice side story to the case."

"Which seems to be all about fathers and sons," Wyatt noted.

Jimmy said nothing, but thought sadly of his own broken fence that could never be mended.

"What's next on your list?"

"Finding the murder weapon."

"Did Mr. Schwindt confirm that he left a maul at the house?"

"I'm meeting with him tomorrow. I thought it should be something mentioned face to face."

"You're right about that. It will be a shock to him if he did leave a maul behind and it turns out to be the murder weapon."

"Forensics found iron oxide in Max's skull. They said it was probably rust from the blade end."

Wyatt nodded then sighed. "You know, it irritates the hell out of me that we weren't able to handle this case without outside help."

Jimmy knew what he really meant. He meant Griffin. Not the RCMP detachment. Jimmy skirted that minefield. "Perhaps Verhagen will see that now. He's pretty proud of this community. Bringing in the RCMP might rub him the wrong way. Maybe he'll get us the money we need for more resources."

"Maybe. What *do* we need?"

"Check with Atkins. He could give you a better idea than I can. Forensics is not my area of expertise."

"No," he grinned. "You're our resident wordsmith and diplomat."

Jimmy thought a moment. "Well, in that case, can I put something to you?"

Wyatt raised an eyebrow. "Go on."

"You might want to reconsider your decision to withdraw Ray from the interview. He knows we're up against it here, and I'm sure he'll do a good job getting more information from the Berdahls without being ham-handed, as you say."

Wyatt rocked back and forth in his chair, oblivious to its squeaking as he considered the request. "No. I don't want to do that, Jimmy. Rossini is a fire cracker, and Berdahl might just light a match. This situation is too delicate to chance it. He'll get over it. You know what he's like."

Yeah. He knew. And now *he* was going to have to deal with Ray's wrath.

Chapter Forty-three

Saturday, July 11th

At first light, the tap, tap, tap of rain drops fell on the bleached-out boulders of Little Man Creek. By the end of the day, only their tips would be visible through the rushing water. The rain, which under other circumstances would be welcomed in the parched town, arrived as everyone was preparing for the Antique Car Show—another of Verhagen's planned entertainments that brought cash to the town's coffers. Because it began as a shower, there remained hope that the event would go ahead. The clouds had other ideas. It was not long before they opened the doors to their secret hoard and shared their coveted treasure. People fled for cover in their shorts and flip-flops.

Ray continued adjusting the roster for his pee-wee baseball team that was scheduled to play at five o'clock. When he could no longer hear over the thunderous downpour, he threw in the towel and began calling parents. Most had already figured out that it was a no-go.

"This is perfect, just perfect," he complained to Georgina sitting across from him at the kitchen table reading the paper. "It's been sunny for weeks and now, just because there's a game, it rains."

"It would have been too hot for them to play anyway if it was anything like yesterday. Maybe it's a blessing in disguise. After all, we need a good rainfall."

"Yeah, yeah, Miss Pollyanna," he grumbled.

She peered over the paper at her husband. "You're a real sourpuss this morning. What's going on?"

He took in a deep breath and blew it out. "A couple of things. First of all, there's Jack. When I told him I'd be coaching today, he got all shirty with me, like *he* was the coach and *I* was the bench coach."

Georgina felt a smile twitching the corners of her mouth hearing Ray using British slang and then imagining the scene. Jack Johnson just might come up to Ray's chin if he stood on tip toes. His baseball jersey hung on his shoulders like a flag on a windless day. But she knew that Ray's attitude about his team skirted the edges of some psychological disorder.

"I mean, it's not like I was completely absent. I was there as often as I could be. He knew that going in."

"Do you remember how we resented Leonora when she came back for Serena? You would have thought she was kidnapping her own baby." Seeing the cloud cross Ray's face, Georgina wished she could have bitten back the words. She knew he would be recalling his sister's arrival from Pesaro years ago to gather up her little girl after leaving her with them for almost a year while she sorted out her life. They had grown to think of Serena as their own. And the entire Italian community had adopted the two-year-old, showering her with love, trying to reassure her that she had not been abandoned by her *mammina*. But at the time, those in the know weren't too sure themselves. Leonora lived a quicksilver sort of life, never settling in one place or on one man for too long. And the father of Serena was just another stop along the way.

When Leonora reappeared, Ray and Georgina became

embittered and their anger was threatening to tear the family apart. Silvana and Umberto had intervened and after more than one meeting and several bottles of wine, they convinced them to accept the reality of the situation. Everyone was devastated when Leonora left with Serena, particularly Silvana and Umberto. She was their first grandchild. But something good did come from it. It became the impetus for Ray and Georgina to start their own family.

"Yeah, I remember. Like it was yesterday."

"Jack is probably feeling like we were. So give him some slack. You should be thanking him, Ray. After all, he took over your responsibilities when you got too busy with this investigation. He's been doing a good job, hasn't he?"

Ray snorted. "His idea of coaching is see the ball, swing the bat, hit the ball, run like hell."

She laughed. "I've heard that one before. Anyway, it's moot now that there's no game."

"Yeah. well . . ."

"So what's the other thing?"

"It's this interview on Monday. I'm pissed that Wyatt gave it to Jimmy. I was itching to get to Berdahl and give him a good grilling."

"Which is probably why Jimmy got the nod. He's more subtle than you are."

Ray snorted. "Like I said, you're a real ray of sunshine."

"Oh, don't be such a jerk. First you were bitching because this murder landed on your doorstep, and now you're whinging because you don't get first dibs at an interview. Get a grip and stop being such a pain in the ass. And if you've finished with your phone calls, go fix that closet door."

Ray levelled a long stare at her. "God. Where did I pick up such a fish wife?" He ducked and laughed, watching the paper sail over his head.

Rain was sheeting down. Jimmy pulled his hood forward as he

dashed under dripping branches to the front of the Schwindt's new house. Jimmy shook off most of the moisture and knocked on a plank-like door.

Seconds later, a man yanked open the door and eyed Jimmy through rimless glasses. "Sergeant Tan?"

"Yes, sir." He held out his hand.

"You're punctual." Gunther Schwindt smiled, clasped Jimmy's hand in a brief vise-like grip, pulled him inside and closed the door. They were in an enclosed porch containing slickers, gum boots, a variety of hats and other outdoor paraphernalia. Jimmy removed his jacket and boots.

"Hang your jacket on that peg." He pointed as he bent and rummaged in a box and quickly came up with a pair of spare Crocs. "I think these'll fit you."

"No thanks. These socks will keep my feet warm."

"Right. Okay." Opening the inner door, he waved Jimmy inside. "Come on in. It's a lot cozier in here." If there were such a thing as a human perpetual motion machine, it would be Gunther Schwindt.

Jimmy entered a spacious room warmed by a blazing fireplace. Large quarry-cut stones reached to the exposed beam ceiling and the raised hearth sported a wooden box on casters filled with split kindling and starter logs. An old black lab with a white muzzle snoozed on the warm wooden floor. Jimmy thought he was the source of the black hairs found in their former home, and murder site.

"That's Caesar," Gunther told him. "He's getting too old to jump up and greet visitors." At the mention of his name, the dog's ears and eyes responded briefly, his tail thumped a few beats and then he surrendered to the call of the floor.

"Have a seat," Gunther said. It was obvious that both upholstered chairs on either side of the fireplace were taken. An open book face-down alongside a pair of rimless glasses on a side table and a knitting basket on the floor identified their occupants.

Jimmy sat on the sofa. It was hard and might have been good for one's posture, but would not have been an inviting place for a nap. Gunther Schwindt, however, did not strike him as the kind of man who took naps.

Lean, and a bit shorter than Jimmy, Schwindt had a head full of curly grey hair, and weather-worn skin that highlighted his vivid blue eyes. His small nose and curved-up mouth added to his pleasant countenance. He had on heavy woolen socks and clogs and was wearing a blue and black checked mackinaw over a white T-shirt. Faded jeans were held up by whimsically patterned suspenders. Jimmy thought they were tiny rabbits.

A robust and attractive woman entered, carrying a large tray holding a carafe of coffee, mugs, a plate of pastries and napkins.

"This is Heather, my wife," he said with a smile. Jimmy could see that he was proud—perhaps of her or perhaps of himself because he had been smart enough to marry her. Or both.

She also wore a shirt and jeans. Although copious, they could not conceal her curves. Her brown hair was pulled back and tied at the nape of her neck. He noticed her hands as she placed the tray on a low table in front of the sofa. They were what Ariel would call "gardener's hands"—tanned and large knuckled.

"Hello Sergeant. I didn't know if you drank coffee. If not, I can offer you something else. I have tea or hot chocolate." Warmth radiated from her hazel-eyed gaze.

"Coffee is perfect. Thank you. This is very nice of you. The pastries look delicious."

"Heather is a magician in the kitchen. It's the reason I asked her to marry me," he said with a twinkle in his eye.

"It was how I trapped him," she grinned.

To Jimmy's ears these were well-worn sentiments but voiced with love.

Taking a few minutes to pour coffee and select pastries served to bridge the gap from the pleasant to the unpleasant. They knew that a murder had taken place in their former home. As with the public at large, they were not aware of how it had been committed. Now with a policeman in their home, they believed they were going to find out—and dreading the news.

When Jimmy said, "Mr. and Mrs. Schwindt," Heather put down her cup. Her husband swallowed his pastry. They looked at him with apprehension.

"I'm very sorry we are meeting under these circumstances," Jimmy apologized. "It's an upsetting situation to learn that Max Berdahl's murder took place in your former home."

"It's more than upsetting. It's shocking," Gunther Schwindt said, face screwed up in a frown.

Heather barely waited for her husband to finish speaking. "Do you know why? I mean, why did he choose *our* house?"

"Because it was empty. And in an out-of-the-way place with no homes around it."

They let this information sink in. "So this, uh, killer is someone local then," Gunther said.

"It appears so. It remains unsolved at this point. However, we have not finished all our inquiries. And until we find the person who did it, they will continue."

They nodded, waiting for the reason for his visit.

"One thing we have yet to establish is the murder weapon. We've been unable to locate it." He paused. "But we believe it was something used to split wood."

Gunther's eyes opened wide. He dropped his head into his hands. "Oh my God."

The meaning of Jimmy's words hit Heather. Colour bled from her face. She clenched her hands in her lap. "Are you saying he was killed with our ax? But that's impossible!" Her voice rose. "It's here—in our shed!"

Gunther looked up, his face drawn and pale. "He doesn't mean our ax, dear. He means the maul ... the old maul I used to use." He turned to Jimmy. "Isn't that correct, Sergeant?"

"We believe so." He paused. Then he asked the pertinent and painful question. "Did you leave it there?"

Gunther groaned. "Yes. Yes I did. It was on the ground wrapped in a piece of burlap ... behind a stack of chopped rounds."

"May I ask why you left it behind when you moved?"

"I don't use a maul anymore. I use a splitting ax. So I thought I would leave it for the new owners." He rubbed his head. "God help me."

Heather went over to her husband and stroked his shoulder. "You couldn't have imagined anything like this happening, Gunther. It's not your fault."

"But I made it easy for him," he reasoned.

Because the man was right, Jimmy said nothing. The killer must have thoroughly checked out the place, found the maul and from there planned how he would proceed. The presence of a weapon was a bonus.

"When was the last time you were there?"

"The first week of June. I went by because I was wondering why it wasn't selling after I dropped the price. The stairs needed a bit of shoring up, but other than that, the house looked fine."

"Did you walk around the property?"

"Yes. I did."

"And you didn't notice anything disturbed?"

Gunther scrolled through his memory. "Well, actually, I did. But I put it down to a bear."

"What was it?"

"There's an unused water tank just past the wood."

"Where the path narrows?"

"Yes. It's not easy to find. You'd almost have to know it was there. The handle was sort of exposed, which was odd. It's probably covered with blackberry brambles now."

Jimmy's mind was racing ahead. "How deep is it?"

"About five feet." Gunther began to follow Jimmy's train of thought. "You think maybe the weapon might be inside?"

"It's a possibility. We'll go back and look."

Jimmy was ready to leave. He was eager to take a look inside the water tank.

What Gunther said next came out of nowhere. "Max was always the unruly one."

This caught Jimmy's attention, his leave-taking interrupted. "Did you know him well?"

"My son was in the same class as Max."

At this comment, Heather glanced at her husband with a frown, her lips pressed together. When she spoke, her words were thick with emotion. "He once did something and asked Curt to take the blame for it."

"Oh, Heather. I told you it was just a teenage prank."

"Maybe," she said belligerently, "but Curt got blamed for it and he had to sit out an important soccer game. He was the goal keeper, too, and they lost that game."

"Curt lives in Britannia Bay, doesn't he?"

"He lives in the township. He's normally up north logging. But he came home when he heard from Stephanie about the murder and the involvement of our old house."

"Do you think he would he be willing to talk to me?"

"I don't see why not. But what could he tell you?"

"I don't know, but we're looking into Max's background for anything he might have done that would cause someone to kill him."

"Well, *I* would've gladly wrung his neck!" Heather said vehemently.

Chalk up another one, Jimmy mused. "I'm curious about something. If you had this unpleasant history with Max, why would you ask him to sell your house?"

The Schwindts exchanged a look then cast sideways grins at Jimmy. "It was penance."

"How so?"

"I laid a guilt trip on him. I knew that house was going to be a devil to sell. No other realtors would take it on without a huge commission. And even then they were reluctant. So I told Max that the least he could do for causing that problem for Curt would be to take on the house sale—"

"—*and* without a commission," Heather said with a note of triumph in her voice.

Gunther's face turned grave. "It will be a frosty day in hell before that house sells now. *If* it ever sells."

As they said their goodbyes, Jimmy looked closely at the suspenders. They *were* little rabbits. He pointed them out.

A smile spread across Gunther's face. "A gift from my grand-daughter."

It might be his last smile of the day, Jimmy thought.

Chapter Forty-four

The downpour put more than a damper on the day. With the cancellation of the antique car show at the last minute, profits took a drubbing as well. All the vendors packed up their food, souvenirs and other merchandise, counting up their losses as they did so. Justine's even closed early. By early afternoon the streets were empty of everything but water. After weeks of constant sun, the ground was baked to a brick-like hardness and could not absorb the inundation.

Georgina was in the den talking to her father-in-law on the phone. "I've called everyone on the reservation list to tell them we're going to be closed. And Marcus has put a sign in the window. I think we've covered everything, Papa."

"We've never been closed on a Saturday night," he said plaintively.

"I know. But it's a monsoon out there. When Marcus came home he said Centre Street was a river." Actually, what he did say, to Georgina's surprise, was that it reminded him of the arroyos in Arizona that had been carved out by flash floods. When did he learn that?

She heard a deep sigh on the other end of the line. "Well, I guess we'll just curl up in front of the fire with a *grappa*."

"Sounds like a plan."

The back doorbell rang. "I'll get it," she heard Marcus yell.

"There's someone at the door, Papa. I can't imagine who would be out in this weather."

"Dad! Mr. Tan is here," Marcus shouted.

"Sergeant Tan is here, Papa. Guess I'll go and see what's up. Have a nice time tonight."

"You do the same."

She opened the bedroom door. Ray, fully clothed, was asleep on top of the bed. Creeping in, she closed the door behind her. "Wake up, Ray. Jimmy's here," she whispered into his ear.

Ray snapped awake. "I'm not asleep. I was just resting my eyes."

"Yeah. And I'm Sophia Loren. Were you expecting Jimmy?"

Ray shook his head then swung his legs onto the floor, stood up and tucked in his shirt. "Maybe he's here to grovel."

"Oh, Ray," she admonished him.

When they saw Jimmy standing in the carport dripping like a drenched dog, they both laughed. With that, some of Ray's resentment melted away.

"There's an old chair," Georgina pointed out. "Drop your jacket on it." She paused. "But don't drop your pants."

"Jeez, Georgie," Ray scolded. "Have some class."

"Oh, come off it. I'm just having fun. I'll bet he's had some *real* propositions in his time. Right, Jimmy?"

"It comes with the territory," Jimmy said, as he took off his boots and entered the kitchen.

"Oh, don't be so modest. Would you like some coffee?"

"No, thanks. I've just had coffee with Mr. and Mrs. Schwindt."

Upon hearing this, Georgina put her hand on her son's back. "Okay. Time for us to get out of here, Marcus," she said, steering him from the room.

There was a moment of discomfort. But during Jimmy's account of his conversation with the Schwindts, Ray's accommodating nods and comments suggested that the rest of his grievance against his partner had dissipated.

"We've got to go back to the house right now, pissing down or not," Ray said.

"We need a couple of extra bodies and forensic equipment."

"And something from my garden shed," Ray added.

Adam Berry bustled about with a damp cloth in one hand and a spray bottle of sanitary cleanser in the other busily wiping the desk that he shared with Simon Rhys-Jones. He smacked his lips in disgust. "Yuck. Here's a piece of Simon's fingernail."

"I'm surprised he has any left," Craig Carpenter drawled, ignoring Berry's high dudgeon while acknowledging the Welshman's habit of biting his nails down to the quick. He rocked back on his chair and put his feet up on his desk knowing how it would irritate the fastidious constable.

Berry gave him a dirty look while he attacked the offending spot liberally and rubbed it vigorously with the cloth. Not for nothing was he called Chary Berry behind his back. "It's bad enough that we have to share our work station," he continued, running the cloth over the computer keyboard, "but couldn't he at least keep it clean for the next person?" Meaning himself.

The back door to the squad room burst open and banged against the wall. "Okay, kiddies," Ray bellowed. "We've got a job to do. Get into your glad rags and heavy boots."

"We're going out in this pisser?"

"Only if you don't want to be demoted, Carpenter."

"I can't go any lower," he grumbled as he got up and made his way to the locker room. Berry had not needed any warning. His adrenaline had kicked in, and by the time Carpenter strolled in he was already fastening his boots.

In the rain, the property's desolation intensified. Rain-laden branches limited what light there was from the leaden sky. The men made their way around the back of the house, placing their steps carefully on the pathway, now slick with mud. Knowing the location of the tank was one thing. Seeing it was another. Just as Schwindt said, it was tucked around the farthest corner of the house and buried beneath brambles. Jimmy could have kicked himself for not noticing this in his previous search. But then, neither had the others.

Ray had brought along his loppers and heavy-duty gardening gloves. He pointed to the vines with thorns as long as three-quarters of an inch. "Carpenter, you get busy cutting those and we'll pull them away." He handed him the loppers. "And for God's sake be careful."

They got about the work, gingerly cutting and lifting and removing the long vines that were intertwined like the snakes on Medusa's head. After half an hour of steady work, the lid was finally cleared. It was approximately eighteen inches square and made of cedar. A hinged metal handle lay flat in an indentation at the centre. Ray gripped the handle and, with a grunt, heaved it off, dropping it on the path. They gathered around and peered inside.

"Gosh," Berry said, "This isn't what I was expecting."

"Me either," Ray agreed.

They were peering into a concrete-lined hole that contained a large oval-shaped urn made of polyethylene. It looked to be about five feet across with a lid nearly two feet in diameter. According to Schwindt it was about five feet deep.

"You want to do the honours, Jimmy?" Ray asked.

Kneeling on the trampled grass, Jimmy reached down, unclamped the lid and levered it until it rested on its hinge. He shone the light into the tank. The hairs on the back of his neck stood up. "It's there," he said softly, and returned to his feet. The enormity of the find did not lead to eruptions of joy. Rather, they were quiet, understanding the magnitude of the moment.

Ray held out a hand toward Jimmy, who passed him the

flashlight. He got down on one knee and ran the beam around until it landed on the butt end of the maul handle. The head was resting in a foot of water. While large enough to hold five hundred gallons, no heavy rainfall for several months meant it was almost empty. "Adam, get that plastic bag ready."

Berry, startled at hearing his given name, fumbled as he unfolded the evidence bag.

Tugging on latex gloves, Ray reached in and grasped the handle. A shiver passed through his body when his hand touched the weapon that only three weeks before had smashed in the skull of a living human being. As he rose, the maul came into full view. The straight hickory handle was bleached and smoothed from years of use. The blade was thick like a sledgehammer at one end and thin and wider at the cutting edge. It bore no obvious traces of its last ghastly job.

Examining it closely, Ray shook his head. "This is really well crafted. Beautiful in its own way. It's a crime it was used to kill someone." After dropping it into the evidence bag, he retrieved it from Berry, who was visibly relieved.

When Chief Wyatt had been informed of the discovery, he immediately called McDaniel and Atkins whose responsibility it would be to photograph and detail the weapon before locking it away. But he knew they would contact a couple of their mates who would want to get in on the action. These were the constables and detectives who were tight with each other. It was a small clique of like-minded officers who were dedicated to the job. Wyatt was aware that this happened in every precinct, and while he did not condone it, he did not discourage it either. Several of them were waiting for the four men when they arrived at the station. They had gathered in the Incident Room looking at the weapon and listening to Jimmy as he once again related his meeting with Gunther and Heather Schwindt.

He was tired. It had been a long, draining day, and he wanted to get home. But he patiently answered their questions. Then he remembered something important and had to excuse himself. His phone call to Curt Schwindt was short and successful. He would meet with him tomorrow and with luck be armed with some facts that the Berdahls or Jari Tikkanen had omitted. He felt in his bones they were getting close to the third element of the crime. They already had the means and opportunity. Only the last one remained—the motive.

Chapter Forty-five

"I'm beat," Jimmy said as he slumped at the kitchen table with his legs splayed open, head resting against the chair back.

"You do look a bit worn around the edges," she said.

"I should be excited, you know? But finding that weapon was like a climax. You reach this pitch of intensity, then suddenly it's over and you're spent and all you want to do is sleep."

"Not according to the movies. The lovers always have a cigarette afterwards," she said.

He smiled at her oblique response. "Do they still have cigarette smoking in movies? I thought that was a no-no now."

"How would I know? When was the last time we went to a movie?"

Jimmy searched his memory. "When did *Crash* come out?"

"Around 2005, I think."

"That long ago? We've got to get out more."

"And go where, exactly?"

"Yeah, right. This isn't exactly Gotham City."

"Maybe not, but you're my Superman."

"Aww, Lois. You say the sweetest things."

Ray and Georgina sat on the floor in front of their free-standing stove drinking *grappa.*

"This was a great idea," Ray said as he leaned back on the sofa's skirt.

"I got it from Papa. He said he and Mama were going to do this tonight since the restaurant was closed."

"You know one of the best things about living here?"

"What?"

"Being allowed to have a wood-burning stove."

"It's only because we're in a rural area. If we lived in a city it would be a different story."

Gabriella sauntered in wearing pajamas. "This looks cozy."

"Yeah, and we're keeping it that way. No more than two persons allowed," Ray told her as he placed a large split log on the fire and adjusted the air flow lever.

"Did I say I wanted to join you? I just came out to get some juice. Sheesh." And she sauntered into the kitchen, ignoring her amused parents.

Ray put his arm around Georgina and listened to the rain beating on the roof. "You know, if we were young again, we'd just get some pillows and blankets and sleep right here."

A few seconds passed. "We're not too old to do that," she said mischievously.

"Yeah, you're right. Why not?"

They pulled off the sofa cushions and placed them on the floor. As they were laying pillows and blankets on top, Gabriella came back in with juice and pastry.

"What *are* you doing?"

"Something we used to do years ago," Georgina said.

Her mouth dropped open. "You mean you're going to *sleep* here?"

"What does it look like?" Ray said.

She shook her head as she left the room. "I have the weirdest parents."

The telephone rang. "Oh, hell," Ray said. Just this one time, he was tempted to let it go to message, but knew he couldn't. When he saw the call display, he was glad he didn't.

"Hi, David. You got news?"

"I do. It appears that Curcio has disappeared," he said.

"I hope you don't mean what I think it means."

Sanders laughed. "No. No body in a block of cement. He went back to Italy."

"He did, eh? Do you know when?"

"Well, from what Bobby could find out, it was several years ago—maybe even right after that property deal."

"Really? That's interesting. Carlene must have known that."

"I don't think so because when Bobby told her, he said she almost fainted with relief."

Ray laughed when he heard that. "I'll bet she did."

"How's it going?"

"We're making progress, David. That's about all I can say at this point."

"Well, good luck, my friend."

"Thanks. And thanks for helping out. We appreciate it."

He returned happily to the warmth of Georgina and the makeshift bed.

"You can't be serious!" Lana's mother said in disbelief.

Lana laughed at her mother's face filled with mock horror. "I know. It's even surprising to me," she said. They were Skyping, something Lana had come to appreciate. A phone call to San Francisco didn't begin to satisfy her thirst to connect with her parents.

"But it isn't as if you're a *Canadian*, Lana. You must still *feel* like an American ... don't you?"

"I'm not sure what that even means anymore. I've lived there and in Paris and Vancouver and now here. I feel more international than national. And what does it matter, really?"

"But Britannia Bay is such a backwater, darling," her mother said, mouth pulling tight.

"Oh, Mom. Don't be such a snob. It isn't like you," Lana chided. "It's charming and has just about everything I want and need."

"But you must miss *something.* It can't have *everything* you need."

Lana did a swift brain scan. "Well, I do miss teaching. I miss the students."

"What about culture?"

"There's all kinds of it, Mom. Little theatre, an excellent concert series, choirs, painters and potters. You name it."

Her mother looked doubtful. "What about men? Are there any marriageable ones there or are they all doddering about on the golf course?"

"I don't want to get married, Mom," she stated, knowing what would follow.

"You can't let that awful experience with Niall ruin your whole outlook. Marriage to a wonderful man would complete your life."

Lana refused to respond, lapsing into silence. Relief from the uncomfortable interlude came by way of her father's voice.

"Claire. Where are you?"

"In here, Robert, trying to talk some sense into Lana," she turned away from the monitor.

Then both their heads were crowding onto the screen. "Hello Punkin," her father greeted her with a big smile.

"Hi, Dad. You look wind-blown and sun burned."

"Of course I do. I was out on the Bay. Perfect sailing weather. So what's this about your mother trying to knock some sense into you?"

Before Lana could answer, her mother turned to look at him. "She says she's never going to return to San Francisco, and that she's perfectly happy in that tiny village full of Britishers."

"Oh, Mom," Lana laughed. "They're Brits. Not Britishers. And as for returning to the States ... I'm not sure where I am with that."

Her father took a moment to absorb the comments. "Is that true?"

Lana felt squeezed in an emotional vise. She saw the pained expression on his face and the concern in her mother's, and suddenly she began to question her own mind. "Well, nothing is written in stone," she said, surprising herself because she had thought it *was*—that Britannia Bay would be her final destination.

After ending the conversation with the usual familial platitudes and a promise from her to think about her decision, she poured a large brandy.

Delilah had drifted off with a smile on her face. The Blue Jays had won 6 to 2 against the Royals in Kansas City, making up for the loss yesterday. They were finally playing five hundred ball and she was looking forward to tomorrow's game. With this rain and her poor eyesight, she was not going to chance slipping or tripping on the pavement walking to church. So the game would be her entertainment for the day. Not the sermon.

She had seen Jimmy coming home during her evening snack of crackers, cheese and grapes. "That poor man seems never to be at home anymore, Tabitha," she said. Curled up on a chair at the other side of the table, the cat flicked her ears upon hearing her name. "I feel sorry for cops' wives. What kind of life can it be for them?"

Her own life had been simple and structured. Melvin went to work at the garage at eight in the morning and came home happy at five thirty, day in and day out. She had gardened, canned her fruit, berries and vegetables, cooked and baked and cleaned, got the kids ready for school, and kicked them out of the house to play during the summer. On rainy evenings, they would play Monopoly together. After buying their first TV, they had all the laughter and drama and news they could want right in their own living room. Life was good.

Thankfully, she fell into a deep sleep before memories lurking in the corners of her mind crept out, tormenting her nights.

Chapter Forty-six

Sunday, July 12th

Robyn Lewitski came close to pinching herself when a clean-cut, clean-shaven man walked into the station early Sunday morning. Close to contemplating retirement after ho-hum years of fielding calls and steering visitors to the appropriate person, she was experiencing the excitement she had dreamed of when she applied for the job twenty years before. That it took a murder to achieve it did take the edge off somewhat. Now when someone came through the door, she wondered: *Is this a suspect or a witness or someone with information?* Rather than: *Is this person going to be a waste of police time?* "Can I help you?"

"Good morning. I'm Curt Schwindt," he said while removing his wet jacket. "I have an appointment with Sergeant Tan."

"One moment, Mr. Schwindt." She walked back to Jimmy, whose head was bent over some documents. "Jimmy, Curt Schwindt is here."

Jimmy grabbed his notebook and pen, and walked to the front with her. When he laid eyes on him, he realized that Schwindt's gangly body easily cleared six feet three inches. Where did his height come from? His parents must have asked the same question. After introducing himself, he led him toward the visitor's room.

Robyn intercepted them. "Can I hang up that jacket for you?"

"Thanks very much. I hope you can find a place where it doesn't drip on everything." He answered in a clear voice, not too soft and not too loud.

"No problem," she said, taking the garment. As he ambled off, she noticed his slight limp and wondered if it was a work-related injury. Logger's lives were filled with danger.

"Thanks very much for coming to the station, Mr. Schwindt."

"Please call me Curt. Coming here was to protect your sanity ... and maybe mine, too." He laughed. "The kids are playing indoors. And we have a new baby."

"Congratulations." He pointed to one of the upholstered chairs into which Schwindt settled his loose-jointed torso. "How old are your other children?"

"Three and six."

Jimmy could only imagine the mayhem in the house. "That's a lot of work."

"We thought we'd have kids early while we still had the energy for it."

Jimmy nodded. "I've heard that before." He glanced at his notepad as a hint that the personal conversation was over for now.

"Just a sec." Curt pulled a cellphone out of his pocket, looked down to check for messages, then changed the sound setting.

As he did, Jimmy noticed that his ginger hair was thinning at the crown and yet his father still had a thick head of hair. His face was long, as was his nose. Nothing about him resembled his parents. He wondered if he were adopted. He wondered if Curt wondered the same thing. "We wanted to speak to you because we need more information on Max Berdahl's personal life. Your dad said you had gone to school with him."

Curt interlocked his thick, long-fingered hands, resting them on his thighs. "Not *with* him. We were just in the same class."

"It's a small school. What about interactions?"

"There weren't that many at first. He spent most of his time with one of his cousins."

"Who would that be?"

"Jari Tikkanen. But when he graduated, Max began hanging around us."

"Who do you mean by 'us'?"

"Well, there was a small group—actually there were several groups of guys. You know, you just sort of gravitate to where you're comfortable."

Jimmy nodded. "How did Max fit in?"

He took his time before responding. "Not very well. He was likeable enough, I guess. But there was always this feeling that he was trying too hard. You know what I mean?"

"I do. Your parents mentioned an occasion when he asked you to take the blame for something he did."

A hardness transformed his face. "Yeah. I was stupid. I still regret doing it because it left a black mark on my school record. And my reputation for a while."

"Do you mind me asking what it was?"

His answer came reluctantly. "Max thought it would be funny if the toilet lids in the men's locker room were glued down."

Jimmy envisioned the scene and consequent fall-out. He started to smile then caught himself, but not soon enough.

"Yeah, I guess it's funny when you look back on it, but it sure wasn't at the time."

"No. I'm sure it wasn't. How did you get the blame for it?"

"The administrators were going to question everyone. Max came to me and begged me to say I had done it. He told me about being a JW and about shunning and things like that. He said what he did was strictly forbidden and that his dad might even be kicked out of the church. Or whatever they call it," he added caustically.

"But why choose you in particular?"

"Because everyone else told him to get stuffed, and I should have done the same thing," he said, regret written all over his face.

"Why didn't you?"

"Search me. I guess I felt sorry for him."

"So you confessed to something you didn't do."

"You got it."

"And missed out on an important soccer game because of it."

"Yeah. The coach didn't believe I had done it, but he was pressured by the principal to punish me by keeping me out of the game. It was the worst thing they could have done." Curt looked at Jimmy. "It still hurts."

"High school is an impressionable time in our lives." Jimmy's mind drifted to Tyler Ashton.

"Yeah. You reminisce at high school reunions. It's like things happened yesterday. And you still have the same feelings."

"So why do you think Max pulled that prank?"

"I think he was making a statement. Like he was one of us. But we wouldn't have done anything like that. He had no idea how we … operated, I guess you could say. He'd only been around us for a few months, not years. We were like brothers."

"What happened afterwards? Did you still let him hang out with you?"

"Hell, no!"

"Did your friends think you had done it?"

"Of course not!"

"What about your teachers?"

"Some of them told me they didn't believe I was responsible, but they didn't suspect Max. Or if they did, they didn't tell me."

"Your dad said he was 'unruly.' Do you know what he meant by that?"

"There were always rumours about him, especially when he and Jaxon got their own place."

Jimmy's alert level picked up a notch. "When was that?"

Curt rubbed the back of his neck then moved it from side to side until it cracked. Jimmy checked his desire to do the same.

"I'm not sure exactly, but Max had already started to work for his dad." He thought for a minute. "It must have been around 2003."

"Did you hear any of these rumours?"

"The only one I remember is that someone gave him a bloody nose. And the only reason I remember that is because I got a good laugh out of it thinking someone finally beat him up."

Jimmy scribbled a note. "Do you have any details about that situation?"

"No. But my sister probably does. She's a nurse and she was working at a clinic when Max came in."

"What's her name?"

"Greta."

"Does she live here?"

"Not now. She lives in Vancouver."

"Do you have her phone number?"

He paused. "You think this is important?"

"It could be."

Curt took out his cellphone, found her number and read it out to him.

Jimmy wrote it down. "Thanks very much. I'll give her a call."

"Just leave a message if she's not there because she's on shift work."

"Okay." He put his pen down. "Looking back, can you think of anyone who would have a reason to murder Max?'

"Maybe my mother." He laughed then shrugged. "No. I don't know anyone who would really do it."

"Thanks very much for this, Curt."

"No problem."

Jimmy rose signalling that the interview was over. When Curt unfolded his lanky frame, Jimmy remembered something. "Have they found a use for the wood damaged by the pine beetles?"

"Yes. Furniture. Some of the patterns are really pretty."

"I'm glad that something good has come out of something bad."

"Yeah. Funny how that works."

They walked into the foyer and Jimmy offered his hand. There was tremendous strength in Curt's hands. So far that was the only similarity he could find with his father. "I hope your new baby is a joy to you and your family."

"She is. She's an absolute delight ... when she's not screaming her head off."

Robyn watched as the pair laughed and shook hands amiably. She sighed with relief. Curt Schwindt was in the clear.

Jimmy closed the door to the Incident Room and called Greta Schwindt. She was home. After a short conversation, she gave him another contact. When he heard the name, his pulse quickened. He quickly thanked her and made a second call.

Agnetha Tikkanen was astonished to be hearing from the Britannia Bay police. She had known about Max's murder, of course. When she began answering Jimmy's questions in detail, he interrupted her. Would she be available to come over for a formal interview? Yes, she could come tomorrow. In fact, she seemed gleeful at the prospect. There was steel in her voice. Afterwards, Jimmy drew three more lines on the white board and entered the relevant information. He then called Ray.

"This changes the complexion of the case," Ray agreed. "It doesn't seem to be about the real estate development at all. There was something going on in his personal life. Something that happened before he went over to the mainland."

"Even so, I think we should mention the money laundering scheme to the Berhdahls. See if they had any knowledge of it. Then we hit them with this new information."

"We?" Ray asked sardonically.

Jimmy felt the jab and answered with more force than he

intended. "Listen, Ray. I'm not happy that Wyatt cut you out of this interview. And frankly, I don't want to carry it all. I'll see if I can change his mind." He omitted telling Ray that he had already tried.

There was a moment of silence on the line. "Don't do that," Ray said. "I don't want you pleading my case for me. I'll call him myself. Besides, I'm used to eating crow," he chuckled. "And Wyatt will love being magnanimous."

"Maybe if you give him the latest information he'll be more agreeable."

His reading was correct. Upon hearing the latest update, Wyatt's comments revealed a softening in his attitude toward his senior officer.

Ray felt it and struck. "Jimmy suggested we split the interview. I take the property deal and he takes Max's fight."

Wyatt waited before answering. "I would prefer that it was the other way around," he said, blithely ignoring his original refusal. "If you think you can do the interview without letting your personal animosity get in the way, then okay."

"Now that we have information that won't allow them to stonewall us anymore, I don't feel that way anymore."

"All right." He grunted a satisfied sigh. "Looks like those goose eggs are finally turning golden."

Chapter Forty-seven

Monday, July 13th

"Okay, everybody. Listen up," Ray said, waiting until the low-level buzz trailed off and all eyes were directed toward him. "We're expecting a woman this morning who may have relevant information on the Berdahl case. Apparently there was an altercation that took place between Max and an unknown person several years ago and Jaxon knew about it. Interestingly, that conveniently slipped his mind. So we're hoping it'll be enough to give him the jab in the bum he needs to fess up. And maybe we'll find out who this person was."

"How does the woman happen to know about this?" Foxcroft asked. "And why didn't she come forward earlier?"

"We only have part of the answer to the first question. As for the second, we hope to find out when we speak to her."

"So, you're not going to enlighten us."

She said this with a blank face, but Ray thought he heard an undertone of challenge in her voice. "You'll be fully *enlightened* as soon as we are," he said biting off his words.

McDaniel had started to say something, but on hearing Ray's

prickly response he changed his mind.

"That's all for now. So stay tuned." With that, he returned to the Incident Room and plopped down next to Jimmy. "You know, there's something about Foxcroft that—" he began complaining when his cellphone buzzed. It was Nigel Wright from Dirt Riders. The biker who had seen an unfamiliar rider on Townshipline Road was back from Ontario and in his shop at that moment. He said if Ray could come there now, the man would wait for him. Ray leaped out of his chair, "I'll be right there." He pocketed his phone. "Bike shop," was all he said to Jimmy before dashing out the door.

Jimmy had checked the ferry schedules and expected Agnetha Tikkanen at around eleven o'clock. When Mary Beth knocked on the Incident Room door at ten thirty telling him that she had arrived, he frowned. He had been planning on a "chance" encounter between her and Jaxon at one o'clock to push him into telling the truth. Now he wondered how long he could drag out her visit to ensure that the fateful meeting and its hoped-for repercussions happened.

"I've put her in the visitor's room," she added.

Agnetha Tikkanen had hung up her raincoat but had not taken the chair offered by Mary Beth. She chose to walk about the small room, filling it with her nervous energy. She almost jumped when Jimmy came in. "Oh!"

"Hi, Miss Tikkanen, I'm Sergeant Tan." He held out his hand, which she shook enthusiastically. "But please call me Jimmy."

"Oh. Okay. Call me Agnetha."

"Thank you very much for coming over."

"It wasn't a difficult decision, believe me," she said, a touch of venom in her voice.

Except for her six-foot height, nothing about Agnetha Tikkanen would have elicited a second look. She had a medium build, medium length brown hair in a simple bob, and a face that could only be described as pleasant. Jimmy guessed her age to be in the mid-thirties.

"You're here earlier than I expected. But that's okay," he assured her.

"I decided to fly over. I didn't want to waste time on the ferry. The airport here is so handy. Besides I don't like driving in the rain." Her quick, short sentences matched her agitation.

"How did you get to the station?" There was no regular taxi service in Britannia Bay, a situation that caused some seniors considerable inconvenience.

"I called an old friend after I spoke with you yesterday. She picked me up at the airport and dropped me off here."

He noticed that she did not say "a family member," yet there were two other Tikkanens listed in the telephone directory. Although she looked nothing like Jari, what were the chances they would not be related? Zero to none. "Would you like a coffee?"

"I would love a cup." Then she smiled self-consciously. "You wouldn't happen to have any of those famous doughnuts around, would you?"

Jimmy saw the opportunity he was hoping for. "I'm assuming you didn't have breakfast."

"No, I didn't."

"Would you like to have something brought over from Justine's?"

She smiled. "That would be great. I could murder a Danish. Justine used to have the best."

"She still does," Jimmy said wondering when she last visited the village. "Let's see what we can chase up." *What luck. This should lengthen her stay.*

When he exited the room, he was pumped. Novak noticed. "You've got a spring in your step, Sarge."

"Things are looking up, but at the moment I'm trying to initiate a devious plot. I need you to do me a favour." He handed Novak a twenty and told him what he wanted.

Later, seated in the kitchen with fruit-filled pastries and a fresh pot of coffee, Agnetha began to relax and talk about growing up in Britannia Bay. She mentioned playing with Jaxon and Max, and Kirsten Saarinen.

"Would that be Kirsten Tikkanen now?" Jimmy asked her.

"Yes. Do you know her?"

"I talked to her husband about Max." Jimmy remained noncommittal about his proximity to the victim and his relatives.

"And I'll bet everything came up smelling like roses," scorn tinging her words.

"You could say that."

"You won't find anyone in the JW congregation who will say a word against him. No matter what he's done. It's a given."

"Then why are you so forthcoming about what happened to Max?"

She wiped a napkin across her mouth before answering. "I was shunned—disfellowshipped. I became a non-person. Everyone, and I mean everyone including family, turned their backs on me." Her voice dripped with resentment. "So in a way, I'm getting back at them."

Ray spotted the road bike outside of Dirt Rider. It was similar to most bikes—cleaned and polished until you could floss your teeth in the chrome mirror. It was a pity that the streaks of rain and spatters of mud from the road destroyed all the hard work.

Nigel Wright was in the back of the shop talking to a short, thin man dressed in rain pants and obligatory black leather jacket. A bright yellow poncho hung on a hook dripping water onto the floor.

"Hi, Mr. Wright," Ray said in a tone he might use with the kids on his baseball team. Friendly. Not authoritarian.

"Hello, Detective Rossini." He turned to the man next to him. "This is Mr. ... uh ... the man I was telling you about." Wright realized for the first time that he did not know the biker's last name.

Cash transactions left no trail.

Ray held out his hand, "Thanks very much for coming forward."

His hand was rough, and his sun-damaged face was criss-crossed with lines, aptly reflecting his vocation. "Yeah, yer all right," he said.

Ray didn't know what the hell that meant, but he did know that the man's words and British accent would have been easier to find in East London than Hampstead Heath.

"As you know, we are interested in anything or anyone unusual you saw on Townshipline Road recently."

"I bin thinkin' about it ever since Nige 'ere told me. I wrote down everything I could remember." He reached inside his jacket and pulled out a folded square of white-lined paper that he opened with as much care as he would an origami flower. He handed Ray the few sheets. The events were numbered, dated and detailed in hand writing that was as neat and even as one would expect from an English grammar school lad—not from someone who more than likely did not even finish school.

After carefully reading all of the notes, Ray looked up at the unidentified man. His smile was genuine. "This is perfect. You have a remarkable facility for detail, Mr. ..."

"Featherstone. Alfred Featherstone." He glanced shyly at Wright, who had cocked his eyebrows.

"And your—" Ray was going to say *writing* but changed his mind. "—penmanship is excellent ... so clear."

Featherstone ducked his head then raised his eyes to Ray. "Blimey. Yer 'avin' me on." A puckish smile transformed his face.

"Not at all."

"Well, me Mum did say it might come in 'andy one day."

"Well, your mother was right. Thanks very much for this." After tucking it away, he held out his card. "Your account seems to cover everything, but if you happen to see or think of anything else, please call me."

Featherstone was trying to remember the last time anyone handed him a business card. *Never* came to mind.

Ray turned to Nigel Wright. "Thank you, Mr. Wright. We appreciate your help very much."

"You're entirely welcome."

As Ray left the shop, Wright turned to the rider. "I didn't know your last name was Featherstone,"

"It ain't, mate. It were Featherstonehaugh. But me ol' man shortened it 'coz it took too long to write."

"I had no idea shunning was so ... so ... inhumane." Jimmy, who was rarely at a loss for words, now found himself searching for descriptions of what he had just heard. Her story had rattled him.

They had returned to the comfort of the visitor's room.

"It's hard for someone outside the JW congregation to comprehend, Sergeant." Her own voice was steady, faltering only occasionally during the discourse. She had spoken of it so often in front of groups that her inclination to cry had long since passed.

Jimmy continued to shake his head with disbelief. "I'm thankful religion hasn't been a part of my life."

"But you know, it can be a comforting thing. You belong to a very tight community that is supportive. You understand each other and know your place and how to act. You socialize and do business together. There is no need to interact with worldly people."

"Worldly?"

"Those who are not Jehovah's Witnesses."

"So from all you've told me, I'm guessing the Berdahls were behind your being forced out."

"Yes. They were."

"You said yesterday that you would be happy to give a statement about how Max got his black eye and cut lip."

"*And* broken finger," she added.

"Would you mind being videotaped as well?

"Not at all."

"There's something else … uh … something rather delicate I would like to propose. And if it's too much, just say so."

She was intrigued. "Fire away and I'll tell you."

"First of all, would it be too emotional for you to see the Berdahls up close again?"

"I don't think it would bother me. But I doubt the opportunity would come up."

"As a matter of fact, Stefan and Jaxon will be here at two o'clock."

Her mouth formed an O and she took in a sharp breath. "Really?"

"They've been asked to come in for a further interview because we were not convinced they told us everything the first time around."

"I'm not surprised."

"The thing is, we were hoping that if Jaxon saw you, he might be pushed into telling us the truth. He would assume you told us the whole story of Max's injuries and so he would have to do the same."

"Ah. So I'm to be the honey trap."

"In a manner of speaking," he smiled.

She tried to suppress a wicked smile, but it got the better of her.

Chapter Forty-eight

Delilah pushed her walker up the wet street, its basket holding a bag of groceries. She hadn't wanted to be out, but the rain had let up a bit and she needed bread, eggs and milk. It was her bad luck that the earlier showers had given way to a cloudburst just as she reached the corner of her street. Her plastic raincoat covered her head and body, but the handles of the walker became slick causing her hands to slip. As she adjusted her grip, her foot caught on a chunk of loose asphalt. She stumbled. The walker slid from under her. She tumbled, throwing out her right arm to protect her face. Landing hard, she yelped in pain.

Pascal, who had been piling pruned branches into his truck bed, saw a wheeled walker rolling down the street. He dropped the last load and ran to see what had happened. An old lady was lying on the pavement moaning, her face and hands severely scraped. He crouched down and gently examined her face and lacerated hands.

"Who are you?" she rasped through her pain.

"Pascal," was all he said.

"I think my wrist is broken," she whimpered.

He took a closer look. She could be right, he thought. "What is your name?"

"Delilah."

"Where do you live?" he asked her.

"Right here." She flicked her eyes toward her house.

"I am going to carry you inside. Okay?"

She nodded, noticing his accent.

"Where is your key?"

"In my right-hand pocket."

He took out the key, lifted her easily while supporting her wrist and carried her inside. A cat leaped off the window sill and fled the room. He was about to lay Delilah on the sofa when she stopped him.

"Put me on that recliner," she said. He carefully placed her in an old pink chair and covered her lap with a pink knitted throw that was lying on the sofa.

"Bend your arm. Put your hand on your shoulder," he demonstrated. "Hold your elbow with the other hand."

Delilah did as she was told.

"I must make a splint and a sling. And clean your scrapes."

"There's a wooden spatula in a jar on the kitchen counter. And I have old sheets in the linen closet. Just rip up one of those."

"You have ice? And pain killers?"

"No, but I have frozen peas. I have Tylenol in the bathroom cabinet, and cotton balls and rubbing alcohol." *For years I didn't use any of this stuff. Now it seems I need it all the time*, she thought.

After Pascal finished tending to Delilah, he said: "I will get someone to take you to the hospital."

"Thank you very much, but first, go and get my groceries, please" she requested. "And my purse," she suddenly remembered. "It's in the basket." Her anxiety overrode any pain she was feeling.

He quickly retrieved the walker. "Now we get you to ER."

"Can you get Ariel from across the street?"

He shook his head. "She is not home. I will get the lady I work for."

"Who is that?"

"Lana Westbrook. She lives behind Mrs. Tan."

Delilah nodded. "I know her. But first put the milk in the fridge."

He smiled. She reminded him of his *grand-mère*.

Lana, making icing, was singing *I'm Gonna Wash that Man Right Outa my Hair* when Pascal rapped on the patio doors and came right in—something he had never done. Lana looked up with surprise. She saw his harried face and shut off the mixer. "What is it?"

"The old woman, Delilah, she is injured. She fell on the street. Her wrist, it is broken."

"Oh my gosh!"

He turned and ran back the way he came. She grabbed her jacket and dashed out behind him. When she entered the living room, Lana blinked. There was so much pink everywhere that it took a few seconds to locate Delilah buried beneath the afghan. "Hi, Delilah. Are you in lot of pain?"

"Not now. Your ... man here took care of everything," she showed Lana her sling and nodded toward Pascal, who hovered like a mother bird over a wounded chick.

Lana glanced at Pascal, wondering if he knew what Delilah was insinuating. His expression hadn't changed. "Pascal takes care of my garden," she explained.

"Are you sure he's a gardener and not some kind of medical person? He knew exactly what to do, you know."

Pascal tensed and a guarded look passed over his face. But he quickly adjusted and attempted a smile.

"I'm sure. Now, I'll take you to emergency." She ran home to get her car.

"Where is my purse?" Delilah became agitated. "It was in my walker basket. It has my medical card in it."

Pascal frowned at her forgetfulness and wondered if she was suffering from early dementia or just in shock. He pointed to the walker beside her chair. "Do not worry, Madam. It is here." She grinned at being called a madam.

They were about to load her and her purse into the car when Delilah turned to Pascal. "You're French-Canadian, aren't you?"

He hesitated, not wanting to correct the old woman. "*Oui*," he replied.

"I don't know much French, but I do know how to say *merci beaucoup*."

While wincing at her pronunciation he graciously responded, "*Pas de quoi*." It was the thought that counted.

As Lana made her way to the highway, Delilah related the details of her fall. "I've talked to Council about the ruts in the road but they're taking their own sweet time getting around to fixing them. I think it's time I spoke to the mayor myself."

Busy adjusting the windshield wipers to accommodate the heavy rain, Lana listened with only half an ear. Not being familiar with the winding highway, her focus was on the road. Not on Delilah's words.

"Pascal is very nice. I've never had much use for French-Canadians. They were nice until de Gaulle came here and got them all riled up about being free ... as if they weren't already. And then everything had to be printed in two languages and it cost the government a fortune to do that. *And* there isn't one single French fisherman on the west coast ... but all the regulations have to include French. They should be in Japanese, or Norwegian. Not French."

Lana finally tuned into her rant. It wasn't the first time she had heard this sentiment about the Québécois, but the instances were gradually waning.

At the hospital, they walked slowly up to the registration desk. "We need a wheelchair," Lana told the receptionist, who turned and shouted out the request.

Seconds later an orderly brought out a chair and helped Delilah into it. As soon as she was settled, she handed over her medical card.

Lana took a seat against the wall. After a few minutes she heard Delilah's raised voice. "Why do you need to know that?" And then: "My neighbours are more helpful than *she* is."

The receptionist was obviously asking about next of kin, and while Lana didn't know much about Delilah, she was saddened to hear her response.

With her intake information complete, Delilah was wheeled through the doors into the ER ward. Curious, Lana peeked into the room teeming with patients and staff. It was then her eyes settled on a very tall man in blue scrubs. There was something familiar about him—was it his hair?—but before getting a good look at him a nurse approached her and said they were taking Delilah to X-ray. She suggested Lana wait in the lobby where it was more comfortable and which had a small cafeteria. At the thought of food, Lana realized she was hungry. It was just past noon.

First she texted Ariel since cellphone use was not permitted. She gave her the news and told her not to come to the hospital as they would probably be back in a couple of hours or so. After buying a sandwich, a Nanaimo bar—something she knew she would regret—and a cup of coffee, she picked up a magazine and found an empty table where she ate while reading the recipes. Washing down the last bite of the bar and thinking it wasn't that bad after all, she checked her text messages. Ariel had invited her and Delilah back for dinner. She gave an update and reply and was putting the phone away when the man she had noticed earlier in the ER came into the lobby. No longer dressed in hospital scrubs, he was holding a helmet and dressed in motorcycle clothing.

Lana froze.

Chapter Forty-nine

Stefan Berdahl's face was mottled with anger as he led Jaxon
through the station doors. Chief Wyatt's phone call requesting them
to come in again was bad enough. But asking him to bring in Jaxon
was beyond the pale. How was his son supposed to heal when he
was being harassed by the police? And for what reason? What could
Jaxon possibly know that would help find the person who murdered
his brother? And what did they have to clarify that demanded a
second interview? He turned to say something to his son but stopped
when he saw his face.

Jaxon's eyes were focused on the foyer. All the blood had drained
from his face. Stefan followed Jaxon's gaze. Sitting outside the
visitor's room was someone he had hoped never to see again. *What is
she doing here?* Puzzled, he pulled Jaxon aside and whispered the
same question.

"I think she knows, Dad," he said, voice quavering.

"What do you mean *she knows*? She knows what?"

Jaxon's head dropped. "I think she knows about the fight."

"What fight? What are you talking about?" Berdahl hissed.

As Jaxon started to answer, Ray interrupted their tête-à-tête.
"Good afternoon, gentlemen. Come this way please."

Berdahl wanted to strangle him.

Filing past Agnetha, Jaxon willed his jelly-like legs to keep moving.

Agnetha was wrestling with her own will, wanting to say hello but knowing nothing good would come from it. The Berdahls walked by her as though she didn't exist.

Seeing the mixture of grief and resignation on her face, Jimmy crouched next to her. "Agnetha."

She tore her sight away from the receding backs. "That hurt, even after all these years of coming to grips with it."

"I'm sorry. Maybe this was a mistake."

"Don't be sorry. It wasn't. I offered to do this. I just thought I was stronger. But I'll be fine. It's actually done me some good because it reinforced my decision to leave this town." She stood, straightening her back. "And I hope I've caused some trouble for the Berdahls," she smiled grimly. "I'll call my friend now and be on my way."

"Do you have time for tea or coffee?"

"Yes, I do. I'd love a cup of tea, thanks."

Jimmy shook her hand. "It was a pleasure to meet you. I know people always say they wish someone the best, but I mean it."

Her hug was awkward but heartfelt. "Thank you."

He went up to the counter. "Mary Beth, Miss Tikkanen will be expecting a friend to pick her up. She's going to wait in the kitchen. Would you mind making her a cup of tea?"

"Not at all." Mary Beth had been watching the drama, and even though she could hear nothing, it had been a mime show worthy of Marcel Marceau. But not in the least comical. She had transcribed Agnetha's statement and her heart went out to her. A cup of tea was the least she could do.

That Ray would be involved in the questioning only added to Stefan Berdahl's exasperation. What was this fight? What did Jaxon mean when he said she knew about it? What did she have to do with my sons? What does any of it have to do with Max's death? "I still don't understand why we've been called in again. And why does Jaxon have to be here at all?" he complained aggressively to Ray, worried for his son and wondering where this investigation was headed.

"I believe Chief Wyatt explained that a few issues have arisen since the first interview, which had us wondering if either of you failed to mention them or just forgot because of the strain you were under."

"I can't imagine we did either," Stefan Berdahl stated.

Ray ignored his comment. "Please take a seat. As with your last interview, this session will be recorded and videotaped." He began the preamble giving the date and time and listing those present. "I'll now turn over the questioning to Detective Sergeant Jimmy Tan."

Hearing that, Berdahl relaxed. But Jimmy cut straight to the chase. "We have discovered some details about Sunnyvale Estates that—"

"Sunnyvale Estates?! Berdahl blurted out. "What has *that* got to do with Max's death?"

"Since the attack on Max appears to be driven by revenge, we were looking for someone who may have had a reason to murder your son and brother. During our inquiries, we were directed to this project because it appeared there were events surrounding it that could have provided us with a suspect."

"I find that very hard to believe. Everything about that development was on the up and up."

Jimmy smiled to himself. Berdahl had just given him an opening. "Did you know that the numbered company that registered the original two parcels was a front for a man in Italy who was laundering money?"

"See here," Berdahl sputtered. "Are you implying that Max was in collusion with a criminal?"

"He may not have been aware of the back story. The owner had purchased that property and he needed to sell in order to get his equity out. I'm simply pointing out that your son was conveniently useful."

"He may have been, but he got that land at a good price," Berdahl boasted.

Jimmy thought of Edna Pitchko and the Ashton family. The choler that had been festering began to bubble up. He took a moment to push it down. "What about the middle parcel? Do you know how your son came to acquire it?"

"Yes, the woman living there had to go into care and so she sold it."

"And do you know *why* she had to go into care?"

"No, I don't."

"Well, let me give you a bit of history, Mr. Berdahl," he said harshly. It was not a bit of history, however, but the detailed account given by Lettie Ashton.

As Jimmy launched into the narrative, Ray was smiling to himself. *And Wyatt thought* I'd *be hard on the Berdahls. He should be watching* this *show.*

Jimmy wrapped up. By now he was gripped with anger. His voice was cold. "And that is how your son came to own Mrs. Pitchko's land."

"How dare you imply that Max would do these things," Berdahl fumed in full denial.

Jimmy pulled out a copy of the transcript of the interview with Lettie Ashton. "It's all here, Mr. Berdahl. You can read it yourself." He held it out.

Berdahl took it but rather than reading it, he looked at the last page. "It's not signed."

"Mrs. Ashton is physically unable to write. The notarized original is being couriered to us. A copy will be available for you should you want it."

He flung the transcript onto the table. "I can't see what this has to do with Max's death."

"His actions seriously affected a family, Mr. Berdahl. You can see why there would be a lot of hatred directed toward him. Perhaps enough to murder him. What he did calls into question Max's character." Then Jimmy stepped out on a limb. "And frankly, we are finding things out about him that suggest he is not the man you thought he was. However, revealing these details won't serve any purpose."

"This is outrageous!" Berdahl recoiled, his face rigid with rage. He scraped back his chair about to get up.

"There's more, Mr. Berdahl. Something that happened *here*. A tragic event about which you know nothing." He paused, taking in Berdahl's startled reaction. "But Jaxon does."

Chapter Fifty

Throughout Jimmy's verbal assault, Jaxon felt faint. He feared what was coming. Seeing Agnetha Tikkanen had shaken him. All the lies that he and Max had told their father would now come out. How could he bear that? How could he face his family? The congregation? He began to quiver. A sheer veil of perspiration covered his face.

Ray noticed his agitation, but had no sympathy for him or for any of the Berdahls. He let Jaxon stew for a few more minutes while he made a show of removing from a folder the printed and signed transcripts of both Greta Schwindt and Agnetha Tikkanen. He placed them on the table fussily squaring them up. Then he looked Jaxon full in the face and fired the first shot. "On Saturday, the fifteenth of July, 2006, Max came home with …" and here he picked up Agnetha's statement. "… a black eye, a split lip and a broken finger. Is this correct?"

"What's this?" a shocked Berdahl interjected, mouth agape.

Jaxon's eyes flew open. He struggled to keep them from straying to his father. "Uh …" He squirmed and looked down, unable or unwilling to speak.

Ray answered for him. "It seems that Max was involved in a nasty altercation with a man that led to a fight and Max wound up going to a clinic to be patched up."

"That's impossible!" Berdahl sputtered as he stood.

Ignoring his outburst, Ray continued. "Did Max tell you what it was about, Jaxon?"

"Jaxon, don't say anything!" Berdahl ordered his son. He waited, prepared to be obeyed.

"I have to tell them, Dad," he pleaded. "It needs to come out."

Berdahl's face paled. He slumped back in his chair watching his carefully crafted world collapse around him.

Ray pressed on. "Are you aware of the circumstances of Max's injuries, Jaxon?"

"Yes, I am," he answered quietly.

"Could you please start at the beginning and give us the details as best as you can remember them?"

Jaxon nervously cleared his throat. "Max came home all upset. His lip was swollen and cracked. There was dried blood on it and his eye was puffed up and black and blue. He said he was sure his finger was broken and we had to get to a clinic right away." The dammed-up words poured out like a waterfall. He took in a deep breath and let it out slowly as his tense body relaxed.

"Did he tell you how he came to have these injuries?"

"Not right away. But on the way to the clinic, he kept repeating, 'Oh, my God.' I knew that it had to be bad because Max would *never* blaspheme."

"What happened when you got to the clinic?"

"We were shown to a cubicle and told to wait a few minutes for the doctor."

"So while you were waiting, did Max tell you what happened?"

"He said he had killed a little girl's dog." He paused. *"It was an accident!"* he protested, defending his brother.

"Where did this take place? And how did it happen?"

"On Landry Road." At this point, Jaxon reiterated Agnetha's information, adding that Max had come around a corner too fast, braked hard and thrown out gravel, which caused the girl to release her grip on the leash.

"What about the fight?" Ray asked

"Max got out to see if the dog was injured. The man was shouting that Max had killed his daughter's dog. Max tried to apologize, but when he saw that the guy was going to hit him, he tried to hit him first. That's when he broke his finger. The guy punched Max in the mouth and then in his eye. If it wasn't for the little girl screaming, Max said the guy probably would have beaten him to a pulp. But he went back to her and Max jumped in the car and got out of there as fast as he could."

A bit of air left the room. Berdahl shifted uneasily in his chair.

"Did he describe the man?"

"He just said that he was big. He towered over him."

Ray thought that wouldn't have been difficult considering that Max had been Napoleonic in height. "How did you keep this incident from your father?"

Jaxon gave a soft moan. "We had to lie to him. We told him that Max got it playing squash." He turned and looked imploringly at his father. "I'm so sorry, Dad."

Berdahl's face was set in stone.

"Thank you." Ray closed his folder and looked at the wall clock. "The interview has been terminated at 2:45 PM."

A distraught Stefan Berdahl got up and walked out of the room, not waiting for his son.

"Can I ask you something?" Jaxon asked Ray.

"Certainly."

"Agnetha Tikkanen was working at the clinic that day too, wasn't she?"

"That's right."

"I thought so, but I wasn't sure until today. She must have overheard us."

"She did."

"I thought she lived in Vancouver."

Ray stared at him evenly. "She does."

There was a beat before a jagged smile creased Jaxon's mouth. The irony was not lost on him.

Chapter Fifty-one

Lana drove quickly, the visions of the biker on the ferry and the man at the hospital blurring together. Was he one and the same person? She wasn't certain, but the similarities were too striking to be dismissed. She needed to talk to Jimmy.

"Sit here, Lilah." Ariel and Lana guided the frail woman to the kitchen table where they settled her into a chair.

"What do you think of this cast? Pretty snazzy, eh?" she said to Ariel. "They gave me a choice of colours, so of course I chose pink."

Ariel laughed. "Of course. Is there any other colour?"

"Cheeky. Mmm ... something smells good," she said, sniffing the air.

"It's lemongrass, carrot and ginger soup," Ariel told her.

"Oh, ginger. I love ginger. I like spicy food. Most old people don't, you know. As a matter of fact..."

She rattled on like someone high on cocaine. Ariel wondered what the hospital had given her. As she turned back to the stove, Lana, who had been dancing with impatience, sidled up to her.

"When will Jimmy be home?" she whispered.

"Any minute now," Ariel said and peered inquisitively at her.

"I need to talk to him right away."

Ariel was ladling out the soup when Jimmy opened the door.

She nodded her head towards Lana and made talking motions with her fingers.

He got the message but first hung up his coat and greeted the patient. "How are you doing, Delilah?"

"No worse for the wear," she chirped and followed Ariel's hands from pot to bowl. "I'll be a lot better when I get some of that soup into me."

"Ariel's cooking could give Lourdes a run for its money." He gave Ariel a quick kiss on the cheek then gestured to Lana to accompany him to the den.

He closed the door. "What's up, Lana?"

She wrapped her arms around herself. Jimmy noticed she was shivering. "Can I get you a sweater or something?"

"No. No. I'm not cold. It's something that happened at the hospital." She pulled out her cellphone. "Do you remember this picture I sent to you? The one I took on the ferry the Friday evening of the murder?"

"Yes, I do." She had Jimmy's full attention.

She took a quick breath. "Jimmy, I'm certain I saw him today in the emergency room, wearing scrubs. Then later I saw him leaving in biker's clothing."

The sterile environment. The unidentified biker. The clues fit together like pieces of a puzzle. "You're certain?"

"Absolutely." That she might have been sharing a table with a cold-blooded killer shook her to her core.

Lana had never been questioned so thoroughly by police officers before. In fact, the only time she had *been* in a police station was to report her car being vandalized when she lived in San Francisco. But here she was, sitting in an interview room being recorded and asked to remember the smallest detail about this stranger. It hit her that she was possibly the only person who knew where the killer had been after the murder and where he was now. It frightened her.

She couldn't stop shaking.

Chief Wyatt brought her a hot coffee and water. She was cold, and her mouth was dry. She needed both. Grateful for her help, he was also solicitous of her safety. "And you're absolutely sure he didn't see you at the hospital?" he asked her for the second time.

"Yes, I'm certain of it."

He nodded. "Then I think we have everything." It was the signal to turn off the recording equipment. "I don't think I have to tell you how significant this information is. It's a huge lead."

She was out of words and could do nothing but nod.

"I can see that you're frightened. But since he didn't see you, you'll be all right."

"We can go now, Lana," Jimmy said to her. "Ariel can warm up the soup for us."

"Thanks Jimmy. I'll take you up on your offer." For the first time that day, Lana could smile. "I'm suddenly famished."

"That's always a good sign," Wyatt said. After the two of them left, he turned to Ray. "So he most probably deep-sixed the evidence off the ferry."

"And you can be sure he knew where the video cameras on the car decks were located," Ray said. "The only wrinkle is that the British biker said the stranger he spotted was riding a Kawasaki dirt bike. The suspect needed a bigger bike with paniers to carry the stuff he brought to the crime scene."

"Not necessarily. Not if he had a good sized back pack. In any case, we'll put a watch on the hospital. Then we'll see what he's riding. He left at around one thirty this afternoon, so maybe his shift starts at five o'clock. *If* he's working, that is." He paused in thought. "Dussault is on graveyard now, isn't she?"

"Yeah."

"Call her and tell her to cover the parking lot an hour before and after five. Have her use her own car. If he shows, we'll get all his vitals from the licence number."

Chapter Fifty-two

When Lana and Jimmy returned to the house, he was struck by how quiet it was. "Did Delilah go home?"

Ariel was taking soup bowls and side plates from the cupboard. "No. She's sleeping in the spare room. First she was flying on whatever drugs they gave her at the hospital. Then she crashed. Her face almost fell in the soup. I had to practically carry her down the hall. She kept mumbling about Tabitha. So I went over to make sure she had enough kibble."

While Jimmy left to check on Delilah, Ariel asked her how the interview went.

"Nerve wracking. I'm just glad it's over. All the details they want you to remember. I mean, your mind goes numb after a while." She started slicing a baguette sitting on a cutting board. "Speaking about details, when Delilah was asked at the hospital about her next of kin, she made quite a fuss about not wanting them notified. Do you know what that's about?"

"Mm-hmm." Ariel began ladling out information as she ladled out the soup. "Lilah has a daughter, Val. And they're not close. In more ways than one. First, she lives in Vancouver with her husband." Jimmy chose that moment to return and sit at the table. "I'm just giving Lana the lowdown on Delilah's daughter," Ariel told him as she put the bowl of steaming soup in front of him.

"Oh. Right. Carry on." He picked up his spoon. "I'll close my ears and open my mouth."

Ariel smiled at Lana. " Jimmy hates gossip."

"Not if it helps solve a crime, I don't. I just don't like gossip gossip."

"Okay, Mr. Self-righteous. We'll wait until you're gone," Ariel said.

"You have to go back to work?" Lana asked with surprise.

"Yep. We need to make plans for tomorrow now that you've provided us with a possible suspect."

They ate. Jimmy left. The dishes were cleared away. "I could do with a scotch. How about you?" Ariel asked.

"I wouldn't mind a *wee dram* after a day like today."

"Right. I've got just the thing." Reaching into the back of a cupboard, she brought out a bottle of Glenmorangie.

Lana laughingly attempted a whistle. Ariel poured a generous portion of the amber liquid into Waterford tumblers.

"Cheers," they toasted and grimaced as the first sip of the strong liquid slid down their throats.

"Aye, this will warm the cockles of your heart," Ariel laughed. Then she picked up the thread of the conversation. "Lilah doesn't see Val and her husband very often. Not that she'd want to," she added.

"I got that impression."

"Val wasn't the daughter Delilah was hoping for. She wanted a nice girl who went to church and believed in the Bible and was charitable. Val wasn't like that at all." She paused. "But Scott was."

"Scott is her son?"

"Was." Ariel sighed.

"Oh," Lana felt the weight of it. "So ... I'm assuming that he died."

"Yes. In 1989 in a terrible plane crash. He was a paratrooper on his way to some kind of military exercise with the Americans in Alaska. It was in the winter and the weather was foggy. The plane plowed into a snowbank and split apart. Some men were killed immediately. Scott was taken to a hospital and lived for a few days. He was only twenty-five."

"God. How awful." Lana looked down, surprised to discover that her glass was almost empty. She drained it. Ariel did the same and poured them another.

"And Lilah still believes in Jesus. This is a big bone of contention between her and her daughter. Val started mocking religion after Scott died because Lilah was praying all the time for his recovery. She would say things like, 'There's no guy in the sky who hears your prayers,' and so on. That's blasphemy to Lilah because she's positive that Jesus guides her daily life and that God has a plan for everyone. Her faith is strong."

" 'The world of fantasy fills the gaps in people's knowledge'," she said.

"That's deep."

"It's not mine. The French writer, Fred Vargas, wrote that."

"Well, he's right."

"He's a she, actually."

"Oh, that's interesting."

Lana thought about some of the uncharitable things coming out of Delilah's own mouth during the trip to the hospital. "Delilah doesn't seem like a particularly pious person to me."

"She's not a nun, that's for sure." Ariel snickered. "She's full of mischief. But she does some really sweet things. At Christmas she goes to most of the houses on this street and gives everyone a box of chocolates. Same for the cashiers at Bayside Foods. Everyone knows her and they all have a nice word to say about her."

"It seems like she's made a sort of family for herself with the people in the town."

"Uh-huh. And in the church, of course."

They sat quietly and finished off their drinks. "Would you like another?"

"Gosh, no. I'm already feeling the effects. I'll be lucky to walk a straight line home."

"Maybe it'll help you sleep tonight."

Lana nodded. "I may have a hot bath ... and a brandy for insurance."

Later, as she soaked in the lavender-infused water and sipped her insurance, Lana thought that in the last little while more brandy was going into her body than into her baking.

Chapter Fifty-three

Tuesday, July 14th

Constable 3rd Class Jean "J.D." Dussault was hunkered down in her brand new Jeep Cherokee eating a warm provolone, tomato and mozzarella ciabatta. A slim stainless steel thermos of steaming black coffee rested in the cup holder. *If you have to be on stake out, at least you can go first class*, she thought. No stale doughnuts and lukewarm coffee for her.

This was the first lone surveillance she had been given since joining the department. In her excitement at the opportunity, she stupidly told her partner about the assignment. The usual lip gnawing and eyebrow knitting evolved into an evening of unrelenting nagging. Quit her job or else. She chose option two. She loved being a cop and nothing and nobody was going to interfere with that. She wasn't wedded to this woman—not like she was to her job. It had been around longer than *she* had, for God's sake.

She was contemplating the sticky business of finalizing the relationship when the familiar rumbling of a big Harley caught her attention. She checked the dashboard clock. Four forty-five. Putting the sandwich aside, she slouched down and watched as the bike pulled around the public parking lot and into the slots for employees. A tall man got off. He took a minute to gather up his belongings before striding into the hospital lobby.

This must be the guy, Dussault thought. But he wasn't on a Kawasaki.

J.D. waited. Maybe there was another employee who rode a bike. She finished her ciabatta and downed the last of the coffee. After she was reasonably certain that no one else was arriving for the shift, she pulled her hood over her head, got out and walked briskly past the big machine. In July at this latitude it was light enough at five thirty to read his plate. She circled around another line of cars and returned to her vehicle. After calling in the information, she started up the Jeep. *Giddy-up pony!* she yelled as she tore out of the lot.

Delilah had had a difficult morning. The cast managed to get in the way of everything she was trying to do. Her left hand had always been weaker and the fingers less dextrous. Now it was being called upon to do things that were nearly impossible. When she tipped a pot of water spilling most of it on the floor, she knew she had to get help.

She got out the telephone book and looked up the number for *Dinner at Your Doorstep.* Making arrangements to have dinner delivered every day for the next couple of weeks made her feel that she was taking charge of her own needs. She wondered what they would bring. She hoped it wouldn't be shepherd's pie with peas and carrots.

"Garreth Andreas. No middle name. Born May 28th, 1970. Six feet, five inches," Ray read off the vitals.

"That was some *big* baby," Craig Carpenter cracked.

Everyone laughed. High fives were exchanged. Euphoria spilled into the room at the news of a possible break in the case. A person of interest was in their radar. "We're pretty sure this is our guy," Ray said. "The only fly in the ointment is the Harley. So, Novak, check with Motor Vehicles and see if Andreas has a Kawasaki registered in his name. McDaniel, get up to the hospital before he leaves his shift. Maybe you can get some close-up shots of this biker *cum* nurse."

"*Cum*?!" Carpenter exploded in laughter."

"A little Latin never hurt anyone," Ray said, trying to keep a straight face.

Jimmy reread the pathologist's report. Max had been a healthy male. The only sign of injury, other than the broken finger, was a broken arm. That would have meant having it set at a hospital. He wondered when that was. From his desk in the squad room he called Mrs. Berdahl. After some teeth pulling, he finally got an answer.

Rejoining his colleagues, he made an announcement. "Mrs. Berdahl has just confirmed that Max broke his arm on Friday, September 13th, 2013, and had it set at Raincoast. We don't know for sure that Andreas was working there at the time, but that's easy enough to find out."

"Friday the thirteenth, eh?" Carpenter smirked.

Ray smiled. "Right. An unlucky day for both of them. Okay, who's left here?" Ray glanced around, ignoring Carpenter, Rhys-Jones and Foxcroft. No contest. "Foxcroft, you'd better head for the hospital, too. Ask the HR supervisor if he was working that day. Also, find out what his current work schedule is. And make it clear that she's to keep a lid on it. Assuming it is a she."

"What if *she* gives me a hard time?"

Not bloody likely, he wanted to say, but bit his lip.

It had been a productive day. Novak had obtained the registration for a Kawasaki dual sport in the name of Garreth Andreas. McDaniel had had time to take several shots of Andreas while he spoke to a colleague who was outside smoking a cigarette. And the Human Resources Supervisor had taken one look at the First Nations police officer standing determinedly in front of her and compliantly given her the information she requested.

It *was* shepherd's pie with peas and carrots. Seeing Delilah's dismay, the woman who brought it explained that they didn't get her order in time.

"Oh, never you mind, dear. I'm just grateful to get something." *I can always doctor it up with ketchup and HP sauce*, she thought, carrying it into the kitchen. "What do I do with the tray?"

The woman looked at her wrist. "Nothing. Normally we ask people to rinse it out and we pick it up on the next delivery. But you're not to get that cast wet."

Delilah held it up. "What do you think? Isn't it pretty?"

"Yes it is. But that's just a gauze covering. The cast will be white," the woman said with some authority.

"Were you a nurse?"

"No." She wondered if she should ask the next question. "Where did you have it set?"

"Raincoast General."

"Was it in the morning?"

Delilah looked at her curiously. "Yes. Why?"

"My ex-husband works there. He could have set it."

"Well!" Delilah exclaimed. "Isn't that something?"

Rather than open a can of worms, the woman quickly made to leave. "I hope you enjoy your meal Mrs. Moore,"

"Thank you very much. By the way, my name is Delilah. What's yours?"

Chapter Fifty-four

Wednesday, July 15th

"Here's our guy," Ray said. Two photographs of Garreth Andreas had been tacked on the board. All eyes were glued to the pictures that McDaniel had taken. The close ups were clear and detailed.

"God, I hate it when a killer turns out to be gorgeous," Davidova said.

"Yeah, you want them to be ugly dirt-bags like Willie Pickton," Foxcroft agreed, "not look like Kevin Kiermaier."

Ray shot her an inquisitive look. "You know who Kiermaier is?"

"You think only white people watch baseball?" she challenged.

Ray, chagrined, chewed on yet another chunk of crow before continuing. "Okay. Here's what we know. He *was* on duty when Berdahl arrived with his broken arm, but he didn't set it. He starts work at five. Leaves around one thirty. Works Tuesday through Saturday. And, he was on vacation during the week of the murder." He paused, waiting for the anticipated comments to die down, then continued. "His job gives him access to pretty much anything he would need for a sterile environment. And he has two bikes. This is all good, but it's circumstantial. All the ends have to be tied up before we go in and grab the guy. This case has had more ups and downs than a whore's drawers. We don't have a motive yet, so let's look at the dog angle. If he *is* the guy who got into a fight with Max, then we also have a person who has carried a grudge for nine years."

"It seems a long time to wait to kill someone who has run over his daughter's dog," Novak said.

"Yeah, it seems pretty far-fetched to me," McDaniel said.

Then Atkins, taciturn at the best of times, spoke. "There's a popular field up on Landry Road where dogs are allowed to run free," he said. "There's a good chance that's where the man and his daughter were headed. Dog people are very chummy. Someone might remember them, even from years ago. That was a pretty dramatic event." He paused then shifted his gaze to McDaniel. "And carrying a grudge over the death of your pet doesn't seem far-fetched to me, Gene. People are devoted to their animal companions and treat them as family members. You obviously have never owned a dog," he added with some acidity. His veiled criticism of the person with whom he worked most closely and who admired him stunned everyone.

The air crackled with tension. Ray knew it could undermine the working relationships and camaraderie of the crew. Before it got out of hand, he chose to carry on as though nothing had happened. "Foxcroft."

She pulled her wary eyes away from Atkins. "Sir?"

He thought she must have momentarily forgotten herself. When had she ever answered according to protocol?

"Do you know where this place is?"

"Yes."

"Great. So go on up there and see what you can find out *if* you can find out anything. We're looking at a gap of nine years here."

Returning to form, she gave him nothing but a curt nod and took off.

By late afternoon the morning buzz had long since died down but picked up when Foxcroft returned. Seeing her arrive, Wyatt joined the others in the Incident Room. Everyone settled down to hear her report.

"Okay, Foxcroft," Ray said. "Were you able to learn anything at that dog walking place?"

She nodded and without any preamble began. "I found two people, a man and a woman, who were there the day of the accident."

The jaw-dropping revelation caused an electric reaction throughout the room. It was totally unexpected and like manna from heaven.

"Their recollections are very similar and still pretty clear in their minds. They didn't see what happened because it took place around a bend in the road. They heard a child scream and then saw a car speeding away. A red sports car. So they ran to see what had happened." She knew everything by heart at this point, but even so glanced down at her notes.

"A man—they called him Garry—was kneeling beside his daughter comforting her. She was in a wheelchair."

"A wheelchair?!" Ray interrupted. "God. This gets worse by the minute." He shook his head. "I wonder if Jaxon was aware of this." He drew a representation of a little girl in a wheelchair and connected it to Andreas. "Carry on, Foxcroft."

"The girl's name was Jenny. Their dog was bloody and obviously dead. What surprised the people was that Jenny wasn't crying. She just kept saying, 'Up, Bailey. Up, Bailey.' They offered to help. Andreas asked them to wait with his daughter while he got his car."

"Good. This is good, Foxcroft. Anything else to add to that?"

"Yes …" Her voice cracked. Everyone froze. Foxcroft was tough and, as far as everyone could tell, devoid of emotions. They barely breathed waiting for her next words. "They said Jenny was about seven years old and had an unusual kind of Down Syndrome. The dog was a specially trained Golden Retriever. He had been her companion since she was three."

Sighs soughed through the room. "Christ almighty," Ray groaned. "I would have killed the bastard myself." And echoes of what Lettie Ashton had said came back to him. *He probably got what was coming to him.*

Ray had been angry on the drive home, stewing over what he had learned about Max Berdahl. But he had calmed down in time to tell Georgina how the case had progressed. Then a sheepish look took over. "You know, I was about to complain to Jimmy the other day about Tamsyn Foxcroft ... something about her attitude. I'm glad I didn't because she's turned up aces."

Georgina waited a moment before saying anything. *Is this the appropriate time? Oh, go for it.* "I remember when she joined the force ... how your prejudices about First Nations came through loud and clear. I was almost ashamed of you then," she said softly.

Ray's head snapped up then quickly dropped. "Yeah. I was a first class jerk. She's really proven me wrong."

"Here's a bit of advice, honey. Don't change the way you deal with her. If you go from being a hard ass to a marshmallow, she won't respect you for it."

"Is that right?"

"Yeah. That's right."

There was a pause. He grinned. "Did I ever tell you that her name matches her face—sort of fox-like?"

"No, but I hope to God you never said anything like that to her."

"Are you crazy? She'd probably scalp me."

"Ray!"

With Molly on her lap, Ariel was on the sofa going over a score when Jimmy came in, Roger trailing behind him. "Oh. Who could this stranger be, Molly?" she said drily.

He sat beside her and took her hand. "Hello, pouty face. I'm sorry. But you know what it's like." He kissed her palm several times.

"Yes, and you can stop doing that right now." She pulled her hand away. "You're not going to get around me with sweet talk ... and stuff."

"I don't know why not. It's always worked before."

In spite of herself, she laughed and then pointed to a piece of paper on a side table. "There's a message for you."

Jimmy read it and smacked his forehead. "Damn! I've been meaning to call him. I'll have to do it tomorrow." He scratched Roger behind his ears. "I'm hungry. Is there any more of that soup from a couple of days ago?"

"There's a container in the freezer."

Waiting for the soup to heat up, he glanced down at the jigsaw puzzle that Ariel had unrolled on the kitchen table. He noticed the missing piece. *Just like us,* he thought.

Chapter Fifty-five

Thursday, July 16th

Jimmy sat ruminating and rolling a pencil back and forth between his fingers as he read over the case file. There had to be a stronger motive for Max's murder than the killing of a dog. Being occupied, he had forgotten to return Greenwood's call. He remedied that. "Gordon? Jimmy Tan here. How are you?"

"Very well, very well. Thanks for returning my call. I know how busy you must be."

"Yes, I'm sorry. I got your message late last night."

"Please don't apologize. I just wanted to tell you that it *is* Tyler Ashton's paintings that are hanging in *Cupcakes and Coffee*. He comes in periodically to check on sales. The owners think he should be in soon because Arts Faire is starting up tomorrow."

Jimmy understood. Arts Faire was held the last two weeks of July. The Farmer's Market would be open every day, chock-a-block full of crafts. Walls of cafés became virtual galleries covered in works for sale. In the town square, artists could be counted on to set up their easels dashing off portraits of passers-by who were captivated by the idea of having an original painting of themselves.

"That's great news. Keep me posted, will you?" Jimmy said.

"Absolutely."

"And please say hello to Eileen for me," he added. When he heard, "Sergeant Tan says hello," he smiled. Were things looking up for Eileen?

Novak and McDaniel filed in from a recce on Andreas's house. All four went back to the Incident Room.

"So what did you find?" Ray asked.

"Well, first of all, we had to stop and check the mailboxes all along River Road," McDaniel told him. "There aren't any addresses. It's a rural route. But we finally found a box with his name on it." He was removing a small camera from a case as he spoke. "He's got a nice little bungalow about fifty metres away from the road."

"It's sort of interesting where he lives," Novak said.

"How's that?" Ray asked.

"Well, Big Man River is on the southern boundary of Britannia Bay. And Little Man Creek, where the murder scene took place, is on the northern boundary. That's ironic, don't you think?"

They smiled at Novak's observation.

"So what kinda pictures you got, Gene?"

Andreas's residence faced onto a dirt road. It was old and made of rough-hewn timbers, almost as though it had started out as a hut. The shingled roof came down over a porch that stretched across the front acting as protection from both heavy rain and hot sun. There were two large windows of identical size placed equidistant from the front door, which was exactly in the centre of the house. Everything about the place was symmetrical, even the pots filled with colourful flowers on the steps leading to the landing.

The man has some house pride, Jimmy thought. *Or he's a neat freak.* He wondered if it were the same inside.

"What kinda coverage is there for surveillance?"

"Lots," Ray said. "There are little pullouts everywhere and lots of bush and trees."

"Any outbuildings in the back?"

"A small garage."

"Did you manage to get any shots?"

"Only of the outside. There aren't any windows."

Ray nodded. "Okay. So we know how to set this up if we arrest him there. Good work."

The delivery woman arrived at Delilah's house just after four o'clock. Weary, she looked forward to a long soak in her hot tub, after which she would have dinner and watch TV. As she rang Delilah's doorbell she was thinking of what to eat. It certainly wouldn't be one of these meals. The smells that accumulated inside the van during the rounds were enough to put her off her food. She got her smile ready as the elderly woman walked in a jerky gait to unlatch the screen door.

"Hi, Delilah. How are you today?"

"Hi, Doreen. Fit as a fiddle. What about you?"

"I'm doing great, thanks." *Liar.* When they entered the kitchen, she noticed a calendar on the wall with the dates crossed off in black ink. Today's date was still clear. This was one way to keep track of the days, she thought. Maybe she should try that. Her days were so alike that when she awoke she had to work to remember what day it was. It had been that way for a long time.

"Did I get my chili con carne?" Delilah asked as she reached for the meal.

"You did. I hope it isn't too spicy for you."

"No chance of that. And I have tabasco sauce if it's too bland."

"Really?" Doreen laughed in surprise. "That's unusual for an old—" she caught herself.

"—an old woman?" Delilah interrupted, an edge to her voice. "Old is a dirty three-letter word, young lady. My body might be a wreck, but my mind is still sharp."

"That's wonderful."

"And I'll tell you how I keep it sharp." she talked over Doreen's compliment. "Every day I count backwards from one hundred by the sevens or nines or fives, you know. One hundred, ninety-one, eighty-two, and so on. And before I go to sleep, I talk to Melvin and tell him all about my day from start to finish."

"Melvin?" *Is that the name of her cat?*

"My late husband. I talk to him all the time. And Jesus, of course. I talk to Him every day, too. I'm never alone, you know."

Doreen didn't know whether the woman was cracked or just an odd ball. "I'm glad to hear that, because loneliness is something I run into on my deliveries. Quite often I'm the only person they'll see all day and they just want to talk. Sometimes it makes me late. But I've got time." *That's all I've got.*

As Ariel snipped the parsley for tabbouleh, images of Maysoon, her friend from Baghdad, came to her as it did each time she made this salad. It was the summer of 1993 just after her second year at Simon Fraser University. Ariel had joined the International Students Association and instantly hit it off with a laughing girl possessing the biggest brown eyes Ariel had ever seen.

To celebrate the end of the semester, members of the club planned a picnic with food from all over the world. Maysoon was making tabbouleh. As Ariel watched her painstakingly chopping a bunch of parsley with a knife, she couldn't stand it anymore. "Why don't you use scissors? It will be a lot faster," She found a pair, took a bunch of parsley and began snipping the curly green ends.

Maysoon laughed. "That's brilliant. But it doesn't matter how long it takes because women in Baghdad have nothing but time. What else are we going to do? We have no jobs."

A few weeks later, Maysoon knocked on her door. Her smile had vanished. Eyes filled with fright. The Americans had launched missiles on Baghdad and all Iraqi males who were studying abroad had to go back. She was afraid her husband, who was doing post-doctoral work in biology, would be forced to join the army. There were frantic days of shopping for as many practical items as could be crammed into massive suitcases. Five days later, they were gone.

Standing in the departure lounge watching Maysoon and Farkad as they turned back and waved at the many friends who had gathered to see them off, Ariel decided that being a carefree student wasn't for her just then.

Was this going to happen every time she made tabbouleh? When would she stop wondering if they were still alive?

Her thoughts turned to the delivery van she had seen leaving Delilah's driveway. The least she could do would be to have her over for meals while her wrist was healing. Putting down the scissors, she walked over. She could see her through the screen door sitting at the kitchen table.

"Lilah! It's Ariel."

Delilah shuffled to the door. 'Hi Ariel. Come on in. What brings you here?"

Ariel could smell the remains of a meal. "I see you're having hot food delivered."

"Yes. I can't cook right now, so I thought it would be a good idea."

"You know, Lilah, we would be very happy to have you join us for dinner."

Delilah was torn because, while she liked Ariel and Jimmy, she would be embarrassed having to use a knife and fork in front of them. Sometimes she made a mess and because she couldn't see straight she might think she was stabbing a piece of broccoli only to come up with an empty fork. Now she mainly used a spoon. While she appreciated her neighbour's thoughtfulness, her problem was how to be tactful—a trait she had struggled with all her life. What could she say? Then an answer came to her, which she later attributed to Jesus. "That's really sweet of you, Ariel. How about lunch instead? We could be two of those 'ladies who lunch'," she giggled as she put the words into air quotes.

Ariel couldn't hide her disappointment. "Are you sure you don't want to come for dinner?"

Delilah shook her head. "I want to give this outfit a try for now. I may need them later on in life … permanently."

Ariel recognized Delilah's reluctance. "Well, okay. We'll do lunch." She gave the woman a brief hug and was about to leave when Delilah stopped her.

"Do you want to hear an amazing story?"

Ariel turned, intrigued. "Sure."

Delilah's eyes fairly fizzed. "The woman who came today with the meal was married to a male nurse who works at the hospital," she began. "I always think that sounds funny, don't you? A male nurse. Never had them in my day. But I guess if you can have female doctors, you can have male nurses."

Ariel felt a frisson of excitement race through her.

"*He* could have been the one who put on my cast!" Delilah exclaimed dramatically.

Ariel's body nearly snapped with tension. But she kept her voice calm. "What a coincidence. What's her name?"

Jimmy looked at the display on his buzzing cellphone and frowned. Ariel was not in the habit of calling him at work. "Hi Ariel. What's up?"

Chapter Fifty-six

Friday, July 17th

Promptly at eight thirty the following morning, Ray and Jimmy pulled up to *Dinner at your Doorstep.* The business was located in a former restaurant that had once been a popular stop on Bayside Drive. With the building of a wider highway inland, it gradually lost its customer base and closed down.

As they exited the car, the scent of frying onions filled the air. The smell would normally trigger Ray's taste buds, but at this hour he found it a total turn-off. They walked in on a portly man dressed in a spotless white shirt and dark tie dotted with naval flags. He was humming along with a 'sixties song on the local FM station. Looking up from his computer, he revealed a chubby, friendly face. His greying brown hair was cut short and neatly parted on the side. He greeted them cheerfully. "Good morning, gentlemen." He seemed a happy man.

"Good morning, sir," Ray replied. "We're with the Britannia Bay Police Department. This is Sergeant Jimmy Tan and I'm—"

"—I know who you are," the man cut in, beaming. "You're Ray Rossini."

"That's right." Ray was surprised. *How does he know me?*

The man's smile pushed up his cheeks, threatening to bury his eyes. "I was there the night Catalani's was opened." He looked up at the ceiling remembering the evening. "What food! What atmosphere! It was heaven. I couldn't believe the town's good fortune. My wife and I have the pleasure of frequenting the *ristorante* on a regular basis."

Ray hid his relief. At least he hadn't arrested him. "I'm glad you enjoy it."

He reached over his desk, hand out. "Buddy Kurtz." Handshakes all around. "How can I help you?"

"We need an address for one of your employees. We know her as Doreen Andreas, but we're unable to find her."

"Oh. That's probably because she reverted to her maiden name after her divorce. She's Hubbard now." He looked at them apprehensively. "I hope she's not in any trouble. She's an exemplary employee. Reliable. Personable. The clients love her."

"No, no. She's not in any trouble, Mr. Kurtz." Ray quickly said, but did not expand on the request.

"Oh. That's good. I'll just bring up her records." As his stubby fingers expertly tapped the keyboard, his mind was spinning. *It must be something to do with notifying next of kin. Maybe her ex has been in an accident.*

As they waited for the printer to be activated, Ray looked around. The office was neat and clean and would certainly pass inspection by the health authorities. He wondered if the kitchen would, as well. Looking at the proprietor, he guessed in the affirmative. Then on a whim, he asked in his blandest voice if he had any idea why they divorced. He knew he was overstepping the boundaries, but would Kurtz know that?

Kurtz frowned. He pressed his lips together wondering how much he should say. "I ... uh ... I think it had something to do with the death of their daughter."

Ray and Jimmy's attention antennae quivered.

"Such a tragedy," Kurtz said, shaking his head.

"When did it happen?" Ray asked.

"November 11th, 2011. Remembrance Day. Imagine having to be doubly reminded of death on that holiday," he said grimly.

In the heavy silence that followed, the printer clacked on, feeding out the paper. Kurtz retrieved it, gave it a quick glance and handed it to Ray.

"Thank you very much, Mr. Kurtz. One last request. We would ask that you not notify Miss Hubbard that we've been here. It's a sensitive issue."

"Yes, of course. I mean, no, of course not. That is, I won't contact her." He was convinced now that it had to do with a family emergency. And more bad news.

As Ray turned over the ignition he turned to Jimmy. "I think we have our motive."

Waiting in the Incident Room for the arrival of his chief investigators, Wyatt was reminded again of their distinctive personalities. When they partnered up, they got tagged Laurel and Hardy. While Rossini was more larger-than-life than large, he seemed gigantic next to Tan. He not only had three inches on him, he also had heft. Tan's muscles, on the other hand, were hidden.

Tan was the big surprise. When he arrived, his quiet demeanour didn't seem suited to a squad room dominated by the big Italian. Rossini's language and gruff manner—even ferocity—could scare the pants off everyone. Except Foxcroft. During her protesting days she had faced down phalanxes of riot police. What was one cop to her? And now she was one herself. Some irony at work there.

Rossini had tried out his bluster on Tan, but whatever he threw at him was calmly deflected. Or Tan would throw back an arcane word or phrase that caught Rossini off guard and cause the crew no small amount of amusement. It didn't take long before they recognized that Tan had a kind of personal authority that set him above Rossini's verbal onslaughts, which, in themselves, were meaningless and simply his way of letting off steam. A few months after Tan arrived, some of the heat from Rossini's rants cooled and equanimity settled on the team.

Wyatt, lost in his reverie, almost jumped when they walked in. "What did you learn from Doreen's employer?"

"That Jenny died in 2011."

Wyatt's face fell. "Oh, bloody hell. That's awful."

"It probably led to their divorce. She reverted to her maiden name, which is why we couldn't find her. We believe we have the motive now," Ray reeled off. He moved over to the evidence board and added the information about Jenny.

"Just wish we had some useful forensic evidence," Wyatt said.

"People have been *convicted* with less than what we've got," Jimmy stated, attempting to mollify his boss. But he understood his apprehension. It was the first murder case in Britannia Bay and it was anything but open and shut. No one wanted anything to go sideways.

"So he's avenging the death of his daughter," Wyatt said.

"That plus the killing of her special dog and the breakup of his marriage," Jimmy pointed out.

"Sounds like we're dealing with a deranged man who works at saving lives," Wyatt said.

"People in the medical field aren't exempt from murdering people," Ray said.

Wyatt nodded. "That's certainly true." There was a momentary pause. "When do you want to arrest him?"

"As soon as we can get a warrant."

Wyatt thought of the time line. "I'll see if we can get it before the end of the day. So work out a watch schedule and I'll get busy on the warrant." Wyatt slapped his hands on his thighs. Pushing himself out of the chair he headed to his office in haste. It was after lunch.

Judge Silverman usually ate at the golf course where the food was above par. Wyatt was counting on that to put the judge in a good mood. "Good afternoon, Mort."

"It *was*. What do you want, Earp?"

Yeah. He was mellow, all right. "That joke is getting old, Zilberkop."

"And that one isn't? It's a wonder I have any hair left with all the crap I see in my courtroom." He sighed. "So, what can I do ya for?"

"I need another warrant."

"What's this one for?"

"An arrest."

"What's the charge?"

"First degree murder."

Wyatt sensed rather than heard his friend's reaction. "So you got yourself a viable suspect?"

"We have."

"How soon do you need it?"

"By the end of the day, if possible."

There was a moment of silence. "I don't need to tell you to make sure you have all the details correct, Bill. All the i's dotted and t's crossed."

"I'll have all my ducks in a row, Mort." Wyatt was well aware that, however off-beat Silverman was, when it came to a person's rights, he was faithful to his fiduciary duty to uphold the law.

Mary Beth ducked into the Incident Room on her way back from the washroom. She looked at the evidence board and saw that Jenny Andreas's date of death had been added. With an ache in her heart, she returned her desk and tapped into her computer's search site. She found what she was looking for, jotted down the details on a small piece of paper, and slipped it into a file folder containing tidbits of information that dispatchers shared with each other.

Chapter Fifty-seven

Jimmy tucked into the short ribs with relish. He separated out a small chunk of meat, stirred the mashed potatoes in with the carmelized onion gravy and heaped his fork with the melange. With his mouth full, he speared a few carrots. There were hints of rosemary in the melted butter.

Ariel smiled as he wolfed down the food. Short ribs weren't summertime fare, but Jimmy loved them, and she wanted to cook him something special that evening.

"There's horseradish, if you want it," she said.

With his mouth full, he shook his head. After he swallowed he said, "Don't need any enhancements, honey. This is delectable as is."

She chuckled. "Would you like a glass of Shiraz?"

Again he shook his head. "Nope. Can you see a farmer drinking wine with his meal? This is down home food."

She guffawed. "And you know this how? Down home for you is noodles. You wouldn't know a rutabaga from a turnip."

"There's a difference?" As he helped Ariel clean up the dishes, he realized that for the first time in many months he felt satisfied with his lot. But then thoughts of tomorrow pushed aside any ideas of contentment. So many things could go wrong and if he dwelt on them, he would never get any sleep. And he needed to sleep tonight.

Ray sat alone at the kitchen table. He had finished the meal Georgina prepared for him before she went to work. Marcus was out somewhere with his mates. Gabriella was in the family room watching TV and texting her friends. Ray felt abandoned and wished his wife were there. Talking things over with her was therapeutic. She had a calming effect on him and he needed that right now. He took another sip of wine.

Gabriella sauntered in and glanced at his empty plate. "You know, you've got it pretty good."

Ray smiled up at her. "You think so?"

"Duh. You don't cook. You don't clean. You don't cut the grass. Mom does all the cooking. I do most of the cleaning. And Marcus does the yard work. What do you do?"

He chuckled at her impudence. "Listen, Miss Smarty-Pants, I bring in money so that you can buy cellphones and computers and iPads so that you can sit and text your friends. And you can do that in a safe town because I catch the bad guys."

She didn't respond, but plopped into a chair. "Dad?"

Ray caught her different tone, and his attention. "Yes, honey?"

"You're going to arrest that man who killed Max Berdahl. Right?"

"That's right."

"How soon?"

"Soon."

"Like tomorrow?"

He smiled. "Like soon."

She sighed then looked down, suddenly fascinated with her cuticles. "Will you be scared?" She didn't want to meet his eyes. She was afraid he might see how fearful *she* was.

He regarded her, realizing she still had a lot of little girl inside her. "Not scared, *cucciola*. Just a bit worried."

She looked up. "About what?"

"Well, sometimes, no matter what you do, things go off the rails."

She frowned. "But you *will* have lots of backup, won't you?"

He smiled. "Yes. We'll have lots of backup." He thought that was the end of it and was about to get up.

"But why did he kill Max Berdahl?" It came out as an anxious whine.

"I'm sorry, honey," he said with tenderness. "I can't tell you that right now. Later on I'll give you the facts because you're gonna hear a lot of other versions of what happened. So, do you think you can wait?"

"Yeah. I guess."

Reluctant for her to leave, he switched gears and nodded toward the bottle of Valpolicella. "Would you like a glass of wine?"

Her dark eyes came to life. "Wow! Yeah."

Ray went to the china cabinet and brought back a red wine glass, but as he was about to pour, she put out her hand. "Wait! I know the proper way to pour wine now. Let me do it." Holding the bottle well away from the lip, she carefully poured out enough to fill a third of the glass. With a flourish, she gave the bottle a slight twist and placed it back on the table.

"Brava, signorina."

She smiled and raised her glass to her father. "*Cin cin.*"

"Oh, I think that's too casual for this occasion, Gabriella. *Alla sua salute,*"and raised his glass toward her.

She blushed with pleasure at the unexpected small step into adulthood.

Rather than talking things over with Georgina, Ray instead shared the evening and a glass of wine with his beautiful daughter, revelling in what a rare treat that was.

Chapter Fifty-eight

Saturday, July 18th

J.D. left well before her assigned watch on Andreas's house. It had been an unpleasant day. Tears had been shed. Not hers. She was shocked at how implacable she could be after sharing hundreds of intimate hours with this person. No pleading could dissuade her. *Yep. Guess she was right. Guess I'm just a cold bitch.*

Drew Hastings had brought her up to date. Andreas arrived home at about the expected time. Watered his plants. Went inside. Had seen him briefly now and then when he passed by the windows.

Just after nine o'clock Andreas closed the blinds. Probably preparing to turn in, J.D. thought. She put on a CD of k.d. Lang and angled her book to capture the last of the sunlight. By nine thirty, the light was too faint for reading. She drank a bit of coffee. At eleven, the evening enticed her out of the car. She strolled along the road, gazing at the stars and planets picking out Antares and tracing the outline of Scorpius. The absence of sound sent her back to the day she had stood alone in the Anza-Borrego Desert, the intense silence numbing her ears. She returned to the car, refreshed but nostalgic. Inserting earbuds, she resumed listening to Lang singing about Western stars. It seemed appropriate. Her head rested on the seat back. Her breathing slowed.

She jumped at a tap on the window, her senses firing on all cylinders. *Andreas?* Fear prickled her body. *God, I'm a sitting duck.* She slid her right hand to her duty belt sitting on the passenger seat and slowly pulled out the OC spray. As she pressed the DOWN window and lifted the canister, a thin sliver of light flashed on the face outside. She exhaled. "Jesus, Simon," she whispered. "What the hell do you think you're doing? You almost got maced." She glanced at the clock. It was a couple of minutes after midnight.

Rhys-Jones giggled. "Perhaps you wanted me to honk first?"

She didn't tell him what she wanted him to do. Instead she told him it had been an uneventful night, started up the Jeep and drove off, deep in thought. *Did I fall asleep?* But if Simon had thought she was sleeping, he wouldn't have chuckled. He was too anal. He would have said something insufferably proper.

Simon was knackered. Erin's morning sickness interrupted what sleep they both managed to get. There hadn't been a chance of a nap for him. Her retching and moaning put paid to that. *Why do they call it morning sickness when it happens morning, noon and night?* He hadn't had a proper dinner again, either. He reached into a brown paper bag and pulled out a Branston pickle, ham and cheese sandwich, leaving one for later on. *At least I can do that for myself.* He washed it down with hot and heavily sugared tea from his Thermos. He set the alarm on his watch for one thirty and within seconds he was asleep.

Waking at the beeps, he got out, took a pee and walked as close to the house as advisable. All was quiet. He returned to the car, and reset the alarm for three. When he awoke, he took out his night vision binoculars and scanned the house. He saw no light, no movement. He ate his other sandwich, switched on an all-night music station and drank the last of his tea. He remained awake. At five o'clock a light went on inside Andreas's house. He reached for his cellphone.

Wyatt perched his butt on the edge of a desk and cast an eye over his officers suited up in Kevlar, ready to hit the road. When Ray answered Rhys-Jones's call and gave a thumbs up, all chatter stopped. Wyatt pushed himself off, handed the search warrant to Ray and squeezed his arm, a gesture that surprised them both.

"Okay, team. This is it." Ray said. "Let's saddle up and move on out." He winced at his reference to horses and hence cavalry, but Wyatt had left the corral. Glancing quickly at Jimmy, he saw him grinning ear-to-ear.

The "posse" was making good time on the quiet streets as it approached River Road. Foxcroft had won the rock paper scissors contest with Carpenter and now sat in the driver's seat. She knew it galled him that a female was in control and an "Indian" to boot. Perfect. For once, he was quiet. Boiling. But quiet.

Ray and Jimmy were quiet as well, anticipating the arrest and wondering if Andreas's state of mind would lead him to do something crazy. They were met by Rhys-Jones at the designated spot. "I can't see any activity because all his shades are drawn."

"Okay. Go on home, Simon. Your work day is over."

"Thanks, Sarge." Exhilarated, he ran back to his vehicle and took off.

Ray signaled to Novak and McDaniel to go around the back. He and Jimmy stepped onto the porch. Ray banged on the door. "Mr. Andreas. It's the police. Open the door." There was no answer. "Andreas!" He rapped again.

Jimmy tried the handle. The door was unlocked. Removing their weapons, they burst through the door looking right then left as they zigzagged their way in. Overkill came to mind. There were only three rooms and a bathroom. Andreas was in none of them. And there was no back door.

"Shit!" Ray blurted. "What the hell happened?" He got out his cellphone and called the station. "Yolanda, get Rhys-Jones and Dussault on the blower and tell them to get their asses to the station!"

Jimmy began a search for something. He found it. "The lights are on a timer, Ray. No telling when he left."

"Well, he was here when Dussault was on watch. She saw activity just after nine. So he had eight hours to slip out."

McDaniel returned looking grim. "I think you'd better come and check this out," he said. Ray followed him to the garage. Jimmy continued looking around the house.

The Harley was sitting sedately to one side. "He's on his dirt bike." McDaniel said. "He could easily walk it to the street and go pretty far before starting it up. No one would hear anything if it has a good muffler," He paused. "Not Dussault or Rhys-Jones."

"But he walked out the front door on their watch."

"No he didn't." They turned to see Jimmy jumping from the bathroom window. Even with all his gear on, he comfortably cleared the frame. "It's not your normal bathroom window. It's an emergency exit. He didn't close it all the way afterwards."

"I didn't pick up on that," Ray admitted ruefully.

Novak sensed a softening in Ray's tone. He thought about the lack of sleep that had Rhys-Jones resembling a zombie. Returning to the station seemed cruel and unusual punishment when they wouldn't be there to question him for a while. "Ray, if you'll give me permission, I'll call Simon and tell him to go home. He needs some rest."

Ray shook his head. "No. We still want to talk to him and Dussault. Just give him the news and tell him he can kip out in the cell. Anyway, he'll probably get more shut-eye there than at home."

Novak called Simon, who was relieved at the news and even thankful. Sleep at last!

After J.D. heard Jimmy's update, her hands were sweating. Andreas couldn't have chosen the minutes before midnight to do a runner. Could he? Surely she would have heard something even with earbuds in. Wouldn't she? God. Just when things were looking up. But even if she was off the hook for a while, she sure as hell wasn't going home.

Chapter Fifty-nine

Ray radioed Foxcroft who told him that Dhillon and Quinn had reported a quiet night at the roadblock. And she and Carpenter hadn't seen anyone. She wanted to know why he was asking.

"He's given us the slip. Took off on his dirt bike. More than likely gone north. God only knows why. It's a dead end."

There was a momentary pause on the line. "Boss, there's an old cemetery up there just below the headwaters of Big Man River and Little Man Creek."

Ray jumped on her words. "A cemetery! Maybe his daughter is buried there. Maybe that's where he is. Tamsyn, you're brilliant."

Foxcroft turned toward Carpenter, the corners of her mouth curving into a smile. He scowled, having heard every word.

Wyatt, however, had passed the scowling stage. "Whaddaya mean he's done a bunk?" he barked into the radio, turning purple as he processed Ray's words.

At her desk, Mary Beth instinctively ducked as Wyatt's fury scorched the walls.

"Whaddaya mean you think he's on his way to a cemetery?"

She was afraid that he would be next—in a pine box.

"Whaddaya mean *if* his daughter's buried there?"

Caught up in the drama and imagining the other end of the

conversation, she finally realized what he was saying. Yanking open the desk drawer, she snatched up a file, pulled out a piece of paper and dashed into Wyatt's office waving it at him. "She *is* buried there," she shouted.

Wyatt's head snapped up from the phone, puzzlement melding with the anger on his face.

"Here." She thrust the note at him.

He took a quick look at it. "Ray, his daughter *is* buried there, in case you didn't hear Mary Beth yelling her lungs out." Winding up the call, Wyatt gazed at his long-serving dispatcher. "Mary Beth, how did you know Jenny Andreas was buried there?"

"I looked up her obituary in *The Bugle's* archives."

Wyatt shook his head in admiration. "I'm beginning to think I should fill this squad room with women."

The search was futile. Finding the grave site had been a no-brainer. It stood out as the only green amongst the desiccated grass. Little Man Creek was close by and there was still a trickle of water after the rainfall. Sitting by the simple grave marker with its poignant words—"Our angel has returned to heaven"—were fresh flowers in a child's yellow enamel bucket. But no Andreas. Dejected, they surveyed the terrain. Except for a small memorial chapel that had seen better days, the site was barren.

"There must be trails leading away from here," Jimmy said. "He wouldn't box himself in."

"No." He sighed. "We'll just have to call it quits and go back to the station. Christ! What a cock up!"

Settling into the van, Jimmy turned to Ray. "How did he know the right time to make a break for it?"

"Beats the hell out of me." At the junction onto Bayside Drive, his cellphone rang. He looked at the caller ID. "I gotta take this," he said. "Hi Mr. Featherstone." He turned on the microphone and jammed the phone into the console cradle.

"You told me to give you a buzz if I saw anything up on Townshipline." He sounded nervous and excited. "The bloke I saw is there now. 'E's pulled in the drive of the empty 'ouse."

"You're sure it's him?"

"As sure as Lizzy's the Queen. Same off-road."

"How long has he been there?"

"Just arrived. I 'appened to see 'im as I was comin' down t'road."

Jimmy snatched up the radio and told the backup units to make a beeline for the murder site. Wyatt had been monitoring the radio transmissions but missed it. He was in the kitchen pouring another cup of coffee. Mary Beth did hear it and ran in. "Chief, Andreas is at the Schwindt house."

"Fuck!" He dropped the cup and rushed out.

Mary Beth blinked, turning crimson. Her mouth open, she remained rooted to the spot. In all the years she had worked with Chief Wyatt, she had never once heard him use the *f* word. She gathered herself together, cleaned up the spilled coffee and returned to her post, slightly shaken but stirred in a way she could not explain.

Wyatt got on the radio. "How far away are you, Tan?"

"All units are about fifteen minutes, max."

That cemented his decision. "Right. I'll be on my way in a couple of minutes. Should be there before you."

Ray still had Featherstone on the line.

"Do you think he saw you?"

"Pretty sure 'e didn't 'coz the front of 'is bike was already in the driveway.

"What about hearing you?"

"I pulled off straightaway and cut the engine."

"Okay. Don't go anywhere near the property."

"You don't need to tell me twice, guv."

"There are going to be several police units arriving in minutes."

"I think I'll go back up, if it's all the same to you."

"Can't tell you how much we appreciate this, Mr. Featherstone."

"I ain't no 'ero. Just want to 'elp out."

Something about Featherstone niggled the back of Jimmy's brain, but it vanished like vapour on a puff of wind.

Ray turned on the lights and siren and stepped on the throttle. "What a break. I'll bet there are trails following the creek from the cemetery to the picnic site. And then all Andreas has to do is go down the road to the house." He thought for a moment. "But why the hell would he return there now?"

Jimmy frowned with worry. "I think he's going to try to take his own life now that he's avenged Jenny's death. Remember the missing key to the front door?"

"But why there?"

"It's where he took Berdahl's life. There's something poetic about it."

Ray chanced a quick glance at his partner. "Poetic? Jeez, Jimmy. Anyway, why wait? Why not do it the same day?"

"We won't know until we have a chance to question him."

"*If* we get the chance."

"If he plans to hang himself, there's a ladder in the house."

"There's a ladder?"

"An old one. In the basement. Another thing that Schwindt left behind."

"Oh, great."

Wyatt radioed that he was at the scene. Minutes later, Ray peeled into the driveway and slewed to a stop. Wyatt's car was there, but he was nowhere in sight. "Oh, Christ. I hope the Chief's not in the house." He cut the engine and bolted out the door.

Jimmy rushed to Wyatt's car fearing that he might be inside injured. Or worse. It was empty.

Ray charged up the steps and tried the door. Locked. He peered through one of the deck windows. "He's on the ladder tying a knot!"

Jimmy sprinted to the front door.

Ray pulled out his gun, unlocked the safety and shattered the lock.

Foxcroft and Carpenter arrived. They tore up the stairs.

Everyone ran inside as Andreas placed the noose around his neck.

Jimmy yelled at Carpenter. "Get up to the loft and cut the rope!"

Ray and Jimmy steadied the ladder.

Andreas tightened the knot. Realizing he might be thwarted, he raised his knees and flung his body off to the side the same instant Carpenter sawed through the rope. "No!!" he wailed as he crashed to the floor.

Wyatt barged through the door. Carpenter clambered down the stairs. Ray kicked away the ladder.

Andreas was big, fit and fast on his feet. He charged Ray and Jimmy, noose around his neck, loose rope trailing behind him. Ray grasped one of his arms while Jimmy latched onto the other, but Andreas had momentum and flung Ray off like a ragdoll. Jimmy quickly released his hold and nimbly leapt aside. Foxcroft deftly sidled around Andreas and stepped on the rope with both feet, momentarily jerking him to a stop. Andreas turned his head to see what had happened. That was all Jimmy needed. With blistering speed, he executed a Muay Thai back leg knee strike to Andreas's groin. The big man collapsed, doubling up and moaning.

Jaws dropped.

"I'm sorry, Andreas," Jimmy said. "But there was no other way."

Later, Ray would say that he never thought he would live to see the day when a police officer apologized for kicking a killer's "jewels." And Wyatt, mortified, vowed to cut back on his consumption of caffeine. He had been in the bush taking a painfully long pee when the others arrived at the scene. The extra cups he drank that morning could have given Andreas time enough to kill himself.

In the weeks following, officers jokingly clutched their crotches when they passed by Jimmy's desk. And pouring a second cup of coffee would prompt some wiseacre to crack: "Be careful. That stuff could be the death of you." But always out of Wyatt's earshot.

Chapter Sixty

Mary Beth gently shook Rhys-Jones's shoulder. "Simon, you have to get up." She heard a faint change in his breathing. "Simon …"

His eyes flickered open.

"I'm sorry, Simon, but you have to get up."

Slowly sitting up, he looked at his watch and groaned. "I've only been asleep for three hours."

"Which is three hours more than you would've had at home."

"Why do I have to get up?"

They're bringing in Andreas. I have to change the linen. Now shift it," she said, laughing.

He shifted it. "So they got him. Where?"

"At the Schwindt house."

"At the Schwindt house? What was he doing *there*?" he asked as she stripped the bed.

"I'm sure you'll find out. Now off you go. I have work to do."

It dawned on him that with the capture of Andreas, he just might get off easy.

Lana Westbrook's description of Andreas as "big and tall" fell far short of the mark. When he was escorted to the cell by the biggest men on the squad—McDaniel and Carpenter—everyone present agreed they looked a mite puny next to him. His T-shirt stretched across a body showing off massive shoulders and arms. Tamsyn Foxcroft, however, had been correct about one thing. He looked like centerfielder Kevin Kiermaier with the same turquoise blue eyes under thick, dark eyebrows.

Andreas had been docile when fingerprinted, photographed and read his rights. It was obvious he was still in great pain. Wyatt, thinking about assault charges on a suspect, was relieved when Andreas shook his head when asked if he would like a doctor to check him. He next asked if he wanted to call a lawyer. Again, he shook his head. "I'll get you some pain medication," Wyatt told him. Andreas nodded.

With that accomplished, the interrogation began. At the onset, his only verbal communications were "yes" and "no" or silence. His eyes, while distinct, had a flat, slightly vacant appearance. But they sparked to life when he heard how the woman who shared a table with him on the ferry the evening of the murder later recognized him at the hospital. He gave a brief, wistful smile, and then closed in on himself once again.

He was taken back to the cell where he stretched out on the cot, his long legs dangling over the edge. Wyatt saw how uncomfortable he looked, and retrieved a couple of chairs to devise a support for them. Then he extracted extra blankets and pillows from the store room. For inexplicable reasons that tilted his moral compass, he felt compassion for Andreas. He was also fearful for the man's life and set up a suicide watch until he was transferred to the provincial remand centre in the morning.

"That was strange, wasn't it?" Ray said as he and Jimmy ate huevos rancheros at El Coyote. "I mean, it wasn't like a normal clamming up. He just shut down."

"I think he's done. Empty."

"Yeah. Like his life. No dog, no daughter, no wife. Just existing until he could get his revenge."

"With a good psychiatrist and support he might have been able to pull himself out of that dark place."

"Don't think so, Jimmy. The hate just ate him up. Gnawed away until there was nothing left. What I don't get is why hang himself? I mean, a hospital has all kinds of drugs. Why didn't he just shoot one of them into his veins? Or pop a shitload of pills?"

"Maybe he was afraid of getting the dosage wrong. Hanging was foolproof. Better to die as intended than wind up as a vegetable."

Ray pushed away his plate and stretched. "Jeez it's already been a bloody long day," he said through a yawn. Do you want to talk to his ex-wife this afternoon, if she's in?"

"Yes. Maybe she'll have the answers to some of our questions. And after that, we need to go back to his house for a quick search."

"Oy vey. Will this day never end?"

Chapter Sixty-one

The neighbourhood where Doreen Hubbard lived had the look of neglect, possibly driven by poverty or despair, or both. Because the houses were located in the township, Ray guessed that several would be rentals. That choice of housing was rare in the village. And if one such vacancy did come up, the rate would be out of reach of most renters. Her residence stood out. It was freshly painted. No sagging gutters. No moss on the roof. Even though the grass had been left to die down, the garden had been kept up. Perennials dotted the openings between tidy shrubs. Colourful annuals graced terra cotta pots by the door.

Doreen had finished washing the few lunch dishes and plugged in the kettle when the doorbell rang. Quietly making her way to the front, she peeked through the peephole. Two men stood away from the door giving her a clear view of the police uniforms. Her heart did a little flip. She opened the door.

The woman didn't fit Ray's vision of what a "gorgeous" man's wife should look like. Although she was wearing makeup, no amount of camouflage could erase the deep crevices that ran down her face or the dark patches underneath eyes the milky colour of moonstones. The shock of dyed red hair emphasized rather than disguised her age. Ray thought she looked more like Andreas's mother than his wife and decided he had better clarify who she was. "Good morning. Are you Doreen Hubbard?"

"Yes."

Old Mother Hubbard came to Ray's mind. "I'm Detective Sergeant Ray Rossini, and this is Detective Sergeant Jimmy Tan. We're with the Britannia Bay Police Department." He showed her his ID. "If it's not too much of an inconvenience, may we come in and speak with you?"

Without asking why, she nodded and held open the door, bringing them directly into a sparsely decorated living room. Nothing matched and everything appeared either a bit worn or scratched up. A sofa, two stuffed chairs, a coffee table, and two end tables were probably purchased from one of the local charities, they surmised.

Other than wearing slippers, Doreen Hubbard was dressed in serviceable clothing—tan slacks, a three-quarter sleeve white shirt with narrow stripes in brown, gold and orange. She looked from one to the other. "I expect you're here about Garry." Although her manner was calm, there was a noticeable tremor in her voice.

Trying his best to keep surprise from his face, Ray acknowledged her. "Yes, ma'am. We are."

She gestured to the chairs. "Why don't you sit down?" The kettle whistled. "I was just about to make coffee. Would you like a cup? It's fresh ground." She tried on a smile. It didn't quite fit.

"That would be very nice. Thank you," he said.

When she left the room, Ray raised his eyebrows to Jimmy and gave a little shrug. Then rather than sitting, he examined the pictures on the mantel over a gas fireplace. They were all combinations of Jenny with her parents and an older couple, perhaps grandparents. In every shot sat Bailey the golden retriever, who had on his dog smile. And in every shot, Doreen was smiling, even radiant.

This is more like it, Ray thought as he held one of the framed photos. *This* Doreen had fashionably coifed auburn hair and had either very smooth skin or perfect makeup. The transformation had been drastic. He wondered how she could stand the reminders of what her world had been. Then he picked up one of Bailey alone mugging for the camera.

"Bailey was the sweetest dog. He was beautiful, intelligent and gentle," Doreen said as she returned carrying a tray with mugs, sugar, cream and spoons, which she placed on a low table. "When he was killed, it was the saddest day of our lives … until Jenny died."

Ray nodded. "I can understand that."

"I'll just get the coffee."

She came back in, poured the coffee then sat on the edge of the sofa. Waiting. Wondering.

"You seemed to be expecting us," Ray said.

"Yes." She picked up her cup. "A letter from Garry arrived yesterday. He told me to call a lawyer in town." Her voice caught, shattering her calm façade. "He said he was going to say his final goodbye to Jenny. I knew what that meant." She trembled. "Has he done it? Has he taken his own life? Is that why you're here? To tell me he's dead?" A bit of coffee spilled as she put down her cup with shaking hands.

Ray rushed to stanch her fears. "No, Miss Hubbard. No. He's not dead."

She looked at them expectantly. "Then, tell me what's happened," she pleaded.

"We arrested your husband this morning," he told her. He realized his error but didn't correct it. And nor did she.

There was a loud intake of breath. "Arrested him? But why? What for?" A spark of anger flared in her eyes. "You don't arrest people for trying to take their own lives, do you?"

"Miss Hubbard. Did you read about the murder of Max Berdahl?"

The sudden change of subject caught her off balance. "No. Why?"

"He was the person who was driving the car when Bailey was struck and killed."

The words landed like a bomb, knocking the wind out of her. "So *he* was the one. And he's dead?"

"Yes."

Her initial shock gave way to bitterness. "Good. I'm glad. He destroyed our lives."

There are those words again, Ray thought. "Can you tell us how your husband dealt with the death of Bailey and its effects on your daughter?" He waited, letting the information hang in the air.

It only took a minute until she put two and two together. Her eyes widened. "My God! You think *Garry* killed this man?"

"We believe so," Ray said.

She shook her head back and forth. "No. That's not right. He would not do that," she said, her voice growing shrill. "He *saves* lives!"

Ray and Jimmy sat quietly, waiting for the full extent of the news to sink in. After a minute or two, Ray carried on. "Did Garry ever say he wanted to kill the person responsible for Bailey's death?"

She nodded. "Over and over again! You know, people always say they want to kill someone. But putting words into action?" She stared at Ray. "Are you *sure* Garry is responsible for this man's death—what was his name again?"

"Max Berdahl."

"How did he find *that* out? He didn't even have his licence plate number."

"Through his job. Berdahl broke his arm—"

"—And Garry set it?" she interrupted, astonished. The words triggered her memory. She glared at Ray. "Did you get my name from Delilah Moore?"

Ray did not answer that. "Your ex-husband did not set Berdahl's arm but he was on duty and would have recognized him. All he had to do was look at the admission form to get his name and other information."

"Then why do you need to talk to me if you have this information?"

"Because he's remained silent since his arrest this morning. We wanted background for his actions."

It was a few minutes before she spoke. Then a torrent of words spilled out. "When Jenny was born, we were numb. You know, you expect a normal child. And then you're handed this imperfect little being. It set us back on our heels. We thought it was the Down Syndrome we were familiar with. But she had Mosaic Down Syndrome. I couldn't understand why she didn't cry like other babies. After tests were done, we learned that she also had Triple X—that's three X chromosomes. Over her brief life she was diagnosed with childhood aphasia, speech apraxia and auditory processing issues. It was extremely rare. She also had to wear ankle braces. It was difficult for her to walk."

Ray and Jimmy sat quietly and listened to yet another family tragedy.

"I quit my job so that I could give her the physical support she needed. And Garry had medical contacts through his work. We got a lot of help." She paused. "The biggest problem was not with Jenny. It was with me. I had had visions of a life for my daughter. You know, normal things—dance classes, skating, graduating from university, a great career, a happy marriage. In the meantime, Garry kept saying things like how sweet and innocent she was, what a little angel and how loveable. And she was. He was absolutely besotted with her." She sighed.

"And that made it all the harder when Bailey was killed. Having that rare form of Down Syndrome, Jenny didn't have the emotional mechanism to deal with that kind of loss. She became angry and anxious because she couldn't get rid of the pain she was feeling. We got professional help and tried to explain where Bailey was. Every day she would keep repeating, 'Bailey in heaven. Going to heaven. Go find Bailey'." She paused. "Jenny had nightmares until the day she died." Doreen stopped as suddenly as she had started, sinking back into the sofa.

Jimmy spoke for the first time. "Did your daughter's death cause your divorce, Miss Hubbard?" His voice was gentle.

Tears began to trickle down, charting out a charcoal trail. She reached for a tissue. "It was the nail in the coffin, you might say. His hatred for the man festered and morphed into a kind of madness. I couldn't deal with it anymore." She turned away. "I left him." When she turned back, there was shame and guilt on her grief-stricken face. She looked from one to the other. "How was Berdahl killed?" she asked tentatively.

"We are not releasing that detail, Miss Hubbard. It will only come out at the trial."

She closed her eyes, imagining the police hauling him off in handcuffs. He would go quietly. That she knew. There would be no fight left in him now. She opened her eyes and gazed directly at Ray. "Garry didn't have to take his own life. He died the day we buried Jenny."

Chapter Sixty-two

"Now we know why he waited before trying to take his own life." In the passenger seat, Jimmy was holding the bagged letter from Andreas. Turning it over to them had caused Doreen considerable anguish. Until the trial was over and it could be returned, she would have to be content with her printer copy. "He was getting his legals in order beforehand. I'll bet he left her everything."

"Yeah. If you count money and stuff as everything."

Jimmy had no answer to that.

Arriving at Andreas's house, they found Adam Berry once again on guard, but not that anyone would notice. Dressed in casual clothes, he had parked his black and white in the back, out of sight. He sat on the porch reading, a battery-powered portable radio at his feet. The two detectives exchanged a smile. Berry's intransigence when it came to electronic gadgets was well known. It had been a battle getting him trained to use a computer. Only the threat of losing his job put the fear of God in him.

The two detectives wanted to do a cursory search, something that wasn't possible earlier in the day. Jimmy's curiosity about the inside of his house was satisfied. It was an unnervingly neat and organized living space. The bed sheets had squared corners. Closets were sectioned off into shirts, jackets and pants. Shoes were lined up underneath. In the linen cupboard, face cloths, hand towels and bath towels were folded in thirds and in colour-coordinated piles. Even his toiletries in the bathroom cabinet had some kind of order.

"You know what this place reminds me of?" Ray asked, not waiting for an answer. "The barracks at Depot in Regina."

"That, or he's obsessive compulsive."

"There's no TV. Who does that remind you of?"

"Barry Ashton."

"Yeah. What is it with these scientific types? Do they have some kind of aversion to popular entertainment?"

"Sort of looks that way. He apparently prefers the written word." He pointed to several bookcases, their contents divided into fiction and non-fiction, the latter of which was broken down by subject—biographies, mythology and astronomy—and various reference books and dictionaries. There were a couple of dozen poetry anthologies, but very few novels. Among them, a spine protruded breaking the neat alignment along the shelf. This bit of curiosity attracted Jimmy's attention. He pulled out a soft cover edition of Henning Mankell's *The Fifth Woman*. A strip of pink satin ribbon marked a page. Jimmy wondered if it was from Jenny's hair. He flipped to the page and read an underlined passage. *Evil must be driven out with evil. Where there is no justice, it must be created.* The words jarred his sense of justice. He showed it to Ray.

"Pretty much explains it all, doesn't it?" Ray said. "He probably figured there was no way Berdahl would ever pay for what he did. So he had to do it himself."

Rifling through the desk drawers, Jimmy found half a dozen notebooks of verse written with blue ink in elongated handwriting, each one signed and dated. The last entry was dated June 26th, the day of the murder. He read it and handed it to Ray.

Stepping into infinity, I soar weightless.
Only my essence remains.
The universe and its glories greet me.
I am bondless. My joy is boundless.
I fly unfettered to my destiny.
A black hole.

"Whoa. If you ever needed proof that this guy was planning to take an early exit, this is it. Jeez, can you imagine having to share a cell with him?"

"He may get solitary in a psychiatric prison."

"In that case, he could get his wish and die sooner," Ray said, referring to the terrible state of mental health facilities in federal prisons. "Or he could sit and write poetry all day long and be as happy as a pig in shit." A leather case on the floor by the window caught his eye. He opened it. "Aha. Here's how he knew when to split." He pulled out a collapsible microscope. "He was doing more than star gazing. Probably spotted Rhys-Jones or J.D."

That might answer one of Jimmy's questions. But there was still the one that had come back to him. What was Featherstone doing on Townshipline Road so early in the morning?

Ariel was at the patio table working on an anagram. In deep concentration, she jumped when a loud, persistent pounding came from across the street. Getting up, she watched as a burly man finished hammering a For Sale sign into the ground. *So, Max's house will soon have new occupants. Hope they're not noisy.* She returned to her task.

Delilah also watched the goings on while filling a water bucket for her fading flowers. As she stood holding the hose, she caught sight of two women with pamphlets heading her way. Being Saturday morning, she knew what they were, turned her back and adjusted the nozzle. When she heard the cheery, "Good afternoon," she casually turned as if to return their greeting then sprayed them with a strong stream of water.

Hearing screams, Ariel rushed onto the street. Two women were running away, pulling at wet skirts sticking to their legs. She saw the hose in Delilah's hand.

"Lilah, you naughty woman. Did you do that on purpose?"

"Of course I did," she giggled. "Jesus told me to do it."

Ariel laughed. "Well, that's one way to keep them out of the neighbourhood."

"I just hope the new people aren't more of them."

Ariel took a look at the sign and recognized the agent's name. *He* certainly wasn't a JW. "Delilah, can I talk to you for a minute?" When Jimmy called to say they had arrested Andreas, she asked him if she could tell Delilah about her role in the arrest, and about Doreen. Armed with an affirmative answer, but with the usual caveats, she decided that now would be as good a time as any.

"You look serious."

"It's just that I noticed a man had delivered your meal."

"Yes, I wondered what happened to Doreen and when I asked him, he said he didn't know. Only that he was asked to sub for her."

Ariel gently took hold of Delilah's arm. "I know why she didn't come."

"You do?" Delilah's face paled. "Has something happened to her?"

"She hasn't been in an accident or anything like that. Can we go inside and sit down?"

"Come through to the kitchen," and she hurried as fast as her weak legs would carry her.

After sitting, Ariel began mulling over how much to tell her.

"Don't dilly dally, Ariel. I'm not getting any younger, you know."

Ariel smiled in spite of herself, then plunged in. "Max Berdahl was killed by Doreen's ex-husband."

It took but a moment for the information to sink in. "What!?"

"Yes. That's why she didn't come today."

"Holy doodle! What a shocker."

"But you must keep this to yourself until …"

"I know. I know. You don't have to remind me."

"Here's the thing." And Ariel told her how her broken wrist had played an integral part in Andreas being found.

Delilah, dumbfounded, shook her head several times. "But why did her ex kill Max?"

Ariel then shared most of what she knew. When she finished, Delilah sighed. "There's nothing worse than losing a child. Believe me. I can understand his grief and need for revenge." She paused. "But it's wrong, you know. The Bible says, 'Vengeance is mine; I will repay, saith the Lord.' And I believe that. We can't go around trying to avenge all the wrongs in the world. There'd be no one left on the planet except critters and little children.

When Jimmy arrived home, Ariel was eager to share the news about Delilah's prank and the For Sale sign in front of Max's house, but his body language and somber face disabused her of that. Levity would have to wait until he emerged from his silent funk. It was enough that he managed to shower, change and eat dinner.

Afterwards, he logged on to the Internet and began reading about Mosaic Down Syndrome. He sat back thinking about the heartbreak a child could bring to a marriage, enough in some cases to cause a chasm too wide to cross. Would Ariel and he have survived if they had had such a child? Besides the danger of his job, here was another reason to opt out of parenthood. They only had each other. He didn't want to lose her. The stubborn weeds of fear, cowardice and selfishness had taken root in his soul.

Chapter Sixty-three

Sunday, July 18th

Outside the station, the early morning air had a salt tang that would evaporate with the warmth of the sun. Inside, Wilma was filling the station with smells of toasted bagels and coffee. The details of Garreth Andreas's life had elicited more sympathy than censure from the kindly grandmother, whereupon she determined to send him off with a smile and food in his stomach. Knowing he was not allowed a knife, she slathered the bagels with butter and raspberry jam. Loading up the tray, she marched back to the cell.

Steve "Rocky" Rivers, who had been given last watch over Andreas, grinned broadly and stood up. "Wilma. You doll. I'm starving." Rivers was on medical leave and due for early retirement. Wyatt, whose crew was catching some well-earned rest, had had second thoughts about asking him to come in, but Rivers assured him that he would be fine. He didn't want to miss out. It would be the last bit of excitement in his truncated career and a piece of cake compared to his years as an RCMP officer in northern British Columbia where armed and dangerous people shot or stabbed people with shocking regularity.

"I'm sorry, Rocky. This batch is not for you." She nodded toward the cell. "It's for Mr. Andreas." Seeing his crestfallen face, she quickly added: "But I'm working on another."

He threw her a kiss.

Andreas had slept peacefully. In the half light of dawn, he awoke and stunned Rivers with a wide smile. Something calming had come to him during the night. He believed that these hardened people understood why he had done what he did. They had apologized for hurting him, saw that he was relieved of pain and made his cell more comfortable. And now, with this thoughtful gesture, he was convinced of it.

Shortly before eight o'clock, Robyn arrived for her shift. Rather than going home, Wilma remained. Ray and Jimmy filed in and were soon followed by Mary Beth and the majority of the squad. At nine o'clock sharp the sheriffs walked through the back door and greeted Chief Wyatt. They handcuffed Andreas and led him through the squad room toward the back door and the waiting Black Maria.

To a person, officers and staff remained still as they watched the scene play out like an old silent movie—but in colour. When Andreas reached the exit, he halted and turned to them. "Thank you for your kindness," he said. Then the sheriffs hustled him out the door.

Everyone found it difficult looking each other in the eye. It was as though a moral mistake had been made and they were responsible for it.

Then a call came in. "Oh, good morning, Mrs. Hoffmeyer," Robyn said.

Laughter, perhaps a little too loud, broke the tension.

Chapter Sixty-four

Ariel was on the phone when Jimmy arrived. "Oh, here's Jimmy now." She mouthed *Gordon Greenwood.* "Yes, I look forward to meeting you, too. I'll pass the phone to him. Bye-bye."

"We're having a couple of guests next Sunday," Greenwood said. "You might find it interesting to join us."

Jimmy noted the plural pronouns and smiled. Things really *were* looking up for Eileen. "Can I assume that one of them will be Tyler Ashton?"

Light laughter travelled along the line. "It's always dangerous to assume, but in this case, you're correct. The other is a gallery owner friend of mine. Your wife said you would be free." He hesitated. "So can *I* make an assumption?"

"Feel free," Jimmy chuckled.

"I'm assuming the case has been wrapped up."

"It has."

Hearing the terse answer, Greenwood understood that that's all he was going to hear. Not one for sensational tittle-tattle, he was fine with it. "Then, will you drop around?"

"You can count on it." Jimmy was cheered to hear good news and eager to meet Tyler Ashton. Ariel added to his upbeat mood as she gave him an account of Delilah's mischievous antics. "Too bad she can't meet Lettie Ashton. I think they'd get along like gangbusters."

"Did you notice the For Sale sign in front of Max's house? The sales agent is Harry McFadden."

"It sounds like you know him," he said.

"Of course I do. He's in my choir."

"Ah. *That's* how I recognized the name when Gordon mentioned it. I read it in one of your concert programs."

"What on earth are you talking about?"

"Harry was with Gordon when Max Berdahl first met Carlene Corrente."

"Oh my gosh. Isn't that amazing?"

"It's just another twist in this tale," he said.

"It seemed more like three months than three weeks," Ray said to Georgina as she slipped into a smart dress for work. He had already showered and was in his pajamas sitting on the edge of the bed.

"Zip up the back, will you honey?"

He did as he was told. "How much did this *schmatta* set you back?"

"A dozen or so lemon pies and chocolate cakes, not to mention a ton of tiramisus."

"Mmm. Some rag."

She checked herself in the full-length mirror then turned to face him. "Now that this case is done with, will you be happy to return to petty crimes?"

"I dunno. If it had been more dangerous, maybe. But most of it was drudge work, you know. It was kinda fun digging down and coming up with some gem of information." He paused. "And we had the stars and planets on our side, of course," he grinned.

Georgina laughed. "Yeah. Of course you did."

"How else do you explain all the coincidences?"

She ran her eyes over his face. "You look like a teenager right now, Ray."

"Hold that thought," he said, playfully, reaching out to tap her on her behind.

Darting away from his hand and out the door, she collided with Gabriella. "Oof! Gabby!" She grabbed onto her daughter before falling.

"Sorry, Mom." she said, steadying Georgina. "I was just coming to ask you something."

"What's so important that you had to charge down the hallway?"

"Me and Andrea—"

"Andrea and I," she corrected her.

Gabriella *tsked* and sighed. "Okay. *Andrea and I* were eating some crostata and we thought we would try baking it. But I can't find any cookbooks."

Georgina smiled. "First of all, I don't have any cookbooks. And second, what makes you think it came from a book?"

Her eyebrows knit together. "Well, duh. Where else?"

"It's from your Nonna's head."

"From her head? So she, like, told Lana how to make it?"

"That's right. And stop using 'like'."

She twisted her mouth and blew some air up, riffling her bangs. "Darn." On the way to the kitchen, another notion struck her. "Maybe Nonna will tell *me*. Should I ask her?"

"You could, but I don't have any baking pans."

"You don't?"

"Why would I? Our pastries have always come from the restaurant."

"Oh." Her shoulders dropped along with her enthusiasm.

"What brought this on in the first place?"

"Watching that British bake-off show. *Andrea and I* thought it would be fun to bake something ... but not anything too hard."

Georgina smiled. "Not hard. And you wanted to start with pastry dough?"

"Yeah. Is that hard?"

"Making pastry dough is tricky, Gabby." Then she thought about it. "I'll tell you what, if you are really serious about learning how to make a crostata, I'll call Lana. Maybe she would be—" she wanted to say "dumb enough" but thought better of it—"willing to show you how it's done. Then you can decide if you want to tackle it yourself."

"That's brilliant, Mom!"

Georgina rolled her eyes, thinking: *Yeah. Right. Lana might bite my head off.*

Chapter Sixty-five

Sunday, July 25th

Curious eyes radiated around the room when Ariel and Jimmy joined the small gathering at Gordon's cottage the following Sunday. Jimmy focused on Tyler, the enigmatic artist who lived off the grid. He wasn't as slight as Jimmy had imagined and if there had been a haunted look on his face, it was no longer there. His relaxed posture matched that of his father, who sat beside him on the sofa. Jimmy introduced Ariel to Gordon, then left to talk to the Ashtons.

Gordon took an immediate interest in Ariel. He had had no information on Jimmy's private life; hence, a pretty woman with springy curls and blue eyes caught him off guard. "I'm very pleased to finally meet you," he said, swiftly masking his surprise.

"Jimmy has spoken of you with affection, Mr. Greenwood. I'm glad to meet you as well."

"Calling me Mr. Greenwood makes me feel very old. Please call me Gordon." He called over a woman who had just entered the room. "And this is my guardian angel, Eileen Haswell."

"Oh, go on with you," Eileen teased, blushing more with pleasure than embarrassment.

After the two women had completed introductory small talk, Ariel brought up Max's former home. "I see that the salesperson is Harry McFadden. He's a member of the choir I'm in and I know he's not a JW."

"No. He certainly isn't. Harry's a good friend. He told me the Berdahls came to him and asked him to sell it. Harry thinks they believe it's tainted now."

Eileen wanted to steer the conversation away from the Berdahls. "So you're in a choir. I used to be in a wonderful choir," she said, eyes lighting up

Gordon gave her a questioning look. "You never mentioned that before."

"There's a lot I've never mentioned before," she answered crisply through a cheeky grin, and turned back to Ariel. "I'd love to be in a choir again, but I think my voice is gone."

"Oh, that's not necessarily the case," Ariel began. "Many people sing well into their eighties."

With Ariel and Eileen keen to talk about singing, Gordon excused himself to join Jimmy and the Ashtons, who were discussing the case.

"I read that you had arrested someone. But there wasn't much more than that," Dean said. He seemed to want further information.

"No. We didn't release any of the details to the press. It was a very sad case, but we didn't think the public would see it that way. We thought the less said about it, the better," Jimmy said with some finality. Then he gestured to the father and son. "But some good has come of it."

"Yes, isn't that the strangest thing?" Dean smiled and touched Tyler lightly on the arm. "It's brought our family together again." Tyler returned his father's smile then turned to Jimmy.

"And I got to meet Gordon. He's introduced me to some of the galleries around here. If you hadn't taken those pictures of the sketches on Grandma's walls, none of this would have happened."

Jimmy only nodded. "When you next see her, will you say hello?"

"We're going over tomorrow. We'll be sure to do that."

On the way home Ariel said, "It's almost like everything has come full circle." Jimmy gave her a sweet smile. *Yes, almost*, he thought.

Epilogue

As the town reverted to its regular summer pattern of golf, gossip and gardening, the residents were experiencing a mixture of relief and regret. While happy that Britannia Bay was not a haven for criminals, they missed the commotion and excitement. It had given them something else to talk about other than who was cheating on their golf scores, what miscreant was watering during prohibited hours, and who was fighting with whom on the Town Council.

Delilah, however, did have something interesting to share with her fellow church goers. Her questionable neighbours had hit the road. A U-haul truck had rolled up and within hours everything had been loaded on and driven off. Until the houses at either side of her were sold, the neighbourhood would be an oasis of peace. But there was still another matter to tackle.

She had marched into the Town Hall and confronted the mayor. Several issues she had brought to his staff's attention had not been addressed. Rather than sluffing her off, Mayor Verhagen guided her into his office, asked her to sit and listened with patience to her litany of complaints. At the end, he told her he had been thinking of striking a committee composed of community members who would come up with a survey for the townsfolk. It would be asking questions dealing with residents' satisfaction with the town and

what, if any, improvements they would like to see. Was she interested in being a member of the committee? *Was she!!*

Georgina had been wrong. Lana had seized on the opportunity to teach Gabriella how to make pastry. When Georgina had called with her request, Lana's mind raced around trying to determine what this might mean. Her first thought was that it would burrow her deeper into Britannia Bay. She had remained on the fence about the town being her final stopping place. What convinced her was the overriding feeling of pleasure at the thought of teaching again. She looked forward to the arrival of Gabriella, a charming, well-brought-up young lady. Even though it was just one student, who knew where it might lead? At the very least she might polish up her Italian.

Pascal read over the Want Ad once again. The Ambulance Service was looking for a paramedic. When he had come to Delilah's aid, he experienced the same rush and the same satisfaction he felt when he had worked as a *paramédical* in Quebec. He seemed to be recovering well from the disaster at Lac Megantic two years before. Working with nature had helped as had the mental practitioners. He knew his skills were still good. But would his English be good enough? He remembered the words of his *grand-mère*. *"Tu dois toujour essayer."* So he would try. That's all he could do.

Alfred Featherstone had been in a quandary. After receiving the Letter of Commendation at the police department in front of the entire squad, he sat at home for an entire day trying to decide what to do. On the one hand, he was a hero. On the other, he was a criminal.

He added up the pros and cons of his situation. He had no education. So what kind of job could he get? He knew how to repair bikes. But how much money could he get doing that? Not much. He wouldn't even be able to afford his own special bikes and gear after paying for his rent, utilities, food, and on and on. But most important, he wouldn't be able to send money to his dear old Mum in England who was now living in a decent retirement home thanks to his financial support.

Then he considered that he probably wouldn't get any aggro from the local constabulary after his "exemplary civic duty." They would probably just honk and wave if they saw him on the road. The pros had it. He would continue his job as a marijuana courier for Tommy and Fiona Grenville.

Jimmy and Ariel were preparing for their first trip together back to Vancouver. On the day they left, Ariel, already packed, was waiting for Jimmy to gather his items together. She sat at the kitchen table with a pencil and piece of paper filled with permutations. He came in carrying a leather satchel given to him by his aunt before his last trip to Penang. It had languished in the back of his closet since then. Peering over Ariel's shoulder, he recognized the crossed-out words, and the scattering of letters arranged in different ways—in circles and lines with empty spaces underlined between letters. Then he saw her solution. With an added apostrophe, it was a chilling two-word anagram of Garreth Andreas.

ACKNOWLEDGMENTS

Grateful thanks to Ann Lemieux, Judy Beyeler and Judy Bosworth for their valuable editorial comments and careful proof reading, and to Mike Langstone in Billericay, England, for giving a voice to one of the characters. Special thanks to Bryce Gibney for his practical advice and support, without which this book might still be languishing on my laptop. To my family, Larry and Noella, and my friends who encouraged me on this three-year journey, I am indebted to you all.

To my readers. If you enjoy solving anagrams, you may want to join Ariel who created an anagram of the name Garreth Andreas. For the solution, please go to www.sydneypreston.com and follow the link to "Contest."